World Light

Book One

The Cleansing

J.W. Elliot

Bent Bow
Publishing, LLC

Bent Bow Publishing, LLC
82 Wendell Ave., STE 100
Pittsfield, MA 01201
USA

ISBN 978-1-953010-01-8

Cover Art by Tithi Luadthong

Cover Design by Brandi Doane McCann

If you enjoy this book, please consider leaving an honest review on Amazon and sharing on your social media sites.

Please sign up for my newsletter where you can get a free short story and more free content at: www.jwelliot.com

May the Light illuminate your path.

Book One

The Cleansing

Chapter One
The Darkness Gathers

"YOUR MOTHER IS a little witch."

I spun around to see Jens Jessop sneering down at me. He was a big kid who had been after me since the fourth grade. His blonde hair fell before his eyes, and his lip curled up on one side. He wore a Cleveland Browns jersey and smelled of Old Spice. Jens hated me because I was the only sophomore in school with a grade point average higher than his. I could usually brush him off as an arrogant windbag—but not after what he'd just said. I clenched my fists as the tingle of adrenaline swept through me.

We had just come out of a history class about the Salem witch trials. He made faces at me from the front of the room during the entire lesson. The hallway surged with students trying to get to their next class. Blue lockers lined both sides of the corridor, and square fluorescent lights flickered overhead.

"That's right, crawfish," Jens said. "I'm talking to you. Your mom is nothing but a midget witch. Maybe we should toss her in the river to see if she floats."

My face burned. The blood pounded in my ears as I launched myself on Jens. My first punch slammed into his temple, and he stumbled backward. The next caught him on the end of the nose. Blood splattered everywhere. He banged into the lockers, scattering his books across the floor. I slipped on one of them, and he grabbed me. I twisted as we fell to the ground, so I landed on top of him. He let go, and his big fist punched into my eye. My vision blurred, but I kept swinging until a big hand collared me and dragged me off.

"Kell Crawford," the math teacher said, "and Jens Jessop. Looks like you two just volunteered to spend your last two weeks of school in detention."

"He started it, Mr. Green," Jens said as he tried to stem the flow of blood from his nose.

"He called my mom a witch," I said as I blinked, trying to get the vision back in my left eye.

"You know the rules," Mr. Green said. "It doesn't matter who started it."

Jens spit the blood from his mouth. "I'll get you for this," he whispered as Mr. Green led us down the hallway to the principal's office.

Mom picked me up after school in her red Hyundai Accent. The sickening pine scent of the air freshener blew from the vents because she had the air conditioning on full blast. She glanced at the big shiner growing around my left eye and gave me that sad, pitying frown mothers use.

"Oh, Kell," she said, "why do you have to fight?"

"He called you a witch, Mom."

Her hands tightened on the steering wheel. "It doesn't matter," she said. "You can't beat up all the ignorant people in the world."

"I can try," I mumbled.

Mom drove me home to our little two-bedroom duplex, gave me a big bag of ice to hold over my eye, and stuck my bruised hand in a bowl of ice water. She was a little woman with an olive complexion and black hair. I had always thought she was beautiful, and Mateo, the cook at the diner where she worked, thought so, too. People told me I looked like her, but I didn't think I did. My skin wasn't as dark, and my hair was more brown than black. I was bigger than Mom, too, by several inches.

She jerked open the yellow curtains on the kitchen window so a shaft of light splashed through to fall on my face. The crystals she'd hung in the window scattered the light into a glittering rainbow of color over the squat refrigerator and the yellow top of the square table.

"The light will make you feel better," she said. "It will heal you." She turned to prepare dinner.

This is why people called my mom a witch. She said weird things like that all the time. She didn't belong to any of the Christian religions in town. Instead, she burned candles and incense and sang sad songs. She started each morning by meditating while sitting in the sunlight. She had prepared for the summer solstice that would happen in a few weeks by decorating the house with all kinds of greenery—pine boughs, sprigs of holly, flowers, you name it. The place looked like a miniature garden nursery and smelled like a forest with the rich odors of earth and decay mixed with a hint of mint and pine.

I kept the ice on my bruises until they got so cold they hurt worse than they had before. Mom slid a plate of microwaved leftovers of chicken and potatoes in front of me, and I dropped the half-melted bag of ice on the table and tucked in.

Sitting deep in thought, Mom didn't say much during dinner and moved her fork mechanically from her plate to her mouth. I wondered what punishment she was concocting. When she spoke, I dropped my fork and watched her.

"Kell," she said, "I have a surprise for you."

Well, that's not what I expected. "Okay," I said as I picked up the plastic cup and sipped the raspberry Kool-Aid.

"Tomorrow, I'm going to work a double shift so I can have your birthday off."

I turned sixteen in two days, and Mom had been dropping cryptic hints about it for weeks.

"It's just a birthday," I said.

She pushed her plate away from her. "No," she said, "this year, you come of age, and I have things I need to tell you—things you need to do."

"That doesn't make any sense, Mom," I said. "Nobody comes of age until eighteen. That's when we can vote. You can't even buy beer until you're twenty-one."

"I've been waiting until you became a man," she said as if the law didn't mean anything, "and we're going to need the whole day to make sense out of it."

My face grew hot. "Wait. We're not going to have *that* talk, are we? I've already had biology."

Mom stared at me for a moment in open confusion and then laughed. She had a wild, joyful laugh that made me want to join her. If I hadn't been so embarrassed, I might have.

"No," she chuckled. "This is more important."

"What's more important than sex?" I asked. "I mean, without sex, there wouldn't be any life on earth."

Mom waved me away and kept chuckling.

I scowled. What did she have to tell me? The only thing I could think of was that she was finally going to tell me about my deadbeat dad who abandoned us when I was too little to remember him.

"Dude, that was sweet." My best friend, Dean, slapped me on the back as we slouched into history class the next day. "I thought they would suspend you for sure."

A wide grin spread across Dean's long, thin face. He liked to wear bright pink shirts and pink shoelaces. When he walked, he kicked out his size eleven shoes in a gangly way that made him look like a giraffe trying to flick the mud off his hooves. He had grown so much in the last year, he was still trying to get used to his own skin. His black hair was tight and curly. He was one of the few black kids in our school. We played on the same soccer team, went out to the river to hunt for arrowheads together, and planned to become archaeologists.

"He had it coming." I slipped between the desks and fell into my seat.

"I think you broke his nose," Dean said, "but man, he gave you a nice shiner."

I poked at the tender flesh around my eye as the announcer on the intercom called us all to stand for the Pledge of Allegiance.

"Makes you look like a lopsided raccoon," Dean whispered.

We ran through the pledge and dropped into our chairs for the announcements.

"I'm gonna miss soccer practice for two weeks." I flipped a

pencil around my thumb. Summer soccer had already started even though school wasn't out yet.

Dean shrugged. "You should have thought of that before you broke Jessop's nose," he said.

I scowled at him, and he raised his hands.

"Don't go off on me, man," he said.

"All right," Miss Kearns said as the last of the announcements blared. "We're going to switch gears from yesterday's class."

She dimmed the lights and clicked on the projector. An image of grass-covered mounds shaped like squares and circles flashed onto the screen.

"Sweet," Dean said.

"Yes, thank you, Mr. Morgan," Miss Kearns said. "Like the peoples of Europe, Native Americans were skilled astronomers. The Hopewell at Newark built these mounds to mark the rising and setting of the moon."

She clicked to another slide of a vast mound city.

"The city of Cahokia has more than 100 mounds built on a true north-south alignment."

She advanced to a slide of two pictures. One had an actual picture of a circular ring, and the other was a drawing of the same ring with big logs stuck in the ground around the circle.

"These wooden henges marked the summer solstice sunrise on Monks mound."

An image of a massive stone circle appeared.

"This is the Big Horn Medicine Wheel in Wyoming, and it is aligned with the solstices.

A picture of an earthen lodge with a hole in the roof flashed onto the screen.

"The Pawnee were some of the best astronomers in North America, and they aligned their lodges so the sun shining through the door on the equinox sunrise would fall on a special altar."

Then she showed a circular mound beside a picture of a stone tunnel with a ray of light shooting through it.

"This is Newgrange in Boyne Valley, Ireland," she said. "This passage is aligned so that the rising sun at the winter solstice shines a beam of light down the passage."

She clicked to an image of Stonehenge.

"Probably most famous of all is Stonehenge, which may have served as a huge calendar marking the rising and setting of the sun and moon." She paused. "So what do you make of all these ancient people so skillfully calculating lunar and solar cycles and being able to engineer their structures so precisely without the aid of modern technology?"

I didn't want to say anything because everyone knew my mom had a weird fascination with light. I couldn't afford another fight. Dean glanced at me, probably guessing what I was thinking. Then he raised his hand.

"Maybe they worshipped light in their religion," he said.

"Perhaps," Miss Kearns replied. "Light certainly had religious significance to many of them. Why else?"

I knew what Mom would have said. She would have told me light was the true power in the universe, and I needed to learn to respect the light. It was an odd way of thinking of things, and I wondered if maybe she hadn't picked it up from some book on ancient religions.

"It also had practical value," Miss Kearns said when no one answered. "Aboriginal peoples used these alignments to mark important times of the year, like the New Year, when it was time to plant or harvest crops, or when certain natural foods became available. Using light in ceremonies might also symbolize the renewal of life."

A girl at the front of the class raised her hand. Miss Kearns nodded to her.

"I watched a documentary that said aliens built all those big monuments," she said.

Miss Kearns bestowed a patient smile on the girl. I smirked at Dean and rolled my eyes. I hated it when people made that argument.

"Those so-called documentaries," Miss Kearns said, "are not based on scientific evidence. They are frankly racist and insulting because they presume that early humans were too ignorant to think complex thoughts and engage in complicated engineering. In this class, we will base all of our assertions on verifiable facts."

Dean raised his hand again.

"Maybe they all had the same religion," he said. He was still stuck on the religion idea.

Miss Kearns pursed her lips and considered for a moment.

"Some people have thought that," she said. "But it seems unlikely, given that early peoples had little contact with one another. They did not share a common culture around the world."

Dean was almost wriggling with excitement as we left class. "That was cool," he said. "We've gotta quit digging around in muddy streams and start looking for the next big discovery."

"Yeah," I said. "I want to see that Newgrange place."

Dean turned to go to his next class. "I'll catch you after soccer practice," he said. "Don't have too much fun in detention, raccoon man."

I wrinkled my nose at him. His pink shirt was unnaturally bright against his black skin. I shook my head and started down the hallway. Dean was crazy. That's why I liked him.

Come. A female voice echoed in the corridor.

I stopped and scanned the kids shouldering past me. None of them seemed to hear it.

Come to me, the voice said again.

"What the…" I jerked my head around to see if Jens had convinced one of his girlfriends to play a prank on me, but the hallway was rapidly emptying of students as they ducked into their classrooms. Maybe Jens had given me a concussion or something.

The shadow approaches, the voice said.

My stomach writhed like a snake slithering through the grass, and I burst into a run.

When I slouched into the detention room, I was gratified to see that Jens sported two shiners to my one, and his nose was swollen. I wanted to confront him about the creepy voice in the hallway, but even if I was right, he would just tell me it was my witch mother. Then, I'd have to punch him again and end up spending two weeks of summer vacation in detention with nothing to do but stare at his ugly mug.

Jens sneered at me now and again, and once he held up a paper that had the words, "I'll get you," written in bold black ink.

"Mr. Jessop," the teacher said, holding out his hand for the note.

Jens paled and wrinkled it up, but the teacher yanked it out of his hand.

"Detention doesn't seem to get through to you," the teacher said. "I'll be speaking with the principal about this."

I gave Jens a triumphant grin. Maybe he would finally have to pay for all the grief he gave me.

They let us study in detention, so I got through everything but my math homework, which I always saved until last. I shouldered my backpack and pushed through the big glass doors of the high school into the late afternoon heat. Soccer was a great game. I loved to play, but it was so hot today I figured I hadn't missed much by sitting in an air-conditioned classroom.

A ray of sunlight slipped through the steel-gray sky and fell on a massive boulder that sprawled on the front lawn of the elementary school. The light cut through the humid air like it had a purpose— like it was trying to show me something. That's what Mom would have said if she had been with me. She would have stopped me cold and told me that a ray of light like that was a message I was supposed to understand. She was different from other moms, and I loved her for it.

I shrugged my backpack higher up onto my shoulder and moseyed down the cracked sidewalk in no hurry to get home. The only thing waiting for me was math homework. Our shabby little town had ten streets, and three of those were dirt roads. The schools all clustered together on the edge of town around the dirt track and baseball fields. The red brick elementary was the oldest school building. Middle school students met in some creamy modules behind the elementary, and the high school was a small two-story affair on the other side of the track.

The forest closed in around the town, nibbling at the edges of abandoned yards and vacant lots. Rusted cars populated the margins, beyond which the green rolling hill country of Ohio spread out—a checkerboard of farmland and forest created by generations of farmers.

That phrase, *the shadow approaches*, kept bouncing around in my head. Why did it make my insides crawl? This was something straight out of a Stephen King novel.

I pushed through the glass doors to the worn out little diner where Mom worked, thinking I might grab a bite to eat and say hi. Sometimes Mateo gave me a slice of pepperoni pizza with jalapeños in place of bell peppers. Dean said I was crazy, but it was my favorite.

A few farmers from out of town, two truckers, and a biker hunched over their plates, tossing the occasional word back and forth as they shoveled the mashed potatoes and meatloaf down their throats. The diner smelled heavenly this time of day, and my mouth watered. I thought I might see if I could sneak a roll or something since I'd be on my own for dinner. Today was the day Mom had scheduled the double shift so we could have her big talk on my birthday tomorrow.

Mateo saw me looking around through the kitchen window and came out, wiping his big hands on his apron. The smell of roasting meat and potatoes followed him, making my stomach rumble. I looked up at his well-sculpted hair and muscular physique.

"She's gone, Kell," Mateo said. He had a crush on my mom, but she always kept him at arm's length. The concerned scowl he gave me now sent a shiver of worry through me. My mom didn't just leave work. She wasn't that kind of lady.

"Did she say where she was going?"

Mateo shook his head. "Nah, but after she saw some weirdo in a long, black cloak, she freaked out. She dropped everything and ran." He pointed to a pile of broken plates and glasses tangled in a mound of spaghetti that had been scooped against the wall. "I mean, she literally dropped everything and ran."

One of the other waitresses came around the counter with a bucket and mop. Her frown and knitted brow told me she was not happy.

I scowled at the mess, trying to decide what to do.

Mateo stepped up to me. "If she's in trouble," he said, "you call me." He laid a heavy hand on my shoulder.

"Yeah, thanks, Mateo."

I dashed outside into the wet heat of an Ohio afternoon in mid-June, where the air was so thick you could chew it. Gray clouds sagged low over the trees, and a distant rumble of thunder growled through the sky.

The flint-colored clouds had closed again, so no ray of light could break through. I tried to imagine what might have frightened Mom so much she would risk losing her job. We had weirdos come through town now and again, but no one around here wore black robes. It was too freaking hot.

I picked up my pace. The sweat dripped from my hair and trickled down my back. Mom couldn't be in trouble. She just couldn't. We hardly knew anyone in town. We did our own thing, never bothering anybody. Then, I remembered Jens. He said he was going to get even with me. Had he played some prank on Mom?

From half a block away, I could see the front door to our duplex standing wide open, but Mom's Hyundai Accent wasn't parked in the driveway. I sprinted the last hundred yards and burst into the living room.

"Mom?" I called. I dropped my bag by the door and checked every room. The house was empty. I stomped into the kitchen and jerked the phone off the hook to call Mateo. We didn't have cell phones because Mom couldn't afford them on a waitress's salary. A piece of paper that had been wedged under the receiver fluttered to the ground. I snatched it up and read.

"Come to the big stone by the elementary school. Bring a shovel and a flashlight. Love, Mom. PS: Don't waste time. Come now! We're being hunted. This is our only escape."

"What the heck does that mean?" I wondered aloud.

She'd scared me half to death by leaving work, and now she wanted me to bring a shovel to the school grounds? Did she think it was April Fool's Day? What did she mean by *We're being hunted?* By whom?

It wouldn't do any good to stand in the kitchen trying to guess, so I hustled to the garage, grabbed a shovel and the big flashlight, and sprinted for the school. Mom's red Hyundai was the only car in the parking lot. I stopped running and tried to catch my breath. At least I had found her, but her car hadn't been parked there when I passed a little while ago.

Thunder rumbled, and a flash of lightning split the sky, illuminating the gray clouds from overhead so I could see through them to the darkening sky above. It was a weird effect. The growl of the thunder built to a crescendo of noise, followed by a loud crack, but no lightning flashed. Had I heard a scream in that thunder? I glanced up at the sky again. Where had that crack and scream come from? The gray sky slouched down upon me as if it were tired. I felt the weight of it and raced off toward the rock. A crack of thunder without any lightning couldn't be good. Maybe it had been a gunshot.

"Mom?" I breathed and broke into a run.

As I pelted around the Hyundai toward the boulder, I saw something black slip behind the school building. I rounded the boulder and slid to a stop. My heart leaped into my throat, and I froze in horror.

Mom sprawled on her back on a pile of dirt. A shovel lay beside her hand. A black hole had been blown into her chest, oozing a dark fluid that soaked her clothes. She gasped, struggling to breathe. Her eyes opened wide. Her body spasmed.

"Mom!" I gasped. I dropped to my knees beside her. What could I do?

Mom had always been a tiny woman with a delicate beauty. Now, her face was so ghastly I could hardly look at her. Clutching my hand, she drew shallow breaths.

"The darkness is growing stronger," she gasped.

I glanced up at the evening sky. "It's just getting dark," I said. "What do I do?"

"No, Kell. You don't understand." Mom struggled to raise herself. "You need to understand."

"Mom?" The panic burned in my chest. We didn't have time for this. I jerked my shirt off over my head and stuffed it into the wound.

"No, don't." Her voice faltered, and her hands fumbled with mine. "If I don't tell you now, you'll never know."

Mom had hinted about my mysterious past ever since I could remember.

"They've found us," she said.

"Who?"

"You need the power to defend yourself." She panted in shallow, wheezing breaths.

"Come on," I choked. "Let's get you to the car. I can drive you to the hospital."

The doctors would be able to do something. I had to believe they could. My mom was all I had—no grandparents, aunts, uncles, cousins. No one. It seemed like we had dropped out of the sky one day. I knew nothing about my mom's past or about my father. I'd never even seen a picture of him. When I asked Mom about him, she always said, "Later. When the time is right."

I couldn't let myself think about her dying now because that would mean I was an orphan—alone in a big, ugly world where no one would care whether I lived or died.

"There's one place you will be safe now, but it's dangerous."

"Come on, Mom." I slipped my hand underneath her head.

"The chamber might give you the power I can't give. But it might take you away. I was going to try on your birthday, but…"

She was talking gibberish. I slipped my other arm under her knees and lifted her against my bare chest.

"Listen," Mom panted, "dig here. It's your only hope."

I glanced at the hole she had cut in the green sod. It was already a good two feet deep and wide enough for me to stand in.

"What are you talking about?" I headed for the car in a stumbling run.

"You can hide there. If you concentrate on the Light, it may come to you. You are your father's son. It is your right."

Mom's fingers spasmed against my bare skin. I grimaced as her nails cut me. Her face twisted in horrible pain. Black streaks expanded on her neck as the black stuff worked its way toward her brain. She panted for air. The black ooze bubbled on her chest and leaked from the side of her mouth down her cheek. I expected the black stuff to smell like rotting flesh or something, but it didn't have any smell at all.

"Hang on, Mom," I said. "I'll get you to the hospital." Tears dripped from my eyes as I stumbled toward the car. Thunder rumbled overhead.

"Kell," she gasped, "we can't run anymore. You have to face who you are."

"Just stay focused, Mom," I choked and stumbled faster.

Her eyelids fluttered. "They're hunting us," she whispered. "Those who escaped." She touched my face. "Go into the chamber. It's the only hope I have left. If it gives you the power, look for your father. He loved you so much."

I glanced around, searching for someone, anyone, to help, but the school was deserted—the red bricks of the building darkened in the fading light. Nothing but the blackened windows watched me, laughing at my despair.

"Help me!" I screamed.

"I love you, Kell," Mom said. She gasped and coughed. "If you find him," she panted, "if he's still alive, tell him I was faithful to the end."

My chest burned. Desperate tears streamed down my face. "Wait, Mom. We'll get help."

"I thought he would come for us," Mom said. Something gurgled in her throat.

"Who?"

"Your father. That's why I stayed here…all these years…near the chamber."

My dad abandoned my mother with a baby and never even sent a postcard or an email. I couldn't understand why Mom always turned away the men who would have married her and made her life so much easier. I couldn't understand her dogged, desperate faith in him. Right now, I didn't care.

"You are his son," she said.

"Hang on, Mom."

I reached the Hyundai and fumbled with the door handle until it unlatched. I used my knee and shoulder to work it open and struggled to get Mom onto the front seat.

"Where are the keys?"

Mom grasped my arm with a trembling hand. It was cold and soft. Her finger drifted to the birthmark on my arm. "You are his son," she said again. "Never forget."

"The keys, Mom."

Frustrated anger distorted her face. "Listen to me," she pleaded, grabbing at my arm. "Do as I say. I waited too long. If the power doesn't come to you now…there is no hope. They will find you… and they will kill you."

"Give me the keys, Mom." I dug in her pockets, found the keys, and jerked them out. They jangled harshly in the humid air. She tried to grasp my hands, but she was too weak.

"I'm sorry, Mom," I said. "Sorry I wasn't good enough." Mom had always been disappointed in my lack of interest in light. I had to tell her before…

Mom blinked and touched my cheek.

"Oh, Kell," she whispered, "you are the only thing that gave me a reason to live."

I thought I saw a yellow light flare around her fingers before her hand fell limp to her lap. Her eyes stopped moving, and her blackened chest stopped struggling to breathe.

"Don't, Mom. You can't go." I dragged her from the car and laid her on the asphalt. I considered doing compressions, but there wasn't much of her chest left. So I propped her head back and blew into her mouth. Nothing happened. I blew again. Nothing.

"Mom," I sobbed. I blew again. Out of the corner of my eye, I could see the air I blew in bubble in the black ooze that filled her chest. It was pointless.

I lifted her head into my lap, bent over her, and sobbed.

The spatter of the raindrops on my head dragged me back to the reality of the situation. Daylight had faded from the sky. The wind kicked up, carrying with it the pungent scent of the damp forest. It seemed wrong that the world should go on without my mom in it. I laid her head gently on the asphalt as a sudden fury burned in my chest.

Somebody had killed her, had stolen away the most precious thing in my life. And they did it just as she was about to reveal something important. Sixteen years of silence about my father and about her past, and all Mom could do was leave me with bits and fragments and a new horror that someone had murdered her and would be hunting me.

I dashed to the corner of the schoolhouse where I had seen the flash of something black disappear, hoping to find the villain so I could pound the life out of him, but the playground was empty. I turned back to the stone and the parking lot where Mom's red Hyundai stood over her lifeless body. A sob escaped my throat. Tears burst from my eyes again. This couldn't be happening.

My mind scrambled, searching for some meaning, some reason for this. The only concrete bit of information Mom gave me was about the stone and some secret chamber where I would be safe and maybe find my father.

I rushed back to the hulking shadow of the boulder, snatched up the shovel, and drove it into the ground only to feel the shock of it striking stone. I cursed and drove it in again, putting all my bitterness and rage into each strike. Something gave. I struck again. Then I jumped up and landed with both feet on the top edge of the shovel. The ground vanished beneath my feet. I let out a yell as I tumbled into darkness.

Dirt and stone cascaded around me. The fall wasn't far, but the landing jarred my bones and rattled my teeth. The shovel handle cracked me upside the head. I blinked the dirt from my eyes and found myself sprawled on the floor of some dark cavern.

How had Mom known this was here? It didn't seem to lead anywhere. I peered up through the hole above me to the darkening sky and the last vestiges of lingering light. Raindrops washed my face. I cursed. Was it just a hole in the ground that Mom said would protect me from whoever or whatever killed her?

The gritty earth coated my teeth, but I didn't care. The only person in the whole world who had ever loved me was gone. I sank to my knees and let myself cry again. The moist darkness enfolded me as if it knew me—as if I had come home.

Come to me, the voice whispered.

Chapter Two
The Promised One

I AWOKE, BLINKING at the column of summer light that filtered through the ragged hole in the ceiling of the chamber. An electrical charge filled the air, raising goosebumps all over my body. Specks of gold danced in the ray of light as it spread like a blanket over me and the pile of rubble upon which I lay. It felt warm on my bare shoulders.

Sitting up, I examined my surroundings. The walls and ceiling of the small chamber were stone. Fine dust swirled and danced in the air. It tasted dank and moldy. Then my gaze fell on a skeleton that stared at me with big, blank sockets, watching my every move.

For one horrible moment, I thought it was Mom's body, but then I remembered I left her by the car.

"Geez," I said as I scrambled to the other side of the pile of rubble. "I gotta get out of here and call the police." I must have slept all night.

A horrible ache rose in my chest at the memory of Mom's body, all covered in the black ooze. I reached for the jagged edge of the hole when a beam of pure white light stabbed across the small enclosure. Where was it coming from? The musty air came alive with power, and the beam landed in a square-shaped cavity in the stone wall. Thin, white writing spread out from each corner, shimmering like a gossamer web.

The lines expanded, growing bolder, moving faster and faster until the light raced around the walls of the cavern with blinding speed, pulsing like the veins of a living thing. Excited interest swelled in my chest. I couldn't help but think of that Newgrange place in Ireland and lowered my arms to wait and see what the light might do.

Soon the threads of white fire covered the walls and the ceiling in an intricate pattern. The air grew thick and vibrated, pulsing with the rhythm of the delicate writing. In the corner by the skeleton, different writing throbbed a pale red hue—like a footnote to the entire composition.

I stared at the writing and pinched myself to make sure this was really happening. Dean would freak out when I told him. No ancient civilization in Ohio had writing like this that I knew of. This was something else—something unknown to modern archeology, and my mom had known about it. I reached out to touch the throbbing white lines when an invisible weight pressed in on me as if the air in the chamber was being pressurized. I fell to my knees and rolled to my back. The writing was everywhere now—all around me. To my surprise, I found I could read it.

"The abyss awaits those who would pervert the Light," I read aloud.

What kind of place was this? Out of the corner of my eye, I noticed the red handwriting by the skeleton pulsing to a different rhythm from the white writing. I shifted so I could read it when a wave of nausea swept over me. My hands trembled. Moldy dust coated my tongue as I tried to moisten my lips. The blood pounded in my temples, and terror filled my chest. I was in danger.

"I gotta get out of here," I mumbled.

This chamber must have had some evil curse on it like the Pharaohs put on their tombs. I struggled to my knees, but a strange weight pressed on my chest, making it impossible to move. I strained to breathe. The air swept in to crush me against the floor. Fear gripped my stomach in a tight fist.

"Help," I gasped.

The invisible force pinned me to the earth, like a butterfly on a mounting board. I was trapped.

"Help!" I choked on the word. My mouth opened in a silent scream of terror and pain. I was suffocating, and I couldn't do anything about it. I heard that people could have PTSD after a traumatic incident, and I thought I might be trapped here by some crazy panic attack until someone found me.

A prolonged ripping somewhere deep within my body engulfed me in agony. Something inside stretched and tore, causing unbearable anguish. White-hot fire burst behind my eyes. A painful snap popped in my chest as if all my ribs had cracked.

Then the pain receded as delicious air rushed back into my lungs. I sucked it in even though it burned my throat. Gasping for air and fighting the terrible ache in my chest, I curled up into a ball. What was happening to me?

Maybe it was a seizure instead of a panic attack. I glanced around the dark chamber. Light streamed in through a tiny cavity in one side—just enough to allow me to see. Where was the gaping hole in the ceiling? How had it closed? How would anyone find me now? I tried to yell, but my tongue stuck to the roof of my mouth.

I blinked at the horrible pressure behind my eyes, and a new horror filled me. I felt a presence. Someone was here inside me, sharing my mind.

It was a man, and his name was Ross.

With that realization came a clarity of understanding. I was possessed by some ancient spirit that inhabited this chamber. Whoever had lived in that skeleton hadn't died—not really. He continued to exist, waiting for some fool like me to come stumbling into his tomb. I curled up and clutched at my hair as the terror and revulsion overwhelmed me. I was going insane. Somehow, watching my mother die had made me lose my mind.

"Help," I whimpered. "Somebody help me."

The two halves of my mind struggled with one another, each trying to seize control.

I fell into the chamber, I thought.

They threw me in, Ross said.

I discovered strange new writing.

I carved the signs of power on the wall.

No one would ever find me now that the chamber had closed around me.

They will be coming.

Shuffling footsteps sounded from somewhere below me. Fear

and anticipation mingled in my throat as I stretched myself, searching for the source of the sounds, afraid that some new horror was going to lunge out of the darkness. I sat up, poking my mud-covered chest, trying to locate the odd presence inside me.

Metal grated against stone. I stared at the floor as the dirt cascaded into a thin line near my feet. I scrambled away from the widening gap in the floor. Every instinct told me to flee, to claw my way out of this hellhole before it was too late, but I couldn't. My legs wouldn't obey me.

The other presence inside me refused.

This is what I have been waiting for.

Ross said inside my mind.

I will have my revenge.

I stood rooted to the cold floor as surely as if I had been glued to it. A strange sense of excitement surged from the other half of me to mingle with my terror.

The scratch of shifting stone ceased, and I stared down into a chasm large enough for two men to enter shoulder to shoulder. A pale red light splashed over a set of stairs. My heart leaped into my throat as my body stepped forward against my will.

"Help," I screamed. I couldn't control my own body. The presence inside me forced me to step forward. He shoved my desire aside and compelled my body to do his will. I watched, as if from a distance, as my feet took the steps one at a time. At the bottom, I found *him* waiting.

The luminous, red eyes blazed from the empty sockets of a smiling skull. Long black hair flowed down his back. His tall, thin frame was draped in a black robe. The overpowering odor of death and decay filled my nostrils. Skeletal hands with no flesh on them reached for me through the darkness. I stiffened. The arms embraced me. An aura of power emanated from this being, strong and pulsating. It reached for me as if wishing to feed off my energy. A deep voice whispered in my ear.

"Welcome, Promised One. We have waited long."

I followed the skeletal priest down the stone corridor. The musty smell of earth and stone permeated the air and mingled with the putrid smell of decay that wafted back from my guide. I sucked in a deep breath, trying to slow my racing pulse. The two halves struggled within me. I wanted to scream and run, but Ross pushed me forward.

"Let me go," I demanded inside my head, but he had seized control of my limbs. I sensed his anticipation.

I can't, Ross said.

"Please," I begged again.

This is my last chance, Ross said.

So I focused on the creature striding in front of me—a skeleton that smelled like death. This could not end well. Was this skeleton or this Ross the voice I had heard in my head in the school? They couldn't be. That voice was female.

We entered a circular chamber, alight with the flames of many candles burning in sconces all around the room. A transparent skull grinned as it floated in the air in the center of the room. Its iridescent gleam reflected off the polished black surface of the walls.

A tremor of terror swept through me and mingled with Ross's shiver of excitement as six more black-robed priests emerged from separate tunnels. I strained against the compulsion to step into the room. Horror forced tears from my eyes.

"Please," I said.

You must, Ross insisted.

The air emanating from the priests assaulted my senses. It contained the confusing and contradictory sensations of fire and water, life and death, earth and emptiness. Confusion and familiarity mingled within me. The priests' eyes shone in all the colors of the rainbow from under the cowls of their black robes. The colors were so bright, so intense, they almost caused me physical pain to look into them.

Ross stopped me underneath the skull as the seven priests closed the circle to stand silent and motionless around me. Power pulsed in the room. A part of me was drawn to it with a desperate hunger like I had never known. I longed to touch it. To hold it. To consume it. To wield it. Is this what Mother had meant when she said I might find power in the chamber?

I trembled and tried to cringe away from the ghoulish monsters that encircled me. Ross made me kneel. The priests extended their arms, exposing pale bony fingers that reached for me.

"Don't touch me," I snarled. My terror was quickly turning to anger. How dare they do this to me when my mother had just died? I strained against Ross and rose to my feet, but my knees buckled, and I slammed back down onto the stone slabs.

Seven bony hands rested on the head of the skull hovering above me. Then seven more pressed upon my head. Their touch burned like fire and ice, sending wild shivers coursing through me. I tried to scream. All the colors of the rainbow flashed against the walls of the chamber before erupting into a brilliant white flame that seared me to the roots of my soul. I collapsed in a gasp of agony.

Chapter Three
The Song of Illurien

ROSS LOOKED AROUND. *Light shone through a large window. His head ached, and his eyes stung like he had been staring at the sun. The memory returned—sluggish at first, then with complete clarity. The new Chosen One was still there, looking out through the same eyes. The sensation of being part of a living being was almost overpowering. Ross had forgotten what it was like to see with human eyes and hear with human ears, to feel the supple reality of a body locked in time and space.*

Yet, something had gone wrong with the words of power. The boy should have read the writing. He should have understood what Ross had done. Ross's memories were supposed to become the boy's own, but his temporary control of the night before had evaporated.

He had managed to compel the frightened boy into the circle of priests, but now as he reached out to him, he sensed a barrier. The seed of power the priests planted in the boy was aware of him and would keep him at bay. It erected defenses against him, isolating him from the boy's motor control and direct thoughts, but he could still feel his emotions and the presence and sensations of the boy's body. He could see and hear what the boy saw and heard.

"By the Sacred Circle," Ross cursed to himself.

This would make his task more difficult. He expected to share his host's thoughts and memories so he could merge them with his own and instruct him on what needed to be done. It was essential that the boy cooperate. Ross alone knew the secret. His friend, Jerome, had risked everything to bring it to him. No one alive understood the nature and purpose of the power. He must succeed this time. There would be no third chance.

I awoke, blinking at the warm light that flooded my face. My head ached, and my eyes burned as if the flash of a thousand cameras had scorched them. I swallowed, trying to rid myself of the odd feeling in my chest—like I had been torn in two, and a strange presence had wedged itself in between. It was like having a bone lodged in my throat, but this was stuck everywhere at once, leaving me divided and incomplete. I swallowed again and clutched at my chest, but it wouldn't go away. The most disturbing thing about the obstruction was that it had a personality. It even had a name—Ross.

This was impossible. I must have been in shock from the death of my mother. I jerked to a sitting position as the memory returned in a sudden, confusing rush. The horrible suffocating feeling of loss forced the tears from my eyes. She died in my arms, murdered by some stranger who blew a hole in her chest.

What did I do about it? Nothing but dig a stupid hole in the ground. She said I would be safe in there and hinted that I might find my father, but it hadn't worked. Everything had gone wrong. The writing. The pain. The sense of invasion. The priests. The strange new power within me that slumbered just below the surface.

I reached out to it, and it fluttered to life in response. My whole being warmed. The energy tingled through me, sparking at my fingertips. I glanced at my hands but saw nothing out of the ordinary. Was this the power Mom thought I might find in the chamber? This power didn't possess color like that of the priests. My power was colorless. This struck me as odd. A rippling tingle across the back of my mind revealed Ross's interest. It was a weird feeling, like a spider scurrying over my skin, only this was on the inside. I didn't like it.

I swung my legs over the edge of the bed that was positioned against a wall under an open window. A table and two chairs filled the center of the room along with a cupboard, and what I guessed was a chamber pot standing against the opposite wall. Flames flickered in a tiny fireplace on the far wall by the iron-bound, wooden door.

It was a simple, yet comfortable, room, awash with light

streaming in through the window. The air blowing in had a scrubbed-clean quality about it, much nicer than the air in Ohio. I had no idea where I was. Had someone found me and locked me up in some insane asylum or a prison cell?

Maybe, but I didn't think so. This was a strange new place filled with power—that much was obvious. Even the light and air coming in through the window pulsed with the energy of life like I'd never experienced. It both invited me and repelled me, but I couldn't stay. I needed to go back to my mother. She lay alone on the asphalt by her car. I jumped off the bed to head out the door in search of a way home.

As soon as my bare feet touched the cool stone, a tingling sensation burst up my legs, followed by a sense of urgency.

"What the…" I cried out in surprise and leaped back onto the bed.

The instant my feet left the floor, the sensation died. I looked around for my shoes and socks but they weren't there, so I touched one toe to the floor again. The same sense of urgency swept up my leg and into my stomach. This time, I heard or felt music. I yanked my toe away again. What was going on? Had I lost my mind entirely? How did a person know if he was crazy? I mean, if you were crazy, you would think you were sane, and everyone else was crazy.

The door opened, and I lunged to my feet to face a thin young woman a few years older than myself with flowing black hair and light brown skin. I expected the urgency and music to erupt again when my feet hit the floor, but nothing happened.

The girl wore a long gray robe with no other adornment. Her stunning beauty made me embarrassed to be standing there shirtless in my dirty pants and bare feet. My shirt was still stuffed in Mom's wound up in the parking lot in Ohio. At least someone had cleaned the mud from my chest.

Her eyes drew my attention. They were large and radiant silver, like liquid mercury, and they glowed and churned. They were not as brilliant as those of the priests, yet they were oddly beautiful. The silver eyes made her all the more alluring. She most definitely was not a skeleton, and I couldn't figure out how or why her eyes would be like that. A thrill of nervous interest swept through me. What was I to do?

A smile flitted across her lips, and I thought she was eyeing the shiner Jens Jessop had given me two days before. I raised a hand to touch my eye and found it still tender. Or maybe she was smiling at the fact I didn't have a shirt on and she could examine my lithe, athletic figure. I had a girl tell me once that my body was well-toned, and I had never forgotten it. I glanced around for something to wear, but there was nothing except maybe the pillowcase.

"Follow me," she motioned.

I hesitated. "Who are you?" I asked.

"I am Lowthelian, a servant of the Light. Come with me." She gestured to me again with her small brown hand.

"Where am I?"

"You are in the Temple of Light," she said. "Now, follow me, Promised One. They will explain."

"My name is Kell," I protested.

She nodded. "Yes, Promised One. Please follow me."

I stared at her for a moment as she half-turned toward the door. "I need to get back," I said. "My mother's there. Someone killed her, and I have to find out who did it."

The memory brought a lump to my throat, and I blinked back the sting of tears.

Lowthelian's smile faltered. She looked confused, but she recovered and gestured to me. What could I do? Maybe these priests would know how to send me back.

As I followed her graceful form, I considered running for it once I was free of the room, but I had no idea where to go. A nervous excitement filled my chest like I used to get when I ventured into the shadows of the spook alleys around Halloween.

This was insane. I knew my steps led me to the beginning of something strange—maybe even dangerous—something orchestrated by a gang of skeletal monsters. And yet, I stumbled toward it because I had no other choice. Some of my mother's last words about my father lurked at the back of my mind. *Tell him I was faithful to the end.* Those words and my own morbid curiosity propelled me onward, despite the trembling fear.

The corridors through which we passed were not dark and musty. They were filled with light. Warm, white light. No decorations, pictures, or furniture. Only cold gray stone. No dust or cobwebs settled here. All was clean and bright and fresh.

A sudden chill swept over my head as a breeze blew down the corridor. I reached up and found a smooth scalp.

"No," I said out loud. "Why did you shave my hair?"

"The Chosen are always shaven," Lowthelian said.

"They let you keep your hair," I protested.

Lowthelian glanced at me with a little smirk. "I am not a Chosen One," she said. "Only the male Chosen are shaven."

"That red-eyed skeleton had hair," I paused. "Wait. How can a skeleton have hair?"

"He is a Keeper," she said, like that explained things.

"Great," I said. I liked my hair, and I didn't appreciate them shaving me bald as a bowling ball without even asking.

"Mind telling me where we're going?" I asked.

Lowthelian said nothing.

"I mean, this is a cool place and all, but I need to go home."

"You are home," Lowthelian said.

I sped up to walk beside her. She didn't look at me. Her dark skin was smooth and perfect. Her hair was thick and flowing.

"My mom just died," I said.

I thought this would elicit some sympathy or surprise, at the very least, but Lowthelian acted as though I hadn't spoken.

"She was murdered," I said.

Lowthelian stared resolutely ahead. My throat tightened, and my face burned with anger. Her callous disregard for my mother's death enraged me.

"Hey!" I yelled. "I'm talking to you."

Lowthelian stopped and cocked her head to one side to study me. "I heard you, Promised One," she said. "Here, you have no family. If you will be patient a moment longer, the Keepers will explain everything."

I scowled at her. Why did the name "Keepers" fill me with dread?

"Keepers?" I asked. "Keepers of what?"

She sighed. "Just come with me, and I'll show you."

She started up the corridor again, and I trailed along behind. The Keepers must be the skeleton priests.

"Why aren't you a skeleton?" I blurted.

Lowthelian glanced at me with an indignant smirk and clicked her tongue as if she thought I was ridiculous. She led me to a square courtyard. A large circle of black polished stones, set at regular intervals amid the gleaming white cobblestones, surrounded a gigantic slab of white stone that stabbed its sharp finger fifteen or twenty feet into the sky, ending at a knife-edge point. It cast a long, thin shadow over the white stones. The plaza was a massive sundial. I stepped after Lowthelian, unable to ignore my interest as I remembered my class yesterday with Miss Kearns.

Seven black-robed priests formed a circle at the center of the courtyard in front of the sundial. The place vibrated with life like no place I had ever experienced.

"Dean won't believe me when I tell him about this," I murmured.

As I approached the sundial, I experienced a tingling sensation that was warm and inviting, powerful and terrifying.

Lowthelian stopped and motioned for me to step into the circle of priests. I hesitated. All I wanted was to return to my mom. She motioned again. I thought about asking them how to get home, but their expressionless, skeletal faces made it difficult to tell how they might react. I considered racing into the corridors to find the chamber myself, but I knew I'd never succeed. Even if I did, how would I get home?

"Hey," I said with an awkward wave of my hand. I didn't know what to say to a bunch of scary priests with weird eyes.

None of them responded, so I took one hesitant step and then another. As I passed between two of the priests, a sense of destiny swept over me. I experienced the terrifying suspicion that I would never be able to step out again.

I stopped in the middle of the circle and examined each priest in turn, trying not to show my revulsion at their appearance. This was worse than Halloween. Kids running around in masks were no threat, but I knew deep down these skeletons could hurt me if they wished. Some of them probably did. When Mom said it would be dangerous, she must have meant these skeletons. I clasped my hands in front of me, willing them to stop shaking.

Then the priests sang. The sound burst out of them in a resonate harmony so powerful that I flinched and stepped backward. The music rang out as clear as a bell in the morning stillness. I expected them to start speaking—to explain why they brought me here and what they intended to do with me—but they only sang.

The song sounded like an a cappella choir, humming in tight harmony. It started low and grew louder. The sound was exquisite. It mingled and mixed and wavered, driving to my heart and bringing tears to my eyes. I had never heard anything so beautiful—not Mozart, not Beethoven, not even my own mother's angelic voice—though the tune sounded familiar.

How could such hideous skeletons create such beauty? The contrast between the exquisite music and the monsters creating it was stupefying. I closed my eyes so I didn't have to look at them and just listened, trying to imagine a choir of monks in a magnificent cathedral. The music carried me away to bright blue skies and deep crystal waters, fluttering flames, vibrant green woods, and freshly plowed earth. In the music, life mingled with death, becoming one.

The priests began to weave a story into the music, which progressed like a ballad, rising and flowing from one stanza to the next—like water slipping over a stone.

Masters of Light, Illurien said, let us sing with one voice,
and so, provide a place for the lesser creations of our song.

The Beings of Light sang into the Darkness,
organizing the chaos, molding, and shaping worlds without number.

They sang to the waters and to the earth,
calling forth all living things and clothing them in Light.

Yet one refused to sing.
She whispered to the darkness, summoning it to smother the Light.

Illurien, who sits upon the Throne of Light,
cast She-Who-Would-Not-Sing from the eternal world.

Now, she roams the darkness.
Ever she struggles. Ever she wanders. Eternal darkness is her home.

Illurien summoned the Beings of Light.

The Song of Illurien

Look upon our creations and see that they are filled with Light.

Yet it will not always be so.
She-Who-Would-Not-Sing will sow darkness and despair.

She will shake the foundations of time and rend the Light.
All creation will perch on the edge of the abyss and the
chaos of unmaking.

But we will not leave the Worlds of Light alone and unguarded.
We will provide Keepers who may wield the Light to
maintain the balance.

And we will send a Promised One in the time of despair,
when the Light fades, and darkness and death roam the land.

He will bear the sign of power,
and so, unite the scattered fragments of Light.

He will purify the Light,
drawing all Light unto himself and so complete the circle of time.

Then Illurien will smile down again upon the Worlds of Light.
The balance will be restored, and Light shall reign untarnished
for all time.

The priests repeated the song once more, then stopped singing the ballad but continued the intricate and delicate harmony for some time. The words filled me with foreboding. The Keepers had called *me* the Promised One. Did they really think some sixteen-year-old kid could do all that stuff? Or was this some kind of religious myth, like Noah's flood? They couldn't be serious. The music ended abruptly, and the priest with the rich yellow eyes spoke in a quiet voice.

"We stand at the center," he said, "the focus of the Light. All earthly light radiates out from this place and fills the world." He raised a bony hand toward the colossal sundial. "This is the Hitching Post of the Sun. It binds the sun to its eternal circle of the earth."

"I think you got that backward," I interrupted. "The earth

actually revolves around the sun."

The priest stared at me with those creepy yellow eyes, and the silence became uncomfortable. I shuffled my feet.

"Well, I just thought I'd throw that in."

The priest continued speaking as if I hadn't said anything. "All power concentrates here in this place. Do you feel it, Promised One?"

"Yeah," I said. I did feel it, but I hadn't known what it was. Warm and tingly, reassuring and good. It wasn't like the nervous, urgent feeling I experienced in my room. This was something else.

"Do you understand the meaning of the song?"

"Uh, well…" I had never heard anything like it before.

"She-Who-Would-Not-Sing," the yellow-eyed priest continued, "has long sought to smother the Worlds of Light in darkness. She will not allow the creation to be complete. We alone hold her at bay. We preserve and purify the Light, and yet, we fail. Still, the nights lengthen, and darkness fills the world. The time has arrived when the Promised One spoken of should come. Long have we awaited your coming. Soon, you will renew the Light and purify it of all darkness, that Illurien might smile down upon this world once again and declare that it is a World of Light."

"Uh, okay," I said. They didn't seem to think the song was just a myth. Nor did they understand that I wanted nothing to do with it.

The priest continued. "You, Promised One, have been sent, and we receive you with gladness. We, the Keepers of the Light, shall instruct you and prepare you to accomplish the purpose for which you came into this world."

My heart skipped a beat. I stared. "Uh, I think you've made a big mistake," I said. I wasn't some savior sent to fight a cosmic battle between Light and darkness. "I'm just a high school student. I need to get home."

The priests shuffled away.

"Hey," I called after them. "Wait!"

They disappeared in between the buildings surrounding the courtyard, leaving me alone beneath the sundial as they melted into the shadows of the temple complex. I considered racing after them, but Lowthelian motioned for me to follow her.

"Come, Promised One," she said. "I will prepare you."

The title *Promised One* now had new meaning to me—one I didn't like. I could feel that Ross was pleased for reasons I couldn't guess.

I tripped after Lowthelian. "They've got this all wrong," I said. "I'm not the Promised One."

An enchanting smile spread over her face, and her silver eyes swirled. "You'll understand soon enough."

"No, it's you who doesn't understand," I persisted. "My mother just died, and I have to get back. She's alone." I choked on the last word, realizing *I* was the one who was alone.

Lowthelian kept walking. I glared at her. Why did she insist on being so unhelpful? So unfeeling? We descended into the brightly lit stone corridor leading to my room.

She opened the door and told me to wait inside. Passing a hand over my now-bald head in frustration, I plopped down at the table. Things had already gone too far. How could I convince them they were mistaken? I couldn't let them believe I was some savior. I wasn't going to save the world. I didn't want to. I wanted to tend to my mother's burial. To hold her hand one last time. To find her killer.

By the time Lowthelian returned, I had decided I was leaving. But when she pushed through the door in a sweep of robes, she didn't give me a chance to speak. She placed a bundle of black robes on the table, like those the priests wore.

"You are to change into more appropriate attire for one who serves the Light," she said. Her gaze wandered over my naked chest. "I will return with something to satisfy your hunger."

"But—" I began to protest, but she flashed a pretty smile and left.

I stared at the robe for a long time. Something about putting them on made my presence here seem final. I stepped out into the corridor. There had to be a way to go back. I could try to escape this temple complex or whatever it was. Maybe if I could find the chamber, it would take me back home. I would just lie down like before, and it would send me back. That seemed the only option. When I turned to stare at the robe, reality came crashing down upon me.

Who was I kidding? I didn't even know where I was. The skeletons didn't follow any of the normal rules of existence in Ohio. I knew about monks in India and Nepal who lived quiet lives of solitude, but this wasn't India. John Carter of Mars managed to gain superpowers by going to a different planet. But this didn't feel like a different planet. Everything seemed to work more or less like it did back home. The gravity was the same. The air was the same. There was one sun. I wasn't any stronger. The real difference was that somehow skeletons without skin and muscles could walk around and speak and sing.

Regardless of what had happened to me, I wasn't going to get home alone. I needed help. Maybe if I played along with them, they would eventually let something slip. Maybe they would teach me how to use this strange power lurking inside of me, and I could use it to return home.

Deep down, I experienced a nagging fear that I wasn't going to be able to get back home—that my mother would have to be buried by strangers without her last remaining family member beside her.

The black robe lay silent and forbidding, the first step down a road whose path I could not see, and yet, it was a path I couldn't avoid. Unless I was willing to walk around without a shirt from now on, I didn't have much of a choice but to wear the robe.

I peeled off my dirty pants and slipped on the robe. It was soft and comfortable with the feel of silk and smelled a little musty like they hadn't been used or washed in a long time. I tried not to think that maybe one of the skeletons had worn them. Lowthelian returned carrying a tray of food. She set it on the table and whirled to leave without a word.

"Wait," I grabbed her arm to stop her. At my touch, she gasped and jerked away. Her silver eyes flashed, and a pulse of power surged from her like a blast of hot air, glimmering like liquid silver as it flared. It differed somehow from the power I felt from the priests and at the stone sundial. It left me feeling disturbed—even threatened. I drew back in confusion and alarm.

"I'm sorry," I said. "I didn't mean to hurt you."

Lowthelian glared for a moment before her face softened, and she smiled.

"No, I'm sorry," she said. "You must understand that you are the Promised One. Your touch causes me pain. Please excuse me."

She bowed low and whirled to leave again, but not before I saw a look of bewilderment, even fear, on her face. She hadn't expected my touch to hurt her.

"No, please wait," I said.

Lowthelian faced me again.

"Can't you tell me what's going on here? I need to get home."

She gave me a patient smile and shook her head. "I am not your teacher, Promised One. You must learn from those who were meant to teach you."

"Then, at least tell me who you are and how you came here."

Lowthelian's smile sagged into a frown. "I'm a servant of the Light," she said. "That's all I am. I came, like yourself, from another place, but I don't know where it was."

"Another place? You mean another world?"

She shrugged.

"Don't you have a father or a mother?"

She shook her head. Her dark hair flowed around her shoulders. "No. I told you. We have no family here in the temple."

"Did the priests come here the same way I did? Have they all been dragged from different places or worlds to serve the Light?"

Lowthelian gave me a condescending smirk. "I am not permitted to be your teacher, Promised One. I will return for the tray. You need time to prepare yourself for your first lesson. I am instructed to tell you to meditate upon the Light and what it would have you do. Prepare well, Promised One."

Chapter Four
Darkness and Light

"WHERE IS EVERYONE?" I asked as Lowthelian escorted me across the compound later that day. The robe flowed around my bare feet. I had kept my boxers on, but I still felt naked under the robes and unused to the draft that kept flowing up my legs.

For such a vast complex, I figured there must be hundreds of monks and servants everywhere, but an unearthly silence hung over the place. No birds called or flapped about. No trash or debris that might hint that anyone had ever lived here could be seen. Even the gentle breeze that blew in with the fresh scent of tilled earth and cut grass didn't make any noise.

The temple seemed to have been forced into a coma-like sleep—an unnatural slumber. Yet underneath it all, a strange energy pulsed in time with the beating of my heart. This place knew me. This place had been waiting for me. I shivered at the realization.

Lowthelian glanced at me but ignored my question about where the people were.

"Come on," I said. "If we're going to be friends, you've got to be more talkative."

She paused for a moment to stare at me, confusion in her expression. Then she gave me a sad smile, and I thought I could like her, even with her strange eyes.

She continued down a long flight of stairs. "We have no friends in the service of the Light."

"All right," I said, determined to learn something from her, "explain to me how skeletons can walk around like these do." I knew it wasn't just their heads that were skeletal because I had seen their bony fingers and toes.

"The Light," she said.

I smirked. "Like that's an answer. Even I know you need muscles and sinews to make bones move. How do these guys do it?"

"The Light animates all things," she said.

I scowled, prepared to insist that she explain when she stopped beside a black door.

"He's expecting you," she said.

"Who?"

Lowthelian gave me a blank stare before turning away.

"Dang that girl," I said to myself as she strode away. This is why I had never tried to date anyone. Girls were too hard to talk to, let alone understand.

I pushed the door open and stepped into a dimly lit chamber. A rectangular depression filled the center of the black stone room. The flame from several candles danced in the darkness.

The priest who had greeted me when I first arrived sat on the floor in the center of the room. His red eyes flashed in the dim light. He still smelled foul—like something that had died. I resisted the temptation to plug my nose and instead tried to mouth breathe. The priest barely acknowledged me. He poked a bony finger toward the floor with an air of disinterested disdain.

As I took a seat opposite the priest on the cold stone, that sense of urgency I felt in my room swept through me. It rose from the very stones of the temple. I struggled to ignore it and focused on the dark cloth draped over a round object that sat on the floor between us. Something about it made me uneasy. Ross stirred angrily within me, and I grimaced at the odd sensation of having an independent consciousness inside me. I coughed and swallowed, trying to dislodge him, but nothing helped.

The priest spoke in his deep, gravelly voice. It was strange— even creepy—to see a skeleton speaking, like someone wearing a Halloween mask. His jaw moved, but no lips formed the sounds that came out. No facial muscles existed to create the expressions living things make. Still, the words came out clear. I shivered. This priest had more the feeling of a demon about him than a righteous monk.

"Today, your testing begins, Promised One," he said. "Hold out your hand."

I jerked in surprise. "Testing?"

"Do not question—simply obey," he demanded in a harsh, threatening tone.

"I just need to go home," I blurted. "I'm not staying here."

"Hold out your hand," he ordered again.

My mind raced. How could they test me when they hadn't taught me anything yet? I considered demanding he take me back to the chamber where he found me, but his swirling red eyes convinced me it would be a waste of time.

Hesitating, I reluctantly extended my hand. The priest grabbed it. The white bones of his fingers were hard and cold. A shudder swept through me, followed by the sudden and frightening awareness of great power—power that wished to suck my life away. To drain it from me like a leech. To feed off the energy and life that was the core of my being.

Terror coiled around my heart like a giant python. I shrank back, but the skeletal hand gripped me like a vice. I would have lashed out had I not realized that the priest restrained the power that sought my life.

"I see that you sense the nature of my power," the priest said in a haughty tone.

He thought my reaction funny—that it was a joke.

"I am called Llaith," the priest continued. "I am the Keeper of the Skull. All life eventually passes into my hands." He let the statement linger in the dank air as if he thought I should draw some meaning from it. "If you are to be the Promised One, you must prove you are worthy."

"How do I do that?" I asked.

He studied me before he dropped my hand and reached for the rounded object. He slipped the black covering from a translucent skull that gleamed a vibrant and painful scarlet, spilling a bloody light over the stone floor. I stared at the gruesome skull, finding myself drawn to it and repelled by it at the same time. I sensed the danger. Something evil and intimidating radiated from that skull.

"The seed of power we have planted within you must be fed and challenged if it is to grow," he said.

"Seed?" I asked. He must have meant that moment when the priests placed their hands on my head the night before. Ever since then, I sensed a power lurking inside me.

"Your courage must be tested," he continued without answering my question. "Now, place your hand on the skull."

I snapped my gaze back to Llaith's face and shrank away from the skull. I didn't dare touch it. It wanted to destroy me. To feed off my energy, off my Light. I could feel a cold hunger prowling within it. A smooth rumble sounded from Llaith, and he shook. He was laughing at me.

"It's always the same," Llaith said. "Everyone fears death—and rightly so. After life, there is nothing. Nothing, but darkness." Llaith threw back his head and opened his white, gaping maw. "Nothing," he boomed. His voice echoed off the stone walls.

I stared in horror. This priest was nuts, completely insane. Dying wasn't what I planned on doing today, and there was no way he was going to make me put my hand on that skull.

"You must begin here, Promised One," Llaith said, now with a note of derision in his voice. "If you are too timid to face your death now, you will fail indeed. Do you think She-Who-Would-Not-Sing will show you mercy? Perhaps you think she will take pity on a mere boy, a whelp, a callow, pink-faced child who can't even wipe his own nose."

He leaned forward. The menace emanated from him like heat from an oven.

"How can you defeat the darkness if you are too afraid to understand it? Face your death now, boy, for you will surely taste it later."

Llaith was mocking me, calling me a coward. I swallowed my terror as anger rose to replace it. I controlled my fear and reached out my hand, keeping it as steady as I could. Every fiber of my being screamed of danger and demanded that I withdraw, that I flee, but I held steady. I would prove to these priests, here and now, that I was no coward.

My hand rested on the round, smooth cranium. Red-hot pain surged through me. Crimson light flashed. I cried out and clenched my eyes shut against the radiating pain. My own power rushed forth, unbidden. The red light flared, seeking an entrance, struggling to get past my protection. Reaching out hungrily for my life—for my Light.

I panicked as oblivion reached for me. The light sought to unmake me—to return me to the cosmic chaos from which I came. My revulsion at the blood-red death and my anger at the mocking priest released my new and untested power in a torrent. I opened my eyes at the strange sensation of heat and light expanding into my arm. I stared at the pulsating, crimson skull. The power emanated from my hand, but I could see nothing. It flared and sparked on my fingertips, yet there was no sign of it. Then the red light siphoned into my hand, drawn in by the irresistible power inside me. I struggled to drag myself from the skull, but my power held me.

The crimson light radiating from the skull dimmed. It turned a faint coral color and then slid toward a pale pink. The power of the skull was being drawn into my own being. Becoming a part of me. Death, decay, darkness, and then emptiness filled my soul. I gritted my teeth. I wanted to scream and shriek at this agony. To call for help. I didn't want to be the monster that sat across from me.

In contrast to the rending agony of the filthy light, the oblivion seemed so inviting, so enticing. I struggled against the desire to slip into it—to slide away beyond being and beyond time. I peered into the great black pit that expanded before me and saw my own destruction. Not my death, but the literal destruction of my being. The extinction of my Light. Was this what Llaith meant by the darkness? Was the nature of the dark nothingness?

This feeling of desperate terror held for a brief moment as I perched on the edge of the abyss, staring into the nothingness before it passed. As the color faded from the skull, something inside me snapped, and the skull fractured with a loud crack. I gasped and snatched my hand away to clutch at the stabbing pain in my chest. The skull lay drained of all color with a great crack cutting across its face. The threat and power of the skull had been broken, and something inside me had changed.

Llaith's mocking laughter died in his lipless mouth. I lifted my trembling hand to wipe at the cold sweat dripping from my brow as I struggled to control my ragged breathing. I gaped at Llaith. He could make no facial expressions to betray his emotions, but I sensed them just the same. The red light I had absorbed built a bridge between us—a tenuous connection like a thin electrical wire that transmitted what Llaith was feeling to me.

Llaith's brilliant red eyes dimmed and churned. A chorus of emotions rushed out of him. Pain, despair, anger, and confusion pulsated in the air, and then hatred—a palpable hatred so intense I scrambled back a few feet, sure he was going to attack me. Llaith didn't speak. He trembled in rage. Then he lunged to his feet and strode away with a disdainful swish of his robes. That's when I realized Llaith hadn't just been angry. He had been disappointed. He intended for the skull to kill me. He wanted his skull to suck away my life.

I struggled to understand what happened. What stopped the skull from killing me? I stared at my hands. The energy still sparked unseen on my fingertips. I could feel it like an electric shock. The power swelled within me. What had been a warm tingling thing now burned hotter—more powerful—more dangerous.

A strange hunger also filled my chest—a hunger to use the power. To wield it. The wild, excited emotions coming from Ross added to my confusion. He, at least, seemed to understand what this meant, though he couldn't tell me. He tried, but something blocked him. A barrier separated us. It let me feel his presence and his emotions but not communicate directly with him like we had the night before.

Not only did I crave this power, I also feared it. It acted on its own accord. I hadn't controlled it. It wasn't really mine. I thought of my mother and remembered a time when I had come in from playing outside with a nice red sunburn. As she applied a cool cloth to my shoulders, she said, "If we do not respect the Light, it can burn us. The Light unseen may be the most powerful of all."

As usual, I didn't understand a thing she said. Now, I wished I hadn't been so pigheaded and ignorant. She had been trying to prepare me for this. How could she have known? I clutched at my chest, thinking that squeezing it might relieve the pressure and the relentless pounding of my heart. I glanced at my hands. My skin blurred. The oblivion that reached for me had tugged bits and pieces of my soul into the abyss of nothingness. I pinched my fingers together, and they felt numb and separate from the rest of me. Was

I coming apart? Would using this power unmake me in the end?

As I struggled to wrap my mind around this strange place and what it was doing to me, the sense of a consciousness prowling inside the stone walls of the temple leaked into me from the stones where I sat. The temple was in pain. Confused. Afraid. I dropped my head into my hands.

What was happening to me? An alien presence lived inside me, and now I sensed some strange consciousness coming from cold, lifeless stones. I'd lost my mind. That was the only explanation. Or maybe they drugged me, and I was in some kind of wild, drug-induced hallucination.

I don't know how long I wrestled with my growing terror—trying to sort through the rising mountain of unanswered questions. Why couldn't I see my power? Why did my power so easily absorb the dreadful power of the skull? Why did Llaith react with such anger?

Maybe I had failed Llaith's test, and they would let me go home—let me escape this nightmare. The sound of rustling robes brought me back from my musing. I glanced up. The priest with the bright yellow eyes loomed over me.

"Come, Promised One," he said.

His voice was soft, almost comforting, but seeing it come from his skeletal mouth provided a contrast more disturbing than Llaith's harsh voice. I rose to my feet, unsteady at first, and followed the priest. I tried to blink the faint red tint from before my eyes. It faded slowly as the priest led me through the vast complex of stone buildings.

As soon as the sunlight touched my face, a sudden burst of energy swept through me. I held up my hands and rubbed my fingers together. The sense of intangibility faded. The sunlight healed me, just as my mother had said.

We reached a long winding staircase that led into a small, circular room at the top of a tower. No furniture cluttered the room save a small writing desk—nothing to make it comfortable or inviting.

One large window overlooked the courtyard where the great sundial stabbed into the sky. Another smaller slit far above allowed the light in. A gigantic column covered in strange, foreign symbols filled the center of the room. Little holes punctured the wall around the tower and cast tiny dots of light onto the column.

The priest stopped before the window to gaze out over the courtyard. I stood beside him and wrinkled my nose at the odor arising from him. It wasn't the nauseating smell of decay that Llaith had—more like burned metal combined with the stale odor of a long-unused room.

"What do you see?" the priest asked.

I glanced up at him, wondering if he was serious. When he didn't stir, I gazed out the window. A beautiful panorama expanded before me. Below in the courtyard, the brilliant white sundial glimmered in the light of the sun, stabbing higher than the tower. The white-tiled roofs of the buildings which formed the complex the priests lived in spread around me for quite a distance. What did they need all that space for—especially since no one but them lived in the temple? Then I lifted my gaze up to the vibrant green of the surrounding countryside.

The temple complex occupied the summit of the largest hill in the center of a city that sprawled out beyond. A wide road wound its way up to the temple complex, through a cluster of buildings with thatched roofs.

A white, gleaming, palatial structure occupied the opposite hill. A checkerboard of fields spread out beyond the city, fading into the distance where a mountain range loomed against the eastern horizon in a dark purple mass. What surprised me most was that the reds seemed to stand out more than usual with a much deeper and richer beauty than I had ever seen.

I picked at a loose piece of stone on the windowsill.

"I see a city and fields and some mountains in the distance," I said.

The priest was silent for a moment and then spoke without looking at me. "I see Light," he said.

I looked out the window again. It was broad daylight, but I hadn't thought that worth commenting on.

"Do you see the Light, Promised One?" The priest spoke with a quiet, reverential whisper.

I shrugged. "Of course."

The priest shook his head. "No. You do not. Come again to this spot just before daybreak. Now go."

I hesitated. What was the point of climbing the tower if he was just going to send me away? I had noticed a growing weariness back in Llaith's dark sanctuary, but now it seemed to bore deep into my very being. I didn't have the energy to argue. All I wanted to do was to lie down and forget about everything.

I staggered into my room on the verge of collapse. My vision swam. My limbs dragged. I fell onto my bed, and, before consciousness drifted away, I wondered what Llaith had done to me. There must have been some poison in that blood-red skull that still sucked the energy from my soul. I fought against the nagging sleep, convinced I'd never awake if I gave in, but weariness overwhelmed me, and I knew no more, save the lurking knowledge I was not alone, even inside my own mind.

"This boy is exceptional," Ross thought. "Already he has defeated Llaith. No one has ever come near such a feat."

A tingle of grim satisfaction swept through him. Llaith deserved to suffer. Yet, it was clear the priests had not expected the boy to succeed. This would change everything. They would be more dangerous now.

The seed of power the priests planted in the boy would have to be nourished. Each contact with an object of power would allow his Light to grow and expand until he reached his potential. What that potential was, no one could now guess. He had defeated the skull so easily when it had conquered all the other Chosen who faced it.

In the past, only the most powerful ever became priests, and none of them succeeded in defeating an object of Light. Some, like Ross, had come close, but only close. In his trial with the skull, Ross managed to draw some of its Light, but Llaith had to rescue him when the skull flashed and sucked away his Light.

Llaith's hideous laughter at his failure had filled the chamber.

"Death," Llaith had said. "You are too weak to face it. Too cowardly to admit your own mortality."

The Keepers told Ross he was the most powerful Chosen One to come in centuries, and yet Llaith mocked his weakness before the skull.

Darkness and Light

"Yes," Ross thought. "This boy is very special. He will grow in power and ability with each trial. The priests must now be questioning what this might mean for them. They had called him the Promised One."

Ross spared himself a moment of triumph. A boy who could defeat the skull on his first trial possessed more power than any of them had ever seen.

"Will they allow him to complete the tests, or will they seek to destroy him before it is too late? The trials will give them ample opportunity."

This thought sobered Ross. Things were not going according to plan. The connection he forged with the boy did not allow him to know the boy's thoughts like it was supposed to. He could see what the boy saw and sense his emotions, but he could not speak to or through the boy.

Ross had been silenced and bound. He needed to communicate with the boy, to teach him, to control him.

"I made an error," Ross thought, "in scratching the words of power into the wall of the chamber. I was already dying, fading fast. I used the last of my energy to scratch them into the stone. My words interrupted the boy's reading of the history of Illurien and the Worlds of Light. Now, he is ignorant of everything. The boy flounders about without any clear idea who he really is and what he needs to do."

It was Ross's fault. He had to admit. Now, a portion of his spirit lingered to inhabit a small fraction of the boy's mind, while Ross's body lay moldering in the dark and dank chamber from which it would never more arise. He would persist to the bitter end because he had no choice. Death would come for him again, but this time, he would finish his task before death could claim him—no matter the cost.

Chapter Five
Rainbow of Light

THE DULL GRAY of the coming dawn filtered through my window, rousing me from disturbing dreams of bleeding skulls. I lay staring at the dark shadows of the rafters above my bed, my mind lingering on the last shadowy image of my dream in which my mother wept softly. She was much younger than I could remember her, and I was a small child. I reached up to wipe away a tear that trickled down her cheek. She grabbed me up in a fierce hug, sobbing into my shoulder.

"My Kell," she cried. "My Kell."

Why had she been so sad? A sudden ache filled my heart. How I missed her. What would they do with her body? I should be there for her now in a last act of respect and love. She had always been there for me, but I abandoned her. Her body hadn't even grown cold, and all I had done was drive a shovel into the earth in despair and frustration. I tried to excuse myself by saying I was following her last dying wish, that I had been delirious with grief. And I had. Yet, here I was in a comfortable bed, while I left her body on the asphalt. I should have run for help, called the police, chased down her murderer.

Instead, I ended up in some weird temple with nightmarish priests who were served by a beautiful and aloof young woman with silver eyes. They all seemed to think I was some savior. I shot bolt upright in the bed. The yellow-eyed priest would be waiting for me. This was my chance to tell them I was going home, that they had to send me back.

I raced to the tower, trying to calm the anxious tickling in my belly. If they thought they were going to make me fight some new monster every time I met with them, they were going to be disappointed. I wanted out.

The yellow-eyed priest gazed out the square window at the coming dawn. I paused at the door, waiting until the priest gave a nod for me to enter.

He pointed to the last star twinkling in the blue-gray sky. "That is Celema," he said, "the first and the last to enter the struggle against She-Who-Would-Not-Sing. It is the Evening and the Morning Star. Now, watch."

The sky slowly brightened. A cool breeze caressed my bald head. A pink flame spread over the distant mountains in a brilliant crown of glory. The priest chanted and waved his hands in a beckoning motion. As he did, the golden ball of the sun rose above the mountains and lifted itself into the sky, as if reluctant to leave its nighttime slumber. Did he really think he was calling the sun into the sky? These skeletons were crazier than I was.

As the priest finished chanting, the gentle singing of a more feminine voice drifted on the cool breeze. I glanced down into the courtyard. Beside the great sundial stood a woman dressed in a white flowing robe. Black hair draped about her shoulders, contrasting with the brilliance of her clothing. She faced the sundial with outstretched arms. Her rich, enchanting voice sent shivers coursing through my body. The power inside me stirred in response to the music, filling me with an overwhelming sense of peace. I wanted to go to her, to find out who she was and why my power responded differently to her than it did to the priests. When she finished, she bowed and strolled gracefully away with her white robe billowing about her.

I couldn't take my gaze from her until she disappeared amid the buildings. Then I faced the priest and found him studying me.

"Who was that?" I asked. "Besides Lowthelian, I haven't seen anyone else here."

The priest's yellow eyes seemed to burn with new intensity.

"She does not concern you, Promised One." His voice rose

in warning. "You must forget those baser things and focus on the Light. The Light is why you have come. You must not lose sight of your purpose."

"And what is that, exactly?" I demanded. "You sing a song and then try to kill me with some magic skull. What you need to know is that I'm going home. My mother just died, and I am going back for her funeral. You have to send me back."

I glared at the priest, daring him to contradict me. My power stirred in preparation for a fight.

The priest raised his white bony hand to silence me. I thought he might start yelling himself, but he said, "You speak as if you did not read the writing in the Chamber of Light."

"What writing?" I stammered. "Where?"

"The chamber from which Llaith guided you. It was written in the language of Illurien that is accessible to all of her creations. Even a child could read it."

What did that have to do with my demand to be sent home?

"I read some of it. I think. But I—"

"Then, how is it you do not understand your purpose here?"

"What?" I shouted. "I was being suffocated by your nice little tomb!"

Then I remembered the messy writing near the floor that interrupted the gossamer white writing on the walls and ceiling. I opened my mouth to tell this priest what happened. To tell him I hadn't been able to read any of the writing because some spirit or demon forced himself into my soul and became part of me.

"Something happened..." I began, but as the words tumbled out, Ross surged up, painful and urgent into my mind. I gasped and grabbed my forehead. Ross didn't want me to speak of it. But why? I swallowed against the nausea caused by his sudden rush of emotion. His reaction sent a wild spasm of fear through me. Had I almost revealed some dreadful secret that the priests would use against me?

"I just didn't understand," I stammered. "It all happened too fast."

The priest contemplated me in silence and then said, "I will answer your questions, but let us first see if you can pass the second test as easily as you did the first."

"You're not listening," I said. "I'm going home."

The priest motioned for me to stand against the wall opposite the window through which the sunlight flowed warm and inviting. Dots of light flickered on the column as the sun rose.

"I don't have time for more games," I said.

"This is no game," the priest answered as he produced a giant, pyramid-shaped crystal, which he held up to the window. As soon as the light of the sun touched its surface, a rainbow of color leaped onto the wall beside me. The colors were so intense they hurt my eyes. They faded and blended into each other with perfect harmony. I stared in awe.

The rainbow reminded me of Mom again. She loved prisms and dangled them everywhere in the house. I remembered her slight figure standing precariously on a chair in the kitchen, adjusting a long crystal so it would catch the light and cast the spectrum onto the wall. The colors skipped around the room and danced in her dark hair as the prism caught the light and sprayed it about. I used to tease her about this strange obsession, but now I missed her so much that the longing ached in my chest.

A lump formed in my throat, and I blinked rapidly. The priest mistook my emotion for admiration of the shimmering colors and was pleased.

"I see you admire the beauty of the Light," he said. "That is good. You must understand that Light is the source of all things. The power that flows through all things. The energy that animates all things. The beginning and the end."

The priest hesitated, shuffled his skeletal feet, and watched me while I fidgeted and glanced around at the room and its sparse furnishings. One small table and a single chair sat to one side. A huge book lay on its polished surface.

At last, the priest spoke in a quiet voice. "Now, Promised One. Reach your hand into the spectrum."

I noted the tension and sense of anticipation in his voice. I glanced at him and then reached my hand into the beautiful rainbow. The instant my fingers touched the spectrum, the colors vanished. I yanked my hand away at the strange feeling of power that surged into me. It wasn't like the terrifying power of Llaith's skull. It was sweet and delicious. I glanced at the priest again, uncertain. The priest waved an impatient hand at me.

"Do it now, Promised One," he commanded. "Take the light."

My curiosity at the pleasant sensation impelled me to thrust my hand back into the spectrum. Again, the colors vanished. This time, I held my hand steady and took a deep breath. The power tingled on my fingertips, tugging at the colors streaming from the crystal. The colors filled my mind and sent it reeling with swirling, blinding rainbows.

Still, my power sucked at the colors, drawing them in, devouring them. Tugging at them hungrily the way a dog worried a bone. I could no longer see the room—only brilliant, blinding color. My head swam, and I teetered sideways as the ground seemed to tilt under me. Something inside me closed. It was over.

I blinked, struggling to get my bearings, and found I was breathing like I had just sprinted a marathon. Perspiration dotted my brow and upper lip. I reached for the wall to steady myself. The colors swirled through my vision, making me dizzy, like I was seeing the world through a revolving kaleidoscope. The priest still held the crystal, but no rainbow of light emanated from it. It sat dull and darkened in his bony grasp.

The priest let out a long sigh, leaned against the wall, and sank to the floor. He cradled the crystal in his lap, sitting motionless with his gleaming skull bowed over his treasure. I blinked again, trying to clear the swirling colors from my sight and then knelt beside the priest.

I reached out to touch him and then hesitated from a mixture of revulsion and uncertainty. The priest raised his head to gaze at me with dim yellow eyes. His sense of terrible loss and even weakness burst over me with such intensity it might have been my own. Tears sprang to my eyes. What had I done?

"It was so easy," the priest said. "It took no effort at all."

That wasn't exactly true. I still struggled to catch my breath. My body trembled with weariness and exhaustion.

"Are you all right?" I asked." I'm sorry if I ruined it."

The priest stared at me with yellow eyes that churned with emotion. Then he gestured to the floor. "Sit, Promised One. I will answer your questions now."

He passed a bony hand over his cranium. His sadness confused me the same way Llaith's anger had. I sat cross-legged on the cool, smooth stones of the floor, wrapping the robe around my legs and leaning wearily against the wall.

"What do you wish to know?" the priest asked.

"Are you all right?" I asked. The priest's sadness was hard to ignore.

"Yes, Promised One. Please, ask your questions."

I stared at him. My desire to demand that they send me back warred with the growing hunger for the power expanding inside me.

"Well," I said, "I want to know who you are, where you came from, why I'm here. Where here even is. I want to know what you think I'm supposed to do and how I'm supposed to do it. And I want to know how to get back to…to where I came from."

The priest nodded, undeterred by my flood of questions.

"I cannot answer you all at once," he said. "You must be satisfied with a little here and a little there. Knowledge does not come in a package. It comes one principle at a time. You must first build a foundation upon which to construct your temple of knowledge."

"But—" I protested.

The priest held up his dull, white hand to stop me. "I will start with your last question." He paused. "You cannot go back, Promised One. There is no way back."

"But—" I tried again.

He spoke over me. "You were chosen to serve the Light long before you were born," he said. "You and many others like you. Many have gone before, stretching back for eons uncounted. Light is not bound by time, Promised One. It simply is and always will be. Unless…" The priest trailed off.

"Were you chosen like me, then?"

"I am the oldest of the Chosen now living. It is so long ago I have no memory of what I did before I served the Light."

"And the others?"

"Yes," he said, "I am Hahl, The Keeper of the Sun. I am the first, and you are the last, the One that was promised. You must purify the Light and defeat She-Who-Would-Not-Sing."

I resisted the desire to jump up and bash him upside the skull. "I heard the stupid song," I said. "But what does it mean? Who is this woman?"

Hahl bristled. "You dare blaspheme the Light," he said, "when you didn't trouble yourself to read the sacred writing on the walls of the chamber that was written to guide you?"

I opened my mouth to snap back at him, but he had a point. What could I say? I bowed my head. "I am sorry."

"I will answer one last question," Hahl said, "because you must know. But you must never use her name. The servants of the Light do not speak her name. It is forbidden. Do you understand, Promised One?"

"Yes," I said.

"Her name is Shaheen," he whispered. Hahl glanced around as if he feared being overheard. "Her power grows, Promised One, and we weaken. It has been long since a Chosen One has come to us to renew our power. If you fail, the Worlds of Light will descend into the darkness and chaos from which they were called."

I stared at him. "You're joking."

Hahl returned my gaze with churning, yellow eyes. I sensed his frustration and turmoil. He didn't believe I could do what he asked. So why all this charade?

"I am not insincere, Promised One."

"I don't care about your world, wherever this is," I blurted. "I care about mine, and I want to go back to it."

Hahl snorted in disgust. "You are a foolish boy," he said. "If we fail here, all the Worlds of Light will fall into darkness—even yours."

"What?"

"If you care about your world, then you will finish what you have been sent to do. If you do not, your world, this world, all the Worlds of Light will be destroyed."

"Why?"

Hahl shifted. "Because this is the first world created by Illurien in the morning of the creation and so is connected by ligaments of time and Light to all other worlds. If we fail here, all worlds will fall."

I stared at him. Was he serious?

"What about my mother?" I demanded.

"You say she is dead," Hahl said. "Then, she no longer needs you."

I jumped to my feet, sick to death of this nonsense. "I'm leaving," I said.

"How?" Hahl asked. He sat there so calm and unperturbed that

I wanted to kick the skull off his spindly little spine.

"I don't know," I yelled. "Put me back in that chamber and send me home."

"We can't."

"Why not?"

"Because none of the Keepers know how to do what you ask. Once there were those who did understand the chambers, but the knowledge has been lost."

My mind reeled. "You mean I'm trapped?" I asked, wrestling with the panic that swirled in my gut. What about my mother, my schooling, my plans to be an archaeologist? Could they keep me a prisoner?

"You can't keep me here against my will," I said.

"I do not keep you here," the priest said. "You were chosen by the Light. You willingly entered the chamber, didn't you?"

I ignored his question. "Send me back," I demanded.

"I cannot. I already told you none of the Keepers remember how to use the chambers."

"You mean there's more than one?"

Hahl nodded.

"But this is your temple," I said. I couldn't believe it. They ripped me from my own world, and they didn't even know how to send me back.

"Yes, Promised One, but we do not control the Light. We merely serve it."

I stared at him. Could he be serious? "You brought me here." I tried again as the hollow pit expanded in my stomach. Was he telling the truth?

Hahl shook his head. "No, we did not. Illurien selects the Chosen. She sends them to us. We have no control over the Chambers of Light."

"You're lying," I said. I had to believe he was lying because I couldn't accept the alternative.

The emotions boiled inside Hahl. I didn't understand how I could tell what another person was feeling, especially a skeleton, but ever since I had confronted his prism, I could perceive his emotions. I braced for an explosion of anger, but he sat, unmoving.

"A wise man accepts what cannot be changed," he said. "Your

education has now begun. You will meet with each of the other Keepers over the next few days until you complete the time of testing. Then you will meet with each of the Keepers once a day, every day until your task becomes clear to you. Learn well, Promised One. You must understand the Light and the nature of the darkness that besets us if you are to accomplish your task. Now go. Ponder on what you have seen and heard."

Hahl turned away from me, picking up the now-darkened crystal. His skeletal fingers clicked against the stone as he caressed it. A wave of sadness and loss passed over him. I whirled away in frustration and anger. I would find a way to get home on my own. Ross seemed pleased with what happened. He, at least, understood. I caught the quiet murmur of Hahl's voice and paused at the door to listen.

"Years beyond number have I shaped you," he said to the crystal. "Years beyond counting, I have molded and perfected you. But now…" his voice trailed off until I could no longer make out the words.

I started down the winding stairwell, lost in thought, wondering if I had been catapulted into some alternate reality where people were afraid of the dark, and everyone had weird, swirling eyes. At some point, the priests must have been like Lowthelian, and that girl I saw singing by the sundial. They must have once had flesh on their bones. When they died, maybe they just decided to go on living—like all the normal rules of life didn't apply to them.

Hahl said I was trapped here, that I could never go home. Now that my mother was gone, what home would I return to anyway? I wasn't what you would call popular. I worked hard to be first in my class because I needed to be better than the rest of them. To be more. Mom wanted me to pursue the hard sciences, but I buried myself in every archeology book or magazine I could find. Except for Dean, I had no real friends. In fact, my world had been small.

Mom had raised me by herself all those years. There had never been any family gatherings at Thanksgiving or Christmas. She never voted in elections, never attended a PTA meeting, never went on a date, or went out with friends. I had been her entire world. Someone must have found her body by now, and maybe they knew what killed her. Maybe they thought it was me.

I cursed at my stupidity. Could I believe anything Hahl told me, or was he just crazy? Was *I* going crazy?

As I worked my way down the winding staircase, my weariness increased. I placed a hand on the wall to steady myself. A jolt of pain lanced up my arm, and I glanced at my hand to find it covered in black dots, like moles, or cancer. I yanked up the sleeve of my robe to find that the dots had spread all up my arms. Had the intense sunlight streaming through the crystal given me cancer? Was the Light going to destroy my body cell by cell? Were the priests killing me slowly, one test at a time?

I stumbled out into the courtyard as a new horror of this power inside me competed with the wild hunger to use it. The sunlight struck my face, and a shiver swept through me. I paused to examine my hands. Some of the spots faded. I reached my room and pushed through the wooden door, ignoring the tray with food and water that sat on the table. Stumbling to my bed, I collapsed onto it. I hungered for the power growing inside me, even though it might very well kill me and leave me an empty shell—maybe even turn me into a grotesque skeleton, living but not alive—suspended in an endless death.

I awoke to the slap of bare feet on stone and the swish of cloth. Lowthelian's slender form in a gray robe bent over the table as she deposited her tray. I struggled to sit up. She flashed me a dazzling smile.

"Good morning," she said and hurried out the door.

Was it still morning? I blinked at the warm sunlight streaming in through the window. It must have been late morning. The aroma of warm bread and sautéed meat made my stomach rumble. A ravenous hunger drove me from the bed to the table. I fell to with such an appetite I didn't think it would ever be satisfied. Lowthelian returned for the tray as I mopped the last of the sauce from the plate with the remaining bit of bread.

"Dang, that was good," I said.

Lowthelian inclined her head. "I will inform the cook," she said.

"Where do you go while you wait for me to eat?" I asked.

Lowthelian scowled at me.

"I mean, you could stay here and talk," I said.

Her scowl faded, and a wistful sadness passed over her face. Her silver eyes swirled. I thought she was going to say something, but she just gave me a melancholy smile that was more ironic than pleasant and left without saying a word.

"Guess not," I said to myself.

It had to get lonely for a beautiful, young girl locked up in an empty temple with nothing to do but serve a bunch of ugly skeletal priests. I found her strangely attractive, and yet I didn't know if I wanted to get too close. She had not responded well when I touched her. Was the other girl who sang so beautifully at the sundial the same? Hahl said I had to forget that girl, but that wasn't going to happen. If Lowthelian wouldn't talk to me, maybe the other girl would.

Remembering the black, painful dots that covered my body, I yanked up the sleeve of my robe to check my arm. The dots were gone.

Well, I wasn't going to find out sitting in my room staring at the walls. Maybe the priests could ponder about the Light all day, but if my mother couldn't get me to do it, no skeletal priest had a chance. If I could find the chamber that brought me here, maybe I could figure out how to use it.

I slipped out the door and paused in the stone hallway, trying to decide which way to go. The warm tingling urgency surged up through my bare feet again, and this time I heard the faint sound of music. The haunting tune led me down the hallway in the opposite direction I took to get to the sundial. I placed a hand on the wall, and the stone warmed to my touch. The music grew louder. I plugged my ears, but I could still hear the music inside my head.

The tune filled me with a desperate longing that made my heart ache. I touched the stone again and closed my eyes. The music coursed through me as I struggled to understand what was happening. The temple itself was calling me. If I was going insane, I might as well know where my insanity would lead me. I crept down the hallway in my bare feet.

A strange, ever-present light that didn't seem to have a source filled the corridor. Dust danced up with my every footfall, which surprised me because the corridor closer to the courtyard was always fresh and clean. The passageway angled downward and was large enough for three people to walk abreast. Dozens of wooden doors populated both sides of the corridor. Here and there, a side passage split off.

The doors drew my attention. They were set in ordered rows— some closed, some ajar. I caught glimpses of furniture inside, much like the furniture in my room. Several of the doors bore blackened streaks left by fire. The sharp odor of burned wood lingered. Others were splintered and broken like someone had hacked their way in.

This portion of the temple appeared to be a residential section where people once lived in large numbers. Where were they now? Why the destruction? This meant the temple hadn't been designed as a residence for the priests alone. A whole city of people must have lived here.

The music in my head ended abruptly as I passed a severely damaged door, so I paused and pushed it ajar to peek in. The rough, damp wood smelled of mildew and charcoal. The latch dangled at an awkward angle, and the hinges screeched in protest. All I could see were odd, hulking shadows, so I shoved the door all the way open to let in the light from the corridor. The room lay in shambles, but it wasn't the normal ravages of time.

Decayed furniture sprawled everywhere, like a strong wind had lifted it all into the air, spun it around and then slammed it back down. A bed frame, much like the one I used, lay broken and moldering in the corner. Stray feathers and fragments of cloth still dangled from the wooden structure. A table and several chairs were overturned and falling to ruin.

Ragged tapestries clung stubbornly to the walls, their tattered ends swaying gently as my movement disturbed the air. Faded images of geometric designs and suns and moons rising over the temple colored the cloth. One of the tapestries had a picture of a woman in a flowing white robe with her hands extended toward me palms up. Something was set in the palms of her hands, but I couldn't make it out.

The odor of mold and decay assailed my nostrils. I explored every room, where I found the same chaos of destruction. Dozens of rooms along this single corridor all showed the definite signs of violent entry. In one, a long black tongue of soot climbed the wall. The reek of burning still lingered in the air, faint yet discernible. I picked up a small fragment of paper that escaped the flames. A single phrase written in a long thin hand survived. "Love of Light is love of life," it read.

"Yeah, well, not much love being shown here," I said.

The music burst into my head again, and I glanced up from the piece of paper to the crumbling bed, when my eye caught something odd in the wall. One of the stones had a gap around it while the others were fitted closely together. The stone trembled with the rhythm of the music, sending a cascade of dust into the air. I stepped over the broken headboard and wiggled the stone loose. As soon as I touched it, the music ceased. The stone came out with a rasping sound and a shower of dust. A musty cloud lifted into the air. I waved the cloud away as I peered into the dark hole.

A tiny glimmer of light flashed inside. Before I could think better of it, I reached in and closed my fingers around a cold stone object. As soon as my hand touched it, the stone burned warm and glowed a soft yellow glow that leaped from the blackness of the hole. I yanked my hand free, scraping my knuckles against the rough stone, and stumbled backward.

How stupid could I get? What kind of archaeologist would be dumb enough to stick his hand into a hole in a wall? I broke off a piece of wire from the ruined bed and poked the object. Nothing happened. I reached in and jabbed it with my finger. The light flashed as my finger touched it and then dimmed. I laid my hand on it, and the warm glow burst through my fingers. I drew it out and held it in my hand. The glow from the smooth round stone filled me with a strange longing and wonder that made my power stir in recognition.

The stone pulsated a steady golden light. Ross surged up in sudden interest, and I had to shove him aside so I could focus. In the center of the stone sat a black spider, like those insects that got trapped in pine resin and turned into amber as they hardened. I flipped it over to find an inscription on the back. The letters reminded me of Arabic script with delicate swirls and dots. It was a beautifully artistic script that was meant to ornament the stone. Around the script, a graceful spider's web covered the surface of the stone.

I reached back into the hole and found a small book with a piece of paper on top. The paper was in a language I couldn't understand, but I was more interested in the book. Dust cascaded off the worn leather cover. If it once had a title, it couldn't be seen now. I lifted the cover carefully, fearing it might crumble if I handled it too roughly. I knew I should have left it alone—that a real archaeologist would have snapped a few pictures and made measurements before touching anything, but I was too excited to care. The same delicate script I found on the stone covered the pages of the book in neat rows.

I slipped the book, stone, and piece of paper into my pocket, and stepped back into the hallway. An unease settled into my gut. Something terrible happened here.

Why were there dozens of rooms furnished like living quarters? Why had they been forcibly entered and turned upside down?

I fingered the stone thoughtfully. My mother said someone was hunting those who escaped. Is this what she was talking about? It didn't seem possible. These rooms, so filled with dust and cobwebs, were too old, too ancient. Everything about this place was far older than my mother.

I didn't bother entering any more of the rooms. The violence gnawed at me. Why had no one cleaned them up? Why had the temple taken me to the rooms and then abandoned me to blunder about? I wandered down the corridor, fingering the smooth stone. I missed my mother now more than I had since she died. A deep sadness came from Ross as I trudged away from the room.

"Tell me what it means," I said out loud. Frustration burned in my throat. "Just tell me." Ross echoed my frustration, but that was all. "What do you want from me?" I said. "Just get out of my head." Ross retreated to mourn, and I was left alone—almost.

The Cleansing

The sight of the golden stone stirred painful memories for Ross. His dear friend, Jerome, had fallen to his knees in front of where Ross dangled, bound to the execution pole, barely clinging to life.

Jerome held up the golden stone that pulsed as if with its own heart.

"The stones are the key," Jerome whispered. "But I am too weak to wield them. I have failed." A sob burst from Jerome.

"You must try," Ross croaked. His voice was harsh, and his throat burned—a gift from Llaith, while the others watched him torture Ross.

"I can't. I tried. I'm not powerful enough. You must use them."

"Look at me," Ross whispered.

Jerome raised his tear stained face to Ross.

"I am dieing," Ross said. "I do not have the strength to wield them. You must do this."

"I can't," Jerome said.

"How do they work?" Ross asked.

Jerome shook his head, clearly at a loss. "It was an accident. They were never meant to come to me."

"Save the women and children," Ross said.

"Here," Jerome tried to shove the golden stone into Ross's hand when a blast of blue flame sent him tumbling over the cobblestones.

"Run," Ross tried to yell. "Save them."

Jerome scrambled to his feet and staggered into the nearest tunnel.

It was a bitter memory—one made all the more bitter by the signs of destruction the boy now passed.

Ross remembered when these rooms were the homes of the Chosen. Memories of happier times filled his mind when the temple housed children who scampered about and played in these corridors. Families worshipped together. Ross remembered the first time he stepped out of the chamber that brought him here when he was just a boy.

In his tiny village, when each child reached the age of six, they spent one night in the chamber alone. The special ones would be gone in the morning—the ones who had been chosen to serve the Light. When the dizziness and heaviness of the chamber left him, and he stepped out to see a smiling priest who embraced him and welcomed him, he knew his parents would be proud of him. He had been chosen.

Then it had all gone wrong. He hadn't seen all the destruction with his own eyes, but he had heard it—listened to the terrible rending cries, smelled the acrid burning, tasted it on his tongue. Now, the sight of the charred doors and ruined *homes filled him with a sadness so deep it seemed to burrow to the core of his being. It had all been his fault. He had done this. So many had died.*

A sudden change in the air made me stop and glance around. Somehow, I stumbled into a huge chamber. Great columns of smooth, white marble supported a vast, domed ceiling. Each pillar descended from a carved sun disk to rest upon a carved moon. A great, white serpent circled the circumference of the dome. Its giant mouth gaped wide as it devoured its own tail. In the center stood a round altar of polished white marble. All around, writing covered the walls. The writing had the same fluid, graceful style of the writing on the walls of the chamber. This writing was golden and broken into long, regular columns.

I stepped up to the nearest wall. As in the chamber, I found I could read this delicate, beautiful writing. It was the story of Illurien and Shaheen, the woman who would not sing, followed by a poem about the Light. I devoured the writing, seeking any clue that might help me figure out how to get home or how to understand what was happening.

An enormous list of names—many tens of thousands at least—covered one wall. I stepped back so I could scan the list. Many of the names repeated, but none of them had last names. I wondered if that's what Lowthelian meant when she said we had no family in the temple. Did we have to lose part of our identity when we joined the service of the Light?

I wondered if my mom's name would be on the wall. It would make sense if she knew about this place, maybe she had lived here. I found four Delwyns before I quit looking for them. Her name was so common here that she could have been any one of them or none of them. Ross's name appeared a few times, and so did mine. In fact, Kell was the last name on the list. I hadn't been here for more than two days, and already my name had been engraved on the wall.

Could this be the Ross that now lived inside me? Had he been a Chosen One a long time ago? Hundreds of names had been etched between our names. How was any of this possible? Did all the Chosen Ones have an older Chosen One living inside them? Why would Ross be locked in a chamber to die if he was a Chosen One? A flash of recognition from Ross and that creepy wriggling feeling at the back of my mind told me that I had guessed right.

A tickle of fear rippled through my chest. Something terrible happened in this Temple of Light. How many of the Chosen had been locked up in that chamber? Hahl said the priests had all been Chosen Ones before they became priests, and no new Chosen Ones had appeared in a long time. What did they intend for me then? They didn't call me Chosen One. They called me Promised One.

The energy pulsing from the altar drew me, and I stepped over to read the golden writing in its center. "The Navel of the Earth."

"Navel?" I said in surprise. I couldn't help but think of the big hairy kid in gym class who used to pick lint out of his belly button and throw it at people. "Well, that's not a real pleasant image," I said. Why would they call a room like this *the navel?*

I touched the writing, and a rush of power raised goosebumps all over my body. I yanked my hand away. This power was greater than anything I sensed from the priests, and it rose in an invisible column from the altar itself. In awe, I glanced up at the domed ceiling. Where was all the light coming from? A room like this, far under the ground, should be as black as pitch.

A sense of amazement and grandeur mingled with the realization of my own smallness and insignificance. I was nothing but a sixteen-year-old boy without a family, forced into a strange world, being consumed by a power I feared as much as I craved. How could I succeed at whatever they expected me to do? I sank to my knees and rested my forehead against the altar, letting its power wash over me.

"Help me," I whispered.

A slow, rhythmic thumping like the beating of a heart broke into my reveries. I scrambled to my feet to stare at the altar's polished surface. Below the original inscription, new letters formed in brilliant gold. I read the words aloud as they appeared. "Pain. Decay. Help us. Time. Help us."

The words burned brilliant gold for a few moments and then faded. I placed both trembling hands on the altar and closed my eyes the way I had back at my room. Pale images flowed into my mind—

wispy figures of a priest with a shaven head before a tiny altar while the world around him seemed to boil with flames.

A little drawer slid open from the altar, and the priest retrieved a silver stone like the golden one I held in my pocket. The vision faded, and the rhythmic drumming returned. A horrible, suffocating dread gripped my chest. I gasped and jerked away from the altar to stare at its polished surface in terror. The temple itself was frightened. It was begging me for help.

Chapter Six
To Withdraw the Light

I FOUND LOWTHELIAN pacing in front of my door when I arrived.

"Hey," I said, trying to put on a smile. But I was more interested in food at that moment.

Lowthelian frowned. "You're late for the evening meal, Promised One," she snapped. "Very late. You would spend your time better meditating upon the Light than in roaming about the temple."

That wiped the smile from my face. I didn't expect her to give me a hug and a big wet kiss or anything, but the hostility and anger annoyed me.

"I thought you weren't supposed to be my teacher," I said.

Lowthelian's eyes swirled liquid silver. Hot anger poured from her. My power stirred like a dog sensing danger.

"Your tray is on your table," she said. She spun with a swish of her hair and her robe and glided away.

Suspicion crept into my mind. Why was her pot boiling over? Was it just that she had to wait for me, or was she worried I would find out things I wasn't supposed to know? Like the room called the Navel or the golden stone and the book?

It had taken me a long while to find my way out of the tunnels, and I only managed it when Ross pushed vague images into my head. He brought me out by a giant carved and painted panel that portrayed a woman in a white flowing robe. She stood inside a silver circle, casting another woman from the heavens. I assumed this must be Illurien casting Shaheen, or She-Who-Would-Not-Sing as the priests called her, from the council. Something about the portrayal puzzled me.

Illurien's hands stretched toward the woman, who cowered in front of her. The woman staggered backward, but what caused her to stagger was not shown. Because I didn't know enough about the priest's religion, I couldn't understand what this meant.

The priests were hiding things from me. That much was obvious after my first couple of days here. But why? My mind worked in overdrive all night—the ruined rooms, the little book, the golden stone, the great vault, the stone panel, and the temple that had a consciousness of its own.

In my wanderings, I also came across a wooden door set in the temple wall. It must have been the way the girl I saw singing by the sundial entered the temple. I needed to find her so I could convince her to help me. If the priests didn't want me to meet her, I figured I should make that very thing a priority. Besides, maybe I could convince her to fill me in on everything the priests weren't telling me.

I jumped out of bed just as the gray of dawn was filtering through my window and dashed through the corridors, my robe flying out behind me until I came to the last shadowed doorway leading out into the courtyard. The girl was already there. I caught the last words of the familiar song. It was gentle and sweet and made me want to lean back against the wall and listen to it forever.

The song ended, and the girl strode from the plaza. I hurried to follow her as she made her way toward the door, but she walked faster than I expected. I broke into a jog and was about to call out to her when a black-robed priest with churning green eyes stepped in front of me. I nearly toppled into him before I slid to a stop.

"Come, Promised One," the priest said.

I was getting sick of that phrase. They seemed to think I was a dog they could just call whenever they wanted.

"What? Now?" I asked. My gaze darted to the door as the girl stepped through and closed it behind her.

"Now," the priest said.

I fell in behind him as he shuffled back into the maze of buildings.

His bony feet scraped and clicked on the stone paving. How had he known to find me here? I glanced up at Hahl's tower but could see no one at the window.

"Where are we going?" I asked. The priest didn't bother to answer. He just kept walking with the quiet, rhythmic clicking of bone on cobblestone.

We walked deep into the temple complex—farther than I had ever been. I followed him past the buildings of pure-white polished stone. We must have walked for fifteen minutes, passing a panel portraying the moon in all its phases and numerous buildings all decorated with the circles and squares and images of the Woman of Light.

At last, the priest led me through an ivy-covered doorway into an immaculate garden. Warm sunlight splashed across the rich greens of the vegetation and the deep purples, reds, blues, pinks, and whites of the flowers. The reds and yellows burned the brightest. The garden pulsed with life, rising and falling, breathing of its own accord. I sucked in a deep breath of the pure, clean air. The garden was alive—really alive. Earth and wood mingled with the sweet scent of blossoms and the sharp tang of herbs and spices.

We continued to the center of the sea of plants. He gestured with his bony hand, and a huge root rose out of the ground to form a chair. I stepped back in surprise. He sat on his strange wooden chair and motioned for me to sit. I looked around for another root chair, but none emerged. So, I tucked my legs underneath me and plopped down onto the white cobblestones.

"I am Einediau," the priest said. His eyes glowed a vibrant green, pulsing with the rhythm of the life of the garden. "I am the Keeper of Life."

That much I'd figured out on my own. I avoided looking at the lipless jaws moving while he spoke. Skeletons weren't supposed to speak. I had never understood why people were afraid of skeletons—until now. They were dead, after all, and couldn't hurt you. But these skeletons were alive with strange, glowing eyes.

It was just wrong to see them talk and move like they had flesh on their bones. I was having a hard time getting used to their creepy animated skeletons.

The priest picked up a delicate little plant with a bright yellow flower. The plant was only about five inches tall. It nestled in a tiny round pot of white marble with golden writing on the side.

Einediau cradled the plant in his hands. "This lily symbolizes the first life and the light of the sun. It was the first plant to grow during the creation. The seed that produced this flower descends from that first flower. The sacred lily grows slowly and can live for thousands of years. I planted this lily when I first became a Chosen, and I have fed and watered it for centuries."

He handed me the pot. It was warm, which struck me as odd.

"Do you feel its life, Promised One? Do you feel its Light?"

I nodded. I could feel the plant pulsing with the same rhythm of the garden. It was alive. That much I could feel, like I had been tuned into the frequency of life.

"Life is Light, Promised One," Einediau said. "This you must understand because Light is also power. It pervades all things and brings them life. Without Light, there is no life."

My mom had said something like that while we were hiking in the hills of Ohio. We had come upon a gigantic rock outcrop that overlooked forested slopes and a winding river far below. She gestured with a dramatic sweep of her arms, taking it all in. "Look at all this," she said. "None of it could exist without Light."

I thought she was talking about the sun, but now I realized how stupid I'd been. She was trying to teach me about the Light. The longer I was here, the more convinced I became that Mom had been here, but I couldn't see how.

Einediau motioned to the lily. "You see. Don't you?"

I sensed the life of the plant and knew I could take it. The thought surprised and disturbed me. I frowned. It was just a plant, but the idea that I should destroy a tiny, helpless thing, pulsing with life, left me feeling base and depraved. Why would I even think of such a thing? Taking its Light would destroy it. I knew I could—and worse, I wanted to.

"Do it," Einediau said in a quiet whisper. His green eyes swam and burned with a painful brilliance. I sensed anticipation and fear in his posture and in his voice.

I glanced down at the lily with its beautiful yellow flower. Clearly Einediau cherished it. A harmless little thing. I didn't need to destroy it.

"Do it," Einediau whispered again. "It is the test."

"Seems cruel," I said.

Einediau pointed at the lily. "Do it," he commanded.

Power tingled on my fingertips. Ross grew tense and expectant. I could feel the pressure of his presence building behind my eyes. I reached out with the power. Einediau stiffened. The invisible power sparked in my palm and probed the life in the little plant. The lily twitched and wilted as the life receded into my palm the way water flows over a stone—calm and unresisting. Light pulsed through me with intense beauty and purity—like taking a refreshing drink of cool water on a warm day.

Then a new sensation broke from the lily, and I sucked in my breath in surprise. I sensed a quiet sadness coming from it. The lily was aware. It didn't want to die. I almost stopped, but Ross urged me on. I had to complete the test. With a deep sense of regret, I withdrew the last bit of life from the lily until it lay shriveled and lifeless on my palm—its once brilliant yellow flower now a limp gray thing that sagged over my hand. I glanced up at Einediau, who stared at the withered lily in horror.

"Such power," he mumbled. "Such power." He reached out to take the lily from me but jerked his hand back as if he had been shocked by electricity.

As the last of the life left the lily, an odd sensation spread through my fingers and toes. I glanced at my hands. The tips of my fingers blurred and elongated. It felt like my toes were extending into the earth, digging into the soil, reaching for nutrients. A tremor of terror swept through me. Using the power was doing something to me again. Taking something from me. I was coming undone.

I struggled to control the sense of dissolution spreading through my body until Einediau lunged to his feet and motioned for me to follow him, but I couldn't move. I had no control over my limbs. My hands and feet stretched for the soil as I wrenched against the knowledge that I was losing myself. Slowly, the sensation passed, leaving behind loose, aching joints while Einediau looked on.

Deciding I couldn't just cast the lily aside, I stuffed it into the pocket of my robe. I had never killed anything other than ants and mosquitoes or the odd bug or weed. But this type of killing was so intimate. I had drawn the Light from the lily and made it a part of my own Light. I didn't like the way it made me feel dirty and mean.

The lingering sensation of looseness persisted. Stumbling after Einediau as he puttered around his garden, I tried to follow what he was saying, but I was too distracted by the feeling that my body kept trying to sink roots into the soil. What was happening to me? Would I become a part of this mosaic of shrubs and flowers?

Einediau strolled along, touching each plant with the tenderness of a father caressing a child. A deep sadness emanated from him. He was mourning the loss of the beautiful lily.

I was surprised now by the brilliant shades of green. When I entered the garden, the reds and yellows had stood out, but now, the greens burned with color. I almost asked Einediau about it, but the fear and sadness emanating from him made me think better of it. I was forming a bond with each of the priests as I passed their tests—a bond that gave me access to their emotions. This made me half-sick. I didn't want to know what they were feeling.

"Now that you have been touched by the Light," Einediau intoned, "you are a part of all things."

"What?"

He didn't hear, or he chose to ignore me. "Light infuses all life," he continued. "When you are one with the Light, you are one with the cosmos. Your individuality merges with the infinite plurality."

Was I supposed to understand what he was talking about? Or was this some weird chant he used? Before I could figure it out, Einediau finished his bizarre monologue and dismissed me.

Gratefully, I left the garden as the exhaustion seeped into my aching bones. Trying to find my way to my room, I got lost, and Ross had to help me with images the way he had in the corridors. Once I was back in the part of the complex I knew, I made a point of passing the little door again on the off chance that the girl would be there.

All the while, my mind kept going back to the little lily in my pocket. By what right did I so casually steal the Light of another living thing—even a tiny plant? I couldn't shake the feeling of being unclean, corrupted.

A tray of warm food waited for me when I arrived at my room. Apparently, Lowthelian had no intention of speaking to me. I placed the book, the slip of paper, the stone, and the dead lily on the table to study them while I ate. I thumbed through the pages of the book. Curiosity about its origins and what it said gnawed at me, but I couldn't make any sense out of the beautiful flowing script.

I slipped the piece of paper into my pocket and hid the book under my bed. I would keep it there until I could figure out what to do with it. Then I picked up the lily. It sagged over the edge of its container, cold, and dead. I had stolen its Light the same way Llaith wanted to seize mine. The act seemed almost brutal, especially since the lily knew what I was doing and wanted to live. It had suffered.

On an impulse, I reached out to the dead lily with my power. I caressed it softly and whispered to it. I tried to push life and Light back into it. The power sparked on my fingers and tingled. The lily's Light seemed distant as if moving away from me, dissipating or losing its strength. I absorbed it into my being and passed it on to the lily. It straightened and swelled as color returned to its stems and leaves. The yellow flower blossomed anew, casting its fragrance into the air. I continued pushing the Light back into the lily until it vibrated on my palm and pulsed with life. My whole body seemed to stretch like my cells were pulling away from each other.

I stopped when I realized I had been singing. The echo of my last words rebounded off the walls of my room. This detail paled in significance when compared to the magnitude of what I had done. A great sense of exultation welled up inside me. I lunged to my feet and paced over the cold stone floor, ignoring the jolting pain in my joints with each step.

This was *real* power. Anyone could take life, but to be able to give it back was something unimaginable. How could I possess the power to give Light and life? What could this mean? Could I draw the Light from anything and give it back again? Or give it to someone or something else?

Still, this power was dangerous. Wonderful things might come with its use, but there was a limit. Each time I used it, it changed me in a way I didn't understand, leaving me feeling damaged and different. I placed the lily on the windowsill, collapsed onto my bed, and let the exhaustion settle over me. The aching weariness dove deep, spreading throughout my body like I had become unplugged from the source of energy that animated my very being. The fog of sleep crept over my mind as I wondered what using the power would finally do to me.

"How do I instruct him?" Ross said to himself while Kell slept. There had to be a way to nudge the boy in the right direction. Kell had the potential for greatness, but that potential needed to be nurtured. He needed to be taught and instructed.

"I've discovered a way to send him vague images of the passageways and grounds of the temple, but how do I teach him what he needs to know?"

The boy had discerned much already. His control and power increased with every test. It wouldn't be long now. Somehow, the boy must discover the secret to purifying the Light. Maybe he would actually be strong enough to do it. Maybe he wouldn't fail like Ross had done. Like Jerome had done. Ross had to be sure he succeeded. There would be no more chances for him and none for the boy.

"The boy guesses," Ross thought. "He is beginning to understand what the power is doing to him."

More than one priest had reached too quickly for too much. Power wasn't free. It had never been free.

"Not even I understand how the power will transform the boy. No one has ever done what he has done. What will the power do to him? What might it demand of the boy? Or will it destroy him before he can complete the task?"

Ross pondered on that last question.

"The boy might die," he said, "but I will keep him alive long enough to finish the work I began. I must."

Chapter Seven
The Light of Illurien

"COME IN, PROMISED ONE."

I jumped and pushed the door open to peer into the dark room. The priest with the orange eyes stepped to the center of the room with a soft rustle of his robe and sat on the floor beside a wavering flame. Another flame burned on an altar of white stone behind him. Golden decorations that looked like a lion's mane or tongues of fire had been etched into the stone. They glinted in the flickering light of the flame.

At first, I thought the two flames must come from huge candles or maybe a gas lamp of some kind. Then I realized they floated in the air with no apparent source or fuel. The room smelled of hot metal and was uncomfortably warm. I followed his example, sitting opposite him.

Lowthelian had left me at the door, ignoring my attempts at conversation with a tight-lipped rebuff. I wanted to tell her to grow up but figured it wouldn't do any good. I felt better today after a long night's sleep—no more of that odd sensation of stretching and coming apart, though my joints still ached.

The orange brilliance of the priest's eyes smoldered and burned like they were themselves ablaze. The priest stared at me over the top of the flame. I could sense his power as I had the others, but I didn't fear it. Something about this priest made me think he might answer my questions.

"Welcome, Promised One," he said. His voice had a melodious quality that made it sound like he was singing. "I am Ufel. Long have we waited and prepared for your coming."

I had heard that before, and it didn't tell me much.

"Before we begin," Ufel continued, "I sense that you wish to speak."

"Uh," I said.

"Please, be at ease," he said. "You may ask me whatever you wish. I will answer if I can."

He caught me off guard. I wasn't used to being told I could ask questions. "Okay," I said, "I need to understand more about the nature of the Light."

The priest bobbed his head in encouragement, so the questions started to boil out of me.

"How can you all control the Light," I asked, "but you each have different colors and interests? Why aren't you all the same?"

"Ah," Ufel said, "these are wise questions. I cannot fully answer them. I will say this. None of us individually can control the Light. We each command one small portion of the Light that fills the expanse and gives life to all things."

"But—" I tried to interrupt.

"Light is truth, Promised One," Ufel continued. "Like truth, Light must be divided and segmented so that it can be understood and used for good. We each control that segment of the Light that is given to us. So, collectively, we are the servants and stewards of the Light. Yet, its power is beyond our control. Indeed, Illurien herself must rely on the cooperation of the other Beings of Light. You have doubtless noticed that our eyes have become the color of the portion of the Light we control."

"Yeah," I said, "no one could miss it."

"This is because," Ufel continued, "the eyes are the light of the body. They reveal our inner Light. Our long use of the power has caused our eyes to change to reflect the portion of the Light that animates us."

Ufel kept speaking, but his voice softened, and his emotions intensified. "You, Promised One, possess a power that may circumscribe all Light. Indeed, we once had a Chosen One who believed…" he paused.

"Believed what?" I asked, leaning forward in sudden interest.

Ufel shook his head again. "No, I have said too much already." He bowed his head and sighed. "Your task is great, Promised One, and our time is short." He raised his head to study me with his burning orange eyes. "We must begin. I am the Keeper of the Fire."

He rose and gestured for me to follow him. He knelt before the white altar and bowed his skull to touch the corner of it. Then he rose and gestured for me to kneel.

I knelt, feeling awkward since I had never been to church in my life. The warmth from the single flame was inviting, calming.

"This is the Eternal Flame," Ufel said. "It has burned since it was ignited on creation's morn."

I glanced at him in disbelief.

"Yes," Ufel said, "it is many millions of years old and has never gone out. It cannot be extinguished by any means we possess."

"But it has to be burning something," I said.

"Does it?" Ufel asked.

"Well, isn't that what fire does?"

"It would appear so," Ufel said, "and yet this flame is truly eternal."

"Okay," I said. I might as well roll with it, but Ufel saw I still didn't believe him.

"This temple," he said, "was called forth from the bones of the earth on creation's morn by Illurien herself. She touched the Great Sundial with her finger and imbued it with her power." He gestured to the flickering flame. "This fire has burned in this place ever since."

I stared at him. Could this be why the temple could communicate with me? Had Illurien given it a consciousness? Was it alive?

"Now, reach forth your hand into the flame."

Ufel said this like it was as natural as asking me to sit down. I considered the fire flickering before my eyes. It was a bright yellow flame with a blue outline. A flame that hot wasn't something I wanted to stick my fingers into.

"Um," I said.

Ufel shuffled his feet beside me. He didn't appear angry, like Llaith. Nor was he nervous and fearful the way Einediau had been. I glanced at the flame again and slowly reached my hand into it, cringing in expectation of the searing pain, but nothing happened. The flames licked hungrily at my hand. Instead of searing and melting my flesh, the flame lapped at my fingers with a cool, inviting reassurance. I stared in disbelief and amazement.

"Extinguish it," Ufel ordered with a sound of excitement in his voice. He leaned forward to gain a better view.

"But you said—"

"Do it," Ufel whispered.

I gazed up at him. How could I explain that I was more afraid of what the power might do to me than I was of getting burned? What part of me would it tear away? I didn't have a choice, so I reached inside where the power slept and awakened it. It rose instantly, tingling on my fingertips before it surged. I saw nothing, but the flame vanished like it had been blown out in a gust of wind.

Ufel let out an exclamation of dismay, and his fiery eyes flashed. I scrambled away from the altar, afraid Ufel might attack me, but he remained unmoving, his orange eyes blazing in the darkness.

"It's true," he whispered. "You bear the sign of power. The time has come."

"What do you—" I began, but Ufel snapped his teeth together in a way that made me half-sick.

"Can you reignite it?" he asked. A surge of anticipation and excitement came from him.

"Is this part of the test?" I asked.

"No," he said in a barely audible voice.

I placed my hand on the center of the altar and called up the flame. It leaped from between my fingers, wavered for a moment, and then burned a bright, steady yellow-orange fire. The strong smell of hot metal filled the room.

Ufel sucked in his breath and staggered away from me. "Oh, Promised One," he said in wonder, "your power is great. So great…"

He trailed off and stared at me for a long moment. Then he returned to his seat by the little flame in the center of the room, and I followed. Ufel leaned in close to me.

"Be wise, Promised One, and think on what I have said. You must seek to understand this power." He waved a skeletal hand at me. "If you do not, you will fail, and all will come to ruin."

Lowthelian wasn't waiting to guide me back as I stepped out, blinking in the sunlight, so I turned to find my way alone. The early afternoon sun spilled warm light over the temple complex, reflecting off the white stone walls. A sudden pain burned on my head, and I reached up a hand to feel something like a crusty scab. I brought my hand down to find that my hands and arms had bits of charred flesh falling off. I stopped and stared in horror. The fire hadn't burned me when I was touching it, but now I could feel the painful burns all over my body as my robe brushed against them with my every movement.

"What is happening to me?" I whispered. Dizziness made me blink at the pale orange glaze before my eyes. The terrible fear at what the power might be doing to me mingled with the overwhelming craving to use it. It was like an addiction. I had heard about heroin addicts who feared and longed for the drug that was killing them. The power must be doing the same to me.

It lurked inside me, expanding with each new task, collecting energy, gorging itself on the Light I was stealing from the priests' treasured objects. With it came a deep, penetrating weariness that seeped into the every fiber of my being. It clawed deep into the marrow of my bones. The most disturbing thing was I knew Ross wanted the power, too. We couldn't be satisfied. The need lingered the way a thirst for water could not be quenched. For some strange reason, I wondered what my father would have done.

I couldn't know, of course, because I had never known much about him. Right now, it would have been nice to have a man I trusted, a man who loved me and wanted to protect me to discuss this with. The only person who had ever loved me was my mother, and she was gone.

As I stumbled through the complex, fighting the exhaustion and wincing at the pain caused by the robe rubbing against the burns, my mind strayed to the young woman in the white robe. Something about the girl reminded me of my mother.

I stepped around a corner near Llaith's room when a sudden tremor of pain and terror swept up through my feet from the stones of the temple, accompanied by a wild, chaotic music that exploded in my mind. Reeling, I clutched my head, trying to shake the horrible feeling, when the air in front of me wavered and shimmered like a strange mirage.

A rent, laced with all the colors of the rainbow, yawned a few feet from me. Something dark stirred on the other side, and the sound and briny smells of the ocean washed over me. I leaned forward in horrified curiosity when a long, curved claw, black as night, snapped through the hole toward my face. My feet tangled as I stumbled backward and slammed onto the cobblestones, banging my elbow. The claws gripped the sides of the rent, trying to widen it, forcing their way to me.

Without thinking, I raised my hand, and a burst of energy surged into the rent. The eyeless face and ragged jaws of some beast flashed back into the hole, and the rent snapped shut. I lay there, trembling in terror. Anxious to get as far away from there as soon as possible, I crawled unsteadily to my feet and staggered across the courtyard and down the long hallway, expecting the air to rip apart at any minute and that horrible black claw to tear into me.

When I arrived at my chamber, I stripped off the black robe to examine my body. The charred scabs were already starting to heal, but the encounter with the clawed beast left me feeling dirty and defiled. Some evil was clawing at the very fabric of reality, ripping through from some other place or time. I shuttered and dunked my head in the silver washbasin. Then I used the linen towel to rub myself down—trying to scrub away the feeling of invasion and fragmentation.

That's when I noticed the birthmark on the inside of my arm near the crease of my elbow. I hadn't looked at it since my mother ran her finger over it as she lay dying, but it had changed. I wiped my arm with the towel again and held it up to inspect. It had always been a pale, white mark shaped like a small six-petal rosette. I never thought much of it. No longer pale, it had grown more vivid and more defined than ever before. Ross stirred inside me, and the pressure behind my eyes grew. I shook my head in annoyance.

"Leave me alone," I said.

The pressure diminished, but Ross kept nudging me to look at my birthmark. I ignored him. After slipping on the fresh robe lying beside the washbasin, I plopped down at the table and tried to understand what had happened. Evil things were not supposed to live in the Temple of Light, but this thing had been trying to tear its way in.

The Cleansing

I studied my hands because I had just used the power inside me to push some monster back into a black hole. If it could do all of these incredible things, what else might this power do? I pointed my finger at the wall and willed the power to strike it. An invisible beam of energy leaped from my hand and punched into the wall. Bits of stone and dust erupted into the air. I peered through the hole into the corridor beyond.

"Oops," I said, looking around like an idiot. It's not like anyone could have seen me, and it wasn't a big hole anyway. I could just hang something in front of it.

The fact that I could use the power that way made me even more curious. I waited to see if some part of me would dissolve or something horrible would happen to me, but I didn't feel anything. It was like doing little things with the power didn't hurt so much, while big tasks took something out of me.

If the power was Light, could I use the invisible power to make light? I imagined a candle burning in my hand. A tickle swept across my palm, and a small ball of pure white light materialized there. It thrilled me. It was incredible. The light warmed my hand and gave me an intense sense of peace that banished the last of the trembling from my encounter with the beast. What were the limits of this power? What would it do to me if I kept using it?

The girl came striding over the cobblestones of the courtyard with practiced grace, her white robe flowing around her feet. Her high cheekbones and large dark eyes with brown skin and black hair contrasted sharply with the white robe she wore. I crouched in the shadows as she knelt and placed the silver platter on the altar, bowed her head, and said something. Then she rose, stepped away from the altar, and lifted her gaze to the sundial.

The rays of the morning sun slanted into the courtyard, catching the crystal sundial and radiating out in a dazzling halo of white. The light glinted off her ebony hair as it waved in the cool morning breeze. I felt like a stalker racing from my room before the sun was up to spy on her, but I forgot all that when she started to sing. Her voice floated through the air, clear as crystal.

My power responded with a warm tingling that swept through me. I closed my eyes. Her voice conjured images of the timeless reaches of space, the great blue vaulted sky, and the flowing of mighty waters. Something earthly, yet eternal, resonated in her voice. The rich, mellow tone left a pleasant longing in its wake. I was surprised to find I knew the song. I had heard it before.

The music ended abruptly, and I jerked my eyes open. The girl stared at me with wide, dark eyes. Our gazes met for an instant before she fell to her knees and bowed so low her long black hair lay like a shroud upon the white stones. I stared for a moment. Then I glanced up at the window to see if Hahl was watching before stepping out of the shadows. When I stopped in front of the girl, she was trembling.

"Hey," I said, "sorry if I surprised you."

The girl stole a quick glance at me and then bowed again.

"Forgive me, Promised One," she said. "I didn't know you were there."

Her voice thrilled me. It contained a musical quality that rang like a silver bell.

"Please don't bow to me," I said. "Stand up."

The girl hesitated and then rose, brushing her hair behind her ears in one graceful motion. She kept her gaze downcast.

"What's your name?" I asked.

"I am called Alana. The Bringer of the Light."

"So, you're a servant of the Light, too?"

Alana nodded, her black hair falling over her shoulders.

"Then why don't you live in the temple?"

Alana glanced up at me like she thought I was slow or stupid.

"You're asking *me*?" she replied. Then her eyes widened, and she dropped her head again. "Forgive me, Promised One. I forget my place."

This was getting out of control.

"Don't worry about me. I'm not one of the priests."

She gave me another puzzled glance. "But you're the Promised One."

"Yeah," I said. "That's what everybody keeps saying, but somehow, I don't really get what it means."

"But—" she began.

I cut her off. "It's like this," I said. "I need someone other than the priests to give me some help."

Alana shook her head. "It is not my place to teach you, Promised One."

Now, she gazed at me with genuine fear. I thought she might bolt.

"Can we take a walk?" I asked. "It probably wouldn't be a good idea for the priests to see us talking."

Alana bowed to the altar and strode out of the courtyard. Once we were in the shadows of the buildings, I grabbed her wrist to slow her down. I caught the fragrant scent of flowers as I stepped close to her.

I needed to convince her to help me understand what was going on. Everything I thought I knew about reality, about life, about myself didn't matter in this world.

"Alana," I begged, "I need your help. Please."

She stopped and turned to study me with a curious expression. "Promised One, I…"

"No, let me finish," I said. "I know I'm the Promised One, but I don't know what that means or what I'm supposed to do. I don't even know where I am." I raised my hands and stared at them. "I have the power, but I…"

"I know," Alana said.

That statement stopped me. "What?"

Alana's face became serious, and her eyes filled with fear. "I know you have the power." She dropped her gaze again. "I saw it."

I stepped back to see her better. Was she pulling my leg? How could she see my power when even I had never seen it?

"What do you mean?" I asked.

Alana motioned toward the sundial. "Back there when you sang with me. I saw it. I felt it."

"Wait. I didn't sing. I was listening to you."

Alan pinched her brow together. "You sang Promised One, and I felt the power fill me like a…like a great cool wind from the mountains." She paused and refused to look at me. "It startled me, so I stopped singing and turned to see who was singing with me. You finished the song with such beauty. That's when I saw the power."

"What did you see?" I demanded. For the moment, I was going to ignore that she said I could sing with beauty because not even my mother liked to hear me sing.

Alana opened her eyes wide again, and she shook her head vigorously.

"Alana, please."

"I can't, Promised One." Her voice wavered, and her eyes were dark and wide. "I must go. I'm very late already."

Chapter Eight
The Mirror

LOWTHELIAN BROUGHT IN my breakfast with the tight-lipped snub which she had now adopted. I didn't bother trying to talk to her after breakfast. I followed her to my next test through a series of passageways into a large courtyard. This wasn't the central courtyard where the sundial stood. It was farther downhill in a cluster of smaller buildings. The air was tranquil amid the buildings, but it didn't smell old and stuffy. Like everywhere else in the temple that was touched by sunlight, the air tasted fresh and sweet.

A clear blue lake shimmered in the center of the courtyard, fed by a gushing spring that spilled from underneath a white boulder and tumbled into the lake. The tinkling sound of the spring echoed off the stone walls. The priest in his black robe stood on the edge of the lake. No air stirred in the courtyard, and the mirrored surface of the crystal waters reflected the pale blue of the sky overhead with the occasional white wisp of cloud.

The priest didn't invite me in, so I strolled right up to him. His brilliant blue eyes flashed in the pale sockets, and his white teeth glinted in the warm, early morning sun. He inclined his head to me.

"Welcome, Promised One." His voice flowed smooth and liquid. I liked the sound of it. It reminded me of the sound of moving water as it gurgled over polished stones.

"I am Durr," the priest said, "the Keeper of the Water." He

wasn't unfriendly, but he obviously had no intention of engaging in pleasant conversation.

"Do you see the fountain that spills into the far side of the lake?"

It's not like I could have missed it. I nodded and glanced to where the spring poured over an immense boulder some sixty or seventy yards away.

"Please stop it."

I glanced sharply at Durr. "Stop the flowing water?" I asked.

"Yes, Promised One. Please stop the water from flowing." Durr's response did not betray any hint of impatience.

Extinguishing the Eternal Flame had left me charred and aching. What would stopping a large flowing fountain of water cascading over a boulder do to me? How exactly did one stop water anyway—even with a strange, invisible power? I considered asking Durr, but I already knew his answer.

I took a deep breath and raised my hand, trying to keep it from trembling. An electric tingle radiated shivers through me as the power leaped from my fingertips. It slammed into the water with tremendous force, sending a spray high into the air. Water tried to flow around the barrier, but I stopped it and forced it back on itself. A churning wall of water curled back, like a dog chasing its tail, spitting and frothing in fury.

I don't know how I did it, but the hunger for the power that skulked in my mind became overwhelming. I wanted to use it. I *needed* to use it. Then the fountain ceased flowing. Simply dried up in a hiss of steam. The silence that filled the courtyard was deafening. I watched as the final ripples of the last splashing water rolled to the edges of the lake.

Durr gasped and then sucked in his breath in a long ominous hiss. "Release it," he said.

I let the water free, and it leaped out gleefully, rolling and splashing into the still waters of the lake. I relished the warm satisfaction of the power as it receded and pulled down inside me once again.

I glanced at Durr, feeling the fear and anger flowing from him. "If the Keepers command the power of the Light," I said, "can't you all do the same thing?"

Durr bowed his head. "No, Promised One. We cannot," he said

quietly. "This fountain springs from the center of the very roots of the earth. It was called forth by Illurien herself on the morning of the first creation and cannot be stayed. Every Chosen One has failed in this task, even after years of preparation and training, and you do it so simply."

It hadn't been simple at all, and though I didn't feel it yet, I would pay for having done it. Every test did something terrible to me.

"I still don't understand."

Durr sighed. "You will, Promised One. You will. Otherwise, you will fail." He paused. "Now, will you look into the Mirror of Light?" Durr motioned to a huge round disk of black obsidian set seamlessly into a raised dais of pure white marble. The dais was stepped so that a person could sit beside the disk.

I glanced at it. "What is it?"

"The Mirror of Light is a window into the past, the present, and the future. Light is truth and knowledge, Promised One. It is not bound by time. The Mirror can show you truth, thus giving you knowledge, but you are left to discern the truth that it shows. Because truth is not always as it seems, you must be careful to decipher the puzzles of truth it will show. You may gaze into the Mirror, but no one can tell what you will see. Do you wish to look, Promised One?"

I still hesitated because I didn't trust Durr. "What if I don't?" I asked.

Durr shrugged. "It does not matter. As the Promised One, you are permitted to look if you choose."

"I wouldn't understand what I saw anyway, would I?"

"It is your decision, Promised One."

I glanced at the black obsidian disk again and then back at the priest. Curiosity propelled me forward. How often does a kid get to peer into the future? The excitement I sensed rising in Durr gave me pause. He wanted me to look. Why? What did he expect to see? I stepped up to the Mirror. This was my chance to get some answers to what was happening to me. I couldn't pass it up.

"What do I do?"

For an answer, Durr snatched up a long hollow reed, dipped it into the lake, and placed his thumb over one end to capture the water. Then he held the reed over the obsidian disk and let the water drain onto it. The water spread out in a perfect circle, creating an even sheet that glittered on the surface and shimmered with tension.

"Sit," Durr said. "If the Mirror accepts you, it will speak."

What was that supposed to mean? Could the Mirror reject me? Durr leaned in so he could see into the Mirror. I adjusted to block his view and bent over, peering at the crystal sheen. My own reflection gazed back at me. I hadn't seen myself with a bald head until that moment, and I suppressed a laugh. I looked like an overgrown baby.

The sheen of water wavered, and images shimmered into existence and then marched across the black surface of the obsidian. A wave of dizziness swept over me. I tried to blink, but I couldn't. My eyes bulged in my sockets. The entrancing silver images drew me in until all sensation left me. Nothing but the surface of the Mirror existed in the entire world.

A light flashed, and I found myself peering down on a man in the same stone chamber I had fallen into a few days before. The man wore a white robe like Alana used, his head cleanly shaven like mine. He crouched in a corner, scratching at the stone. Then I saw myself lying on my back with my gaze fastened on the ceiling as it glowed with the beautiful, white writings.

The silver thread swept through the image, erasing it, and a woman with dark hair and a white robe materialized. She fled through the temple courtyard, clutching a bawling baby in her arms. I couldn't see her face, but something about her struck me as familiar. The thread spun again, and I saw men and women dressed in white robes dashing about the temple in obvious panic. Some carried children. Others lay in crumpled heaps. A great black cloud of smoke rolled over their heads from some huge fire.

The images streamed past, and I looked down on the city that surrounded the Temple of Light. A vast army marched through the city gates—rank after rank. Lances and armor gleamed in the sun. A wave swept through the scene, and I saw the great army descending on a city nestled among the crags of the mountains. The army filled the plain before the city, whose defenders seemed insignificant before the great host.

The surface of the Mirror shimmered, and I saw soldiers carrying away great treasures and leading prisoners with chains around their necks. They were mostly women and children.

I saw the priests gathered around the sundial singing. Then I was in a valley filled with mounds of earth covered in green grass. A woman lay upon an altar. I leaned close, but I didn't recognize her.

A light flashed, and I found myself gazing at a beautiful woman clad in a brilliant white robe. Her face radiated a soft glow. She had a delicate, porcelain-like appearance. The Light emanated from her being—pure, beautiful Light that wrapped itself around me and enfolded me in its glory. The Light shone warm and comfortable. Then she sang.

Her voice echoed like the purest crystal, plunging deep into my heart. I had never experienced such radiance and beauty. Everything ceased to exist, but the glorious music and the delicious Light. The woman reached out to me with her glowing white hands and beckoned to me. I wanted to go to her—to bask in the brilliance and beauty of the Light and the sound of that voice. I reached one hand toward her. As I did, a thin outline of darkness formed around her figure. This surprised me. I hesitated. Something was wrong.

A jet of icy cold water slammed into my face, tossing me away from the Mirror of Light. I stumbled backward with a cry. My eyes bulged, and for a moment, I thought they had been ripped from their sockets. I sprawled on the cold stone, dripping wet, blinking up at Durr through a silver-tinted haze. His blue eyes flashed so brightly I couldn't look at them. Anger emanated from him like heat from a hot furnace. I rubbed at my eyes, trying to understand his rage. What had I done?

"Fool," Durr growled. "Would you go to her so easily? Would you deliver the power into her hands?" He trembled, and I realized he wanted to attack me. My power responded, and I became alert.

"Leave here," Durr whispered, pointing toward the entrance to the courtyard. A column of water rose from the lake and bent toward me, spitting and churning. Had Durr used the water to knock me away from the Mirror?

"What's the matter with you?" I yelled. "I didn't ask to come to this temple and play your useless games."

"Is that what you think this is?" Durr demanded. The column grew closer.

I scrambled to my feet. "I did what you wanted," I said. "If you don't like it, stop asking me to do it."

"Get out." Durr jerked his bony hand toward the entrance with such fury I thought his finger bones might fly off.

"What is happening to me?" I demanded.

Durr remained motionless before me, and I could sense the confusion and terror boiling inside him, just like the column of water he held in check.

"Please," I said.

Durr whirled away from me and let the column of water collapse back into the lake with a splash. "You should consider what I have said and what you have seen," he said.

I snorted in disgust and spun away with a swish of my robe. The nasty, ugly skeleton could go stuff his head in his silver fountain and blow bubbles for all I cared. I was sick and tired of their secrecy and animosity. If I was the fulfillment of some prophecy, the least they could do was show me a little respect.

As I stomped back toward my room, my robe rubbed against the new sores that burst out all over my body. I lifted my sleeve to find big, oozing blisters had formed. It was like my cells had turned to water and were leaking out through these angry sores. I didn't know how much longer I could do this. I still had two more tests. With each test, the power grew, but so did the feeling that I was coming apart inside—that the power was stretching me, turning me into someone or something else.

Chapter Nine
The Roinan

THE LINGERING PAIN punctuated my every step as I hurried through the morning shadows the next day to wait at the sundial for Alana. I jerked up my sleeve as I walked to check the blisters from the day before. Most were gone, but a few were still scabbed over. My body was trying to heal itself, but the injury from each task seemed to take longer to heal.

A sudden burst of fear swept over me, and I stopped. Silence filled the temple. A palpable hush rang in my ears. Sweat beaded on my brow, and I examined the shadows. Something watched me— something I couldn't see. I felt like a deer when it knows the wolf is creeping up on it. Every muscle tensed. My power flared to life and sparked on my fingertips. The darkness rippled and wavered, and I bolted.

As I rushed around a corner, I nearly ran over Lowthelian. She shrieked in surprise and cowered away from me like she thought I had come to hurt her. I slid to a stop, panting. I glanced back, but the churning fear had gone.

Lowthelian recovered and passed her hands over her gray robe, trying to appear unconcerned, but her churning eyes betrayed her emotions.

"You startled me, Promised One," she said. "I seldom meet anyone in the temple, and no one rushes around corners like that."

She tried to smile. "No matter, follow me." She waved her hand at me.

"Right now?" I said, trying to still the nervous trembling. I hadn't been that scared since my Mom died.

She cocked her head to one side. "Yes, now. Were you going somewhere more important?"

I glanced back. "Did you feel anything just now?"

She wrinkled her nose at me and cocked her head sideways, clearly thinking I was just stalling.

"I haven't eaten yet," I protested. How did I explain that I was feeling evil things roaming the temple?

Lowthelian raised her eyebrows and gave me a knowing smirk. "That didn't stop you from leaving your room so early to rush around the temple. Did it?"

I tried not to blush, but I could feel my face growing warm. I wanted to say something witty, but spontaneous sarcasm was not one of my strengths.

"Well—" I began, but she waved her hands in front of her, trying to ward off my reply.

"It doesn't matter," she said. "I've been sent to bring you. You must come."

I glanced up the corridor to where the sunlight brightened the courtyard beyond. Alana would be coming, and I worried about her coming to the temple alone if something evil was lurking about. I checked to make sure the evil presence was gone. But I hadn't actually seen anything, and the feeling of terror had disappeared.

"Oh, all right," I said and fell in behind Lowthelian as she stepped down a side corridor.

I had given up trying to understand her. She made it obvious I annoyed her, but now she had smiled. She hadn't been exactly friendly, but then, she hadn't snapped at me either. I sensed something else in her that I couldn't identify. She was connected to the larger questions I struggled to understand, but until she was willing to talk to me, there wasn't much I could do about it.

"Why don't you wear a black robe like the priests?" I asked as we walked.

"Only the Keepers wear black," she said.

"I'm not a Keeper."

"You are the Promised One," she said.

"So, who wears white?"

She glanced at me suspiciously. "Have you seen someone wearing white?"

I shrugged. "Why?"

"You are not supposed to be disturbed," she said.

"Well then, just explain why your robe is gray," I said.

Lowthelian scowled at me. "The Chosen and the other servants wear white," she said. "I am…" she paused as if searching for the appropriate word, "different. I serve the priests. I am…in between."

"What the heck does that mean?"

Lowthelian sniffed at me in irritation and strode ahead. She led me to the back of the temple complex to a wide courtyard with a tremendous stone of black marble hewn into a perfect orb. The stone dwarfed me. It must have been three stories high. Its glassy surface shone in the light of the rising sun. A million diamonds seemed to sparkle within it.

The priest skulked to one side. His indigo eyes burned in their otherwise empty sockets. I was getting used to the look of them, but they still spooked me—especially after what just happened. Could it have been one of them lurking in the shadows?

"Welcome, Promised One," he said.

I raised my eyebrows at him because I knew by now none of them meant it.

The priest motioned for me to sit. I collapsed onto the stone floor with my legs crossed and my hands folded in my lap. I wanted him to hurry. Maybe I could still catch Alana.

"I am Dairen, Keeper of the Earth," he said. His voice rumbled deep and gravelly, from the very earth itself.

"Please, hold out your hand, Promised One."

I obeyed. By now, I had learned that it didn't do any good to ask questions.

Dairen stretched forth his long, bony hand and dropped a heavy object into mine. My eyes opened wide as he withdrew his hand to reveal a glimmering diamond. It was huge—about the size of a goose egg. It had been cut with such skill that it grabbed every ray of light and sent each one off in a thousand jets of glittering light.

I had never seen a diamond so valuable, let alone touched one.

I could buy a small country with a rock like that. I didn't even try to hide my amazement. If the priests could play with such wealth, how much did they have hidden away in this temple complex?

"I see that you appreciate the beauty of finely cut stone," Dairen said.

"Yeah," I said. I didn't want to tell him that I had been thinking about the value of the stone, not its beauty.

"It is the Light that gives it its beauty, Promised One. It is the Light that beautifies all that we see. The stone itself is nothing."

Disagreeing with him would have been pointless, but a diamond like that wasn't worthless.

"Let me teach you something of the Light before we begin," he said. "You have seen Hahl's crystal?"

"Yes." I didn't mention what I had done to it.

"Then you know that light in its purest form is white, but that it can be split into many colors. You have also noted that each of the Chosen possesses one of the colors of the Light?

"You can't miss it," I said.

"All things possess the capacity to absorb some of the colors of light while they reject others. This is what gives color to all things. The sky absorbs all colors but blue, which it reflects back. The same is true of the leaf and flower. Do you understand, Promised One?"

Of course, I did. I grew up with a woman who was obsessed with all the properties of light. "Yes," I said. "I've learned something like this before."

Dairen's eyes swirled, and he seemed surprised that I should know something so basic. He apparently thought his observations were profound.

"Now, look at the diamond," Dairen said. "The reason it is so beautiful is because I have carefully shaped it to reflect every color of the Light."

I shifted the diamond, and color erupted from its myriad facets and then combined and split again. It was the most beautiful stone I had ever seen.

"It's magnificent," I said.

Dairen's eyes swam with pleasure for a moment, then intensified. "Yes. Now, crush it, Promised One."

"What?" I gaped at him. He couldn't mean it. "It's impossible,"

I said. "It's a diamond."

"I know what it is," Dairen said. "I know better than you what it truly is. Crush it." His voice echoed through the courtyard, deep and commanding. His eyes swirled and brightened the way all the priests' eyes did when they were feeling intense emotions. The power emanating from Dairen was solid, firm and immovable, drawn from the earth itself.

"Crush it," Dairen ordered again, his voice level.

"Fine," I said. Even if I could do it, I knew he was going to be upset with me. None of the priests liked it when I did what they ordered. Closing my fingers around the glittering, priceless gem, I braced myself for some new and terrible thing the power would do to me. I just had to survive two more tests.

The power flared. I squeezed, and the power surged into the diamond, and then it was over. I opened my hand. A fine black powder spilled between my fingers, flowing like water to the floor. I hadn't crushed the diamond. I returned it to its original state of simple carbon.

Dairen let out a long hiss. Once again, I sensed that same fear and awe the other priests had displayed. There had to be a way to keep them all from hating me for destroying their most prized possessions.

"Sorry," I said. Somehow no matter how hard I tried, I seemed to ruin everything. In desperation, I placed my hands over the pile of black dust and called forth the power again. It wrapped around the dust, and I squeezed.

When I picked up the diamond and offered it back to Dairen, he stared. He wouldn't touch it. The emotions emanating from him were overpowering and confusing, but fear dominated them—an overpowering, paralyzing fear.

"I'm sorry," I said again. "Did I do it wrong?"

Dairen shook his head and spoke with a quaver in his gravelly voice. "No, Promised One. You have more than passed the test." He paused for a moment and then continued. "I am the Keeper of the Earth. I created the Diamond of Light. I have bent all my power upon its creation. I have made it harder than any diamond. I have cut and shaped it to show the beauty and majesty of the Light. For years I cannot count I have labored, and now you…" he paused, "now you come and undo all my labor and then redo it again without effort. Please go, Promised One. I wish to be alone."

I placed the diamond on the ground and rose to my feet, hesitating and scowling at the sudden stiffness in my joints. With great effort, I took a step. Then another. My steps were labored, and they jarred my teeth. I felt so heavy, so sluggish, like a giant granite stone. As I lumbered from the courtyard, I glanced behind me. Dairen leaned forward as if in pain, but he would not touch the diamond.

Struggling against the rigidity in my limbs, I made my way through the temple. Every breath brought stabbing pain as if my lungs were turning to stone. I stopped and leaned against the wall of the temple to rest when that sense of urgency seeped into me again. I faced the wall and placed my hand on it, trying to understand what the temple wanted to communicate. All I received was a confusing mixture of fear and pain. I pulled my hand away, took several steps, and stopped.

There on the wall was a long, jagged, black scar. I stepped up to it, half-expecting a monster to climb out of it, but nothing happened. I placed my hand on the wall again, and a powerful surge of pain and terror swept into me, accompanied by a wild, desperate tune that made me shiver. Something was attacking the temple itself. It was afraid.

"What do you want from me?" I asked. The music grew louder. I waited for words to materialize on the wall like they had on the altar in the Navel, but I waited in vain.

I jerked my hand away in frustration and reached out a finger to touch the scar. A flash of utter blackness swept into me, and the emptiness of eternity reached for me. Vast, all-encompassing despair stretched toward me. I yanked my hand away and stumbled backward, crying out at the pain that surged through my stiff joints.

"What the heck is going on?" I said. When no other communications came from the temple, I tried to run, but could only stumble. The breath stabbed at my lungs, pierced by millions of tiny needles. Despite my best efforts, all I could manage was a slow lumbering jog. I ignored the pain, driven by the horror of that grasping emptiness.

Ross experienced a moment of pure terror as the nothingness yawned before them. The very Temple of the Light was now threatened. The darkness of She-Who-Would-Not-Sing infiltrated the holiest and most powerful sanctuary of the Light. The boy wasn't ready. He poised on the edge of the greatest accomplishment in the history of the Light—passing the tests—and he had no idea what to do. The boy might fail in his final, most difficult task of purifying the Light. He might die in the attempt. The nothingness might destroy him. If he died, the temple was doomed. Nothing could save the Worship of the Light or the worlds whose very existence now hung in the balance.

"I must push him harder," Ross thought. "Time is running out."

I ate a long, slow breakfast of the fruit and bread Lowthelian left for me while sitting in the rays of light coming in through my window. The light drained away the feeling of heaviness and rigidity. I needed answers. With one test left to go, I still had no idea what was going on or what I was supposed to do. I didn't know if the last test would finish me—if my soul would blow apart.

To make matters worse, the temple seemed to be haunted by some strange power that did not belong, and the temple was begging me for help. My situation couldn't have been more confusing or frightening if I had been dropped into some alternate reality.

I stared out the window at the clear blue sky. Once, when I was just a boy, I had been staring out the window like this on a beautiful fall day. The breeze had rustled the curtains, inviting me to come outside, to feel the cool grass tickle my toes. To soak up the warm sunlight and smell the life all around me. Mom had other ideas. She usually did.

As a five-year-old, I didn't want to sit at the table when I could be outside. Mom made me sit while she dropped a yellow ruler into a glass of water. Then she dribbled some oil into the water. The oil pooled on the top of the water without mixing with it. Why this should interest a five-year-old with dirt, grass, and bugs on his mind, I didn't know. She insisted that I explain what I saw in the glass.

"It's broken," I said. "The ruler is broken."

Mom smiled. I always liked her smile. She was a small, beautiful woman with dark hair, sad eyes, and an intense, passionate love of the Light.

"That's right, Kell," she said. "Light travels at different speeds when passing through air or water or oil. The ruler isn't broken. The light you see is being bent as it passes through the different substances." She wiggled the ruler around, and the numbers on the ruler stretched and elongated.

I grabbed the ruler and swirled it around, trying to see if I could get it to go back together. I couldn't, so I gave up and glanced out the window. The breeze still beckoned me.

Mom grabbed my chin and pulled my face back around. She scowled. "This is important, Kell. You need to understand this."

Then she poked her finger through the oil. It looked like her finger had broken into three pieces.

"Ouch," I said.

Mom smiled again. "It doesn't hurt. It's an illusion. It isn't real."

I stuffed my hand into the glass and watched as my wrist broke into three pieces. "How come it doesn't hurt?" I asked.

"I told you," she said. "It's the beautiful light that is all around us. It's the power that makes all worlds possible."

I looked out the window again at the pale blue sky and decided I wanted to go play in that light. I yanked my hand out of the glass, knocking it from the table. Oil and water flew everywhere. Mom jumped, trying to catch the glass.

"Kell," she yelled. Her voice sounded more desperate than angry. I gazed up at her. She was disappointed in me again. She always said she loved me, but I knew that I wasn't good enough. She wanted me to be more than I was. And it had to do with the Light.

I rubbed the mist of tears from my eyes. Had my Mom and Dad been mixed up in this religion? Had they been driven from the temple? If so, then Mom hadn't been delirious when she said someone was hunting us. It could only be the Keepers, but if they didn't know how to use the chambers, how did they find us? Why would they kill her, but not me? Did they know I was her son?

A wave of homesickness swept over me. I had lost everything I loved. I was alone in a temple with hostile priests who hated me, pursuing a power I didn't understand yet one I craved like I yearned for food and water—a power that was changing me in ways I couldn't comprehend. Mom also expected me to find news of my father here, but I hadn't even seen a man who wasn't a skeleton. If the priests had been responsible for my mother's death, I was going to find out.

My mind drifted toward Alana again. If I could get her to talk, I might be able to figure out what was going on and how I could find a way home. I might be able to ask her if she knew anything about my father. I closed my eyes and surrendered to the exhaustion.

A clang and a thump startled me to wakefulness. I jerked upright as a knock sounded on my door.

"Come in," I said.

I was glad for the interruption. Even if Lowthelian didn't talk much, at least she was a person—a real human with flesh and blood. When a small boy pushed through the door, I was so surprised I just sat and stared for a moment. His skin was a dark, nut brown, and his head was shaven. He couldn't have been more than nine or ten years old.

The boy bowed deeply and stepped into the room, carrying my lunch tray. His wide, dark eyes stared at me.

"Hi," I said. "I haven't seen you before."

"No, Promised One. I do not serve in the temple."

The boy's voice rang soft and melodious like he was on the verge of a song. I wondered if everyone here sang like the priests and Alana.

The boy spun to leave.

"Wait," I said. "What's your name?"

"We are the Roinan, Promised One."

"We?"

The boy stared at me.

"There are others like you?"

The boy nodded shyly.

"Where do you normally serve?"

"I serve in the kitchen of the Palace of Light."

"The palace? You mean the one over on the other hill?"

"Yes."

"Is that where my food is cooked?"

"Yes. The Keepers of the Light do not need to eat and drink. They live forever." The boy lowered his voice as he spoke and glanced over his shoulder at the door.

"You don't happen to have pizza and jalapeños over there, do you?" It was a long shot, but I hadn't had my favorite meal in a while.

The boy shook his head, shuffled his feet, and stared at the floor. He didn't want to talk to me, but I was so desperate for information that I plowed ahead anyway.

"Where is Lowthelian?" I asked.

"She could not come."

"Why not?"

The boy fidgeted and glanced at the door. "I don't know."

"What else does she do in the temple?"

The boy shrugged.

"Okay," I said, trying to hide my growing frustration. "Where did you come from, Roinan?"

The boy shook his head. "Far away," he said.

"Do you remember it?"

A frown tugged at the sides of his mouth.

"Did you choose to come here?" I asked.

Now, the boy glared at me.

"No, Promised One. Does anyone *choose* to serve the Light?"

The question so stunned me that I just stared after him as he retreated through the doorway.

Chapter Ten
To Touch a Star

AFTER THE BOY left, I couldn't sit still. I didn't have another test until the next day, and I wasn't about to sit around in my room forever. I wandered up to the sundial. The sun had long since disappeared. I must have slept longer than I thought. The cool night air and twinkling stars greeted me. I stared up at the sundial as it glistened pale white against the night sky. My mother would have loved a night like this, pointing out the constellations and going on about the different colored stars.

I turned to wander the temple complex when Lowthelian emerged from the shadows.

"Please follow me, Promised One," she said.

How did she always know where to find me? I glared at her. I was getting sick and tired of her telling me where to go.

"Again?" I demanded.

Lowthelian raised her eyebrows. "I've been sent to bring you."

"Where?"

"To be tested."

"Today?"

Her silver eyes swirled. "Please come, Promised One. He's waiting."

"Where were you earlier today? Why didn't you bring me my lunch?"

Her eyes flashed. "I have other duties, Promised One. I am not your slave." Then she gave an exasperated sigh and clasped her hands in front of her, struggling for self-control.

"How did you know to find me here?" I asked, suddenly suspicious that she might have been spying on me.

She stiffened, and her lips drooped into a frown. I thought she might scold me, but she just said, "Please come, Promised One."

"Oh, all right," I said. I liked Lowthelian—despite our rocky relationship—though I didn't understand her. She had become impatient and prickly ever since I touched her, and it got worse after I came back late to my rooms. Now, she was acting more friendly. What did she want from me?

"How come Llaith has hair?" I asked. "I mean, he doesn't even have a scalp."

"He is a Keeper."

"That's not an answer."

"He can do as he likes."

"Come on," I said, "you can answer one little question."

Lowthelian stopped to study me. Something in her expression had changed. "Perhaps he took it from someone."

I started to laugh, but she was dead serious. I touched my bald head in horror. "Is that why my hair won't grow. Did he steal it?"

Lowthelian scowled in confusion, and then she laughed. It was a bright, bubbly laugh. "Not from you," she said. Then she stopped laughing, and her face grew serious. "I think you know he can take things even when they are not offered. He can hurt and unmake."

"I guess," I said, genuinely surprised she was telling me this.

"Anyway," she said as she whirled to continue walking. "You have more important things to worry about now."

"You mean this is my last test?"

She glanced back at me, her face tight with concern. "It's the most dangerous, Promised One."

"What is it?"

"You know I can't say."

I followed her slender form through the dark temple, struggling to still the nervous flutter in my stomach as I contemplated what the last test might be and why it would be held at night. Then it hit me. Maybe the last test wasn't a test at all. Maybe she was taking me to a chamber like the one where Ross had been locked up. Maybe the priests had tired of me and were going to get rid of me under cover of darkness.

The thought sent my blood racing. Would they kill me? Ross had been left to die in a chamber. Would they sacrifice the Promised One? Yes, they would. In fact, maybe that is what the Promised One was supposed to do—gather all the Light into himself and then let them kill him to set it free. That would make sense.

Lowthelian stopped before a doorway that led up into a narrow tower. She motioned with her hand. "He waits at the top of the stairs."

She spun to leave, then stopped and turned back. An unusual expression I couldn't read crossed her face.

"I wish you success, Promised One," she said in a quiet voice. "I really do." Then she scurried away. The sadness in her voice surprised me. She knew what they were going to do to me tonight.

I waited until she vanished into the shadows before I faced the stairs. My heart still raced. If I climbed those stairs, I might never come down again. Still, I had nowhere else to go, and that craving for the power tugged at me. Ross nudged me toward the stairs. One more test and it would be over, one way or another. I started to climb and kept climbing.

By the time I reached the top, my heart was pounding, but not from fear anymore. Sweat dripped from my bald head and dribbled down my back. I found the priest on the roof of a high tower where the expanse of the heavens opened before him.

Pausing in the doorway to catch my breath, I gazed up at the beautiful sky. Never before had I seen the sky so filled with stars. They glittered against the inky background of space. Some burned with a silver-blue light, while others glowed with a dark red fire. Still others flickered in pale yellow or green light.

A bright band filled with millions of stars stretched across the sky. I knew enough to know it was the Milky Way, and I recognized some of the constellations my mother taught me. The Big and Little Dippers filled one corner of the sky. The large, irregular W formation I knew as Cassiopeia floated near the small cluster called Pleiades or the Seven Sisters.

My breathing had almost returned to normal when I stepped

through the door. The priest faced me. His eyes burned a deep and beautiful violet.

"That's some climb," I said.

"I take it one stair at a time," Seren said.

I paused to study him. "Was that a joke?"

"You look like you ran up them."

"Not really," I said.

As I approached him, I could sense a great serenity about this priest—something none of the others had. He wasn't anxious or excited or angry. He raised his arms in welcome like he wished to embrace me.

"Welcome, Promised One," he said. "You have finally come. I am Seren, the Keeper of the Night. I am left to the last because I am the youngest. I alone among the Keepers still remember my life before the choosing."

"Before?" I asked.

"I know how you must feel," Seren said. "Don't worry. You'll soon understand, and with understanding will come acceptance. With acceptance, peace. Now, come stand beside me, Promised One, and let me introduce you to the beauty of the night."

His demeanor surprised me. Only Ufel had been kind. I stood beside Seren as he pointed out individual stars with his long bony finger, speaking their names with quiet reverence. Then he pointed to the little cluster that I knew as the Seven Sisters.

"Do you see those seven bright stars clustered together?"

"Yes."

"Those are the Seven Tears of Illurien," Seren said. "She shed them as she cast She-Who-Would-Not-Sing from the Kingdom of Light. The tears remain as guardians to keep the way against her return. The Seven Tears mark our most important responsibilities. If we do not heed their warnings, She-Who-Would-Not-Sing may return and destroy the Light. It is I who inform the others of their movements in the heavens and interpret what they would say to us." He looked down at me. "I foretold your coming, Promised One. It was written in the stars."

"*You* told them I was the Promised One?" I blurted.

"Yes. The time has come for the prophecies to be fulfilled. The stars do not lie."

When I just stared at him, he continued. "Now, Promised One. We must begin the final testing. Are you prepared?"

There wasn't any way to prepare, so I just shrugged. The nervous flutter returned to my stomach.

Seren pointed up to the sky. "See that bright star there, near the horizon?"

"Yes," I said, "that's Venus." The star pulsated, outshining the others.

"We refer to it as Celema, the first and the last. The morning and the evening star. Now, stretch forth your hand and catch its Light."

I knew better than to question, but I couldn't help it. This was the most incredible thing any of the priests had asked me to do.

"You're not serious," I said.

Seren gazed at me placidly for a moment. "Stretch forth your hand, Promised One, and seize a portion of its Light." His voice remained calm and even, yet insistent. I couldn't avoid it. Stretching out my hand toward the star, I focused on it, reaching for the power.

The power came slowly, warm and taut with energy. It built up on my fingertips until I thought my hand would explode from the pressure.

Then it leaped out with a surge that knocked me backward. I staggered and caught myself against a pillar with my other hand and waited as the power flowed out of me. I didn't try to check it. I didn't try to control it. I just let it flow.

As the power gushed from my hand, a hollow, hungry feeling crept in to replace it. My chest ached. My fingers burned. Ross stirred, sending a creepy tickle across the back of my brain, and I tried to shove him aside. I couldn't afford to be distracted.

My arm grew heavy and my knees weak. I sagged against the pillar. A slow panic coiled around my throat. Maybe this was how they were going to kill me. They were going to let the star absorb my Light and leave me an empty shell. I remembered the shriveled lily and struggled to control the rising dread.

I had failed. The last test had been too much for me. I would die in the attempt. Sliding to the ground beside the pillar, I struggled to keep my hand outstretched. The world spun around me. The edges of my vision blurred and darkened as I perched on the brink of consciousness. Then it happened.

A tingling sensation brushed my palm, settling there and growing warm. The power poured back into me with renewed energy. I gasped at the painful rush of power as it filled me to bursting with light and energy. I closed my eyes against its overwhelming tide.

When the flow stopped, I opened my eyes to find a small ball of silver light materializing in the palm of my hand. Seren murmured something I couldn't hear. The warmth from the light washed over me, driving the weariness away, renewing not only my energy but also my body and mind. I scrambled to my feet and thrust my hand toward Seren in triumph.

He didn't move. I had expected him to display the same awe that I experienced, but that wasn't the emotion coming from Seren. He was sad. His violet eyes dimmed.

"Thank you, Promised One," he said. "You may release it."

I hesitated. This thing in my hand was so majestic and beautiful, so pure and delicate, I didn't want to let it go. I wanted to show Lowthelian and Alana—let them see the majesty and glory of the star. Seren stared at me until I released it. A thin silver strand unwound itself like a ball of yarn and threaded its way back toward the star from which it came.

I stared at the thin tail of Light as it trailed away into the inky blackness of space. An incredible feeling of grandeur and glory overwhelmed me. My eyes misted with tears. I had touched a star— the most beautiful manifestation of the Light I had yet witnessed. I sensed the magnitude of what I had done. The awe and humility filled me to overflowing.

Seren laid a heavy skeletal hand on my shoulder. I glanced up at him as his sorrow pierced me.

"It is the end," Seren said. "All things will now change for good or ill. It is beyond our power to say which it will be. That power now lies in your hands, Promised One. Only you can now choose our fate. Choose well, Promised One. The destiny of all worlds rests upon your shoulders."

"I don't get it," I blurted. "I've passed all the tests, but I still have no idea what they mean. Why have I been tested? What were the tests for?"

"Be at peace, Promised One." Seren gestured to the floor. "Sit, I will explain what I am permitted to explain."

I dropped to the cold stone, grateful to be able to sit. Weariness spread through my body, and I shivered as a deep chill filled me. I glanced up at the sky and realized it was the penetrating cold of space that somehow seeped into my soul. Seren's image blurred. I blinked, trying to bring him back into focus.

"Promised One?" Seren asked.

His voice muffled like he was speaking through a wad of cloth. I reeled and slumped to the floor as the emptiness of the heavens reached for me and tugged at the fibers of my being. Agony burst through me as my soul ripped apart, and I tumbled into the bitter void of space.

I drifted in emptiness. Alone. Undone. A tiny speck of Light in the vast cosmic darkness. The power had finally ripped me apart. I had reached beyond my strength in grasping the Light of a star.

The web of space and time pulsed around me, silent and brooding. Something was out there, lurking in the folds of time. I couldn't see it, but it perceived me. It knew me. It had been waiting for me. The presence shifted and approached, creeping like a spider along the strands of its web, responding to the vibrations of its prey as it struggled in the snare.

"Promised One?" The voice sounded distant and hollow.

The presence hesitated. "Promised One?"

Some other presence was down their tugging me back, begging me to return.

Ross, I thought.

Pain surged back into me. I gasped. Warmth radiated through the top of my skull to spread throughout my body. I shivered uncontrollably, and, for a moment, I saw my shuddering body twitching on the cold stone with Seren bent over me. Then I rushed back.

"Promised One," Seren said. "Can you rise?"

I blinked at the horrible sensation of bitter cold and struggled to a sitting position.

"What happened?" I mumbled, trembling from cold and exhaustion.

Seren shook his head. "I cannot tell you because no one has ever called the Light of Celema to their hand."

"It's like I was coming apart and drifting away," I said.

Seren nodded. "To use the power of the Light can be taxing. We each experience it differently. Perhaps you have discovered the limits of your power."

"How long was I…like that?"

Seren folded his bony legs underneath him and sat. "Several minutes," he said. "I thought we had lost you."

I hugged myself against the trembling cold. I thought they had meant to kill me, but I remembered the warmth on my head. "What did you do?" I asked.

"As the Keeper of the Night, I can call upon the Light of the celestial bodies to heal and restore," he said.

"You saved my life?"

"I restored it."

None of the other priests, except maybe Ufel, would have bothered. If they feared me so much, why would Seren save me?

"Why?" I asked.

Seren studied me with his swirling violet eyes. I sensed his conflicted emotions. He had been tempted to let me die, but he had saved me anyway.

"Thank you," I said.

Seren inclined his head in acknowledgment.

"Can you heal any injury?" I asked.

"No, only those that damage the Light, and even then, my power is limited."

"Will you please tell me what I'm supposed to do?" I asked. I shivered again and tucked my hands under my armpits in search of some warmth. My head throbbed.

Seren sighed. "As you should have learned by now," he began, "you are the last of the Chosen. We have not had a Chosen survive for so long that we've forgotten when it was. Each of the Chosen have been tested. When they failed, we trained them for many years, and then we tested them again to see which quality of Light they possessed. Each color has different attributes that align with the

Chosen's personality, strengths, and weaknesses. When they failed again, they either joined us as Keepers of the Light if they were powerful enough or..." Seren paused, "or they left the service of the Light."

I noted the way he paused and the odd tone that came into his voice as he spoke the last phrase. Seren was hiding something from me. I shivered but struggled to control it.

He continued. "I was Chosen long ago. I failed the tests. Many times, we have had Chosen Ones who came close to passing one of the tests. Yet no one ever has. Never has one of the Chosen come near to capturing the light of Celema. It is a feat of power beyond imagination."

Seren paused and then lifted a bony hand toward me. "You do it with such ease."

I grunted. Having my soul ripped from my body could not be described as easy. Seren didn't notice because he kept speaking.

"Truly, you *are* the Promised One," he said. "There can be no doubt. The signs of the prophecy have been fulfilled. The end is now come. It will be a time of renewal or of destruction. It is in your hands to decide."

I didn't bother to remind him that if he hadn't been there, I would have died for sure. Somehow, Seren's explanation didn't help. I tried not to let my frustration show because Seren was a nice priest. He wasn't furious with me—at least not yet.

"I still don't understand," I said.

Seren sat more erect and sang. His voice started low and then rose in volume. It rang bright and clear and yet was filled with fathomless depth. At first, I thought he was going to ignore my question. The tune and the lyrics were so familiar—like I had been singing the song all of my life. I had also seen the words etched on the walls in the Navel of the Earth, but hadn't known what they meant.

> The pulse of life, the coldness of death.
> A touch, a song, a simple breath.
> The eternal flame will burn no more.
> Water cannot flow o'er the shore.
> The strength of the earth he will sift like sand
> The light of the star will fly to his hand.

The seven colors will cease to be.
Only the Promised One will be able to see.

Life and death are one in his hand.
Fire and water obey his command.
Earth and star, he molds with a touch.
Rainbows fade in his clutch.
The lost and forgotten shall return.
Upon his palms, the light will burn.
Light unseen descends from the skies.
Only the Promised one will hear their cries.

Seren finished and stared off into the star-filled night. Ross's emotions punched into me, causing my headache to flare. I pressed the heels of my hands into my temples, trying to shove him aside. The words of the song bounced around in my head, but my mind kept stopping on that last line. Whose cries was I going to be able to hear? Why would I be the only one to hear them?

"Now, Promised One," Seren said. "You have fulfilled the tests. You are now prepared to fulfill your destiny."

"That's it?" I said in disbelief. "After all of this drama about the tests, and that's all you have to say?"

"What do you want me to say?" Seren said.

"I want you to tell me what it's all been for. What am I supposed to do?"

Seren averted his gaze. "It is not for me to speculate," he said. "Remember the song, Promised One, and choose well. Go now. I wish to be alone."

Chapter Eleven
The Apprenticeship

IN THAT MOMENT, *when Kell slipped into the oblivion of space, Ross faced the true horror of extinction. He had gambled everything on this one chance. It couldn't end this way. He clung to the fragments of Kell as his own being slipped away. Before he floated into the void, a cool light enfolded the boy's Light and brought it back.*

"This vulnerability is intolerable," Ross thought. "If Kell dies before he accomplishes the task, everything is lost."

The testing was now over, and the boy was still alive. Ross remembered his own testing with perfect clarity. The Keeper of the Night had been Arell then, a loud, demanding man.

"You have failed," Arell sneered in his pompous voice.

Ross clutched at his chest, where the pain of the effort seemed to stretch every ligament in his body.

"You're no better than the other sniveling failures."

Later, Ross discovered Arell carrying a bundle that looked disturbingly human, and Ross began spying on him, partly out of spite and partly out of morbid curiosity. The day Arell found Ross lurking in the shadows, he became dangerous. He forced Ross's hand.

Now, Kell had accomplished what no other Chosen had ever done, and it had almost killed him.

"I have to do something. The boy may have survived the testing, but can he survive the fury of the priests?"

The Apprenticeship

Ross had failed there, too. They had overcome him and locked him up to die, but he had frustrated their designs. Though he had been mortally wounded and too weak to use the chamber to escape, in a last act of desperation, he had written the words on the wall and so forced his soul to remain. His body was no more than a pile of bones and earth, but his spirit lived on, trapped in the tomb, waiting through the endless night until the boy came crashing through the ceiling.

"I had control," Ross thought, "and I squandered it. The boy shuts me out."

Yet, the barrier diminished while the boy was asleep, perhaps Ross could use this to his advantage. He would begin tonight. The boy had to know, and Ross would make him understand. He had to before it was too late.

That night, the dreams burst into my sleep, boring irresistibly through my exhaustion. At first, the images swirled around me in a confusing blur, but they slowly took shape—a long line of black-robed priests that stretched off into the distance farther than I could see. There must have been tens of thousands of them, but these priests were not skeletons. They were men and women, boys and girls of every size, color, and age. Their eyes were normal, like mine. I gazed along the column until I came to the last and recognized my own face.

These were the Chosen stretching back for years uncounted into the past. I wanted to ask them who they were and where they came from. To ask them how the priests I knew could live forever if the tens of thousands that had gone before them had died. What had changed? I wanted to ask them what was expected of the Promised One.

The dream shifted, and I stared up at the sundial. A soft humming came from it, as it glowed with an internal light. A priest rushed past me, and I spun to follow him. This priest didn't have a skeletal head and colorful eyes. He was just a man, though his head had been shaved. I followed the priest through a maze of corridors until he stopped before a set of stone stairs where the passage ended. The priest waved his hand, and a panel in the ceiling slid aside. A small boy descended the stairs, his eyes wide and his expression confused and frightened. The priest embraced him.

"Welcome, Chosen One. We are glad you have come," he said.

The priest then led the boy to the same room where I had been taken, and the priests laid their hands on the boy's head and performed the same ceremony.

The dream accelerated. I rose up on the wind carried from place to place within the temple complex, watching as Chosen Ones attempted the tasks I had performed. Time after time, it was the same. They failed, though one Chosen came closer than any other. The dream surged forward and sped through the lives of thousands of Chosen Ones until they were an unintelligible blur. Behind the dream lurked the ominous feeling that I was racing toward a doom I could not avoid or control. One I would rather not face.

I awoke unrested. The pale glow of morning filled my window. I leaped off my bed and dashed from the room. I couldn't miss Alana again. I had too many questions. The silent temple greeted me as I raced through the door into the cool morning air. My robe flapped around my knees, and my bare feet slapped the cold, smooth stones.

"Alana," I called as her hand rested on the latch of the small door. She jumped and spun to face me. I lurched to a stop in front of her and tried to catch my breath. She studied me with her head cocked to the side. She was beautiful, with her dark hair spilling over the white robe, her smooth brown skin, and her deep chocolate eyes watching me expectantly.

"Promised One?" she asked. She peered over my shoulder like she expected something to be chasing me.

I raised a hand. "Just a minute," I panted. I bent over and rested my hands on my knees. Sweat dripped off my smooth, bald head to splash onto the white stones. I was a soccer player. A little jog like that shouldn't have winded me. Then again, I had never called the Light from a star before and nearly died. "I just need a minute," I said again.

When I straightened, I saw a smile dart across her face.

"What?" I asked.

"You're very strange," she said.

"That's what people tell me," I said. "Have you got a moment?"

Alana glanced at the door with a look of apprehension.

"Yes, Promised One. Only a moment."

I stepped closer to her and breathed in the fragrance of flowers. Speaking to a girl that was so much more attractive than I was proved difficult. Girls like her had never said "boo" to me in my life. She was studying me with large, beautiful eyes and a guarded interest. She didn't sneer or scoff. For a fleeting moment, I wondered what my mom would have thought of her.

"I'm sorry if I scared you the other day," I said. "I just wanted to ask for your help."

Alana frowned and shook her head. Her face tightened. "I am here to serve the Light, Promised One. I'm not meant to be your teacher. If the priests knew we were even speaking, I…" Fear crept into her voice.

"Why are you scared of them?" I asked. "What would they do?"

She shook her head. "I cannot tell you Promised One, but I do not want to face their wrath. It can be terrible."

I sensed she was right. I was placing her in danger merely by talking to her. Did I have the right to do that? I perched on the edge of indecision, needing so badly to have someone I could talk to, but not wanting to cause her harm. I had spent so much time thinking of this vision of a girl, hoping she would be my friend and help me unravel the mysteries of the temple and this religion, but… I bowed my head.

"I'm sorry," I said. "I won't bother you again."

I turned to leave when she laid a cool hand on my wrist. Her skin was smooth and soft, her grip firm. A shiver rippled through me. I glanced up at her, and she smiled in a way that made my heart skip a beat. Dang, she was beautiful.

"I'll help you if I can, Promised One," she said, "but not now. I must go, or they will suspect. After sundown, I have a few hours to myself. I can come then. Will you meet me here at the door?"

I hesitated. She was willing to risk the wrath of the priests to help me. Why? I knew I should refuse, but I smiled.

"Thank you, Alana. I'll wait for you."

She squeezed my wrist and stepped through the door. The lingering fragrance of flowers held me to the spot as I stared stupidly at the closed door. Elation warmed my chest. I had found a friend in the temple at last—someone who would help me. I ambled back toward my room, lost in thought, until I noticed the click of skeleton feet on the stone.

I stopped and listened. The priests didn't wander around the temple. What caused them to do so now? The sound came from a side corridor off the main courtyard. I turned to follow. I hadn't gone far when the clicking stopped. An eerie silence filled the temple, and a feeling of confusion and fear reached for me. It wasn't from the temple this time. It was Seren.

Each of the priests had a distinct feel about them. Seren's was usually calm and peaceful, but right now, he was agitated and alarmed. I peeked around a corner and found him staring at a long, black crack in the wall, just like the one I had seen earlier. This one stretched all the way to the top of the wall. Seren reached up to touch it and jumped back with a yelp of dismay. He shuffled away.

I sat down with my back to the wall to contemplate what I had just seen. The priests didn't have any more idea what was happening to the temple than I did, and Seren, at least, had no idea what to do. He must have seen the great abyss that was connected to those cracks or scars. I considered touching it myself to see if I could heal it, but the memory of that horrible emptiness stopped me. I waited to see if the temple would send me some message, but silence echoed off the white stone walls, filling my ears until I rose and made my way to my room.

I arrived just as the Roinan boy with my breakfast tray knocked on my door.

"Good morning, Roinan," I said. I waved him into the room. The boy set the tray on the table and bowed low.

"I am to tell you, Promised One," he said, "that you must report to Hahl this morning after you break your fast."

I dragged my hands over my face and moaned. I had planned a nice long nap this morning.

"Thank you, Roinan," I said. "Sit down, please."

I gestured to the other chair. The Roinan opened his eyes wide and shook his head. He stepped backward. His obvious terror made me feel guilty, but I persisted.

"I'm not going to hurt you," I said. "I just want to find out about the Roinan and who you are and what you do."

The boy puckered his brow in confusion. "Why does the Promised One not know?" he asked.

"Ah, well, there's a lot I don't know," I said. "I came from far away—like you."

The boy scraped his boot on the stone floor. "We're just boys and girls who serve in the palace and the temple."

"What do you do?"

The boy scratched his ear, still confused. "We serve," he said.

I sighed. This kid was a literalist. "What else do you do besides bring me my food?"

"We wait at the king's table and clean the palace and the temple. We also sing at the high celebrations, and sometimes special Roinan enter the service of the Light like a Chosen One, even though they are not."

Now, we were getting somewhere.

"What are the high celebrations?" I asked.

The boy averted his gaze. "I can't talk about them, Promised One. Surely you know they are sacred."

"Of course," I lied. "Then tell me what happens to a Roinan, who is selected to be a Chosen One."

"He leaves the service of the Light," the boy said.

"Leaves?" I asked.

The boy bowed. "I have been gone too long, Promised One. I must return."

I let him go, but I ate my breakfast thoughtfully before traipsing up to Hahl's tower. If these Roinan servants or slaves cleaned the temple, why hadn't I seen them? What happened to them when they became young men and women? I shoved these questions to the back of my mind as I climbed the stairs to Hahl's tower because I knew he wouldn't answer them.

Hahl met me with a casual wave of his hand that beckoned me into the room and to the window where he stood. His swirling yellow eyes barely looked at me. The now-colorless prism sat on a stand in the middle of the room. Hahl apparently couldn't bear to part with it even though it had been drained of its power. I didn't feel so bad about it now that I knew it had been prophesied that I would do it. Even if Hahl didn't like it, he still had to accept it. As I waited for him to speak, I sensed resignation and determination emanating from him, but I didn't understand why.

"I congratulate you, Promised One," he said. "You have done well." He stared out the window at the city beyond the walls of the temple.

"Thank you," I said. The tone of Hahl's voice told me he wanted to say more but held it back.

"You didn't expect me to survive, did you?"

Hahl never looked at me. "No," he said. "No one has ever passed the tests, but now that the testing is over, your training will commence. You will meet with each of the Keepers every day until you are prepared to purify the Light."

This seemed like such a letdown. Here I thought if I passed the tests, I would know what to do—how to fix this mess, and maybe even find my father.

Hahl faced me, his yellow eyes seething with emotion. I stepped back at the intensity of his gaze.

"The future of entire worlds now rests in your hands, Promised One," he said in a low, deep growl. "We have no choice but to trust you. You must set aside *all* other concerns and concentrate on understanding and accomplishing your task."

At the word all, an image of Alana flashed into my mind, and I knew he was referring to her.

Hahl continued. "Time runs short, Promised One. The signs we have waited for all these eons have been given at last." He waved a pale, white hand in an all-encompassing gesture. "The darkness gathers. If we do not receive renewed strength, it will prevail."

"What darkness?" I blurted. "The sun is rising. The stars were shining last night. I don't see any more darkness than usual."

Hahl stared at me and then motioned with a white, bony hand toward the floor.

"It's now time," he said. "Sit, Promised One. I will explain."

Hahl sat facing me, and I folded my legs under me. It's about time he actually helped me. I tried not to notice the way his robe draped over his bony knees. It was a grizzly sight.

The Apprenticeship

"In the beginning," Hahl said, "Illurien emerged from the chaos that filled the universe and began to sing. You must understand that the natural state of matter is chaos, disorganization. Illurien sang to the unorganized turbulence and called forth a spark of Light. From that spark sprang all creation. Illurien then called forth the Beings of Light. One by one, she took the most intelligent particles of matter, called them forth, and clothed them in Light, endowing them with a portion of her own Light. Together, they brought order to the chaos and organized the Worlds of Light."

"How many worlds are there?" I asked. Could this mean I was on a different planet, not just some distant, alternate dimension? Could it mean aliens really existed?

"Worlds without number did Illurien and the Beings of Light create," he said. "However, in the creation, She-Who-Would-Not-Sing refused to lend her voice to the song. She secretly desired to possess the power of Illurien and to take her power unto herself.

"So she called to the darkness even while the Beings of Light sang. She interlaced the darkness with the Light, ensuring that the creation would remain forever incomplete. Too late, Illurien realized what she had done. She cast She-Who-Would-Not-Sing out of her presence, but the damage had been done. She could not set it right. All of the Worlds of Light would have to endure periods of darkness and cold when the Light would have to struggle to keep from being devoured by the darkness."

I raised a hand to stop him. "You're talking about winter?" I asked.

Hahl nodded. "Each year during the Time of Sorrowing, the days grow short. The Light fades. The darkness seeks to gain supremacy over the Light. At these times, we must unite our power and receive renewed strength to turn the darkness away and renew the Light."

I couldn't believe what I was hearing. I had been thinking they had some great secret to tell, and all this time, they were scared of the winter solstice. Did Hahl believe the priests could use their power to control the cycles of the sun and the stars? Hahl must have seen the skeptical smirk slip across my face because he stopped talking.

"You doubt what I say, Promised One?" His yellow eyes swirled.

"Look," I said, "on my world, wherever that is, we call the Time of Sorrowing 'winter' and the shortest day of the year, the 'winter solstice.' We have no Keepers of the Light, and the sun never fails to rise and set. In fact, it isn't the sun at all that causes the change of seasons. It's the way the earth revolves around the sun and rotates on its axis."

My mother's teachings were becoming useful.

Impatience and even anger emanated from Hahl. "The learning from your past will not serve you here, Promised One," he snarled. "You must forget it." He straightened. "The reason you have no Keepers of the Light in your world is because *we* are here. This is the First Place, created before all of Illurien's other creations. What we do we do for all of Illurien's creations. She has selected us—including you—from different Worlds of Light to come to this world to constantly renew the Light so She-Who-Would-Not-Sing will not claim victory by returning the Light to the chaos from which it came."

"But didn't Illurien create her?" I asked, refusing to be cowed by him. "Why doesn't Illurien just sing her out of existence?"

Hahl clicked his teeth together in a way that made my stomach roll over. I shivered.

"Now, you begin to ask intelligent questions," he said. "Illurien granted the Beings of Light a portion of herself to be held for all time. If she took the spark that she freely gave, she would cease to be Illurien. She would fall into the chaos from which she emerged, and all that she created except the Beings of Light would cease to be. Only their true self would remain.

"Their essence would endure because that cannot be unmade, but the Beings of Light would no longer have the ability to create Worlds of Light. She-Who-Would-Not-Sing would use her command of the darkness to rule over them and bend their power to her will. For all eternity, they would do her bidding and never again would Light beautify the heavens."

Hahl paused and glanced out the window. "Even now, the Light weakens. She-Who-Would-Not-Sing has found a way to keep the Chosen from coming to renew the Light. It has been more than ten years since a new Chosen One has survived to reach us."

My mind stalled on the word *survived*. Seren had used the same word. "What do you mean, *survived*?" I asked.

Hahl ignored me and kept speaking. "Our power fails, and the Light darkens. Can't you feel it in all of the Keepers? We are afraid. We all feel the loss of power. The Time of Sorrowing comes earlier each year and lasts longer. We have to find new sources of strength to hold it back."

"So, is this happening on all the Worlds of Light?" I asked. "Because I don't think earth is having this problem."

"It begins here," Hahl said, "and then spreads to all the Worlds of Light."

He paused and ground his teeth together. A strange emotion came from him, leaving me feeling nervous and frightened. Danger lurked somewhere in what Hahl had just said. I sensed it like I could feel the warmth of a fire. I kept waiting for him to explain the black scars on the walls of the temple, the monster that came through a rent in the air, and the evil presence I felt the night before, but he didn't.

"Now, you have come, Promised One. You have passed the tests and fulfilled the prophecies. You will purify the Light and initiate the time of renewal promised by Illurien."

"Hang on," I said. "I don't even know—"

Before I could finish, Hahl raised his pale bony hand to wave my words away. "I do not know how you will accomplish your task, Promised One. It has never been revealed to the Keepers of the Light. *That* you must discover for yourself."

"Great." I threw my hands into the air. "We could be waiting a long time before I figure that out."

"That is your task," Hahl said.

I left Hahl, feeling depressed and frustrated. It sounded like the priests felt frightened by a simple changing of the climate or a shift in the earth's rotation. How could I correct that? I glanced down at my hands. Even with this new power, I knew I couldn't do anything like that. Touching the Light of a star had nearly killed me.

Hahl didn't even mention what I thought was the real problem. The temple itself was under assault. Something dark and dangerous lurked in the very air of the temple, and the temple was desperate for someone to help it. How could he be ignorant of all of this?

Lowthelian clung to the shadows as Kell stepped out from Hahl's tower. He strode with a determined grace, his black robe flying behind him. She had spent years waiting on and serving the priests. They disgusted her—foul smelling, demanding, uncompromising, hideous. The Promised One was young, closer to her own age, strong and handsome. She couldn't help but be drawn to him.

There was precious little company in the silent temple where even the fall of her bare feet echoed off the walls, and there was no affection. She could look forward to nothing but the daily mind-numbing monotony of pleasing the priests. No one here cared for her. No one knew how her heart ached for companionship, how her tears wet her pillow at night. Lowthelian's gaze followed the Promised One's lithe figure as a strange, unfamiliar hunger grew in her stomach. He was kind to her, tried to talk to her. But he could never know what she had suffered. He could never understand what she had done.

Fear and anger grew among the priests. Lowthelian caught snatches of their hurried conversations. The Promised One unsettled them in a way she had never seen. He was different, unassuming, reckless. Maybe he *would* change everything. Maybe he would set her free.

"So, the priests are scared of winter," I said as I flopped onto my bed after returning from Hahl's tower and rested my head against the cool stone of the wall. "This is nonsense. I can't control the earth's orbit or its rotations."

The temple sent a surge of urgency into me from the wall where my head rested. I jerked away.

"Knock it off," I said. "I don't know how to help you. Why don't you do something useful like show me where my father is?"

A moment of silence came from the temple, followed by a blinding stab of pain behind my eyes that drove me to my feet. I reeled as an image of a large building flashed into my mind. I knew the building but had never gone into it. The temple nudged at me, and I stumbled out of my room, curious to discover what the temple wanted and unable to resist the horrible pain.

The building stood to one side of the courtyard and was several stories high. I followed the image in my mind, which led me around to the side opposite the courtyard. I gaped at the huge windows that had been shattered. The jagged fragments of glass stabbed out from the frame like fangs.

Black smoke stains smeared the white stone in long streaks. The blackened door sagged on its hinges, and I edged my way through the crack, being careful not to step on any broken glass or sharp pieces of wood. A long hallway led to another doorway as I stepped over the broken doors and stopped. The room smelled like an old campfire. Great beams of light fell in through the shattered windows.

I couldn't believe what I was seeing. Ross surged into my mind with an overwhelming sense of despair that confused me. Why would he react that way to a library? Did he love books the way I did? I wanted to asked him, but we couldn't really communicate like that, so I tried to focus on the immense library.

The remains of bookshelves and reading tables covered the bottom floor. Rows of shelves ten or twelve feet high lined the walls with the remains of ladders allowing access to the highest shelves. I gazed upward at the next floor where blackened beams of carved wood stabbed up and up for five stories. This must have been a magnificent library with tens of thousands of books.

Yet, everything had been charred. Piles of ashes with the remnants of books lay everywhere, like someone had gone through making huge bonfires. I stepped into the devastation, feeling the burned fragments of paper crunch under my bare feet. The fine gray powder that settled over everything drifted up to tickle my nose.

"Why?" I whispered. "Why would anybody do this?"

I stepped over broken chairs and around overturned tables. A bit of white paper poked out from a gray pile of ash, and I bent to pick it up. Pieces of burned pages fell away. Words were still legible on one of the largest pieces.

"The Temple of Light will groan under the dominion of those who should have cared for her," it read. "He will come to purify the Light by..."

A sick warmth spread through my chest. The text was talking about me. Someone had known how to purify the Light, and they had destroyed the book. I rummaged through the mountains of debris with a renewed sense of desperation. The answers had been here. Everything I needed to know had been in these books. I yanked the piles apart and ransacked the shelves until I was covered in ash and choking on the dust that coated my throat and stung my eyes.

When I couldn't endure the coughing and wheezing any longer, I retreated to the fresh air of the courtyard. I stared at the library for a long time before returning to my room to change and clean the filth from my body. Ross's sorrow added to my own to weigh me down.

If someone had been destroying everything that would tell me how to do what I needed to do, then how was I going to figure it out on my own? What did the library have to do with my father? Why would the temple lead me there after I asked it to show me where my father was? Perhaps it wanted to tell me that my father died there in the terrible fire.

The sight of the destroyed library sent a shiver of dread through Ross as he remembered the pain of his failure. Even while he sagged in the ropes that bound him to the sundial, the Keepers had embarked on a rampage of destruction. The shrieks of terror and pain, the begging for mercy, and the heavy clouds of smoke that reeked of roasting flesh and burning parchment choked the air.

Now, the sight of the once-glorious Library of Light fallen to ruin with the wisdom of thousands of generations of Chosen left him with a deep sense of despair. He had come to the library as a child to study with the other children. It had seemed so huge and important. The books lined the walls from floor to ceiling. The beautiful woodwork carved with all the symbols of the Light and the high stained-glass windows produced a sense of grandeur and awe that never left him. Yet, now it was a blackened skeleton, gutted and destroyed by the very men who should have treasured it, and they had done so because of him. With the knowledge of the ancients lost forever, it was even more important that Ross teach Kell what he needed to know. Ross had set the whole thing in motion. Now, he had returned to finish the task.

Still shaken from my encounter with the library, I stepped into Durr's sanctuary with the lake and the waterfall. He waved for me to take a seat with an air of disdain that told me he was not going to forgive what I had seen in the Mirror. The gentle, watery rolling of his voice that I had liked on my first meeting was now guttural and threatening, like waves crashing against cliffs. Durr started right in without any pleasantries. He wanted to get the meeting over with as much as I did.

"We'll begin with the symbology of the Light, Promised One, so you can add understanding to the power you now possess."

"Okay," I said. I shifted to get comfortable.

Durr's eyes churned as he struggled to control his anger. This priest was psycho. I didn't trust him. The ever-present sensation of power prowling inside me was reassuring, because I might need it if I angered him again.

"Water is the first form of all matter," he said. "All water symbolizes the motherhood of Illurien. Water is the liquid counterpart to light, and so it can symbolize forgetfulness because it dissolves, abolishes, and purifies. Therefore, we each wash before we engage in any sacred function. Do you understand?"

"Yes," I said. "But I've never seen the priests wash." I tried not to think of a naked skeleton standing in the lake, trying to splash water over his body, or worse, trying to swim. The thought was comically grotesque.

Durr's tone rose as he replied. "It is a *private* ritual, Promised One," he said. "One that you must assume, as well."

Well, I wasn't opposed to a bath, since I had just taken one, but I would rather have a regular tub than some little washbasin like they left in my room. I wasn't about to strip naked and dive into the lake with a bunch of psycho priests watching me. By the smell of Llaith, I don't think he bathed very well at all.

When I opened my mouth to ask Durr what this ritual washing included, he snapped his teeth at me impatiently. I recoiled in disgust.

"Please, allow me to continue, Promised One."

"Sorry, proceed," I said, anything to keep him from clicking those ghastly teeth at me again.

"Water is the foundation of blood," Durr continued, "and it is essential to life. Like the Light, all living things must possess water, or they will die. The life-giving waters of the Fountain of Life rise from the root of the Tree of Life that Illurien herself planted in the center of the Paradise of Illurien."

He held up a hand toward the sky.

"The rain is the fertile power of Illurien, and the dew is her benediction upon the world. Flowing water symbolizes the Water of Life flowing from the presence of Illurien."

I glanced at the little waterfall on the far side of the lake.

"Yes, Promised One, this fountain symbolically recreates the fountain that flows from the presence of Illurien, from the Tree of Life. Water, like all good things, can be turned to the dark." Durr's voice rose in volume as he continued. "Water can kill. It can erupt into chaos and wreak destruction upon the earth. It is a power to be reckoned with."

Durr paused again, and I was sure he had said that last bit for my benefit. Was he trying to scare me?

"Lakes and seas are also the abode of the dead who must cross the Great River dividing the living from the dead and so pass into the Eternal Depths."

"Really?" I said before I could stop myself.

Durr's irritation was evident in his swirling blue eyes.

"Well," I tried to think of something to say, "I mean, does everyone go to the same…what did you call it?

"Eternal Depths," Durr said in a flat tone. "No, there are levels of reward in the depths. Only those who are purified by the Light will be able to ascend to the Paradise of Illurien."

"What happens to those who aren't purified?"

Durr glanced at the water and shook his head. "Not today, Promised One." He rose to his feet. "Come stand beside the pool, and I will teach you how to wash."

I frowned at Durr. He was being deliberately unhelpful, but I followed him to the lake, ready to bolt if he started stripping off his robe. He didn't, though, and I watched as he went through the motions. The cleansing ritual was simple. It consisted of washing the parts of the body, starting with the hands and then the head, and so on while intoning a few lines about Illurien and the Light. Frankly, I didn't see any point in it, but I humored him.

When I dipped my hands into the water to wash, something malicious and evil rushed up to meet my fingers. I yanked my hand back and spun to stare at Durr. He stood impassive, but I could feel the anger and vindictiveness coming from him. I wondered if the priests knew I could perceive their feelings.

"It is simple enough," Durr said. "Surely, the Promised One can wash."

I ignored his sarcasm and glanced at the water again. Something was prowling in its depths. Something dark and dangerous. Its malice had reached for me when my fingers penetrated the surface of the water, but it wasn't a single malice like the one I had felt in the temple the night before. Millions of angry beings swarmed in the water like a huge churning school of fish. I wanted to ask him if this was the Eternal Depths he had mentioned or just some holding place he created for the dead, but I no longer trusted anything he might tell me.

He knew I had sensed it, that it startled me, and he was enjoying his little victory. My mind spun. What had he done? What was he hiding in the lake? Dairen and Hahl had fashioned beautiful manifestations of the Light. Had Durr spent his energy and power, creating some creature of the dark?

"I'll wash in my room," I said.

Durr stared at me.

"I'll just go now," I said, pointing toward the entrance.

Durr spun away from me and strode toward his fountain. The click of his bony feet on the stone sent a shiver up my spine.

My meeting with Llaith proved mercifully short. The hatred and anger emanating from him were palpable in the close chamber of his dark sanctuary. Llaith's blood-red eyes smoldered. The rancid odor of decay still rose from him and filled the room. I wanted to suggest he do a more thorough washing next time he performed his private washing ritual.

The translucent skull was gone, and Llaith did not explain its absence. Beside him lay a bowl of a thick red liquid that I was sure was blood. I didn't want to know where he had obtained it.

When he spoke, his voice was deep. "Blood is the rejuvenating force of both body and spirit," he said. "It is nourished by the Light of Illurien. It is the source of life in all things that draw breath."

Llaith paused and lifted the bowl, holding it out in front of him like he was preparing to drink it.

"Drinking the blood of another allows one to absorb the other's power. But drinking the Light is more powerful. It can extend one's…" He stopped and turned his head to gaze directly at me for the first time.

What did he mean *drinking the Light*? If someone "drank" the Light of another person, wouldn't that person die—like the lily?

His eyes churned, and his hatred focused on me. I returned his gaze. My power tingled on my fingertips. Llaith was trying to frighten me, and I would *not* be frightened by him—not anymore. My power had defeated him once before.

Llaith continued without finishing his thought. "Blood is strength and weakness. It is blessing and calamity. It is warfare and destruction. It is rejuvenation, vengeance, and martyrdom. It is renewal and death."

He said this last word slowly and quietly, relishing the sound of it. Then he set the bowl down in front of me and jumped to his feet.

"You have one hour to meditate upon the quality of the Light that grants life and permits death."

Then he strode away, stirring the air of the small chamber with his foul reek. This time, I covered my mouth and nose. I had no intention of sitting in his dark, fetid chamber for an hour, staring at a bowl filled with blood. Llaith was clearly a psychopath. How he could be a psychopath without a brain, I didn't know. But then I didn't know much of anything anymore.

While I waited to make sure Llaith had gone, an awful music filled my head. The stones beneath my bottom became painfully cold, and a deep unreasoning fear surged into me. The temple was afraid of Llaith and what he did in this chamber. I wondered if it had anything to do with the scars on the walls and the monster that had tried to get through the strange mirage.

I jumped to my feet, fighting the nauseating terror and the goosebumps that jumped out all over my body. The incongruity was too much. How could the Temple of Light be afraid of one of its priests? I snuck out of Llaith's chambers and raced to find Einediau's gardens. At least there, I would find living plants instead of blood and death.

I wondered what Llaith meant about drinking Light. Is that what had happened when I stole the Light from the yellow lily? Why had he focused so much on renewal? How could taking Light from another being renew someone? I hadn't been renewed when I stole the Light of the lily. I had felt defiled and dirty.

As I strode through the temple, strange noises floated over the temple walls. Shouts, cries, and what sounded like hoots of laughter drifted in from the city below amid the ringing of bells or the crash of hammers on metal. It sounded like some great party was going on outside. I was tempted to sneak off to join it. Anything would be better than finishing these meetings with the priests. Worries about what Durr was hiding in his little lake and what Llaith was doing to the temple competed with my growing desperation to talk to Alana.

I found Einediau pruning a purple bush. He didn't seem to know I was there. I cleared my throat, and he whirled around as if he had forgotten I was coming. His garden contained an incredible array of plants, most of which I had never seen before, even though my mom had kept a garden.

Still, I could feel the energy and life that filled the garden.

It was so fresh and clean compared to the dark malevolence of Llaith's skull and his blood-filled dishes or of Durr's menacing lake. I touched a purple leaf. Its life force pulsed under my fingertips. It was gentle, quiet, and beautiful. I experienced a deep connection with every plant in the garden—their roots reaching deep into the rich soil—their leaves breathing in carbon dioxide and exhaling oxygen. The energy of the garden was so soothing that I almost missed the odd feeling coming from deep within the garden.

Something lurked in Einediau's garden, like that strange thing hiding in Durr's lake. I closed my eyes to get a better feel for what was wrong, reaching out with the power. The garden was sick. A festering disease lurked amid the tangle of roots, like a dormant virus waiting for the right moment to multiply and spread.

When I opened my eyes, Einediau studied me as if he expected me to withdraw the life from his plant. I yanked my fingers away, annoyed that he would think so little of me and uncertain if he even knew about the sickness. Einediau began immediately, hurrying to finish so he could return to his plants.

"This garden," he said, waving a pale hand, "symbolizes Paradise. It is a mirror of the Paradise of Illurien."

I followed him to the center of the garden and stopped before a beautiful little fountain that gurgled up from somewhere into a silver basin. The basin nestled amid the roots of a large, shapely tree.

"This," Einediau said, "is the Silver Fountain that flows from the roots of the Tree of Life."

A single white blossom decorated the tree.

"This tree will bear fruit when the one worthy to partake stands before it."

He glanced at the blossom as if he expected it to burst into a fruit right then.

"Why?" I asked.

Einediau studied me like he was trying to decide something. "It was first planted by Illurien herself, and her power abides in it. No one knows what the fruit will do."

"So, you've never seen the fruit?"

Einediau's eyes swirled. He thought my question was impertinent. He shook his head. "It has never borne fruit," he said and continued to meander amid his plants. He mumbled to himself as he went, trimming one plant here, poking in the soil of another there. I followed, uncertain what I was should do.

He turned, saw me, and jumped back. "What are you doing here?" he demanded.

"Um. I've been here for an hour," I said.

He kept walking. Could he be senile?

"Have you ever thought upon the color green, Promised One?" he asked.

That struck me as an odd question. Did anyone ever "think" on the color green or any color for that matter?

"Not really," I said.

"Did you know that it is a compound of blue and yellow or of heaven and earth? It is the color of abundance and vitality. It is the color of immortality and hope."

"That's interesting," I said.

Einediau stopped and faced me. "It is *my* color, Promised One, and I am bound to it." He said this as if he thought I intended to steal it from him. His liquid green eyes swirled more intensely. I scowled as Einediau left me. I considered telling him about the sickness in his garden and then shrugged the idea away.

Just when I thought I understood something of what the priests feared, I discovered that I knew nothing at all. The temple was trying to tell me that the whole place was sick. I could see the disease, or whatever it was, everywhere. I paused at Einediau's door and placed my hand on the cool stone walls. I heard screeching music like someone was drawing a bow over an out-of-tune violin and realized that it was a cry of pain and anguish from the temple. The sadness and despair brought tears to my eyes. I wanted to help. I really did, but I didn't know how.

Lowthelian sat at the table in Kell's room staring at the tiny lily in its white marble pot. The lily confused her. It should be dead, yet here it was vibrant with life.

She had shooed away the Roinan who had come to clean the room and had done it herself. Being in his room let her feel closer to him. The silence echoed in her ears, but she could still feel the presence of the Promised One. The power he wielded left an aura behind, especially in the places where he had used it. She couldn't see it, but she could feel it. The power the priests had given her stirred whenever she was near it, sending a wild, thrilling chill through her. She was not nearly as powerful as the priests. They never permitted any rivals, but her power was drawn to that of the Promised One. It longed to be controlled by him, but it also recoiled whenever he came too close. What could it mean?

She tried to imagine him enfolding her in his arms. Tried to imagine what it might feel like to have a man care for her—to have anyone care for her. Did her power know he was meant for her? Was it trying to help her overcome her fear and uncertainty? But would he love her when he discovered what she was, what she had just done? She replaced the lily on the windowsill. The Promised One was keeping secrets, as well.

Chapter Twelve
Flame and Smoke

I FOUND UFEL bent over his little orange flame in the center of the room. The Eternal Flame still burned on its altar behind him. An emotion of warm greeting emanated from him.

"Welcome, Promised One," he said as he rose to his feet. "How are you?"

For just a moment, a cloud of loneliness swept over me. No one had asked me how I was doing since I arrived here. My mother had been murdered. I had been torn from my own world and forced into this terrifying role of the savior of all worlds with priests who hated me and who were intentionally making life difficult in a temple where evil things seemed to pop up everywhere. I had been forced to accept a power that threatened to tear me apart.

How I missed my mom. What I would have given just to have her drape an arm around my shoulders and tell me everything would be all right. To smell the gentle, vanilla-scented perfume she wore. To feel her warmth and hear her quiet voice, but I tried not to let any of this show. Ufel waited.

"Frustrated, actually," I said.

Ufel motioned for me to sit. "May I be of assistance, Promised One?"

Well, if any of them were going to talk to me, it would be Ufel.

"Yes," I said. "I need to know what you know or guess about

how I go about saving all of creation. You all go on about the symbolism of your ceremonies, but you never bother to give me any information I can actually use."

I glared at Ufel, daring him to contradict me.

"I understand your frustration," he said. "But I am not permitted to…"

"What does that mean?" I interrupted. "It means you won't. Why? Who is stopping you? Why won't any of you help me?" My voice echoed in the stone chamber.

"Let me finish, Promised One." Ufel paused until he saw that I would listen.

"This knowledge regarding the symbology of the Light is essential to you," he said. "How can you understand the task that has not even been revealed to the Chosen if you do not first understand the symbols that teach us so much about the Light? That is the power of symbolism. It encapsulates so much knowledge into an object, or a word, or a color. Through the symbolism, you can gain a deeper understanding of the power you possess and how it is to be used."

"Maybe, but—" I started to protest, but he held up a bony hand, cutting off my words.

"We can't tell you how to use this power you possess because none of us have ever possessed it. No one knows what it can and cannot do. All we can do is share with you the knowledge we have acquired through long ages of study in the hope that this knowledge may assist you in understanding the task Illurien has set for you."

"Illurien?" I said.

"Of course. Who did you think sent you?"

"Well, I never really thought about it."

Hahl had said something like that, but I hadn't thought of it that way before. Then I remembered that feminine voice I heard back at the high school in Ohio. *Come to me* it said. Had Illurien literally called me here?

"Then think about it now, Promised One," Ufel said. "Illurien Herself has selected you from among all of Her creations to perform this task. That ought to give you courage. She would not have selected you if you were destined to fail. You will succeed in due time. Meanwhile, learn all that you can. Every bit of information, knowledge, and experience will come to your aid when the time is right."

Ufel fell silent. I studied my hands folded on my robe.

"But I didn't choose this," I said.

"No, you did not," Ufel said. "Neither did I. But you may still choose to finish your course or abandon all worlds to ruin. *That* is your choice, Promised One."

I studied Ufel now. Was that really my choice? Who did I think I was? Some hero with a superpower? A power that tried to kill me every time I used it. What would I have to become to do what Illurien asked? I already sensed the power changing me, transforming me into a tool. Power or no, I didn't think I had what it took. I had never done anything more difficult than run track and play soccer.

"If that's true," I said, "Illurien is taking a big risk. I'm just a kid."

"We're all taking a big risk," Ufel said.

Something about the way he said this caught my attention. Maybe it was the subtle shift in emotions I perceived coming from him. There was an edge of fear to it now. If Ufel trusted me, then I would do what I could.

"I'm listening," I said.

Ufel's eyes churned with orange flame, and I sensed that he approved of my decision.

"I am the Keeper of the Fire, as you know," he said. "Fire does not possess a Light unto itself. It is not a living thing. It draws its Light from things that live or have lived in one form or another. When it consumes the Light, it leaves behind the waste that had once been animated by the Light."

All I could think of was the way a campfire turned a tree into a pile of ash. It made sense.

"So, fire is a transformer, a purifier," Ufel continued. "It represents the life-giving, generative power of the sun and the renewal of life with each new dawn. It is power and strength, but it is also destruction and corruption. Through flame, many kinds of offerings and messages are conveyed to the divine presence of Illurien. The flame is the breath of life and the sign of death. For upon the death of a human soul, the flame of Illurien leaves the body. When I kindle a new fire once each year at the winter solstice, it represents the rebirth promised by Illurien to all those who are purified. Fire is the soul of man. It is splendor and glory. It is the consuming power of Illurien. Do you understand, Promised One?"

I guess I did. Maybe that was what I had done to the tiny lily. I had taken its Light, its soul, if it had one, though I still hadn't told any of the priests that I had been able to give it back.

"So, if the Light or flame leaves the body," I said, "where does it go?" I remembered all too well the moment my soul had left my body up on Seren's tower. Maybe I hadn't died because Ross remained behind, keeping me alive.

Ufel was silent for a moment and then shrugged his bony shoulders.

"This question has been debated by the Chosen for many eons. I will not confuse you with the many sides in the debate, but I will give you my opinion of them."

"Okay."

"I believe," Ufel said, "that the Light or Flame of Illurien that inhabits and animates all living things returns to Her presence. By this, I do not mean the inner self. I mean the life force that animates the body. I believe the inner self, or the first essence that Illurien called forth from the chaos, persists beyond death and will also return to the presence of Illurien at the end of time in the form of the body that it once inhabited."

"Wait," I said, "isn't the inner self the same thing as the Light?"

Ufel shook his head.

"I do not think so. Long ago we had books—"

He stopped. I knew he referred to the books in the library I found destroyed.

"Once," he continued, "a special and very learned Chosen One taught that the reason Illurien created physical bodies was to provide a home for the immaterial bodies of Light she had already created, and that death is nothing more than the separation of these two bodies. The Light that animates them departs and returns to Illurien, while the immaterial body, which is also made of Light, goes to the depths to await the ending of time."

"Okay," I said. "Durr told me about a river that had to be crossed to reach the depths."

"Yes," Ufel said. "The Great River separates the living from the dead. The dead will be gathered and judged according to their doings. Those that have purified themselves in the Light will be reunited with their bodies and join the Beings of Light."

I scowled. "Uh, sounds like Christianity mixed with a bit of Greek mythology to me."

Ufel stared at me with his huge orange eyes. "I do not know these words."

I started to explain and then decided not to. Mom never participated in any religion, and I didn't know that much about Christianity, except what I learned in school.

"It's just a religion on the planet or place I came from."

"I see," Ufel said. "They must have lost the true teachings of the Light and gone astray."

This made me smile. I didn't think many Christians I knew would have liked that description and, in fact, would have thought the opposite.

"There's another thing I don't understand," I said.

Ufel waited, and I could sense his curiosity. He was enjoying our discussion, which was quite different from the other priests. He might have been a good college professor if he had lived in a different world and time.

"You all say that you are stewards of the Light and what you do holds back the darkness of She-Who-Would-Not-Sing, but I haven't seen anything like that. Your ceremonies don't help anyone that I can see and…" I hesitated, uncertain how much to tell him about what I had seen in the temple. "And there is evil in the temple. I have felt it."

"Aah," Ufel said. "This is an important question, but a difficult one to explain." He shifted and clasped his bony fingers together in preparation for a long lecture.

"In the beginning, the seven Keepers were chosen for three reasons. They symbolically represent the Seven Tears of Illurien and the seven Beings of Light, who sang the song of creation. They also represent the seven colors of pure Light when it is split into its smallest segments. Hence, each of the seven Keepers can use only one-seventh of the Light. Our use of the power to do good and to create enhances that portion of the Light we control. None of us can control all Light because it would kill us. We each affect the Light differently. You have already guessed this, I think."

I nodded.

"I, for example," he continued, "can create flame and consume things. When I use the Light for good, my flames burn away the darkness leaving only the Light. But I must be careful. As you have also discovered, I think, using the Light too greedily can be dangerous. If I were to use the Light without restraint, the Light would consume my body, leaving only the ash behind."

"Yeah," I said. "I got that."

"So, you see that each of us using the Light helps to strengthen the Light and diffuse the gathering darkness. This is how we keep it at bay, how we keep it from gaining too much strength. Hahl's Light enhances the growth and health of living things. Einediau's provides energy and vitality to all life. Durr's purifies and cleanses. Dairen's provides stability and strength. Seren's creates connections and pathways that unite all time and space, thus holding them together. We bind people to one another, to nature, and eventually to Illurien Herself in one great net of power and Light. To keep the darkness at bay, we must have seven Keepers who each purify and strengthen the Light."

"You left out Llaith," I said.

Ufel bowed his head. "Llaith's power is different from the others."

I waited for Ufel to continue, but he just sat there.

"We will speak of this another time," he said.

Why did his reluctance to tell me leave me with a feeling of dread?

As I left Ufel's sanctuary, a column of black smoke billowed above the walls of the temple into the clear, blue sky. I stopped and stared at it before rushing to Hahl's tower. Maybe the party I heard earlier had gotten out of hand.

The images of destruction I had seen in the Mirror and in my dreams returned to me. Could something more sinister be going on? Maybe the city had been attacked. I leaped up the steps two at a time. I didn't even pause at Hahl's door, but strode, breathless, to the window where he stood rigid as stone. Anger boiled from him.

On the far hill, tongues of orange flames leaped above the roofs of the palace complex. Black smoke curled and rolled into the sky. The pungent smell of burning wood and tar wafted through the air.

"What happened?" I asked.

"Rebels," Hahl said.

"You mean rebels attacked that palace over there?" I asked. "Are they going to come here?"

"They wouldn't dare come here."

The threatening edge to his voice reminded me that Alana had said the priests could be dangerous. I believed her.

"This is a symptom of the growing power of the darkness, Promised One. It is what you have come to correct."

"But—"

"Let us begin," Hahl interrupted. He turned to me. "Sit."

"But where did the rebels come from?" I asked.

He ignored my question. "The sun symbolizes Illurien's universal feminine power," he said.

"Wait," I said. He couldn't just ignore me. I wouldn't let him.

Hahl paused, and his golden eyes simmered in anger. "If you wish to understand what you have seen, then you must allow me to teach you," he said.

"All right," I said, but I wasn't finished. I dropped to the cold stone and crossed my legs.

Folding his hands in this lap, Hahl continued. "The sun represents both life and death and the renewal of life *through* death. Its symbols are the revolving wheel, the disk, the radiant circle. In recognition of their power and status, we call the royal family who live in the palace the Children of the Sun, and the King bears the title of the Sun King. So long as Illurien smiles upon their reign, they rule by Her will."

"It's a mandate of heaven, then," I said.

"I suppose you could call it that."

"How is the mandate lost?"

Hahl tapped a bony finger on the floor. "It has never been lost in this kingdom. The Children of the Sun have reigned for at least a millennia. Illurien would not permit a family to reign who had lost her approval. She would remove them."

"How?" I persisted.

His yellow eyes flared, and he waved a hand to dismiss my question. "That is not my concern—nor yours. What concerns us now is the symbology of the sun."

Hahl paused as he regained his composure.

"The sun also represents intellect, faith, and goodness." His gaze seemed to bore into me. "But also, treachery, treason, and jealousy. It signifies the renunciation of desire and the revelation of truth."

I studied Hahl. Why was it that all these symbols had both good and evil sides to them? Were they trying to warn me or scare me? If the Light was good, where did the darkness I found in the temple come from?

Hahl handed me a dark crystal about the size of my fist.

"Look at the sun through this," he said.

My mom played this game with me once during a solar eclipse. We had used some funny glasses to stare at the sun as the moon's shadow crept across its face. I turned to the window and held the crystal to my eye. It magnified the sun as good as any NASA image I had ever seen. I could see sunspots and even solar flares. The sun was more orange than yellow in the crystal, and a halo of glory surrounded it. I wondered why Seren didn't have one of these.

"As you can see, Promised One," Hahl said, "the sun is a living, changing thing. It is a power unimaginable for both life and death."

Hahl grabbed the crystal from my eye and dismissed me with a wave of his hand. "That is enough for today," he said.

"You never explained—"

"I said that is enough for today," he snapped. "Return tomorrow."

I stomped from Hahl's tower, more annoyed than anything.

The temple now reeked of burning as the smoke from the palace drifted over the walls to settle amid the white stone buildings. I could taste it on my tongue. How could rebels attack the palace without first having conquered the city? Unless it had been a simple act of arson. Hahl didn't seem overly concerned, and he was supremely confident of his safety inside the temple. Still, what would political unrest have to do with me and the Light? Maybe it didn't concern me, and maybe it did. If people were dying, shouldn't we be doing something to help them?

Lowthelian strode through the temple toward Hahl's tower. The message from the palace fluttered in her hand. She remembered well her first month after being sent to the temple. She had been so young, so foolish. Freshly enslaved and grieving for her parents, she had refused to carry Llaith's bowl of blood to him. It frightened her as much as he did. Llaith's wrath had been terrible. His skill and delight in causing pain was immense.

He spared her because Ufel intervened. Ufel insisted that they compensate her for her suffering with a portion of the light to which she was so clearly drawn, but she had never abandoned her hatred. She found other ways to resist their tyranny, other ways to remain sane. Ways that not even the priests could fathom.

Lowthelian waited while Hahl read the message. He was the senior priest, the one who maintained correspondence with the King and led in the priestly ceremonies. Hahl raised his swirling yellow eyes to hers. He seemed supremely satisfied with himself. She had worked with the priests long enough to judge their moods. It had been a necessary skill to survive in the temple. She wanted to ask him what he was planning, but she knew better. Hahl didn't like it when she questioned anything he did, so she bit her lip and tried to figure out what had so pleased him.

Now, that the Promised One had come maybe she could use him. Maybe she could convince him to help her once he witnessed the ceremony. What would the Promised One do when he realized what they planned?

"Tell them to begin preparations," Hahl said.

Lowthelian tried not to scowl. She knew what happened at the celebration. She had become accustomed to it, but the Promised One would not like it. He might do something crazy. He might provoke the priests's wrath. Hahl waved her away, and she spun with a flutter of her robe. Should she warn the Promised One? Did she dare?

This day of revelations left me with a growing sense of dread. The priests were correct, something was wrong with their religion. This whole temple complex remained empty of any worshippers—except the Keepers and Alana. No one I could see benefited from anything the priests did. Then there were the unsettling brushes with evil I experienced within the temple complex. It was wrong—especially here in the place where I sensed the timeless beauty of the Light.

On my way to Dairen's chamber, I found several more of the black scars on the walls and floors. I considered touching them again but worried this time I wouldn't be able to pull back from the emptiness that lay hidden there. I did stop when I found a pool of the same black ooze I had seen on my mother's chest seeping from the base of a great column carved like a twisted rope. Once again, I wondered if the priests hadn't had something to do with my mother's death. I bent close to examine it. I didn't dare touch it. The sickness was everywhere, expanding. Sad, plaintive music whispered in my head, and I jerked upright and spun away.

"Get out of my head," I snapped.

I was growing tired of the temple and Ross playing with my mind. I wanted to be alone in my own head.

Dairen led me through some strange ceremony where he placed chemicals in the bowls of a huge candelabra with seven arms and set them aflame. He wasn't very talkative, so I let him do his thing while I fidgeted and tried not to breathe in the acrid smoke from the burning chemicals. Then, I hurried away to Seren's chamber. The sun had gone down, and a cool evening breeze blew through the temple. It still tasted of ash and burning.

"Come, sit beside me," Seren said as I emerged from his long stairwell. "Let us talk for a while."

I folded my legs under me as I flopped to the ground, panting from my climb and glanced up to where a few stars glittered in the evening twilight. The clear cloudless sky tinged with gray was oddly beautiful.

Looking back at Seren, I noted that he had followed my gaze. "It is a thing of wonder," he said.

"Yeah," I said. I tried not to show it, but I was hoping Seren *wouldn't* talk too long. I hadn't eaten anything since earlier that morning, and I didn't want to miss Alana again. Seren must have read my expression.

"You must be tired," he said. "We won't take much time. I still remember how it feels to be weary and anxiously awaiting the next meal."

I nodded gratefully. How must it be to never feel hunger or weariness? Did the priests even sleep?

"Well, let us add a bit more to your knowledge before your day is done," Seren said. He raised his hand in a sweeping gesture that took in the great vault of the sky.

"The night is my domain," he said. "I alone among the Chosen ponder the heavens. There is much to learn and many mysteries to pursue. The moon is the masculine creative power that controls the rhythms of time. It is the eye of the night as the sun is the eye of the day. It symbolizes the dark side of nature, and together with the sun, it represents the sacred union of night and day, light and dark, male and female."

Seren waited until I bobbed my head in understanding. It seemed like everything in the temple came down to the celebration of opposites.

"The darkness of the night," Seren continued, "is the cosmogonic darkness that preceded the creation. It is the chaos from which Illurien called the Beings of Light. It represents her enveloping maternal and feminine power—the protective covering she maintains around her creations. It is also the chaos, death, and disintegration that She-Who-Would-Not-Sing seeks to impose upon the creations of Light. The darkness preceded the Light and may yet envelop it in oblivion. Do you understand, Promised One?"

I shifted and straightened my back. "Okay, but if the darkness preceded the Light and can envelop it, isn't it more powerful than the Light?"

The question seemed logical enough to me, but Seren fidgeted, and his eyes churned, which was unusual for him.

"No, Promised One, it is not," his voice had an edge to it. "The darkness possesses no creative power. It is empty and inanimate. It is timeless and thoughtless. It can prevail only when we allow it to do so. Only when we willingly subject ourselves to it."

Seren's eyes churned more powerfully as his anger grew. It pulsed from him in waves like heat from a furnace.

"That is the danger, Promised One. When we choose the darkness, we turn from the Light, and the darkness will devour whatever Light we possess until we are left empty shells with no being, only pain and desolation."

Seren's passion surprised me.

"I'm sorry if I offended you," I said. "I'm just trying to understand."

Seren studied me as his anger turned to confusion. He sagged.

"No, *I* am sorry, Promised One. There is too much fear among the Keepers. I have allowed it to cloud my judgment. I see that your question was an innocent one. Do you understand now, Promised One?"

Innocent? What did that mean? "Yeah," I said.

"There's still something I don't understand," I said. "If She-Who-Would-Not-Sing destroys the Light, wouldn't that destroy everything she wants to dominate? Wouldn't she destroy herself?"

Seren violet eyes churned. Slowly, he nodded his head.

"Your question is very perceptive, Promised One," he said. "She does not seek to destroy the Light so much as to dominate it. To weave the darkness so thoroughly through the threads of time that only she can determine what and who survives. Those who will not serve the darkness will perish. Chaos will reign over all creation, and she will revel in the confusion and suffering."

"Wouldn't it be easier for the Keepers to band together and just kill her?" I asked.

Seren shifted, and I could see that my question disturbed him.

"She cannot be killed, Promised One."

"How do you know?" I asked. I was starting to wonder if she even existed.

"She is a Being of Light," he said like it would explain everything.

"Then there's no hope," I said.

"There is always hope," Seren replied, though I didn't feel any radiating from him. "We have you."

I slouched. Me? That was a slim hope, indeed.

I raced through the temple until I slid to a stop beside the little wooden door in the wall. It was closed. Alana hadn't arrived for our meeting yet. I swallowed my disappointment and settled down into the gathering shadows to catch my breath while I waited. I drew the golden stone from my pocket to study it. Its yellow glow pushed out into the darkness that collected inside the bone-white walls of the temple. A strange weight settled over me.

Something about this darkness was different. It reached for me, pressed against me, curled around my arms and legs. The breath caught in my throat, and my chest tightened. I recognized it as the malevolent evil I had found skulking in Durr's lake. It had escaped.

Lunging to my feet, my power stirred in preparation for the attack I knew was coming. I searched the darkness for the source of the growing menace, but I was alone. Still, the contradiction of it unsettled me. Some evil lurked out there, some malice that prowled the temple dedicated to worshipping the Light. Nothing like this should exist in the Temple of Light.

A few tiny dots of silver and blue lights floated into view, dancing in the palpable darkness. These dots were hunting for me. I tensed, ready to bolt, when the distinctive clicking of bony feet on cobblestones burst through the suffocating darkness. Soft voices echoed off the pale walls. I recognized Llaith's deep and threatening tone coming from the direction of Hahl's tower. I crouched closer to the wall, trying to become part of the shadows.

"We must not wait," he growled. "He is becoming too strong. We must be replenished before it is too late."

My heart leaped into my throat. Llaith was talking about me. I knew it deep down in the marrow of my bones. Ross's anger rose, mixing with my own. I tried to ignore him and edged to the corner of the wall, hoping to catch a glimpse of them.

Another voice interrupted Llaith, rolling like softly flowing water.

"Patience," Durr said. "We have waited so long. A few more days or weeks will make little difference. Besides, the others must consent, and a suitable Roinan must be found before we can…" Their voices faded, and I couldn't hear anymore.

I started after them. The dots of light scattered, and the dark cloud swirled away, startled by my sudden movement.

A Roinan for what? What were they planning to do? I strode after them when the click of a latch sounded behind me. I spun and crouched, ready for a fight. A dark shape slipped through the small door and glided toward me—the sweet scent of flowers blew before her.

Chapter Thirteen
Planting and Weeding

"ALANA," I WHISPERED.

She wore a black cloak over her white dress.

"Shh, not here," she said. "I know a better place."

Alana grabbed my hand and dragged me behind her. She led me back through the door and out onto the hillside. I hadn't been outside the temple walls since I arrived, and I experienced a sudden rush of elation like I'd just been freed from prison. Her hand was warm and smooth in mine.

The lights from the city glittered in the darkness as Alana skirted the wall and angled downhill on a trail paved with white stones and bordered by miniature trees, shrubs, and flowers. She slowed as we reached a small, white building with a cone-shaped roof that crouched beside the trail. She lifted the latch on the door and slipped inside.

I followed, closing the door behind me. Alana drew back the hood of her black cape and looked at me. Her hair spilled out over her shoulders like flowing water. I couldn't tell if she was glad to see me or afraid—or maybe a little of both. Rays of moonlight slipped in through a narrow window in the wall and fell across her brown face and high cheekbones, giving her an angelic glow. She sat on the bench and pulled me down beside her.

"Sorry it took me so long," she said. "I couldn't get away. There was a..." she paused, "a problem at the palace."

"I saw the fire," I said. "What happened?"

Alana frowned. "Some rebels infiltrated the palace staff and set fire to the stables. My father lost his best horses, and five of the stable hands were burned to death."

"I'm sorry," I said. "Is your family all right?"

Talk of her father made me a bit jealous that she had one. I knew I was being stupid, but she must have seen the expression on my face because she gave me a sideways, suspicious glance before she nodded.

"Look," I said, "I don't want to make trouble for you, but I need your help."

That scared expression crept back into her eyes. She fidgeted. "I'll help you if I can, but we must not be discovered."

"I know," I said. I shifted, trying to stop the trembling in my belly. Why was I so nervous? I cleared my throat. "I need to know where I am."

Alana frowned.

"No, really." I hurried to explain. "I mean, I feel lost in this world. Like I'm drifting—like a kite without a string." The words came in a rush, and I felt foolish. "I'm sorry," I said. "I..."

Alana clasped my hand and squeezed it. "What do you wish to know, Promised One?" Her voice thrilled me. The promise of a song always seemed to linger just on the edge of her speech.

"Who are you?" I said.

She sat back, startled, and cocked her head to the side. "I thought you knew," she said.

"No." I shook my head.

"I don't see how this will help you, but I'm the daughter of Kalanon, the Lord of Light."

"The what?"

Alana gave me a curious smile. "My father is King of this land. I am his oldest daughter. That's why I serve the Light. Always it is the oldest."

"So, you live in the palace?"

"Yes. I'm also responsible for the Roinan and the others who serve in the temple."

"Others? What others? I haven't seen anyone but Lowthelian

and the Roinan boy."

"I know," Alana said with a look of satisfaction. "You aren't supposed to see us. We would disturb you. The priests do not like to be disturbed."

I threw up my hands. "Okay, tell me everything," I blurted. "Start with the palace and your father and then tell me about these Roinan before I go crazy."

Alana grinned at my exasperation.

"What?" I asked.

"You are very different, Promised One."

"Geez, I hope so," I said. The thought of being like the priests was alarming.

Alana kept smiling and settled back onto her seat. "As I said, my father is Lord over this land. He rules from the Treasure House of Light." She paused at my puzzled expression and gave me an exasperated smirk that said, how can you not know the simplest of things? "That is what the palace is called," she said.

"Right," I said. "Keep going."

"Well, from there, he plans the weeding and the planting each year."

"Uh, sorry," I said, "but is he a farmer as well as a king?"

Alana scowled. "I don't understand you, Promised One."

I shook my head. "Weeding? Planting?"

"Oh," Alana said. "The Seeds of Light must be spread to all the peoples of this world if the darkness is to be defeated. All must worship the Light to strengthen it against She-Who-Would-Not-Sing. But they must be purified of their ignorance first. My father prepares them and then teaches them how to serve the Light."

"He 'prepares them,'" I repeated. "This preparation is the weeding?"

"Yes." Alana wiped at a lock of hair that fell into her eyes.

"What does he do to prepare them?" I asked.

"He must first send his armies and show them the power of the Light. Then he purifies them of all those who will not serve the Light before he teaches them."

She said this like she was reciting a harmless recipe for pancakes or something. As she spoke, the vision I had seen in the Mirror of Light of the brown-skinned soldiers marching out of the city flashed before my mind.

"In other words," I said, "he engages in campaigns of conquest." I tried not to let my voice show my annoyance, but Alana cocked her head to one side in confusion. I didn't want to distract her, so I urged her to continue.

"So that is the weeding. What is the planting?" I asked.

Alana scowled at me. She didn't understand me. "We send teachers to show them the way," she said.

"You mean priests like these?" I asked, waving my hand toward the temple.

"No. Of course not," Alana said. "He sends people to live among them."

"Aah. I get it. He colonizes them. Conquest, then colonization. Of course. How nice."

Alana frowned. "Promised One, you are confusing."

"I'm sorry," I said. "I've never liked conquerors. They're too much like bullies, and I've known enough of those." My shiner had healed, but I secretly hoped Jens's nose was still broken.

Alana drew back in surprise. "But we bring them the Light, Promised One. Surely, that is a good thing."

"Well, that's what all conquerors say, isn't it?" I said. "That's how they justify what they do. In my world, a people called the Europeans convinced themselves that enslaving Africans was okay because it was better for them to live in slavery and to be Christian than to live free and be pagan."

I leaned my head back against the wall.

"They even liked to call it the white man's burden. When in reality, all they did was exploit the people they conquered and colonized, made themselves rich, and made those people poor. Most of the world they colonized is still a mess."

I took a breath to continue, but a glance at Alana stopped me. She couldn't possibly follow what I had been saying, but she apparently understood more than I realized.

"Promised One," she snapped, "to bring Light to people in darkness is a good thing. They may suffer at first, but they will thank us in the end. Once they truly understand."

I opened my mouth to argue, but then closed it. I had offended her. I couldn't afford to lose her goodwill.

"I'm sorry," I muttered. "Go ahead."

Alana stared at me with a glower of defiance on her face, but she continued.

"My father causes them to construct a great stone circle in their sacred high places. Once a year, he travels through his lands and walks the circle in both directions twice to retake possession of the land."

"What does he do with the people that have to be weeded?"

"He allows them to serve the Light."

"Is this where the Roinan come from?" I asked.

"Of course."

"Then they're slaves, forced to serve the Light against their will?"

Alana gave me a calculating look, and the puzzled expression crept back into her face. "Why are you angry, Promised One? I don't understand. This is the way it has always been. We have always worshipped the Light and struggled at great sacrifice to bring it to the other peoples of our world."

I rose, trying to figure out how to help her understand.

"I don't believe that conquest and slavery are good things," I said. "They're bad. They're always bad, no matter who does them. They allow a few to dominate and exploit the many, and the many always suffer."

Alana still studied me. I thought she wanted to grasp what I was saying. I reached over to take her hand.

"Alana," I said, "how would you feel if someone came and killed your family, destroyed your city, took you as a slave, and then forced you to worship their gods?"

She tilted her head, skeptically. "There is no one who could do such a thing."

"What if there were," I persisted, "and they did? Then they made you work for them to make them rich so they could be lazy. How would you feel?"

Alana clenched her fist. "I would not serve the barbarian gods."

"Exactly," I said. "How do you think the Roinan feel, who know that your father killed their families and forced them into slavery to serve in the palace and the temple?"

Alana's eyes flashed. She lunged to her feet, yanking her hand out of mine. She glared at me.

"The Roinan are happy serving the Light," she demanded. "They could do nothing better. They would have continued to live in ignorance and squalor if we had not sown the Seeds of Light among them. How can you say such things? *You* are the Promised One." She said this last phrase like an accusation and a reprimand.

I sat back down, knowing I should be silent, but I spoke anyway. "If serving the Light is so wonderful, Alana, then why are you always so afraid? Do you enjoy living in fear?"

Alana glared at me. She stepped toward the door, stopped, and glared at me again. Then she sank onto the bench. She dropped her gaze to the floor and settled her hands into her lap. "I don't know," she said.

I reached out and lifted her hand again. She stiffened and then relaxed.

"Don't you see?" I said. "The Light is supposed to bring life and health and happiness to all people. Light should be good and beautiful. It's supposed to be pure and sweet. Isn't that what you feel when you sing to the Light?"

She glanced up at me with an expression that told me I had guessed right.

"Have you never wondered how such ugliness and brutality can have their source in such beauty and gentle power?"

It surprised me to say this. I had never thought of it before, but it made sense. That was what kept bothering me about everything I had seen. It was all a huge contradiction. Everything was a contradiction—the priests, the political order, the rituals, the evil lurking in the priests' creations. None of them connected with what I knew and experienced from the Light. That evil had invaded even the temple itself. It came searching for me.

Alana stared at the floor. I squeezed her hand, but she wrenched it free and lunged to her feet. "I must get back before I'm missed." Her voice was even and distant. She led me back to the door in the wall, never giving me the chance to say anything more.

"Will you come again tomorrow?" I asked.

She averted her gaze. "I don't know," she said as she spun and strode down the hill.

Chapter Fourteen
Knock, and It Shall Be Opened

IN MY DREAM, I knelt beside a black-robed figure sprawled on his back—violet liquid leaked from his eyes. A pool of blood spread over the stone floor. I stared at his lifeless face. What had I done? I wiped my hands on my robe, wishing I could clean them. I had to do it. The priest had known, and he threatened my family.

A white light flashed, and I sagged against the ropes that bound me to the sundial. Five priests circled me like a pack of hungry wolves. Their eyes churned a kaleidoscope of menace. But these priests had faces, old faces that were wrinkled and sagging. Their bald heads shone dully in the morning light—the reek of burning filled the air. Fear, anger, and loathing surged through me. How dare they presume to command me? I couldn't overpower five of them together.

The dream spun forward again, and I was alone—locked forever in the stone cell. I was dying, too weak and injured to escape. Despair and terror stabbed at my heart. I would die alone. My family would never know what happened to me. I reached out to the cold stone with a finger glowing white with the power and etched the signs of power into the wall. This will not happen again. I will make it end.

I awoke with a jolt. The blood throbbed at my temples. Warm dots of light flickered in the inky, blue sky visible through my window. For a moment, I thought they were the evil lights coming back, but they were just stars. The beautiful yellow lily sat on the windowsill, pulsing with life. I closed my eyes, trying to shut out the horrible dream, but I couldn't. The images were now a part of my memories. They were a part of Ross's past, and Ross was showing them to me for a reason. If he was a servant of the Light, why would Ross kill a priest? What had they done?

Alana never came back to the little door in the wall. The courtyard before the sundial remained silent and empty as the sun rose into the sky. How could she stop performing her ceremony just to avoid me? Maybe I had offended her more deeply than I guessed.

When she didn't arrive, I rushed through my lessons with the priests, searching for some clue that would help me unravel the confusing and contradictory information I was getting from the priests, from Ross, and from the temple.

Ufel and Seren remained pleasant and helpful. Einediau was just confused. Sometimes he forgot I was there, or he would tell me the same thing he had told me the day before. Dairen kept me at arm's length, while Durr and Llaith sneered at me in open hostility. Hahl was resigned. All of them remained agitated and annoyed.

One thing did change, however. I first noticed it in their eyes. I was sitting with Ufel in his dark chamber, and I realized that his eyes were less bright. The persona that always emanated from the priests seemed weaker. Ufel hunched his shoulders like he carried a heavy weight and moved like a 100-year-old man on sedatives.

When I asked him about it, he just brushed me off.

"It's nothing, Promised One. I am very old," was all he would say.

I tried to ask Seren, too, but he gave me the same treatment, although he seemed ashamed about it. Now that I noticed it, the condition worsened as the days wore on. Something was happening to the priests, and I wondered if I was the cause. That would explain why they feared and hated me so much. Maybe, when I passed the tests, I had drawn their power into myself, and they were growing weaker. Maybe they were dying.

Each night while I waited for Alana by the door, I found I had to hide from the tiny dots of blue and silver light that floated about in a writhing cloud of evil. Somehow, they knew I would be there. I sensed their malevolent desire to harm me. My power stirred each time, and I tried to decide how I might use it against this groping evil. The dots drove me from the wall twice before I discovered they would not approach me too closely if I held the golden stone in my hands.

Something about its light kept the oppressive darkness and the tiny dots of evil at bay. I kept the stone out and toyed absently with it, watching the blue and silver lights float about, advancing and then retreating every time they came too close. What were they? Why did they hunt me? And what would they do if they ever caught me?

As I wandered back to my room on the fourth day after my meeting with Alana, the temple drew me down a corridor and through a maze of tunnels. Though I had become accustomed to the way the strange music played inside my head, and the temple sent me images of where I should turn. The experience was disturbing. If I told anyone about this back in my world, they would have thrown me into an institution. Dean would have snickered and called me crazy. Maybe he would have been right.

I followed the promptings until I faced an iron-bound door. A strange smell I couldn't place came from the door—a mixture of mildew and decay. I hesitated to open it. By now, I knew the temple wasn't going to show me anything happy or uplifting, and I was growing weary of the constant dread. Still, my curiosity overcame my hesitation, and I pushed the door open to stare into utter darkness.

The stale air in the chamber wafted over me, and I gagged. It smelled of death. I called up a ball of light, and my blood turned cold. The temple had brought me to an underground tomb where corpses had been piled in rows like cordwood. There were hundreds, if not thousands, of bodies. Some still had the flesh clinging to their skulls. Most wore the same white robes I had seen in my dreams and that Alana wore, but some were dressed in strange clothing, and one had on a pair of jeans. Some skulls had fallen away from their bodies to roll across the floor. I covered my mouth and backed away. I didn't want to see any more. A deep sense of sadness and guilt came from

Ross. He must have understood what happened here. These were the bodies of the Chosen Ones—the ones the priests said had not survived.

Ross tried not to let his emotions interfere with what the temple was showing the boy, but the sight of all of those Chosen so rudely piled in a dark room, forgotten and disrespected, stirred his deepest sense of revulsion.

"I probably knew some of them," Ross thought. "These had to be the bodies of those murdered in the purge, but the others in the strange clothes must be the others who were Chosen only to arrive murdered in the very chambers that brought them."

The horror of it was astounding. Someone was murdering the Chosen before they could be collected by the priests. Ross had not seen it because no one had been sent to the chamber where his bones lay until Kell arrived to trigger the Words of Light he had scratched into the wall. If the Chosen were being slaughtered in the chambers that brought them here, then some great evil was at work in the temple. Something more than the priests—some evil that threatened the very foundations of the Temple of Light.

"The Light preserve us," Ross said.

As I rushed back the way I had come, the temple nudged me in another direction. I resisted because I didn't want to see any more dead bodies. Eventually, I gave in and followed the promptings. The priests refused to teach me anything about what happened here, but at least the temple was trying to educate me. It brought me to a stop in a small room near the Navel of the Earth. The floor was covered in a fine dust that lifted into the air as I strode in. I raised a ball of light to find myself facing a huge painting. Why anyone would create a painting down here where no one would ever see it, I couldn't guess.

A glimmering white tower soared above a rocky coastline where waves beat against the cliffs. Perched on a great boulder in the wash of the sea sat a gleaming skull. Orange light splashed through the sky where the sun and the moon rose together, casting dancing shadows over the fields beyond the temple that was strewn with bodies and the refuse of war. Above the temple, two disembodied hands with round eyes set in the palms faced outward as if in a sign of warning. It was a strange Picasso-like painting.

"What?" I said aloud. "What does it mean?"

I received no answer, just a plaintive music in my head that brought tears to my eyes. How did I stop something that no one could explain? What did it have to do with the sun and the moon? Maybe it didn't matter. All those people were dead, and the temple knew their deaths were connected to the evil that threatened it.

That night as I slept, the haunting music of the temple filled my dreams, rising and falling to the rhythm of the yellow and orange flames dancing in the darkness. Black-robed priests threw books of all sizes and colors onto a huge bonfire as sparks and ashes jumped into the darkness. The flames licked hungrily at the dry pages, curling the corners and twisting the writing before it devoured them. Tome after massive tome perished in the inferno.

One priest stood to the side with his back to me while the others circled the bonfire and sang a beautiful song that jarred against the destruction in front of them. Someone screamed, and the sound echoed off the soot-stained walls of the library as the lone priest spun to face the bonfire. His orange eyes shone bright in the darkness.

I awoke with a sudden dread about the book I had hidden under my bed. I had forgotten about it in all the drama of the testing. The pale light of dawn spilled in through my window as I crawled under my bed and searched for the book with my hand. It wasn't there. I stuck my head under my bed, peering into the shadows. Nothing.

Sitting up, I tried to remember if I had moved it, but I was sure I hadn't. Then I remembered that I had smelled burning in my room that was different from the normal smell of the burning wood in the fireplace. I scrambled to the hearth, and there in the ashes were charred fragments of paper and the edge of a book binding.

Who would destroy my book? How would they even know I had it?

I cornered the Roinan boy that morning when he brought me my breakfast.

"I've decided to call you Roy," I said. The boy's eyes grew wide, and he backed toward the door. A red blush crept into his cheeks, and he shook his head.

"It's cool," I said. "I'm the Promised One. I can change the rules." I don't think I convinced him because he still clung to the doorway. It was pitiful to see how frightened the boy was. The priests did more than meditate on the Light. I was sure of it.

"Do you know Princess Alana?" I asked.

Roy nodded.

"Why hasn't she been singing at the temple?"

"She prepares to receive the Gift of Illurien," he whispered.

"The what?" I hadn't heard anything about this.

"The gift will be given soon, and she must prepare."

"What is the gift?" I asked.

Roy shook his head, and his cheeks burned bright red. "I can't speak of it, Promised One." He paused. "May I go?" His fingers clutched at the door jam.

"One more question," I said. "Did you find a book in my room?"

"No," Roy said.

"Has anyone mentioned a book?"

He glanced at the door and shook his head. "May I go, please?"

Pity filled my heart. He hadn't burned my book. I picked up a roll from my tray and held it out toward him. "Only if you'll eat this for me," I said.

Roy hesitated, but a sudden flash of desire slipped across his face. He raised a slow hand, casting a furtive, fearful glance at me and stuffed the roll into his mouth before he fled the room.

I tried to concentrate on my lessons with the priests, but they were pretty much the same as before. My mind wandered while they droned on. What was the Gift of Illurien if it wasn't me? I was the Promised One, wasn't I? What other gift did they need? When I finished with the lessons, I crept back into the tunnels to inspect the rooms one more time before dinner.

I had just returned to my room when a knock sounded on my door. I yanked it open prepared to quiz Roy again about Alana. But Lowthelian beamed at me, and I stumbled back from the doorway in surprise. I hadn't seen her in over a week. She held my dinner tray out to me.

"Where's Roy?" I asked.

Lowthelian's smile faltered. "The Roinan is attending to his other duties," she said.

"Right. Where have you been?"

"Attending to *my* duties, Promised One."

"I haven't seen you around the temple for days."

Her silver eyes swirled leisurely, and a conspiratorial smile lifted at the side of her mouth. "Just because you didn't see me, doesn't mean I didn't see you."

I lifted my tray from her hands. "Were you watching me?" I asked.

"Well," she said, "skeletal priests aren't as nice to look at."

My face warmed in embarrassment, and I turned to set the tray on the table. This was a new Lowthelian I had never met. I dropped into the chair. She had been testy with me, then sad, and now she was flirting with me. I shoved a warm roll into my mouth so I wouldn't have to say anything.

Rather than rushing away as she usually did, Lowthelian dragged out the other chair and sat down. I stopped chewing and stared at her. Lowthelian smiled sweetly and rested an elbow on the table, leaning her chin into her palm. I swallowed the lump of bread in my mouth. She watched me with her liquid silver eyes churning languidly.

"Um, don't you have to rush off somewhere?" I asked.

She shook her head.

"Can I do something for you?"

"No, I've already eaten. I'll watch."

Pausing in mid-bite, I swallowed my food and was surprised a how loud it sounded.

"Watch? Why?"

She shrugged and batted her eyelashes at me.

I sat back in my chair and set my spoon on the table. "I can't eat with you staring at me."

She rose and wandered over to the window. She clasped her hands behind her back and studied the wispy clouds that floated in the pale blue sky, swaying from side to side while she hummed a quiet tune.

I picked up my spoon and tried to eat the stew without slurping. Lowthelian made me so self-conscious I finally gave up. Lifting the bowl to my lips, I drank its contents. When she heard the clunk of the bowl on the tray, Lowthelian returned to the table and sat down.

"I don't want to sound rude," I said, "but, well, you usually don't hang around while I eat. Is there some reason why you have tonight?"

"I finished my work, and I'm bored."

"Really? I didn't think you were ever finished."

She glared at me. "I'm only human," she said.

"Uh, right. Sorry." I searched for something to say. I had known her for weeks now, and I still didn't have anything to talk about.

"Um, do you know every way in and out of the temple?" I blurted.

She grinned, and I found that I liked her smile. She had small, white teeth, thin lips, and one tiny dimple. She was pretty. Not as attractive as Alana, but she was nice to look at. I hardly noticed her silver eyes anymore. They made her exotic.

"I know more ways than the priests," she said.

I smiled back at her. "Any chance you'd be willing to show me something interesting?"

A wicked grin spread across her face. "Come on," she said.

Her sudden enthusiasm so startled me that I blinked stupidly at her as she rose to her feet.

"Come now, or I'll not show you," she said.

I lunged to my feet, nearly knocking the chair over and followed her down the maze of corridors toward the empty rooms with the broken doors. I guessed where she might be heading, but I didn't

154

want to say anything. Her bare feet made no sound. She didn't seem to notice the doors or anything else. It surprised me how quickly we arrived at the great domed chamber I had stumbled into on my first night of wandering. The golden light from within spilled out into the corridor.

Lowthelian waited for me to enter the room and then raised her hands above her head in a great sweeping gesture that included the huge marble columns, the domed ceiling, and the walls filled with golden writing. "This is the Navel of the Earth," she said.

I struggled not to laugh. "Navel?" I said. I had seen the phrase written on the altar last time I was here, but hearing her say it out loud seemed really funny. "What is that supposed to mean?" I asked.

She glanced at me and narrowed her eyes suspiciously. "That's all you can say?"

I gazed up at the great snake that devoured its own tail and tried to act surprised and awed, but since I had already seen it, I wasn't very convincing.

"Wow," I said. "How come none of the other buildings in the temple are like this?"

"You don't know where you are, do you?"

"No, not really."

"You remember the Hitching Post of the Sun?" she asked.

"The sundial? Yeah."

"We are directly beneath it. Can't you feel the Light?"

"Of course," I said, "but why call it the navel? I mean, that's kind of disgusting." I wasn't sure I wanted to be standing inside a navel. Navels were hairy places were lint and sweat gathered.

Lowthelian smirked at me. "It's the center," she said like I was the biggest idiot she had ever met. "All Light is focused on this place."

"So, navel just means center?"

"All the symbols teach of the Light. Look." She pointed to the columns. "The great columns of light shine down from the greater light of the sun and rest upon the lesser light of the moon, showing their sacred union. The writing teaches about the creation and celebrates those who have given their lives to the Light." Then she pointed at the great serpent that encircled the dome.

"The world serpent endlessly creates and devours himself—

155

forever moving and circling just as the Light never remains still and is not contained by time or space."

"That's actually really interesting," I said.

Lowthelian beamed.

"What's the altar for?" I asked. I hadn't forgotten that the altar had written words to me last time I was here.

Lowthelian glanced at me sharply. Her smile faded, and she looked away. "That I cannot tell you. But you'll learn soon enough. The priests will show you."

Now, I studied her. Why wouldn't she tell me? It seemed like everyone was hiding something in this place.

Her sour mood passed swiftly, and she smiled again. "There," she said. "I've shown you something interesting. Haven't I?"

"Yeah," I said. "The priests are still hiding things from me."

I hadn't meant to say it, and I prepared myself for another one of her tongue-lashings, but she didn't seem to be annoyed.

"Perhaps they are waiting," she said, "until you are ready to understand what they have not yet taught."

My face burned, and I wanted to snap at her, but maybe she was right.

"Sorry," I said.

"We all get impatient, Promised One," she said. "You'll understand everything one day—perhaps more than you want to."

"Which means?" I asked.

Lowthelian gave me an indecisive frown, and I could tell she wanted to say something, but she shook her head. "I've already said too much."

She spun to leave, and I reached out to touch the altar when her back was to me. An image of a slender figure racing through the temple, carrying a long black stick and wearing a black robe with the hood pulled up, flashed through my mind. A sense of danger surged into me, and I snatched my hand away. What could that image mean?

That night I dreamed of stone chambers like the one I had fallen into—dozens and dozens of them. Disturbing music played in the background as, time after time, I saw a boy or girl lying on the cold stones, dead. A black stain spilled across their chests, just like the one that killed my mother. These were children of various shapes, sizes, and even skin colors, but they were all lying in the same attitude of death.

Were these the Chosen, dead even before the priests came to collect them? How could this be? Who would kill them just after they arrived at the Temple of Light? Why would they do it?

Then a sun and a moon rose into the sky together and just hung there the way they had in the picture the temple had shown me. It was bizarre and unnatural, but it left me with the lingering feeling that the temple expected me to make it happen somehow—which didn't make any sense. It had to be symbolic, like everything else here. These images didn't come from Ross. They came from the temple. What was it trying to tell me?

Chapter Fifteen
The Gift of Illurien

THE PHRASE, THE Gift of Illurien, haunted me as I fidgeted in the shadow of the wall by the little door the next morning, hoping Alana would come. Why did the idea of this gift disturb me so much? There was something sinister in it and the way the Roinan boy behaved when he talked about it.

When I couldn't wait any longer, I jogged across the courtyard to Hahl's tower. The Hahl that greeted me was dramatically changed. I paused to stare at him. He hunched over in weariness. His yellow eyes still smoldered, but the light was dim. His internal flame was going out, and the long years he had defied death were finally creeping up on him.

"What happened?" I blurted.

He waved away my question and shuffled past me to descend the tower stairs. I followed him as he labored down each step. His bony feet clicked off the stone. I breathed in the cool morning air and considered escaping through the small door to lie down on the hillside amid the flowers, in the warm sun.

I followed Hahl's clicking, shuffling gait as he made his way amid the buildings, until he came to a building shaped like a cube. We entered without pausing, and I found myself in a dimly lit square room with a large circular hole in the ceiling, through which a great column of sunlight streamed. Four fires burned in four round holes in the floor. A column of light beamed directly down onto one of the fires.

Other than the fires and a single, three-legged stool in the corner, the room was empty. I glanced around at Hahl, wondering if he wanted me to sit on the stool and stare at the fires all day. Hahl's now-dim yellow eyes churned.

"This is the House of Perfection," he said. "It marks the four corners of the year with exactness. Do you know which corner it marks now?"

I tried to understand the strange mixture of emotions emanating from him. He was anxious and excited at the same time. Ross stirred in interest. At least he knew what was going on. It sure would have been easier if Ross could just talk to me in my head.

"It's the longest day of the year, isn't it?" I said.

Hahl nodded. "Our most sacred ceremonies occur at the four corners of the year. Tonight, we celebrate the Day of Victory and prepare for the Time of Sorrowing. As the Promised One, you must attend. The people will want to see you."

"The people?" My stomach lurched.

"Yes," he said. "They all know the Promised One is among us. You must comport yourself with dignity. Do not speak to them or look at them. You must not lower yourself from your high station. You are special, Promised One. Do not forget it."

Well, special was one thing I was not. I didn't like this idea of being paraded about like some trophy the priests could hold up as evidence of how well they were doing at serving the Light—especially since I knew they weren't. Hahl stepped toward the door.

"You'll have no lessons today," he said. "You are to return to your room. Lowthelian will come soon to help you prepare."

We stepped out of the little chamber to find another one of the long, jagged scars on the wall of the temple. Hahl paused to study it.

"What is it?" I asked.

"The darkness," Hahl said. "It has even entered the temple." A cold fear, mingled with despair, emanated from him.

"It will not be long now," he said, "if the Promised One cannot see." He shuffled away with a quiet clicking of his feet on the polished stone.

Lowthelian arrived at my room just after I did, carrying a large wooden box. She grinned as she set it on the table. This new friendly Lowthelian still made me jumpy. I couldn't decide how to behave toward her.

"Are you nervous?" she asked.

I passed my hand over my head. "I don't think the people are going to be too impressed when they see me walking out of the temple."

"You won't disappoint them, Promised One," she said. "You are...special." She whispered the last words with a blush.

A rush of affection for Lowthelian swept through me. How long had she been waiting on a bunch of grumpy skeletons? Her life must have been so lonely. Then again, if she was comparing me to skeletons, I suppose it wasn't much of a compliment that she flirted with me. I mean, anybody would have seemed attractive in comparison.

"Well," she said, "I've been given permission to teach you, at last." She said this like it was a treat for which she had long awaited. Then she bent over the box and withdrew items as she spoke.

"The ceremony begins at high noon and ends at midnight. You will eat and drink nothing for the rest of the day."

"What?" I blurted.

She glanced at me. "I hope you had a good breakfast." She gave me a knowing smile.

I smirked. "If I'd known you were going to starve me all day, I might have eaten more of it." The truth was I hadn't eaten much at all because I had rushed out to see if Alana would come.

Lowthelian held up a pure white robe. "You will need to change into this robe." She handed it to me and waited expectantly.

I raised my eyebrows. "Now?" I asked.

Lowthelian flashed me another smile. "We only have a few hours, and you have much to learn."

"Uh. Do you mind?" I said.

She shook her head, giving me a fiendish smile.

"Can I please have some privacy?" I said, stabbing a finger toward the door.

"Oh, all right," she said, "but hurry."

I changed quickly and let Lowthelian back into the room.

She pulled a circlet of shining silver from the box. It had a square knot tied in the center.

"This is the knot that ties heaven and earth together, just as you are the link that will restore the balance and bind them together forever."

She set it on the box. I picked it up and placed it on my head so that the knot sat in the center of my forehead. I couldn't help but feel like some twisted beauty pageant contestant. I knew I looked ridiculous.

Lowthelian withdrew an iridescent cloak, which flashed all the colors of the rainbow, with a golden sun disk clasp.

"All the colors are united in the Promised One," she said, "who alone can wield their power."

I reached to take the cloak from her. Our hands brushed. My power flared. Lowthelian screamed and flew backward like a rag doll. She hit the wall hard, slumping to the floor. Ross awoke. A sudden and overwhelming desire to kill surged through me. The power rushed menacingly to my fingertips. My breathing came fast. The blood pounded in my temples.

What was happening? I rushed across the room, trying to suppress the awful rage that snarled within me. I knelt beside Lowthelian's crumpled form, where she remained unconscious, unresponsive. Ross pushed against my mind, urging me to destroy her. But I couldn't. I had to help her. It had been an accident.

I reached out to touch her but stopped. If I touched her, I would not be able to restrain the power, and I might kill her. Ross struggled within me. The pressure built up behind my eyes. He insisted that she must die, but I held him back.

"Leave me alone," I said.

Fear and horror replaced the rage. What had I done? Why had the power reacted this way? Why had it attacked her? She was here to help me. She served the Light. Why would it attack with so much more force than before, and why couldn't I control it? Why was Ross so desperate to kill an innocent girl?

I shivered in horror at what the power was trying to do and glanced at the door, considering whether I should run for help. What could the priests do anyway? Then the image of the little withered lily came back to me—the power to take Light and to give it.

I couldn't touch her like I had the lily. So, I closed my eyes. Though I didn't know the words or tune, the song came to me. The singing filled me with a deep sense of goodness and happiness—a peace that enfolded me like a warm blanket. This is how serving the Light ought to feel.

The power caught the Light that flowed out of Lowthelian. She was dying. Her Light was leaving her. I willed the power to heal her. It wrapped around her Light as I tenderly put it back where it belonged. This overwhelming gentleness of the power was so different from the awesome and brutal display of a moment ago. The contradiction confused and frightened me. I had never had the desire to kill anyone, and yet, I had just experienced a nearly overwhelming passion to destroy.

As my power enfolded her Light, I noticed something wrong with it. The plant's Light had been healthy, vibrant, and pleasing. Hers seemed to be damaged, sick, like Einediau's garden. I couldn't tell what it was, but something was not right. The silver Light I ushered back into her soul was unnatural, tainted. Perhaps serving the priests all these years had left a mark on her.

The last of her Light fell gently back into place. My song ended. I opened my eyes and blinked at the sweat that dripped into them. Lowthelian leaned against the wall, staring at me. Her silver eyes swirled. Tears spilled down her cheeks. She bore an expression of the utmost dejection. I resisted the urge to wipe the tears away and to drape a comforting arm around her shoulders.

"Are you okay?" I asked.

She nodded.

"I'm sorry," I said. "I didn't mean to. Can you stand?"

She struggled to her feet.

"Please, sit at the table." I grabbed a chair and pushed it toward her before stepping away so she could approach it without fear of touching me.

"I didn't mean to hurt you," I said again. "The power just flared up. I couldn't stop it."

Her continued silence left me feeling even worse. What could I say to make her see that I hadn't meant to hurt her?

She wiped at the glistening tears. "I know, Promised One."

"Can you tell me why I can't touch you?" I asked. "Why does my power react so strangely to you?"

New wet streaks slipped down her cheeks. "It is who I am, Promised One. That is all."

"But—" I tried to continue, but she crawled to her feet.

"We don't have time, Promised One. We must continue. I..." She choked back a sob. "I thank you for saving my life. Your power is beautiful. I only wish..."

She wiped away the tears, and, taking a deep breath, reached into the box. She withdrew a short rod with a golden orb perched on one end and a clear crystal pyramid on the other. She set it on the table.

I picked it up in frustration. How could I help her if she wouldn't trust me?

I waited for the consequences of using the power to hit me. I was tired, and a little achy, but nothing else happened. Maybe using the power during the testing had increased my capacity and tolerance for it, so things like drawing and replacing Light didn't have such a negative effect on me.

Lowthelian spoke in a monotone voice, all the excitement and energy drained from her until she had dressed me in the ceremonial clothing and educated me in what I was supposed to do—which wasn't much. A sense of deep sadness, even pain, radiated from her. This surprised me because I hadn't been able to feel her emotions before like I could the priests. While she spoke, she swiped at the occasional tear.

"Are you sure you're okay?" I tried again when she finished.

She ignored me. "You must be at the Hitching Post of the Sun before high noon," she said and turned to leave.

"Please, Lowthelian. I want to help you, but I can't if you won't let me."

She faced me. Another tear slipped down her brown cheek. She shook her head. "There is nothing you can do that would help me," she said. Then she spun and rushed from the room with a rustle of her robe and a sob.

Lowthelian tripped and stumbled to her chambers and threw herself onto her bed. Bitter tears soaked her pillow. Her one chance to have a real friend, and the priests had managed to destroy that, too. They had stolen everything from her. She couldn't even enjoy the touch of the one person in the world whose touch she most craved. Once, she understood the danger, she had tried to keep her distance from him. She had tried not to think about him, but she couldn't do it. Now, his power had nearly killed her, and the Promised One had saved her. Awakening to hear his beautiful song and feeling his power overwhelmed her.

The concern and caring that had shown in his face made everything worse. He did care for her—really cared for her. No one had given one moment's thought to her or her needs and desires since she had been torn from her mother's arms so many years ago.

Why had he saved her? Why hadn't he let her go and released her from the suffering and loneliness? She would have rather died than live knowing she was destined to waste her life until her youth and capacity to love had shriveled away, leaving her an empty shell as ugly and brutish as the priests.

Lowthelian sat up and struggled to control the racking sobs. She blinked at the blank walls of her room, her prison. She tried to remember what her mother had looked like and failed. Even that sweet memory had been fouled by the priests. She clenched her jaw. The priests. It was always the priests. She had been fighting her own private war with them since they had damaged her. Now, she would fight for the Promised One.

The priests were already assembled when I stepped out into the bright courtyard, dressed in the radiant cloak and white robe. I carried the short staff in my right hand, as Lowthelian had instructed.

Hahl wore a bright yellow robe. A silver band with a pyramid-shaped diamond set in the middle encircled his skull. He carried a golden cube in one hand and a crystal sphere in the other. A golden sash lay across his shoulders, and a golden belt with the words "Light and Life" engraved upon it circled his middle where his waist should have been. Since he didn't have any flesh to hold the belt up, it sagged until it caught on his hip bones. The image sent a sick, disgusted flutter through my belly. With their loose robes on, I could sometimes forget the priests were nothing but bones.

The rest of the priests wore the colors of Light they controlled. I was the only one who wore pure white, though I had a cloak with all the colors of the rainbow. All the symbolism I had seen thus far indicated that my power should be white because it united all the colors of the Keepers. Then why was it invisible?

The priests had never seemed so imposing as they did in their royal regalia with the colors of their power burning in their eyes. They still hunched over, and their eyes were dimmer than before. I shivered. Their kingly attire made them more grotesque. Llaith was the spookiest of all with his black flowing hair and angry red eyes.

I found Ufel watching me, and I nodded to him. He nodded back, but I sensed a deep turmoil inside him, unlike the other priests who seemed excited and expectant. I wanted to ask him what bothered him about this ceremony, but I didn't get the chance because Hahl motioned for me to take my place. I stood beside Hahl while the other priests spread out behind us in a V with three on each side.

As the shadow from the sundial fell across the midday mark, we marched forward. No one gathered inside the temple, but when we left its gates, it seemed like the entire population had turned out to watch the ceremony. People packed into every possible nook and cranny, looking on in absolute silence.

This wasn't at all what I had expected. I thought there would be cheering and applause. Instead, I met stone-faced silence. I tried not to show that I was studying the people, but I couldn't help it. Most of them had the same deep brown skin as Alana and black or dark brown hair. Here and there, I caught glimpses of others with red or blonde hair packed in among the crowd. I guessed they were the products of the weeding from far countries that Alana had told me about. As we passed, mothers hugged their children close. The children stared with wide, frightened eyes at the skeletal priests. Several children started wailing.

The priests marched on, not looking at anyone. As soon as they passed the gate, they lifted up their voices and sang. I had never heard the song, but it raised over the crowd in a beautiful harmony, lifting and falling with a slow, haunting cadence that filled me with wonder. Again, I marveled at how such hideous beings could produce such impossible beauty. They sang as we wound our way through the streets.

A troop of soldiers dressed in shining mail and carrying colorful banners followed behind, keeping the press of people at bay. The buildings huddled close against the cobblestone street and reminded me of pictures I had seen of medieval European cities. Greenery decorated the doorways and windows, giving the streets a festive air that contrasted sharply with the stench of filthy city streets. I tried not to think of what I was stepping in when something cold and wet squished between my toes.

As we climbed the other hill, the buildings became more ornate, and the street widened. Two- and three-story buildings with columns on either side of their doors loomed over us. Sunbursts and half-moon designs decorated the doorways. Some of the upper windows had balconies where men and women in fine silk clothes waved handkerchiefs. They, at least, seemed to be enjoying the procession.

As we passed a large, stately house, a commotion erupted in the crowd. Something flew over the heads of the onlookers and struck me in the chest. I stopped. The priest's song ended abruptly. Whispers of surprise stuttered through the crowd. I glanced down at a doll that lay at my feet. Its face had been cut to ribbons, and a large needle protruded from its chest. Of all the things I might have expected, this would never have occurred to me. A doll?

I searched the crowd, but the soldiers were already forcing their way through. People staggered out of their way until they grabbed an old woman and dragged her toward the palace.

I glanced at Hahl. He didn't look at the soldiers. None of the priests did.

"What..." I began, but the surge of anger and annoyance gushed from Hahl so powerfully that I didn't finish. I wanted to pick up the doll, but I didn't know what Hahl would do with all those people watching, so I just stepped over it. As soon as I did, the priests took up their song again as if they had never been interrupted. I understood now that this procession wouldn't be like a papal visit, where people hoped for blessings from their spiritual leaders. These priests weren't revered because they were loved—but because they were feared.

We passed under the great, arching gates of the palace and into a vast courtyard. The immaculate palace grounds contrasted with the rancid debris and odor of the streets. The sweet aroma of flowers wafted on the air.

The Roinan had been kept busy here. This palace combined the high round towers of medieval castles with Gothic arches and delicate floral designs. It made the stately houses we passed on the road seem shabby. The palace left me with a feeling of elegant grandeur and beauty. In fact, the palace reminded me of Alana—distant, beautiful, mysterious. The crowds packed themselves into the palace grounds and spilled out around the edges of a raised wooden dais in the center of the plaza.

We climbed the stairs and filed out along the dais, looking out over the masses of people. The soldiers placed their banners around the platform where they snapped and fluttered in the breeze. As they placed the last flag, the priests ended their song abruptly, but the resonance drifted on the air until it was swallowed by the palpable silence that followed it. No one stirred for a long moment.

Then a man stepped out from one of the wide palace entrances and strode toward us. He was tall with deep brown skin and long, black hair. A golden crown set with many precious stones encircled his head. His silver cape fluttered out behind him as his black boots clicked against the cobblestones. He strode with his head high, refusing to honor anyone but the priests with a glance. Alana trailed behind him, carrying a huge glass disk, her silver robe rippling in the breeze and flowing about her bare feet. Two guards wearing purple robes and polished plate armor escorted them until they reached the stairs, where they stopped and stood at attention. Alana also stopped at the foot of the stairs as the King ascended.

I tried not to stare at her, but she was so beautiful. I hadn't seen her since I had upset her, and I wanted to know that she wouldn't hate me forever.

Now was not the time to worry about Alana, though, because the King made his way toward us. He inclined his head to Hahl, who nodded in return. This seemed odd until I considered that these were the two most powerful men in the kingdom. Clearly, neither man would concede supremacy to the other. The King then stepped in front of me. I had to bend my neck to gaze up at him. His black eyes were hard and penetrating. They narrowed as he studied me. I guessed he was sizing me up, and he didn't like what he saw.

I hadn't been prepared for this moment. This man was a reigning king, and he looked the part. I was just some stupid kid in a situation that was way beyond my understanding. If I had known how to get home, I would have rushed off that platform, stripped off the ridiculous robe, and run for it. I tried not to show any sign of weakness as my stomach churned. The King then spun on his heels to face the crowd. He raised his hands and spoke in a deep and resonating voice.

"People of the Light," he said, "today we celebrate the Gift of Illurien. We thank her for the new hope she brings us in our time of trouble. We have been faithful in our service to the Light. We have spread the Seeds of Light to almost every land, and still, the darkness lengthens. This day is the longest day of the year, and yet, it is two thirds as long as it was ten years ago. Our crops wither in the field from want of light. Our people flee famine in the north countries. Life grows dim and trouble brews. We must weed the Field of Light more frequently. She-Who-Would-Not-Sing stretches out her hand to claim us."

He paused.

"Yet, we have hope. Illurien has sent us the long-awaited Promised One."

He gestured toward me, and I wanted to crawl under the dais and hide.

"He will soon turn back the darkness and bring balance to the Light. Until then, we must continue as before. The Time of Sorrowing approaches, and Illurien has offered yet another gift. We accept it with honor."

The crowd parted to let a child step forward. He wore a long black robe, and his head was shaven. He could have been a smaller version of me if it hadn't been for his darker skin. He climbed the steps of the dais and knelt before the King with a bowed head. I took an involuntary step forward before realizing what I was doing and stepped back. The Gift of Illurien was none other than Roy, the little Roinan who brought me my meals.

Chapter Sixteen
A Beacon and a Tomb

I TRIED TO CATCH Alana's gaze, but she looked away, her face betraying no emotion. Obviously, she was still angry with me. I peered around at the other priests. The eagerness that emanated from them turned my stomach sour. Something wasn't right. Ross stirred inside me, and his rage created a painful pressure behind my eyes. Questions tumbled around in my brain. Questions I couldn't answer.

How could Roy be a Gift of Illurien? What would this mean for him? Were they going to make him like Lowthelian with swimming, colored eyes and make him serve in the temple? Why did this ceremony so enrage Ross when the other ceremonies hadn't?

My thoughts broke as I realized Alana was now gliding across the dais, carrying the great circle of glass. She wore a loose-fitting robe of silver with a golden belt around her slender waist. A circlet of delicate white flowers crowned her raven head. The morning breeze stirred, catching at her robe and hair, making her look like a soaring angel as she glided forward. She bowed low to the priests and then to her father before handing him the great disk of glass.

The King took it and raised it above his head. "We light the beacon of hope," he said.

The polished glass flashed as the King caught a beam of light from the westering sun and directed it toward the eastern tower. He held it steady. After a few moments, a thin wisp of smoke fluttered into the air. The smoke grew darker, and then a flame leaped out. Men on the tower fed the flame, which soon became a great bonfire. I couldn't decide if the trick had actually worked or if the men had started the fire on their own. It didn't matter because the people burst into cheers so sudden and so powerful that my ears rang. The King held up his hand to quiet them.

"Tonight, the Gift will be accepted, and the sign will be given," he said.

Then he spun on his heels and marched out of the courtyard. The guards and Alana followed. The priests burst into song again as we filed out of the courtyard and back toward the temple. This time, Roy shuffled along in the middle of us with his head bowed. He kept his gaze on the cobblestones, but his face was tense, and his shoulders drooped. Roy, at least, seemed to know or guess what was going to happen to him.

The priests kept singing the same song until they passed through the temple gates and reached the great sundial. Then they switched tunes without a pause and sang the Ballad of Illurien with little Roy cowering in the middle of the circle—alone and forlorn. I wanted to comfort him, to protect him.

Lowthelian appeared out of nowhere. She handed Roy a translucent skull like the one Llaith had used. When he lifted it in his small hands, he swayed under its weight. Roy raised his gaze to meet mine for just an instant. His eyes were sad and frightened, but his expression was resigned. He looked like a trapped animal that knew he could never escape. I struggled to understand what I should do. I couldn't avoid the peculiar dread that gripped my heart. No one had told me about this part of the ceremony.

The priests shifted songs again to one with no words. This tune had a haunting quality that sent a wild shiver coursing through me. It seemed more appropriate to the grotesque skeletal faces that sang it than the beautiful music I heard before. It possessed no beauty, only a deep and abiding emptiness fringed with despair. This was not the type of music I had come to expect from the servants of the Light—a power coursed through the song—a dark power that gave me goosebumps.

This time, Lowthelian led the procession with Roy behind her, followed by me and the priests. My insides were churning. The warnings and rumblings from Ross were ominous. I knew I should do something, but what?

Lowthelian led us to the great underground room called the Navel of the Earth. The boy stepped forward and placed the skull on the altar over the words chiseled into its center. Hahl raised a hand. A door slid aside at the center of the domed ceiling, casting a warm beam of rich yellow light onto the skull. It pulsated and burned with a deep golden fire.

All the priests encircled the skull and laid their hands on it. Their colors flared beneath their hands for a moment, followed by a flash of white light. The priests parted to let Roy retrieve the skull. As soon as he touched it, he reeled and staggered in a faint. Lowthelian caught him and supported him as we filed back out of the tunnels toward the courtyard.

I stepped close to the altar, trying to brush my hand against it to see if it would tell me anything about what was going on. Haunting music burst into my mind, along with the image of a sundial aflame with a brilliant white light. I had to pull my hand away before I could see more because the priests were already moving, and I had to follow them into the tunnels.

When we reached the courtyard, two guards clad in gleaming, silver armor, and purple cloaks waited with a stretcher. Lowthelian helped Roy lie down on it. She cupped his hands around the now-golden skull that perched upright on his chest. His eyes were closed. His chest rose and fell.

The priests sang the eerie wordless song again as the guards lifted the stretcher and filed off toward the gates of the temple. We paraded through the city again, this time winding downhill to the valley opposite the Palace of Light. Crowds of people looked on with silent, grim faces. Some openly wept. As we drew near the city gate, a shriek of anguish rose above the sound of the priests' haunting music, and someone shouted something I didn't understand. Several guards from the back of the column pushed through the crowd in search of the person who dared defile the procession.

We passed under two huge arches that spanned columns carved to resemble ropes tied in knots. The people remained behind at the gate. When I glanced back, they stared after us—motionless, expressionless, expectant.

The procession advanced along a dirt road into a landscape that had been transformed into thousands of earthen mounds punctuated by standing stones. I had seen this place in the Mirror of Light. We wound in and out of the green mounds until we came to a large one that must have been somewhere in the middle. The King and Alana waited for us there with a retinue of guards clad in purple cloaks and glittering armor.

The King carried a large torch that spat and popped, casting up the nasty reek of burning pitch and tar. No one spoke. He led the two guards carrying the stretcher into the entrance tunnel. I glanced at Alana, but, again, she refused to look at me. I wanted to scream at her to do something. They were going to shut Roy up in this chamber alive just like they had done Ross. Trying to think of something to do, I looked at Hahl and then around at the other priests. Something was happening. They were no longer bent over but stood erect.

The sound of boots scraping on gravel brought me around. The King ducked out of the entrance, still carrying the torch. Then the guards rolled a large stone over the entrance to the tunnel. The King nodded again to the priests and then strode off toward the city. The priests didn't follow. They encircled the mound and sang as the sun sank into the western horizon.

My gut instinct told me to rush up and shove the stone aside. Roy would eventually die from thirst or starvation. I had to get him out. I couldn't let them do this. Ross also roiled in fury, but instead of wanting to react with violence, like he had with Lowthelian, he seemed content to watch—content to let me see this.

I controlled myself because I knew if I tried to do anything now, the priests would stop me. Later that night, I would come back to save Roy. I would find some way to get him out of the city. Roy wouldn't die in there. Even if it meant I would be hunted by the priests for the rest of my life, I would save him.

The sun had fallen behind the mountains in a glorious display of corals and lavenders before the priests broke their circle and promenaded back into the city, still humming the same haunting, wordless tune. They filed into the temple until we encircled the great sundial. As they chanted, their song grew louder and more vibrant. The old fire returned to their eyes. They stood straight and tall.

The hours dragged by in tortuous minutes. My feet ached, and my knees wobbled. My stomach groaned and pinched my spine. My head pounded. I kept shuffling my feet and glancing back toward the gates of the temple, trying to figure out how I could save Roy without the priests knowing.

I was getting ready to make a break for it when the song ended abruptly. The priests stared up at the sundial where a small dot of light grew on its point—brighter and brighter until it became so brilliant that I couldn't look at it. It shone like a beacon in the darkness, pushing it back until the temple courtyard was bathed in pure white light. Then the light flashed and blinked out.

The instant the light vanished, a great roar exploded from the city. Music burst forth. People shouted. Fireworks blossomed in the inky sky above the temple. The booms echoed inside the walls. The celebration of the Gift of Illurien had begun. All I could think of was little Roy locked in that chamber and how terrified he must be.

The priests filed away. Ufel stopped once and glanced back at me. Something in his demeanor made me uneasy. Guilt emanated from him. Not anger, not sadness, but guilt. I stepped toward him to ask him what they had done, but he turned away. I considered following him to demand an explanation, but I needed to get back to Roy.

Racing to my room, I ignored the burning in my eyes and the weakness in my legs. I had to get out of this flashy robe and silly crown and change into my plain black robe. I would be harder to see in the dark that way. I yanked on my black robe, guzzled a glass of water, and rushed out the door.

Lowthelian was outside my door. She jumped back as if struck by lightning, and I stumbled around her, doing everything I could to avoid touching her.

When I regained my balance and faced her, I said, "I'm glad you're here. I need your help."

"I thought you might try something," Lowthelian said, "so I came to stop you."

"What?" I couldn't believe it.

"There's nothing you can do," she said. Her voice was flat like she was trying to keep emotion out of it.

"I'm going to get Roy out of there before anything happens to him. I need you to help me."

"Roy?" she questioned.

I gestured impatiently. "You know who I mean."

Lowthelian shook her head again, her black hair swishing about her shoulders. "It's no use, Promised One."

"Then, I'll do it myself." I brushed past her coming recklessly close to touching her, but, at the moment, I didn't care.

She cowered against the wall and then rushed after me. "Wait," she called.

I ignored her.

"Wait. You can't go that way. The guards will be watching all night."

I stopped and faced her.

Tears trickled down her face. "I'll show you," she said. "But it's too late."

A huge rock landed in my stomach. "Why do you say that?" I asked. He had been alive when they shut him in. There would have been plenty of air. He couldn't have suffocated in such a huge chamber.

Lowthelian shook her head and turned back down the corridor. I followed her, trying not to think about what I might find in the tomb.

The instant we passed beyond the walls of the temple above, the cool light that filled the corridors beneath died. I called up a small ball of light into the palm of my hand. Lowthelian never paused until she stopped by a small wooden door and pointed at it. She said nothing.

I lifted the latch and ducked inside. The ceiling of the chamber was low, forcing me to crouch as I shuffled over to a ladder. I climbed up until my head thumped against a wooden trap door. Pushing it aside, I clambered up into the stuffy darkness.

The white light I conjured spilled over the huge slabs of stone that had been set on end, forming an octagonal chamber. A long stone altar upon which Roy lay with the skull still clutched on his chest filled the center of the chamber. I strode over to him and let the ball of light float in the air above us. I bent low over Roy's face. He seemed to be asleep—no sign of pain or fear or injury. Maybe I had overreacted. Maybe he was fine.

I shook him, but he didn't stir. "Roy," I whispered. "Roy, it's me, the Promised One. I've come to get you."

Still, Roy didn't stir. I picked up his little hand. It was cold—cold as death. Horror clutched at my chest. I knocked the skull from Roy's body. It thudded to the packed earth. Grabbing Roy by the arms, I shook him. "Wake up, Roy. Wake up."

I tried to remember what I had learned about CPR. I tilted Roy's head back and blew into his mouth. Nothing happened. Tears spilled from my eyes. "Roy," I whispered. I blew into his mouth again. I experienced that horrible wrenching helplessness I had felt when my mother died. It seemed like I should be able to do something. His little body was uninjured. How could a little boy die just like that? A rustle sounded behind me, and I spun to find Lowthelian watching me.

"What have they done to him?" I demanded.

The light glinted on the tears that slid down Lowthelian's cheeks.

"I told you it was too late," she said, her voice thick with emotion. "The Gift has been accepted." Her lips trembled.

I stepped toward her. It took all the restraint I had to keep from grabbing her and shaking her to death.

"You helped them do this," I said through gritted teeth. "You helped them."

She stood her ground. "So did you, Promised One."

I stared at her. The awful realization hit me like a freight train. I staggered against the altar. A wave of horror and guilt choked me. She was right. I had helped them. Tears dripped from my chin. I fell to my knees and grasped my head with my hands. How could I have done it? I had suspected—no, I had *known*. Ross had been warning me for days, had tried to tell me in my dreams what they were capable of. This is what Ross wanted me to stop. He had known. He had known all along. How could I have been so stupid?

Then I remembered what I had done to the lily and the way I had been able to find Lowthelian's Light after my power attacked her. I scrambled to my feet, brushing savagely at the tears that blurred my vision. I leaned over Roy and sang. The power came forth, warm and comforting. I had done it before. The power would let me do it again.

When I searched for the Light that was Roy, I couldn't find it.

A Beacon and a Tomb

The power filled the room and pushed beyond its walls, searching for his Light. It found nothing—only a great emptiness where Roy's beautiful Light should have been. My song faltered, and I fell silent. I reached down and picked up Roy's little body. I held him close and wept.

Chapter Seventeen
The Light Unseen

"THE TRANSCENDENTS WILL someday overcome death itself." Arell, the Keeper of the Night, sneered at Ross and the small group of Chosen who had come to study the stars in Arell's tower.

The Keepers and their group of close followers among the Chosen, who called themselves the Transcendents, had long argued for a complete reorganization of the worship of the Light. Only the Keepers, they said, should mediate between Illurien and the people. They alone could participate in the ceremonies.

Arell's statement puzzled Ross. If the Keepers were extending their lives, why were they growing older—more bent and wrinkled?

"The time will come," Arell said, "when the Keepers remain forever providing eternal continuity to the worship of the Light."

"You mean," Ross asked, "that you are now seeking immortality?"

Arell gave him a condescending smirk. "The Light is eternal, so why shouldn't those who guard it also be eternal?"

Horrified curiosity had driven Ross to spy on the Keepers. What were they doing in their search for immortality? How did they plan to accomplish it?

One dark night, he crept into Llaith's rooms and found the dead child with Llaith and Arell looming over it. The child's breathless chest and blue lips revealed the unimaginable depravity to which the priests had descended.

That moment of discovery set Ross on the path of destruction. Now, the Promised One had seen it for himself. Now, he finally understood.

The next morning, I paced in an alcove near the little door waiting for Alana. My eyes burned, and my head throbbed. I hadn't slept all night and was in a dark and reckless mood. If she didn't come this morning, I was going to the palace to find her. I didn't care anymore.

The door cracked open, and she slipped through to stroll gracefully to the sundial without seeing me. I let her make her offering and then sing her song. It didn't sound so beautiful this morning. Nothing could shake the dark cloud that settled over me. I wanted answers. I wanted revenge.

I stepped in front of the door and waited for her to come. When she saw me, she stopped. Her face remained impassive, but her eyes widened. I thought she might try to defend what they had done, but she just watched me, calculating, waiting.

"He's dead," I said.

She still said nothing. She only stared at me with her big, dark eyes.

"You helped them kill him," I accused. "You knew they were going to kill him."

Alana licked her lips. Fear crept into her eyes.

"Did you pick him yourself?" I yelled. "Did you pick him because I asked him questions? Because I liked him?" The power flared in response to my anger. I wanted to lash out—to punish her for what she had done. I could believe anything of the priests, but not of her. I couldn't forgive her.

Alana backed away, raising her hands to ward me off. The fear transformed into open terror as I stepped toward her.

Alana shook her head. "No, Promised One," she stammered. "Please, no."

I reached out to grab her. She would pay for murdering the little boy.

"Kell, don't," she said.

I stopped. No one had said my name since I came here. How did she even know it?

Determination, even defiance, settled on her face. "I didn't choose him," she said. "Hahl always chooses who will be the Gift of Illurien."

"But you knew they would kill him."

"Of course, I knew. It's always the same."

The anger burned inside me again.

"Why did they do it, and how did they kill him so quickly?"

Alana glanced around. "Not now, we'll be seen."

"I don't care," I yelled. "I want answers, and I want them now."

Alana glanced around, panic stealing into her eyes.

"Okay," she said. "I'll go first to the little building we used last time. I'll wait for you there."

She slipped out the door and was gone. I was still in a brash mood, so I only waited a moment before I followed her through the door. Alana raced down the path as if Shaheen herself chased her. I waited until she entered the gazebo-like building. Then I strode after her. When I stepped in and pulled the door closed, she was standing on the far side, watching me—expectant and fearful.

"Tell me why they did it," I demanded.

Alana clutched her hands in front of her and took a deep breath. "Every so often, the priests must renew their power. If they go for too long without renewing it, they will die."

"What?" I couldn't believe what she was saying. "I thought they had already died and were now immortal."

Alana shook her head. "The priests didn't used to look the way they do now. They once looked like you and me."

I remembered my dreams. "I know," I said.

"When a new Chosen One came," Alana continued, "they were tested to determine which aspect of the Light they could command—which fit their personality most closely. Those that had a true aptitude for one aspect of the Light apprenticed to that priest until he died, and then he took his place. The other Chosen who didn't become Keepers studied the Light, wrote books, and taught classes. The temple used to be filled with Chosen Ones—whole families of them."

Alana paused and ran a hand through the dark hair that spilled over her shoulder.

"I shouldn't know any of this, but my teacher, who is also

the guardian of the palace archive, once explained it. He said this continued for thousands of years. Then one of the priests discovered that he could draw the Light from living things and so draw strength from it.

"I bet I know who," I interrupted.

Alana shook her head. "I don't know who did it. First, they used plants and animals, but their Light isn't strong enough. As you should know, human Light is the strongest of all."

She licked her lips and smoothed a wrinkle in her dress.

"As the Chosen Ones came, instead of apprenticing them, the Keepers withdrew their Light and renewed their own strength. Over time, the Keepers changed until they came to be as they are now. Something happened, and the Chosen Ones stopped coming." She paused and shuffled her feet. "Well, at least the priests said they stopped coming. The Roinan have told me that they have been forced to remove bodies from the chambers and store them somewhere in the temple. So, I think someone or something is killing them."

I thought immediately of the room filled with bodies and the evil in Durr's pool, the malicious specks of silver and blue lights that hunted through the corridors. And there were black monsters trying to rip their way into the temple. But could those creatures leave the black oozing wounds I had seen? Were these monsters killing the Chosen? Had *they* killed my mother?

Alana continued speaking. "So, they had to find a substitute. That's when they started using the Gift of Illurien."

I snorted. "Why is it that evil people like to give nasty things nice-sounding names?"

"Still," Alana continued, "they prefer to use the Chosen Ones, as their Light is more powerful and pure. But when they weaken, they choose a pure Roinan and use him or her."

"Wait a minute," I interrupted. "If I hadn't been the Promised One, they would have killed me in the same way?"

Alana nodded, her eyes wide, her face grave. "Probably."

"They left the service of the Light," I whispered, remembering something Hahl told me. Now, I understood what he meant. That's why I couldn't find Roy's Light. The Keepers had drawn it into themselves to renew their strength and extend their lives.

"A Chosen One has not survived for many, many years. When

they found you, they thought you must be special because you survived and because you are the only one to come to the most sacred chamber in the temple."

The image of Ross crouching in the corner, writing on the wall, crept into my mind. He had been the last to die there, hadn't he? As Ross stirred within me, I knew I was right.

"Seren said he had predicted my coming in the stars," I said. "Weren't they expecting me?"

Alana shrugged. "They've been expecting you for hundreds of years."

"Right. Okay," I said. "So, the song they sang allowed them to suck away Roy's Light?"

"Yes."

"The Light I saw on the top of the sundial was Roy's Light?"

"Yes. It was the sign that the Gift had been accepted."

I growled and almost shouted. "I am sick of this double-talk. Just say what it is, and stop hiding behind empty clichés. Roy was no Gift of Illurien. He was murdered so these pitiful priests can live forever and wander around their temple, muttering about the Light."

Alana's eyes grew wide again.

"That's what it is, Alana," I said. "It's murder. Cold-blooded, calculated murder. And I'm going to stop it." My power welled up again, and Ross joined in my anger.

"You're frightening me, Kell," Alana said.

When I glanced back at her, she had fallen against the wall with an expression of fear and vulnerability in her eyes. I studied her now. I didn't like scaring her. It made me feel unclean and underhanded. I shifted my gaze to the dirt floor.

"Sorry," I said. I raised my head to peer at her. "Wait, why did you use my name?"

Now, Alana dropped her gaze. "I want to help you," she whispered. "I can't forget what you said about the Light, and I want to help you purify it. This…this…evil use of the Light should end." A tear trickled down her cheek. Then she spoke in a rush. "I see that the Light is beautiful and good, but I can't justify what my father and the priests are doing any longer. It hurt me to see the Roinan—I mean Roy—die. I have worked with him since he was a small child. He was always so good and eager to please. But now…" A ragged sob escaped her throat.

I stepped forward. I wanted to hold her, but I didn't dare. Alana grabbed my hand in a tight grip. "There's one more thing I must tell you," she said.

I waited.

"Once you asked me what I saw while you sang with me at the Hitching Post of the Sun."

"Yeah?"

"I'll tell you what I saw." She swallowed. "I saw the power."

"What?" I glanced at my hands. Even *I* couldn't see the power. "What did you see?"

Alana licked her lips. "As you sang, a brilliant white light such as I have never seen surrounded you and then..." She paused again as a flicker of fear swept across her face. "Then you faded until all I could see was an outline of white light around your person. But you were gone."

"That's not possible," I said. I studied my hands again.

"Yes, Kell, you disappeared, and all that remained was a bright outline of beautiful Light. And the overwhelming sense of...of... goodness and peace. It was beautiful. That is how I knew you were the Promised One. That is what I have always expected the Promised One to bring."

My mind reeled. This would explain why the priests had been so shocked when I passed their tests. When I drew deeply on the power, I became invisible to those who watched.

"And," Alana continued in a quiet, fearful tone, "today when you became angry, you began to vanish again. That is why you frightened me."

I dropped onto the bench, staring at my hands. Why would the Light make me disappear? Maybe something had gone wrong.

Alana sat beside me. "This is important, I think," she said. "Can you tell me what it means?"

I shook my head. None of the priests ever mentioned an Invisible Light. None of them ever said I glowed and disappeared when I used the power. In fact, I couldn't see that they had told me much at all that would help me understand how to purify the Light. I wished Mom were here. She would have understood all of this.

"Kell," Alana said, "I must go. I have duties to perform."

I rose with her and grasped her hand in mine. "Thank you," I said.

Alana smiled and reached for the latch.

"Wait," I said.

She paused as I held out the little piece of paper I found with the stone. "Can you read this?"

Alana took it and studied it. Then she shook her head.

The flicker of hope died in my chest.

"But I know one who can," she continued. "I have seen this script before."

"Really? Where?"

"This is an ancient language spoken long ago. I was told that it belonged to a great civilization renowned for their learning and wisdom. I've seen a book with this writing only once. The master who showed it to me can read it. I think he's the only one left who is able to, but no one speaks it anymore."

"Do you think he would be willing to translate it?"

Alana smiled sweetly. "He will if I ask him."

I grinned. "Thanks."

Her smile drew me in, and I found myself leaning toward her, looking at her moist lips, feeling a rush of warmth in my gut. I wanted to kiss her. Did I dare? What would she do if I did?

Alana squeezed my hand, and she was gone, leaving behind the sweet fragrance of flowers and a quiet ache in my heart. I was such a fool.

I hesitated and then sat with my back to the wall to wait. I had no place to go, and I needed to think. If Alana had seen my power, then the priests certainly had, and so had Lowthelian. I had everything all wrong. I thought my light should be white because that was all of the colors combined, and the priests also seemed to think so. That would explain why they had been so upset when they couldn't see my power. What could it mean?

Leaving the little hut, I wandered back to my quarters. Hahl peered out from the window of his tower when I came through the door, but I kept walking. The priests had lost whatever moral authority they may have had over me. A confrontation was coming. The power swelled inside me, responding to my sense the danger was near. I wanted to use the power again—to wield it to punish the priests. I craved it the way a person could desire a cool drink after days of thirst. They deserved to be punished after what they had done to little frightened Roy and countless others like him. Roy's cold, dead face and limp body would haunt me as long as I lived.

The symbols that populated the temple reached out to me as if the temple was trying to communicate in a different way. Circles and squares were everywhere, etched into the walls, and even forming the structure of the buildings. Pyramids, knots, cubes, and wheels filled my mind. They symbolized eternity and wholeness, perfection and stability, light and time, purity and power—invisible power.

I found myself outside Durr's sanctuary without realizing I had been tending that way. Durr wasn't there. The pale blue sky reflected off the mirrored surface of the water. The obsidian Mirror of Light shone in the morning sun. I had the right. I could look in the Mirror now without any priest peering over my shoulder. The Mirror could tell me what this invisible power was. I glanced around again and strode up to it.

The lapping and splashing of the fountain on the far side of the lake whispered through the chamber. I lifted the reed from its little holder beside the black obsidian disk and dipped it into the lake. Then I let the water dribble onto the disk and spread out. Leaning in, I gazed at the liquid silver sheen, seeing my reflection. Then the surfaced shimmered and drew me in. I became senseless to my surroundings. Several images swept past and then settled on the huge panel of Illurien casting She-Who-Would-Not-Sing from the heavens. Of all the things the Mirror could show me, why would it show me this? A simple decoration in the temple.

Then the images swirled again, and a young man, maybe fifteen or sixteen years old, stood on a beach. He held a broken piece of stone that bore the image of the serpent devouring its own tail. The young man raised his dark eyes to look up at me, and his face registered shock and fear. The boy had seen me. He had peered through the Mirror and seen me looking down on him. The picture shifted, and the young man gazed at a room filled with clocks and timepieces of every kind.

The image spun away and was replaced by another of a young woman bent over a charcoal drawing of a serpent swallowing an egg. I couldn't see her face, only her soot-stained hand scratching frantically at the paper as the drawing took shape.

The picture shifted, and a great snowstorm raged in front of me. It covered everything in a thick, frozen blanket. I realized I was seeing a cornfield. The silken tassels were coated in snow and ice. The stalks bent under the weight. Then, I saw multitudes of people begging for food at the king's gate, and then, thousands of starving men, women, and children, with sunken eyes and bloated bellies stretched on the earth awaiting death. Great shadows of darkness in human shape—some with wings—slinked amid the desperate people claiming a victim here and a victim there. I couldn't see what they did to their victims, but when they passed on, only the shell of a person remained. The light churned again, and I shuddered at a sudden sensation of danger.

I dragged myself out of the swirling silver light and spun to see what was wrong. Reeling, I clutched at the edge of the dais for support as a wave of dizziness swept over me. Silver streamers flecked the edges of my vision. I blinked to clear them away and found clouds of light filled with thousands of tiny dots hovering over Durr's lake.

They were studying me. New dots lifted from the surface of the lake like steam. So, I had found the source of the malevolent specks of light that haunted the temple. They must hide here in Durr's lake during the day when they weren't hunting for me. It was now broad daylight, and I could see them clearly. The malicious evil that emanated from them washed over me like the heat from a fireplace. They wanted to hurt me. They wanted to destroy me because they feared me. I reached for the golden stone in my pocket when the distant sound of skeletal feet clicking against stone reached me. I spun and fled Durr's sanctuary before he could find me there.

I didn't stop until I reached the great panel of Illurien, expecting to hear the harsh clicking of bony feet on cobblestones or to see the ominous clouds of evil lights swarming after me. Only the cool wind blew through the temple. I leaned against a twisted pillar to catch my breath and wiped at the sweat dripping off my shaven head with the sleeve of my robe. I never appreciated how useful hair was at catching sweat until I found myself without it. And my hair didn't seem to be growing back like it should. Maybe I could find a way to borrow someone else's like Llaith had done.

The stone pillar was cool and pleasant after my long run, and I breathed a sigh of relief. That had been close. Had Durr known I was looking in the Mirror and come to stop me?

The shadow of the pillar beckoned me, and I slipped closer to the wall and faced the panel of Illurien. There must be some clue here that I had missed—something the Mirror had tried to show me. I studied Illurien and the way she stretched forth her hands as she cast She-Who-Would-Not-Sing from the heavens. Something about her hands caught my attention, but what? I studied it until I spun away in frustration and strode to the square room with the fires that Hahl had shown me the day before.

As I watched the beam of sunlight inch its way across the floor, something clicked in my mind. Invisible power meant Invisible Light. I tried to imagine the beam of sunlight as an invisible beam. Invisible Light. I glanced down at my hands—Invisible Light.

That's what had been strange about Illurien's hand. She must have used this invisible power to cast She-Who-Would-Not-Sing from the heavens.

"If Illurien's Light was invisible," I said, "and her power was invisible, that meant I had…"

I stopped myself. It couldn't be that. I must be stretching for it. If I wasn't supposed to combine the Light that each of the priests held into some pure white Light, then maybe this invisible power had some other purpose.

I set off down one of the tunnels that Ross had shown me—not because I was going anywhere in particular. I just needed to think. My robe flowed around my legs, and the cool air of the tunnels rushed over my head. I called up a small ball of light, even though I didn't need it. The natural light of the tunnels was enough to see by.

What had my mother said about Invisible Light? For some reason, I couldn't dredge up the memory. All I could remember was the way she smelled of vanilla and the dark stain on her chest as she lay dying on the asphalt. I still didn't know who had killed her or why, but if she came from this place and had been afraid to return, either the priests had her killed or one of the evil things haunting the temple must have done it.

It didn't make any sense, though. Alana said it had been years since a Chosen One had survived. How could my mother have had anything to do with this? How could she know about the chamber? Why had she kept going on about my father and how she thought he would come for us, that I might find him here?

As I wound my way through the underground labyrinth, a sound worked its way into my consciousness, and I stopped to listen. By now, I was deep beneath the temple in a tunnel I had never been in before. I had no idea what to expect in the bowels of the priests' complex.

The sound resembled a cat meowing. I followed it down a side passage, suspicious that the priests had locked up someone else to die in the temple. I thought of the woman that threw the doll at me during the procession. If they were going to kill her for that, I was going to stop them now.

I let my ball of light go out as I peeked in through the crack of an open door. Someone huddled inside, and she was speaking. A pale yellow flame from a candle flickered on the walls and filled the small chamber with golden light. A bed sat against the far wall, but that was all I could see in the room except for the small form kneeling on the floor, wearing a black robe with the hood pulled up to conceal the face.

"I don't want to do it. Not him." I recognized Lowthelian's voice. Why was she wearing a black robe? A sob wracked her body. "Not him. Not after what he did. I can't."

She shrieked in terrible pain and crumpled to the floor, writhing in agony. I reached to push through the door to go to her aid, but Ross stopped me. I wasn't supposed to know this was happening. It would be dangerous to reveal myself. I stepped back and cringed at her shrieks of pain, fighting the urge to help her.

I had grown fond of Lowthelian. We had become friends in the last few days. If she hadn't kept pushing me away, we might have been better friends. Her shrieking lasted so long I was afraid she might be dying. I reached for the door again, but Ross surged into my mind. I shook my head to dislodge him when the shriek faded back to the agonized whimpers I heard before.

"Please, no more," she gasped. "I'll do it. I'll do it."

She lay still, and I peeked through the crack until her breathing returned to normal. Then I slipped away and retreated to my room more horrified than I cared to admit and confused about what I had witnessed. What were the priests forcing Lowthelian to do?

Chapter Eighteen
Blood and Bones

I AWOKE WITH a start late in the day. The soft rustle of movement seeped into my sleep, dragging me toward wakefulness. Long shadows stretched across the floor. Something moved in the room. I sat bolt upright to find Lowthelian standing in the doorway. Not knowing what to expect, I jumped to my feet. She didn't smile or take her gaze from the floor. Her long black hair hadn't been brushed, and her gray robe was wrinkled. Redness rimmed her eyes, and the silver light did not shine and swirl. Her face was pallid as death, and her shoulders drooped.

"Are you all right?" I asked..

"Hahl commands your presence," she said. Then she spun and left.

"Lowthelian?" I called after her, but she ignored me.

Hahl was at his window, as usual, gazing out over the city when I arrived. When he turned to face me, the brilliance of his yellow eyes shocked me. He was powerful and confident once again—glutted on the Light of a child. I ground my teeth to control my rage.

"You've not been to your lessons today," Hahl said.

"No."

"You've been outside the walls of the temple."

"Yep," I said.

"What have you been doing?"

I wanted to grab his darkened crystal and shove it right into one of his swirling yellow eyes. Instead, I decided to tell him the truth—at least part of it.

"I've been thinking," I said. "Pondering on what I have learned and what I witnessed yesterday, trying to understand what the Light would have me do."

Hahl was taken aback. He clearly expected a more flippant reply.

"Have you reached any conclusions, Promised One?"

"Yes, I have. It seems to me that the worship of the Light has become dangerously polluted."

Hahl's eyes swirled, but I plowed recklessly ahead.

"It's time to begin the purification of the Light, by purifying its worship of all ceremonies that contain darkness."

Hahl's yellow eyes blazed. Anger came off him in waves.

"What do you know of the ceremonies, Promised One, or of the darkness? You are an ignorant child."

"You're right," I said. "I want to see all of the ceremonies so I can know what needs to be purified."

Hahl stared at me in enraged silence. "If that is your wish, Promised One. You will begin tomorrow."

He didn't bother to dismiss me. He turned his back on me as if I wasn't there. The emotions emanating from him were different today. The old sense of resignation was gone. He seemed more crafty. I would have to watch my back.

"I don't like any of this, Kell," Alana said after I told her that evening about Lowthelian and my meeting with Hahl. We sat close together in the little building on the hillside.

"What do you know about Lowthelian?" I asked.

"Not much," she said. "I don't even know when she came. She has been here as long as I can remember. She assists in the ceremonies, and she relays messages between the temple and the palace."

"Is she a servant for the priests then?"

Alana cocked her head to the side. "I don't think so. She seems to be more of an assistant."

"How did her eyes get to be like the priests?"

"I don't know. Maybe she was sent as a Chosen One and was given a different role to play."

"Does she ever go out in the city or do anything?"

Alana thought for a moment. "Not that I've heard, but I think Hahl can communicate with her wherever she is. I've seen her talking and then suddenly stop and hurry away. I've always thought Hahl was calling her."

"So, she could have been talking to Hahl when I found her?"

"Who else could it be? She's a servant of the Light."

"Yeah," I said. "It's like them to cause pain to anyone who disappoints them, isn't it?"

Alana clasped her hands together. "They can do terrible things," she said. "I've seen it."

"Like what?"

Her eyes grew wide. "I won't speak of it."

"Okay. Then tell me what other big ceremonies are coming. Do they plan to sacrifice someone at every solstice and equinox? I need to know how much time we have."

Alana shook her head. "No. The two largest celebrations are the solstices. The Gift of Illurien may come at either solstice. I've seen it at both. Years usually pass between these gifts." She hesitated. "I think you drained their power when you passed the tests."

"I think so too. What else?"

"Well, the two solstice celebrations are the most important, but the New Year celebration is also significant."

"So, what happens?"

"It begins at the winter solstice with a sacrifice to renew the Light."

"Wait a minute," I interrupted. "Even if they sacrifice at the summer solstice, they'll do it again at the winter solstice?"

Alana flattened a crease in her robe. "It's not the same thing. This sacrifice is to renew the Light and to push back the darkness of the Time of Sorrowing. The priests don't use it to strengthen themselves."

"I bet," I said. "Is this sacrifice done the same way?"

"No." Alana shook her head and lowered her eyes. "A Roinan is again chosen and locked up in one of the tombs until he dies as an offering to the Light. No parades. No procession."

"I can't believe this," I said. "You mean every year they kill someone as an offering to the Light?"

Alana pushed her hair behind her ear. "This is only the beginning of the New Year ceremony. All the people come to the Palace of Light. On the last day of the year, my father, the King, wages ritual combat with She-Who-Would-Not-Sing. He's always defeated at first, but he finally prevails. Then he descends into the tombs to show he can overcome death."

She glanced at me to make sure I was following, and I gestured for her to continue.

"He must endure utter darkness and silence for three days. This is symbolic of a world without light. A female queen then sits upon his thrown for three days, and no one leaves their homes for fear of her punishment. They eat and drink only what is needed. Then the King emerges triumphant, and the priests sing the Hymn of Illurien. There's much feasting and celebration. The priests cause a brilliant light to shine all night from the tower of the sun to show that the Light will eventually prevail."

I grunted. "Might be interesting, if they left out the human sacrifice."

"It's a huge festival. The people always enjoy it. The King gives them food and wine to help them celebrate."

"So, it's like the Roman bread and circus trick," I said. "Distract the people with fun, games, and food so they won't think about how the system is stacked against them. I don't suppose you have gladiators and gladiatorial rings, do you?"

Alana scowled. "I don't know what you mean."

"Uh, big arenas where people fight and kill each other for the pleasure of the crowd."

Alana glowered at me. "Why would we do such a thing?"

"Sorry, just checking. Then it isn't as bad as it could be."

Alana studied me until she saw that I had run out of questions. "Are you done quizzing me?" she asked.

"Sorry," I said.

She handed me a folded piece of paper.

"I had the note translated," she said.

"Already?"

"I have him wrapped around my little finger," she said with a mischievous grin.

I snatched the paper, unfolded it, and read it out loud.

> My beloved husband,
> I have taken the children through the chamber to the place
> we discussed. Come to me quickly.
> Your loving wife. Mihela.

I read it twice more, and then I gaped at Alana. "What does it mean?"

She bit her lip and frowned. "I don't know, but I have to go, Kell."

I liked the way she used my name instead of calling me Promised One.

"Thank you," I said. I didn't dare try to kiss her again.

That night the dreams came again. Ross crouched in a dim corner of a square room. He was a thin-faced handsome young man with a shaved head. His attention focused on his hands. Light skipped across his fingers. It was a pure white light, but it flickered the way a flame might lick and writhe along a log in a fire. It flashed and disappeared, though it still tingled on his fingertips. The Light had become momentarily invisible. Then it flickered back to pure white flame. Why did it do that? The words of the poem came back to Ross. *Light unseen descends from the skies.* This was the secret. It had to be. Ross would ask Ufel.

The image wavered, and Ross sat across the flame from Ufel and held out his hands. Ufel was an old man with a deeply wrinkled face and eyes that were turning orange. He recoiled at the sight of the light sparking sometimes white, sometimes invisible. He jumped to his feet and paced.

"Chosen One," he said. "I have never seen such a thing. I can feel the power, but I cannot see it." He placed a bony hand on his wrinkled chin, and his orange eyes flashed. "I wonder," he said. "I wonder."

As I drifted toward wakefulness, I became aware of a presence in my room. It hovered over me, probing, testing, seeking an entrance. The malevolence turned my blood cold, and I snapped my eyes open in terror to find the evil lights churning above my face, darting in and then drifting back to the churning mass.

I scrambled off the bed with a shout of surprise and grabbed for the stone in my pocket. The golden light flared, and the lights swirled and drifted away, passing directly through the wall. My heart pounded, and my breathing came fast. They had been trying to get inside my head, in my own room.

Then a rhythmic clicking sounded. I jumped to the door, flung it open, and raced into the hallway. No one was there, but I was sure I had heard the click of running skeletal feet. Returning to my room, I flopped into the chair at the table to think. Had I gone too far? Were the priests going to try to kill me?

A cold sweat covered my body, and I remembered the dream. Ross had been forcing his memories into me while I slept. He had wielded a mixture of white and Invisible Light. But how? Ufel had known about it, but this had obviously happened before he became a skeleton, though he had been very old. I determined to ask him about it today during my lesson. I couldn't understand how a Chosen One could have two different qualities of the Light. Nothing I had learned would permit it, but I was going to be doubly on my guard now. One of the Keepers had sent those lights into my room.

Llaith greeted me that morning with his usual air of disdain and hatred. So, I was surprised when he handed me a cup filled with a red liquid and told me to drink it. I took the cup and peered into it. It was filled with blood, I could smell the metallic odor.

I stared up at Llaith.

"You're joking," I said.

"If you would learn the ceremonies, you must participate," Llaith said. I could sense his anticipation.

"I don't think so," I said. There was no way I was drinking blood of any kind—and certainly not blood Llaith offered me. I wondered

194

if he might not be the one that sent the lights into my room.

He snatched the cup from me and poured the blood over a translucent crystal skull. Then he dipped the cup into a nearby basin and kept pouring, rubbing the blood into the skull with his boney fingers until it turned black.

"What's the point of this?" I asked.

Llaith jerked his head toward me so violently I thought it might fly off. His creepy black hair flew about his skeletal face. The hatred flowing from him was so overwhelming it made me feel sick.

"Do not question me," Llaith said in a cold, harsh voice. "I will not tolerate your interference. How dare you question those who have dedicated eons to the study of the Light?"

Llaith paused, gathering himself, and then surged to his feet, waving his pale hand threateningly. Droplets of blood sprayed everywhere. "Get out of my presence," he roared. "Do not come to me again. I have nothing to teach you. Get out."

Llaith's power lashed out at me, and my own power flared. I came to my feet. I was done being scared of him.

"You're right," I said, and I spun on my heels, striding purposely from the room. Llaith's anger boiled after me. I half-expected him to attack me, but he let me leave.

What was in that cup besides blood? Had he tried to poison me? Or was he just asking me to do things he knew I would find repulsive to annoy me?

Durr treated me to a similar reception, but he, at least, managed to control himself. Durr's morning ceremonies consisted of bathing in the waters of his lake and polishing the surface of the Mirror of Light while singing a quiet and beautiful song. His mellow, watery voice flowed in and around the words. Since Durr didn't invite me to participate, I just watched and listened. Where Llaith's ceremonies had been dark and threatening, Durr's song reminded me of quiet lakes nestled among wooded hills and gently flowing streams bubbling and skipping over little smooth stones.

When he finished polishing the Mirror of Light, he focused on me.

"Will you look, Promised One?"

"What?"

"Will you look into the Mirror of Light?" Durr's voice did not betray what his emotions did, but he was anxious and irritated, daring me to do it again.

"No, thanks," I said as I rose to my feet.

"Promised One?" Durr said. I stopped and stared at him. "Remember what you saw in the Mirror," he said. "She-Who-Would-Not-Sing desires the power you wield. You must guard against her influence. She would seek to deceive you. Beware, Promised One. Beware. There may even be those inside the temple who might seek to lead you astray."

I scowled. "Who might that be?" I asked. Did he mean Ufel? Seren? Durr refused to answer, but I hadn't missed the veiled threat in his words.

As I left Durr's chamber, the temple tugged at me again. The impression did not possess the pain I experienced in Llaith's chamber, but the urgency of it pulsed through me. The temple wanted to show me something again.

Since I had time before my next meeting with Einediau, I followed its directions down into the tunnels. Things had grown considerably more dangerous in only two days, and I needed all the help I could get. My curiosity about the people who had written the note and hidden it with the stone had been piqued. Would the temple show me something to help me understand the stone, and who made it and tried to hide it? I pulled the golden stone from my pocket. Its deep yellow light shone off the walls and warmed my hand. Who was the family mentioned in the note? Did the man ever find the woman and children? Why would she leave without him, and where had she taken their children?

The temple led me back to the room where I had found the golden stone. Nothing had changed in my absence. It still lay in shambles. I stepped over the broken furniture to the wall and pushed and tapped on every stone I could reach, examining every corner before I turned my attention to the broken furniture. Rummaging in every cupboard or pile of ruin yielded nothing. I hefted the shattered table to push it aside when I saw the body. I gasped and jumped back, letting the table fall with a bang.

Steeling myself, I lifted the table and set it aside. A crumpled, moldering body lay facedown with one arm outstretched and the other concealed beneath it. A terrible gash sliced through the back of the skull as though the person had been hit with something sharp and heavy. Dust floated up to tickle my nose.

Dried and shriveled flesh still clung to the bones. My stomach rolled over, and bile rose to my mouth. Before coming to the temple, my mother was the only dead person I had seen. Now, bodies popped up everywhere I went in the temple.

This man or woman had died a violent death, and they appeared to be reaching for the wardrobe a few feet away when they died. I tried to swallow the bile and reached a trembling hand to turn the body over. The first touch made me gag. I gave it a shove and jumped back at the eruption of dust. The bones rattled, but the shrunken tendons and flesh held it together. I covered my mouth and nose with my robe, waiting for the dust to settle.

A bright crystal object glinted where it lay clutched in the newly exposed hand. I bent close to peer at it, despite my revulsion at its bearer. It was a beautiful clear stone with delicate silver writing. A spider web pattern had been etched into its surface, and, at the stones center, a geometric shape with a full circle in the middle and a half-circle on either side pulsed a silver light. The stone seemed alive. I reached over to touch it. As soon as my finger made contact, it burst into a brilliant silver light. The bones of the hand fell apart as I lifted the stone free.

I withdrew the golden stone from my pocket and held one in each hand. They both glowed and then pulsed together like each had a tiny heart that beat to the rhythm of my own. The beauty and peace emanating from the stones astonished me. Goosebumps stood out all over my body. The stones emitted a pure, undefiled Light. They knew one another—like they were meant to be together. And even more startling, they knew me.

I glanced down at the body of the person who had held the stone and realized that a tiny scrap of paper had fallen to the floor when I picked up the stone. I grabbed it up and unfolded it. To my surprise, I could read it. It wasn't like the other writing at all.

"Fourth chamber from the Navel. Three left, five right, one left, two right." Then it had a symbol—an eye set in the palm of a hand.

Chapter Nineteen
The Coming Night

MY MEETING WITH Einediau was mercifully short. He showed me how he raked sand in a square room with golden walls. I couldn't see any point to the ceremony, but what disturbed me was the black sickness. Where it had been deep down in the roots of his garden before, it was now coating the branches and smearing the leaves of his plants. It was like the temple was rotting from the inside out.

I had to know what was going on. Since the Navel was the center and the Light was strongest there, I figured that was the best place to communicate with the temple. Besides, that was the only place the temple had actually written real words to me. So, I rushed to the Navel, not caring if I was late for my meeting with Ufel.

I burst through the door and placed both hands on the altar.

"Tell me what to do," I said.

Writing appeared no the stone of the altar one word at a time in golden letters.

"Dying. Help. Us. Sun. And. Moon. Unite."

"That's not helpful," I said. "Can't you write a complete sentence?"

"Dying," it wrote again.

"You mean you're dying?" I asked.

"Yes."

Ross surged into my mind in sudden terror like he had never

quite figured out the temple was in trouble.

"How do I stop it?" I asked.

"Sun. And. Moon. Unite," it wrote.

I blew out my air in disgust. "Can't you do anything but write in riddles?"

"Please," it wrote. "Before. Too. Late."

I snatched my hands away and spun to leave. This was ridiculous. I was talking to a building again, expecting it to communicate like a human.

"You've gone totally insane," I told myself. Maybe, if I was lucky, I would wake up and find out this had been one long nightmare.

"Where are they?" the man demanded. Ragged clothing hung from his gaunt frame, and he clutched a huge cudgel in his scarred hand. His shoulders hunched over as if wearied by heavy labor, but they were broad, and his neck was as thick as my leg. He scowled at me.

"Where are they?" he demanded again.

I had been on my way to Ufel's chambers when I stumbled upon him. His appearance gave me pause because I had never seen anyone besides the servants of the Light in the temple, and this man did not belong.

"Who?" I asked.

The man's gaze passed over me from head to toe. In the ensuing silence, the scratching clicks of skeletal feet on stone echoed amid the buildings. The man jerked his head toward the sound and scurried off in a lumbering jog. I stared at his retreating back in startled silence for a moment before I tore after him. If he met up with one of the priests, they wouldn't play nice. Maybe I could escort him out of here before they found him.

As I reached the corner of a square building, a roar filled the air. "My son," the man screamed.

I came around the corner in time to see a column of water slam into the man. He flew through the air to bounce off the cobblestones.

Durr sent a burst of blue light to stab into the man's chest. Then he stalked up to where the man lay crumpled on the wet cobblestones with his legs and arms twisted at unnatural angles. The man's chest smoked, and he coughed. His cudgel hadn't been much use against a Keeper of the Light.

Sprinting the last few steps, I knelt beside the groaning man. He grabbed my hand in a vice-like grip. The blood pooled under his head.

"They murdered him," the man whispered. "Someday, the Light will destroy this evil."

I glanced up at Durr. "What did you do to him?" I demanded.

He waved a dismissive hand at the man. "The guards will clean up this zealot," he said and strode away.

"Guards? What guards?" I said. I hadn't seen anyone like that in the temple.

The man stared at me with large, dark eyes.

"Let me help you," I said. I rolled him on his side and saw that his scalp had split open, but I didn't think he would die. I tore a piece off his ragged shirt and held it against the wound. I glanced at his leg. It bent at an unnatural angle.

I placed my hands on his arm and closed my eyes to see if I could heal him when the slap of running feet and the jangle of metal approached. I glanced around in surprise. Where had they come from?

The man struggled to sit up. "You're not like them," he said.

I shook my head.

The guards grabbed him by his armpits and dragged him away.

"Wait," I said, but they ignored me.

The man craned his head around to stare at me. "Light will prevail," he called.

I knew something was wrong the moment I stepped into Ufel's chamber. The little dancing flame that usually burned in the center of his room wasn't there. The Eternal Flame still danced on its altar, but Ufel crouched in a far corner, looking like a pile of discarded robes with the odd bone bulging out. Light streamed in through windows I hadn't seen before. His chamber had always been so dark. Was he dead?

"I can't see you today," Ufel said. "Come again tomorrow." His voice was strained, and the emotions emanating from him were of intense pain and sadness.

"Are you okay?" I asked. I considered saying I would call a doctor, but that wouldn't do any good. A skeleton had no flesh or organs for a doctor to treat.

"You cannot help me," Ufel said. "Come again tomorrow."

What could I do? I stared helplessly at him for a few moments before working my way back to Hahl's tower. The sun stood directly overhead. Its light shimmered off the polished stone, making the passages between the buildings feel like an oven. I experienced a terrible sense that something was escalating, swelling like the pressure in a hot soda can, and I was supposed to relieve it.

When I entered Hahl's room, he rose from where he knelt in apparent meditation and motioned to me with his long white fingers. I followed him into a side chamber where candles flickered in golden sconces. On a large, polished bookstand sat a tremendous volume that must have contained at least 2,000 pages. Hahl opened the book and flipped through the last several hundred pages before he pointed to a chart with dates on the bottom and hours of light on the left side.

The graph showed that the hours of the day had been diminishing for the last several decades, at least. Hahl flipped the page again and showed me another chart of the year 10,848. Each month was labeled, and the days had been getting shorter even more rapidly.

I stared at Hahl in wonder. "Is 10,848 this year?"

"Yes."

"You've calculated all of this?"

Hahl's yellow eyes swirled in pleasure. "Much of it," he said with obvious pride.

"Your graphs show that the daylight hours diminished just this year by two hours. How long were the days when you started?"

Satisfaction radiated from Hahl at my interest.

"When I began my service to the Light, the darkness only held for about six hours per day year-round. Now, it lasts more than double that, and it is even shorter during the Time of Sorrowing."

"So, this is why you think the power of She-Who-Would-Not-Sing is growing?"

"It is only a matter of time," Hahl said, "before crops will no longer grow. Already people have been driven from the north country by the frost."

I remembered my vision of the cornfield in the Mirror of Light.

"Why do you think this is She-Who-Would-Not-Sing? Aren't these kinds of changes normal?"

"Because I *feel* her power growing, Promised One."

I scowled at him. "How do you know she even exists?"

Hahl's eyes churned. "You ask me this after she appeared to you in the Mirror of Light? After she tried to lure you into her power?"

"I...I..." What could I say? Durr had hinted she might try to corrupt me. "You think I would give up the Light to join the dark?" I asked.

"It has happened before, Promised One."

I narrowed my eyes. "You feel it in the temple, don't you?" I said.

Hahl spun away.

"Why can't you admit it?" I demanded. "You saw the nasty black crack. What have you all done?"

"Get out," Hahl said with restrained calm. Anger, frustration, and shame surged from him.

"Please," I said.

"Just get out."

"If you won't help me, who can I trust?" I asked.

Hahl whirled and left me standing beside his book. All along, I had thought they were being paranoid, but his records showed a significant decrease in the daylight hours. I pondered on what this might mean as I made my way to Dairen's chambers.

His ceremony consisted of scratching quotes about the Light into his big black rock. He wrote, "Matter without Light is inert and powerless. Light without matter cannot take form. Sun and moon are one in thine hands. We, the children of Illurien, each possess a spark divine."

Then he circled the stone three times in each direction and washed his hands in a basin before coming over to sit beside me.

"What is the significance of three?" I asked before he could speak. The priests often did things in threes, and I wondered why.

"The sun, moon, and stars represent the three sources of cosmic light," he said. "The power of the Light requires the union of the soul, the mind, and the heart. No one can use it fully until the three are one."

"How can the sun and the moon become one?" I asked in sudden interest.

"It is symbolic," he said.

I wasn't so sure. The temple didn't seem to think so.

"What is happening out there?" I asked Alana that evening as we talked in the little building. It was so dark I couldn't see her face, so I called up a flame like Ufel used in his corridor and let it dance in the air. Alana stared at it.

"Sorry," I said. "Do you want me to put it out?"

"No," she said. But she couldn't take her eyes off it. The flame cast a warm, yellow light over the painted walls. Images of soldiers and priests wielding beams of light surrounded us. The dark wooden benches glinted in the light. The little building smelled of old charcoal and incense.

"So, what's going on?" I asked again.

"What do you mean?" she said.

"A man tried to club Durr today," I said, "and Hahl says people are fleeing starvation in the north. Did you know he has records that go back hundreds of years, showing that the daylight hours are growing shorter?"

Alana smirked at me from where she sat on the bench with her hands folded in her lap. "Why do you think we struggle to worship the Light as faithfully as we can?" she said. "My father is facing rebellions all over the kingdom. The crops in the west failed last year from a blight, and this year the cold came early in the north. People are starving and dying every day."

"I'm supposed to stop all this?" I asked.

She nodded. A lock of hair fell before her face, and I suppressed the sudden urge to grab her hand. I wanted to feel her smooth skin and smell the delicate fragrance of flowers, but she was a king's daughter.

"How?" I said. "What can I do? It sounds like your world is experiencing climate change or something. There's nothing I can do about that."

"Yes, you can," Alana said. "You are the Promised One."

"Alana," I said, "I'm a sixteen-year-old kid."

Alana moved to sit beside me. "I felt the same," she said, "when I was dedicated to the service of the Light at the age of seven. I've done my best, and now I also manage the service of the Roinan. The truth is that you don't know what you can do."

I glanced at my hands.

"At least you have some native talent," I said. "You can sing like no one I've ever heard."

Alana beamed. "I live in a song," she said. "Music fills my mind and my soul. I sing for my father's court and at many of the ceremonies. It is the aspect of serving the Light I most enjoy."

"Your voice must be a gift from Illurien," I said, "so the worship of the Light can be beautiful."

Alana bowed her head, but I could tell my compliment pleased her.

"Can I ask you a weird question?" I asked.

"Sure."

"Has the temple ever…" I paused, knowing how crazy this would sound. "Has the temple ever spoken to you?"

Alana gaped at me in surprise and shook her head.

"I know it sounds insane, but sometimes it sends me feelings and plays music in my head. It even wrote a message to me on the altar in the Navel of the earth."

"You've been there alone?" Alana's eyes widened.

"Yeah," I said, wondering why she seemed so surprised.

"No one is allowed there except during the high ceremonies."

"Well, the temple took me there," I said. "And it showed me the burned-out library."

Alana stared in apparent confusion. "There is no library in the temple," she said.

"Not anymore," I said. "Someone burned it along with all the books"

Alana shook her head. "No one would do such a thing."

"Well, someone did," I said. "Look, something is wrong with the temple. It's sick or something. It keeps warning me that something is going to happen. It's like pressure is building. It knows that it's in danger. It's afraid."

"It's a building," Alana said in disbelief.

I lowered my head into my hands. "I know it's a building," I moaned. "And I know it shouldn't be able to talk to me, but there are a lot of things happening here that shouldn't be able to happen."

We sat in silence for a long while.

"Do you know what the phrase 'sun and moon are one in thine hands' means?"

"No."

"Dairen wrote it today on his big black rock, and I keep seeing references to the sun and moon all over the temple. What does it mean?"

"They are the two great lights in the heavens," Alana said. "One is male, and the other is female, maybe that's what it means."

I studied her. She was so beautiful. I wanted to touch her. I hadn't had any real human contact in weeks.

"As a servant of the Light, are you permitted to marry?" I asked. I hadn't meant to say it out loud.

Alana glanced up with a guarded expression." No," she said. "The priests could marry if they wanted to, but they stopped doing so many hundreds of years ago. I only know about it because Ufel told me once that if he were young again, he would ask my father for my hand."

I chuckled. It was such a grotesque idea.

Alana shivered and scowled at me. "I didn't think it was funny."

"Sorry," I said. Trying to deflect attention away from my stupidity, I added, "tell me about yourself."

She smiled. "What do you want to know?"

"How old are you? What do you like to eat? What's it like living in a palace? You know—everything."

Alana laughed. "I'll be seventeen in a few months. I like pork fried in butter and honey, and the palace can be very suffocating."

"Suffocating? Why?"

"Because everyone expects me to be perfect. I don't have much time to myself except for coming to sing at the temple. At times, my father can be overbearing."

"I never knew my father," I said.

Alana frowned. "I'm sorry," she said.

"My mom thought I might find him here."

Alana cocked her head to one side and studied me. I fiddled with the hem of my robe.

"How could that be?" Alana asked.

"I don't know," I said.

"What's his name?"

"I don't know that either. Mom never told me."

In some ways, Alana reminded me of my mother. She was beautiful and confident, but also possessed an air of sadness. As I strolled up the hill toward the temple after our meeting, I remembered one of the times I'd found Mom crying. I thought she liked the guy who brought her flowers. It was Mateo, the cook at the diner where she waited tables. He came by now and again, but that night he brought Mom a dozen red roses.

Even as a ten-year-old, I understood this was serious. I had seen the way he watched her. He liked her a lot, and I knew why. Mom was young and attractive with dark brown hair and sad, brown eyes.

Mom shooed me away when he knocked on the door, and I curled up against my bedroom door with my arms wrapped around my knees, trying to listen to what they said. I heard the words "love" and "respect" and "kindness" and "think of the boy" before he said, "I'm sorry to have bothered you." The door closed, and the silence only ended with the sound of my mother sobbing.

I was afraid he had hurt her or something. He was a big, handsome man, and my mother was tiny and fragile. I slipped out the door and tiptoed up the hallway, trembling with fear. What would I do if he had hurt her? I was just a kid.

Mom hunched over in the rocking chair with her back to me. A bouquet of bright red roses dangled in her hand, and her shoulders shook. I wanted to wrap my arms around her and tell her it would be okay. That's what she did for me when I needed her, but her stuttered whispers held me back.

Mom had always been a mystery to me. At the time, we lived alone in a two-bedroom dump on the edge of town. It was all we could afford. My mother didn't have a picture of my father in the house. We didn't have pictures of anyone but me. It didn't make any sense—like we had been dropped out of thin air into a world Mom desperately tried to pretend wasn't there. Why?

"He will come for me," she sobbed. "He *will* come for me."

My heart seemed to stop beating. The ache rose into my throat. Who would come for her? The cook? I didn't think so. She must have meant my deadbeat dad, who had left us penniless and alone.

"I want you to be like him someday," Mom would say to me. How could I be like a man I knew nothing about? Did I want to be like him? Whenever I asked about him, she would say, "When the time is right."

If she thought this would make me excited and curious, it didn't work. Secrets don't make friends. They breed distrust. My father must have been a monster. Why else would she hide the truth from her own son? My childish imagination ran wild with all the things my father must have been—a mass murderer, a cult leader, a bank robber.

"He has to come," she sobbed again. "I can't do this alone."

That's when I understood what she was talking about. *I* was the problem. If she hadn't had me to worry about, she would have run off with the cook and lived happily ever after—or gone in search of my father on her own. I was a burden. It isn't that she ever said as much. When I didn't understand some of the strange things that she tried to explain to me, she would pucker her brow and frown. She was desperate to get me to understand, but I didn't share her crazy fascination with rainbows and prisms.

Even though I knew I disappointed her, I still loved her fiercely. She had been all I had in the entire world. That's why it hurt so much when she left me—when she died and left me alone without ever telling me who I was or who I was meant to be.

Maybe it didn't matter anymore.

"Is it possible there are different kinds of light?" I sat cross-legged on the cold stone in Seren's tower beneath the great vault of the star-dusted sky. He had shown me a diorama of the temple complex and taught me that it was a symbolic representation of the cosmos.

"Yes, Promised One," Seren said. "I believe there may be different kinds of light, but I don't know what they are."

I tried to choose my next words carefully because I didn't want him to realize that I knew he had seen that my Light was invisible.

"Is it possible that we cannot see all the different types of light?"

Seren gave a pensive nod. "I think it is possible. The Hymn of the Promised One speaks of unseen Light. You are venturing into fields that have not been adequately explored. No one knows all the ways of the Light. We had a Chosen One once who…well, never mind."

He shifted nervously and waved a hand at me. "I am afraid that I must ask you to go. I have other duties to attend to before dawn. Thank you for your questions."

His abrupt dismissal angered me. I jumped to my feet. "If the priests would be more helpful," I said, "I might be able to do some good here."

I spun on my heels and left. I had forgotten about the hymn. "Light unseen descends from the skies," it said.

Unseen Light meant Invisible Light. The priests had known from the beginning that the power of the Promised One would be invisible. Then why were they trying to hide this from me?

Now that I had finished observing their ceremonies for the day, I rushed down into the corridors, drawn by the lure of the two stones and the cryptic message I found with the silver one. I'd been putting it off all day, but I was going to follow the directions I found with the silver stone. The pale light that always illuminated the corridors directly under the temple lit my way.

Fourth chamber from the Navel. Three left, five right, one left, two right, and the symbol of the eye set in the palm of a hand.

When I reached the Navel, I stood in the doorway facing the corridor. Two small side passages led away from the main corridor—one angling to the left and the other to the right.

Well, there was only one way to figure out what this meant. I would have to check all of them. An hour of searching turned up nothing. I had given up when the temple surged into my mind, nudging me back down the passage I had just explored. The word "chamber" came into my mind, and I slapped myself upside the head. "Chamber," I said out loud. "Not passage."

I strode back down the narrow passage on the right where I had seen several doors. This time, I counted them and pushed open the fourth door. It screeched on its hinges, and I found myself in a tiny room with several doors leading off in different directions. I yanked open each door only to find they all opened onto narrow passages.

"Three left" had been the next clue. Three what, doors? I circled the room, inspecting each door carefully. There had to be some clue, but I could find nothing. Leaning against the wall, I slid to the floor in disgust.

I had decided to abandon my search when I saw what I was looking for. Just under the latch of one of the doors was a small hand. I couldn't see it from a standing position because the latch on the door had concealed it in shadow.

Scrambling on hands and knees, I knelt before the door. The small hand with an open eye in the palm had been etched just beneath the latch. It was the same symbol the temple had shown me in that giant painting. I yanked the door open, rushed down the corridor to the third door on the left, and shoved through it to find a similar room, only larger. Circling the room, I found the sign of the hand scratched on the bottom of one of the doors near the floor.

This continued until I entered the last room and found it bare. No doors. No furniture. The ceiling sagged so low that I had to duck to keep from scraping my head. I cursed to myself. It had been a waste of time. I had been played by some trick left with a stone hundreds of years before.

I don't know what I expected, but an empty, useless room wasn't it. In frustration, I called up the power and demanded that it show me the way. The power surged upward and burst through the ceiling, sending a shower of broken rock down onto my head. A large piece struck me a glancing blow that sent me sprawling to the floor. I curled up into a ball, coughing and choking on the gritty air until the rain of debris subsided. The warm blood slid from my head to drop off my cheek. I crawled to my knees and called up a ball of light to help me see through the thick dust.

"Good grief," I said. I had ordered my power to show me the way, and it blew a hole in the ceiling. I ignored the blood trickling down my face and jumped into the hole. Hooking my elbows over the side, I dragged myself up. The chamber was square with a round altar of white stone in the center. The ceiling hung so low I couldn't stand in the chamber. Where the power blasted the hole, I could see the remains of a ladder. It looked like this chamber had been intentionally hidden, made difficult to access. I crawled over to the altar. The golden outline of the eye in the center of the hand had been carved into the top of it.

I touched the altar with my finger and probed it with the power. I snatched my hand away as another power pushed back. How was that possible? How could an altar have a power of its own? It wasn't like the power of the sundial or the Navel. It felt older, more pure, like the power coming from the gold and silver stones. This was another sacred chamber like the one I had come through—only much older.

I spread my hands on the altar and reached out to it tentatively so as not to provoke a reaction. The power in the altar pushed back, repelling my attempts to communicate with it. I couldn't get in. The power of the altar held me at bay. I wiped my dirty hands on my robe and pulled the stones from my pocket.

They both glowed. I set them on the altar to see what would happen. They kept glowing, even after I no longer touched them, and began pulsing. The power of the altar responded. It glowed a dull white like a fire had been kindled inside it. The altar and the stones throbbed in unison like a beating heart. A bright white light throbbed from somewhere deep within the white stone altar.

I crawled away from the altar to wait and see what would happen, huddling in the dusty chamber, wondering what this could mean.

"I should ask Ufel," I said.

Ross let me know that he disliked the idea, but why? He had been right about Roy. Maybe he was right about Ufel. I shook my head so I could concentrate when a loud click sounded. Stone grated against stone, and a small drawer popped out at the base of the altar. I bent to peer inside. On a scarlet piece of cloth lay a book similar to the one I found in the room with the furniture tossed about. I hesitated to pick it up, but I couldn't control my curiosity. The book was warm and smooth—it was alive with power. The plain cover had no markings other than a small golden symbol of the eye in the hand on the front cover.

I lifted the cover. The same beautiful script inscribed on the stones filled every page, but this script was written in gold. I couldn't read it like I could the writing on the wall of the chamber that brought me here and on the walls in the Navel of the Earth. It was infuriating.

A single piece of paper slipped from the pages. I unfolded it and found I could read the following lines.

"My dearest, why have you delayed? They are coming for us. I cannot wait any longer. Come to me."

All I could think of were my mother's words that night, the handsome cook, Mateo, had proposed to her. "He will come for me." But he hadn't. No one had come.

I thumbed through the pages of the book. Someone had made marginal notations here and there. Some of them I could read. I stopped on a long note scribbled sideways in the margin.

"This passage refers to the Cosmic Stones, also known as the Eyes of Illurien," it said. "They have been lost to all but the caretakers who have a sacred duty to protect them until the time when they shall be needed. Since the stones can only work for the One they have chosen, they are of no value to anyone who seeks them for power or profit."

I glanced at the two stones pulsing side by side on the top of the altar. Were these the Cosmic Stones? Had the temple shown me the stones because I needed them to save it?

I slipped the stones and the book into my pocket. I would keep them with me at all times. No one was going to burn *this* book.

"I will not teach you my ceremonies, Promised One." Ufel's orange eyes danced like the flame between us.

I had waited for Alana at the sundial that morning. When she didn't come, I came straight to Ufel's chamber. I hadn't bothered going to meet with Llaith, and I was concerned about Ufel after the way I found him yesterday.

"Why won't you teach me?" I asked.

"Because that is not why you are here, as I think you are beginning to see." He pointed toward my hands with one bony finger.

I had guessed right. The priests had seen and understood my power.

"What can you tell me about Light that cannot be seen?" I asked.

"I thought so," Ufel said. "One other time have I been asked this question. It came from a Chosen One, much like yourself. He was very intelligent and very powerful for a Chosen One. I thought he might be the Promised One, but I was wrong. Yet, he came nearer to passing the tests than any other. Then he fell, and his Light could not continue."

Which meant they killed him. An image of Ross flashed into my mind, and I realized that Ufel was speaking of him. That would explain how Ross knew so much and why he forced himself upon me.

Ufel grunted. "Did you know that in our most ancient tongue, the name for the Promised One is Anweledion, which means *invisible*?"

I just shook my head. Obviously, I hadn't known that, but it now made perfect sense to me.

"Well, Promised One, I can only tell you what I have guessed about this unseen Light. We do not speak of it. The other priests would not like me to mention it to you. You must not tell them I have spoken to you about it."

"Of course," I said. I didn't mention Seren because I had already talked to him about it.

"I study the Light of the flame, Promised One. Do you notice that the flame causes things we cannot see?"

"Yes."

"Can you feel the effects of the flame without touching it?"

"Yes," I said again.

"Can you see what happens when the flame takes a sound piece of wood and reduces it to a pile of ash?"

"No."

"The others study aspects of the Light that are visible," Ufel continued. "I have spent years I cannot count searching out the reason for the invisible effects of the Light. Why is it that we cannot see the Light that animates all things? All matter is inert and helpless without this Light. We know this, but why do we not see it? There must be some other form of Light that permeates the universe and gives life. I do not know what to call it, but I have named it the Light of Illurien because I believe this Light is the true power. I believe this is the Light that Illurien used to create the universe and still uses to govern it."

Ufel leaned toward me and lowered his voice.

"We had another Chosen One once who gave me great insight into this question. He was a skilled craftsman with glass and crystal. He manufactured a tube he called a Light Glass that allowed him to see what he called particles of Light. I peered into his glass once before he fell, and I saw round golden particles. They were so small that the naked eye could not see them, but the Light Glass somehow magnified their size so they could be seen."

"You mean an electron microscope," I said. "What happened to the priest and the Light Glass? Why did he fall?"

Ufel sighed. "You must understand Promised One, that not all of the priests found his Light Glass as compelling as I did. Some even called it heretical."

"Heretical," I said. "Why?"

Ufel shook his head. "There are some mysteries that ought not be explored too deeply, even by the Chosen. To do so is to mock the power of Illurien. It is arrogant to think that we might understand all that she does or the means by which she does it. The Keepers informed him that he must destroy the glass. He refused. It was taken from him, and he fell."

"Couldn't they see he had proven that light which may be invisible to the human eye not only exists but can be seen if it is magnified?"

"That is how I saw it," Ufel said. "But my voice did not carry the day." He waved an impatient hand. "That isn't important now." Ufel shifted in his seat. "I have come to the conclusion that the light we see is a pale reflection of this much greater Light, which is beyond our capacity to see or even to fully comprehend. I believe that Illurien can see it and control it. We cannot." He paused and then scooted closer to me and whispered, "but you, Promised One, wield a portion of this Light. Do you not?"

In that moment, the pieces fell into place for me. That's why I couldn't see how Illurien had cast She-Who-Would-Not-Sing from the heavens in the great panel. Illurien's Light was invisible. Could I possess the same power?

"I think so," I said.

"As do I," Ufel said. "We are speaking of very sacred things, Promised One. I hope you understand this. You have been sent to use this Light of Illurien to bring back stability and balance. The feeble Light that we priests control cannot do it. I have long believed this, and I have been shunned for saying it. Only then can we cast off the darkness that grows around us."

"How do I do it?" I blurted. "I'm just a kid. I'm not smart enough." That was the one thing I knew for certain. I always sensed my mother's distress that I didn't love the Light the way she did. Now, Ufel sat there, telling me I had to do something impossible.

"I do not know for certain," Ufel said. "The other Chosen One who asked me this same question guessed, I think. That is why he fell. He tried to do what he did not have the power or the right to do."

I tried to recall the dreams Ross had sent me. Ross pushed into my mind the image of a young man in a white robe looming over a dead priest. I had seen the image often enough in my dreams. I realized what Ufel was suggesting. The priests had something to do with the growing darkness, and Ross had intended to kill them, one by one. That is what he had tried to do. It was the only way.

I stared at Ufel with a growing sense of dread. I couldn't do something like that. I had never killed anything bigger than a cockroach. The bottom dropped out of my stomach. I struggled to breathe. The power had tried to kill Lowthelian. I couldn't become a killer. I wouldn't.

Ufel read my expression. "I fear that it must be so," he said quietly. "So do the others. That is why they fear you and hate you so much."

I thought of Roy and how furious I had been that the priests had killed him. How could I do the very thing I hated them for? How could Ufel sit there with his churning orange eyes and tell me that I had to kill him?

"May I see your right arm, Promised One?" Ufel asked.

I hesitated, shocked and dismayed, but I raised my right arm and pulled back the sleeve. Ufel grasped my hand with his cold, bony fingers and turned it over. He stared at my birthmark—the pale white, six-petal rosette that sat just below the crease of my elbow.

Powerful emotions surged from Ross—disbelief, awe, consternation.

Ufel dropped my hand and clambered to his feet. He waved a hand for me to follow. I was still stunned by the implications of what Ufel said, but I followed him through a small door at the back of his chambers.

Ufel stopped before an altar where a candle cast a trembling yellow flame and touched the sun disk inset into the wall beside it. The sun disk flared bright orange. A portion of the wall slipped sideways without a sound. We stepped through into a small room with bookshelves filled with books.

"I thought the library had been destroyed," I said. "I've seen it."

Ufel shot me a surprised glance and turned to his books.

"There used to be a great library," he said, "filled with the knowledge of the ages—the study and thought of thousands of servants of the Light kept and revered for millennia. This is all that remains. These are forbidden books that I have kept secret for many centuries. Save for the books Hahl uses to record his observations, the rest have all been destroyed."

Not all of them, I thought.

"Why, Ufel?" I asked. "Why would the servants of the Light destroy such a valuable treasure?"

"Fear, Promised One," Ufel said. He reached out and touched the spine of a huge volume. "If you succeed in your task," he said, "there are things you will need to know. Much of it is here. Keep this place secret, Promised One. You must speak of it to *no one*." He emphasized the last words. I somehow knew that he also meant Lowthelian, but I wondered if Ufel knew about Alana and the archive at the palace.

Ufel retrieved a large leather-bound book from a shelf and set it on a low table. He flipped through the pages. "Here is a record of the Chosen. The Keepers of the Fire have always kept this record, and I have continued to do it."

"Here it is." He pointed a bony finger at an entry. I bent forward to read.

"Ross Celyn, born 10,039, Chosen in the year of Light 10,048 and Delwyn Rees, born 10,040, Chosen in the year of Light 10,046, married in the year of Light 10,060, child Kell Celyn born 10,061 marked with the sign of his father."

Beside the last statement had been drawn a six-petal, white rosette. I yanked up my sleeve to compare my birthmark with the image in the book. I stared at Ufel in confusion. Ross surged so forcefully into my mind that I couldn't concentrate. Raw emotions swept through me.

"Why is my mother's name in this book?" I stammered. "What are you saying?"

"I have wondered many times what became of Delwyn and her child," Ufel said. "Now, you have come back to us at the fading of the Light."

Horror, shock, and despair filled Ross with equal measure.

"My son. The boy is my son? How is it possible? Oh, Delwyn, what have I done? I sent you away to protect you. Now, you are dead, and our son has been dragged back to the temple where he was born. He has been delivered into the

power of the priests."

The raging tempest of emotions engulfed him.

"Why? Why did you send him back?"

Unknowingly, Ross had seized control of his own child in the chamber and forced him to receive the power of the Light. He had set him on a course from which there could be no return—a course that could end only in his death.

Chapter Twenty
Pollution

EMOTIONS FROM ROSS exploded into my mind. Pain. Loss. Grief. Shock. I grabbed my head at the sudden pressure behind my eyes, thinking my head might burst open, and sank to my knees. The anguish bursting from Ross drained the strength from my limbs and forced the tears from my eyes.

I was weeping harder than I had ever wept in my life—weeping for father and mother. Mom had never told me much about my dad—other than that he had been a scholar. She hadn't even had a photo of him. My mother spent my entire life longing for him to come for her, and I had hated him for it. I had imagined that he was some loser drug dealer or useless drunk.

All those years I had longed for a dad and believed that he had deserted us. All those years I had hated him—only to learn now that he hadn't come because he couldn't. He had died—murdered by the Keepers—locked in a chamber to perish alone.

Shame at my lack of faith in my father burned as hot as my misery. I was such a small-minded numbskull, and my mother had lived all those years knowing what he had remained behind to do and knowing he had probably died. How could she have lived with so much sorrow alone with a snotty boy who refused to understand?

"Father," I said, hoping Ross would hear me. "Mom said to tell you she was faithful to the end."

Pollution

Ross longed to hold his child—to comfort him. Delwyn had waited for him, and he had never come. And now she was dead, and he had forced his son to become the sacrificial lamb. The Keepers had wanted to murder his son all those years ago, and now Ross had delivered him into their power. The shame and horror were too much to bear.

When I managed to regain control from Ross, I dragged myself to my feet and clung to the wall for stability. Ufel's orange eyes blazed.

"I'm sorry," I said. I brushed at the tears, ashamed at my weakness. "Tell me about my parents?"

Ufel closed the book and led me back to his little chamber to sit beside the fire.

"I don't know where to begin, Promised One. The tale is long." He paused. "Many centuries ago, the Chosen could marry if they wished. The firstborn child was always dedicated to the service of the Light, and so was marked with the sign of the Chosen. If the Chosen was his father, as in your case, the child carried the father's mark. Always this mark was placed on the inside of the forearm just below the elbow."

"That was 800 years ago," I said. I had seen the date in Hahl's books.

"Yes," Ufel said.

"It's not possible."

"I have long believed," Ufel said, "that time and light are intertwined in ways we cannot know. Ross Celyn must have found a way to use one of the sacred chambers to send you and your mother to a different time as well as a different world and thus hide your whereabouts from any who might seek you."

Ufel must have seen my inner struggles because he reached over to lay a cold hand on my arm. I shivered at his touch.

"I'm sorry to tell you this Promised One, but it is time you understood."

I swallowed at the knot in my throat. Now was the time to tell Ufel the truth.

"Ufel," I said. "Ross's spirit survived."

"What?" Ufel said.

"My father's spirit survived and lives inside me."

"But—" Ufel began.

"Listen," I insisted, "he wrote something on the wall of the chamber that allowed him to possess me. That's why I didn't read the writing on the wall. He forced me to receive the power, and he's been trying to help me."

Ufel sat so still and silent I almost thought he had finally died. Then his mouth opened and shut. His teeth clicked. His eyes swirled orange fire.

"I…" he began. "I've never heard of such a thing. Are you sure?"

"Positive," I said.

"Well then," Ufel said. "I'm going to tell you something I've never told anyone. I sense the time is near at hand."

He paused and seemed to shrink. His whole being assumed such an aspect of dejection and despair that I felt sorry for him.

Ufel whispered. "*We* did it, Promise One."

"Did what?"

"We polluted the Light."

I didn't know what to say. I had guessed as much, but to hear him openly admit it left me speechless.

Ufel straightened, a new courage and determination entering his voice. "We turned from the path of Light. We allowed our desire to live and continue serving the Light to lead us to feed on the Light of others. We said we would transcend the ancient worship of the Light with a new, more powerful form of devotion that would allow the Keepers of the Light to continue."

He paused.

"It is a dark and evil deed to steal the Light from another soul.

In fact, I think it is unforgivable. We shall pay, Promised One. We shall pay dearly when we stand before Illurien to make an accounting of our stewardship. Oh, yes, we shall pay."

He said these words with deep conviction.

"The Chosen became divided over petty theological issues. The Keepers sought to elevate themselves to the center of worship and to act as mediators for the rest because we believed the people were too ignorant and weak to worship on their own. We called ourselves *Transcendents* in an arrogant declaration that we would transcend the original and, what we called, outdated worship of the Light. The rest remained true to the original teachings and called themselves *Mystics of the Light* because they believed that we should approach Illurien through service and self-sacrifice."

Ufel shifted nervously, and his eyes churned with intense emotion.

"Some of the Keepers searched too deeply for things that we could not understand, and we lost control of our power. In our fear and greed, we followed someone who wanted to exploit us to gain power over us and over the people of our world. Once we sinned against the will of Illurien, she rejected us. She withdrew her mantel of protection and direction, and we lost what knowledge we possessed until we have descended into this cycle of ritualized performances that none of us understand and which help no one."

Well, I had reached the same conclusion after observing their rituals.

"Now, look at me, Promised One." He held out his skeletal hands. "Look at what I am. I'm a monster. I'm a creature of death and destruction when I ought to have been a giver of life and Light."

He wrung his hands together with an awful scraping and clicking.

"Oh, we justified our evil by saying we did it to increase our strength in defense of the Light and to keep the knowledge and power which we had acquired intact instead of recreating it with each new generation.

"Our pride and foolishness have had the opposite effect. The new Chosen Ones brought renewed life and Light that restored our power for a time, but always we needed more. We became parasites, preying upon the Chosen Ones that Illurien sent to serve the Light. Each time we fed on the Light, we diminished. We needed to feed more frequently. We lost our focus and spent our days creating objects of power and beauty instead of teaching and caring for the people of this world."

Ufel paused. His orange eyes swam.

"You see, Promised One. So long as we exist, the Light cannot be pure. *We* are the pollution that must be removed. This is what your father discovered. He was the first to suspect that we were the source of the contamination. Somehow, he sent you and your mother away to protect you. I came to believe that he had hidden you somewhere on this earth, but I underestimated his power. I do not know what he planned to do, but once you were gone, he attempted to purify the Light."

"You mean he tried to kill the priests?" I asked.

Ross's emotions were still swirling within me, and I struggled to concentrate. His despair and sorrow mixed with my own astonishment. I didn't want to believe any of it.

"Yes," Ufel said. "He was far more powerful than any one of us alone, but, together, we overcame him. He slew Arell, but we stopped him." Ufel paused and shifted nervously. "I'm afraid we ensured that he would die before we imprisoned him in the most sacred of our chambers. It is from this same chamber that you came to us."

The knot had risen in my throat again, and with it came all the anger, sadness, and desperation I had bottled up inside. My entire life, my father had been a mystery, a blank slate upon which I had scratched all of my frustration and hatred. Now, Ufel claimed that he was a hero. That he sent my mother and me away to keep us safe while he sacrificed his life to purify the Light. That he had died trying to save us from the Keepers—trying to stop them from murdering innocent children.

Ufel shook his head. A deep sadness emanated from him. "The others were so angry and so determined never to let such a thing happen again that they purged the temple of all the other Chosen and their families."

I remembered the vision I saw in the Mirror of Light of the temple with people scurrying everywhere amid great clouds of smoke. I thought of the burned library, the ruined rooms, and the piles of corpses. There were also the two stones in my pocket and the desperate letter I had found in the drawer beneath the altar. Someone else had found a way to escape the priests with some children.

"It was an awful scene that I will never forget," Ufel continued. "The Keepers preying upon the Chosen in a hideous act of butchery that still cries from the earth for vengeance and justice. Even while they attacked the Chosen, the Keepers emptied the great vault and burned the library. Tens of thousands of books that stored the knowledge of the ancients were tossed into the flames. I refused to join them in their purge. I managed to save some of the most valuable books, but I could do little else. The fire burned for two weeks, and a great, reeking cloud shrouded the temple all that time, leaving black soot on everything. Sometimes I think how ironic it is that we, the servants of the Light, should shroud our own temple in darkness."

Ufel stopped speaking and stared into space.

"I still don't understand why they destroyed the library," I asked.

"Because," Ufel said, "they feared that some new Chosen might discover the secrets your father had uncovered, and we would face another dangerous adversary. You must remember that we had already committed ourselves to a path of murder to extend our lives. Once a man has descended to such depths, it is not easy to climb out again."

"But Ufel, this all happened hundreds of years ago. How could I be the son of this Chosen One?

Ufel's great orange eyes churned. "As I said, I do not know how your father accomplished the task. He must have sent you to a world that exists far from this one, perhaps in a different time."

If Ufel was right, I had been born eight hundred years ago on this world, but only about sixteen in mine. Did time pass at different speeds on different worlds? Or was there some other explanation?

"You bear his mark and the invisible power that was, at least in part, his. There can be no doubt, Promised One. You are his son. You were born here in this temple. You have been sent back to finish what Ross began."

"My mother told me just before she died," I said, "that I was my father's son. This must be what she meant. That's why she took the day off. She knew I wouldn't be able to accept such a wild story."

Ufel stared at me for a few moments before nodding.

What would she have done if she had known my father had died alone in a dark cavern after altering the writings in the chamber so that some part of him would remain and inhabit the next Chosen to enter the sacred chamber that had become his tomb?

The incredible irony of the situation churned in my stomach, making me sick. What remained of my father had taken possession of a part of my soul. He lived inside of me. He had chosen to face a second death so that he could complete the task of purifying the Light. My mother had never known that he had failed.

She waited all those years for my father to return—to come get us and take us back. Now, I understood her strange fascination with light and why she pestered me to study it. She had always expected to come back here to the temple—to bring me back to the place where I was born. She had wanted me to find my father and tell him she had been faithful. Faithful to what? To him? To the Light?

She hadn't made it. Someone had killed her, too. *They are hunting us,"* she had said. *"Those who escaped."*

I stared at Ufel in horror.

"Did the priests kill my mother?" I asked.

Ross's grief made me reel again, but this time I was ready for it, and I wanted an answer.

Ufel didn't stir, but his eyes churned more fiercely. "Is she dead then?" he asked.

"She was murdered," I said.

Ufel's eyes churned. "I know nothing of this, Promised One. I don't think any of the Keepers know where Ross Celyn sent Delwyn and their child."

"Then who killed her?" I demanded. "She said she was being hunted. Someone blasted a black, oozing hole in her chest, just like the stuff I found in Einediau's garden."

"This is alarming news," Ufel said, his eyes churning with surprise and concern. "I don't know what to tell you. Many escaped the great cleansing, but I know of no one who pursues them. We have long lost the knowledge of how to use the chambers."

I couldn't speak. My own emotions mingled with the anger and desperate misery coming from Ross. I could barely breathe. Ufel watched me struggle for a moment and then continued speaking.

"The time has come Promised One," he said. "When you are

prepared, you must finish your father's work. You must purify the Light. Then new Chosen Ones will be sent. A new order will arise that will return to the pure worship of the Light without ambition and greed. The Chosen Ones will serve instead of being served. They will protect liberty and freedom—freedom without slavery. The people will flourish and prosper because they will respect the rights and freedoms of others. They will learn that to serve the Light means to serve one another. That is how it used to be, Promised One."

Ufel rose and paced back and forth in front of his flickering flame, his skeletal feet clicking quietly against the cold stone. "This is the long hoped for time of renewal," he said. "The time we have awaited and feared. I wish I could live to see it fulfilled."

He stopped and studied me with orange eyes that churned and boiled. I realized what he had just said and my blood ran cold. I didn't want to believe him Ross pressed again with dark desires for revenge. I tried to push them aside. Could I kill Ufel?

"Ufel, I—"

Ufel silenced me with a raised hand.

"It must be so, Promised One. It is all clear to me now. I have long seen it, though I would not accept it. I believe the others have all seen it, as well. But you must not act before it is time. I will help you if I can. I only ask this of you, Promised One."

He paused to make sure he had my attention.

"When my time comes, make it quick. And remember that I willingly set my life aside this time. I have lingered far too long upon this earth as it is. I no longer wish to remain." He paused again. "Not at the price that we must pay."

I stared into the dancing flame. I didn't think I could do it. My mother may have thought I was my father's son, but I was no killer. I yanked up my sleeve to stare at my birthmark—the one I shared with my father. It had become distinct now—a small, white, six-petaled rosette.

"What does it mean?" I asked Ufel.

Ufel gazed at me. "The rosette has always represented the rejuvenating power of the Light of Illurien. It is the divine Light of the universe. You are marked with her mark. Now, do what she has sent you here to do."

Ross listened with a mixture of dread and resignation. He couldn't turn back now, not after all that he had sacrificed. Delwyn had remained true to the Light and true to him. She could have kept Kell safe even though he had been dedicated to the service of the light when he was born. Ross would not fail her now.

He remembered the first time he met Delwyn. She had been up in a tree on the hill outside the temple in her white robe, hanging crystals from the branches.

"What are you doing?" Ross asked.

She glanced down at him and smiled an enchanting smile that warmed his heart. She was slender with delicate features and light brown skin. Ross had never seen a more lovely woman.

"Beautifying the temple," she said.

"You'll fall and break your neck."

"Not with you down there to catch me," she said.

They had grown close over the years as people whispered that she would be the logical choice to succeed Hahl when he passed away.

The memory left him with bitter longing. How had everything gone so wrong?

Chapter Twenty-One
Torment

AS I MADE MY way from Ufel's chamber, Ross's emotions quieted to a desperate sadness. A permanent knot lodged in my throat. I didn't want to believe anything Ufel had told me. I couldn't. I couldn't be Ross's son. I just couldn't. I was an orphaned kid from Ohio that had been dumped in a huge mess way over his head. I wasn't a killer. I could never *purify* the Light as they called it—not if it meant murdering people—even if they were skeletal priests. To talk of killing was one thing. To face the reality that I would be expected to do it—and soon—was quite another.

I found myself beside the small door where I met Alana before I realized I had been heading there. It was too early for her to come, so I slipped through the door and down the path to the little building. I curled up on the bench to wait for her. I needed to be alone, and yet, I didn't want to be.

In the cool shadow of the pavilion, amid the lingering smell of Alana's flower-scented perfume, I allowed myself to cry. I wanted to hate my father for abandoning us and my mother for never telling me the truth. But Ross, my father, stirred and sent me an emotion of serenity and peace. It filled me with warmth like a cup of hot chocolate on a cold winter's day. This was a different emotion than I usually felt from Ross. I guess it felt like love.

A portion of my father survived alone for eight hundred years, so he could be here to tell me that he loved me. How could I love a father I had never known? How could I *not* love a father who had sacrificed everything to keep me safe, to right a terrible wrong?

"Mother, why?" I whispered. "Why didn't you tell me?"

She tried to tell me at the end, but she had been murdered before she could. I wish I had known so I could have comforted her in her loneliness and grief.

That my mother had been a Chosen One explained everything. Her weird fascination with light. Her ability to do seemingly impossible things. Like the time I was very young and very sick, and she laid her hands on my head and sang a beautiful song. Her warmth filled my body, and I was healed.

With the memory came the realization that the reason the music I heard in the temple sounded familiar was because she sang those songs or hummed those tunes. When she did, her garden became more productive. We were healthier and happier. How had I missed all of this?

Ross and I sat alone in the gathering darkness. The experience of having another consciousness had always been disturbing, but now it was just awkward. I had so many things I wanted to ask this remnant of my father, but I didn't have any way to do it. He could only push images and emotions into me, not words. Talking to myself didn't seem like a good option. It would be too much like surrendering to insanity.

When darkness settled over the city, I stepped out onto the trail. Crickets chirped. The bushes rustled in the evening breeze, but nothing else stirred. Watchfires twinkled at the palace on the far hill. Lights glowed in windows all over the city. They had all gone on with their lives—already forgetting the dead little boy. They could ignore the priests again until the next celebration when another of their children would be chosen to serve the Light.

Alana hadn't stopped at our meeting place, but she hadn't known I would be there. Maybe she was waiting for me by the little door. I strode up the hill to the door, but Alana wasn't there either. A nagging doubt warmed my chest as I stared up at Hahl's window.

"*Come with us,*" *Delwyn had begged.*

"*I can't,*" *Ross said, while clutching her tight.* "*Arell will come for us no matter where we go. I have to finish this now. I have to put an end to their filthy, murderous rites.*"

The slap of running feet brought Ross's head up, and he stepped in front of Delwyn as she snatched up their baby from the bed. Arell slid to a stop before them, breathing hard. His eyes had turned a deep violet color.

"*The Keepers require your child,*" *he said. Violet light sparked on his fingertips, and a sneer spread over his face.* "*Do not defy the Keepers.*"

Ross let his own power rise. It flickered as it shifted from white to invisible. Arell gaped when he saw it.

"*You?*" *he said in amazement.* "*You have Invisible Light?*"

Ross stepped toward him, and Arell raised his hands.

"*The child will die,*" *Arell sneered, and a violet jet of light jumped toward Kell and Delwyn.*

Ross leaped to intercept it. His power flashed, and the white and violet lights collided in a shower of energy, sending globs of power flying like molten stone.

Then Ross drove his power through Arell in a savage attack that ripped his chest open as he flew across the hall to crash into the wall.

Delwyn's cries fell on deaf ears. This is what Ross had been born to do. It was his calling. He glanced down at the light flickering on his fingertips as the certainty of it filled him to bursting.

"*It had to be done,*" *he told himself.* "*I had to do it.*"

Delwyn grabbed his arm. "*Oh, Ross, what have you done?*"

Ross spun and grabbed Delwyn and Kell into a tight hug.

"*I have to get you out of here,*" *he said. He rushed them to the nearest chamber.*

"*I will come for you,*" *he said.* "*I promise.*" *He kissed them both stroking their cheeks with his fingers.* "*I love you,*" *he whispered and sent them on to a distant place, where they would be safe.*

Now, his son had returned in search of the father he had never known, and Delwyn had died before she could tell their son who he was. It was a wound too deep to be borne. The Keepers of the Light would finally claim them all, and there was nothing Ross could do to stop them.

The next morning, I waited in the shadow of a twisted column for Alana to arrive. As the sun touched the knife-sharp point of the sundial, I finally admitted to myself that she wasn't coming. Just then, a figure stepped out of the doorway leading to Hahl's tower. Even in the early morning light, I recognized him.

He strode with purpose and authority. His black boots thudded against the cobblestones. The morning light glinted off his polished armor. The King had come to the temple, and he was not happy. A scowl twisted his face.

By the time I remembered that the King was Alana's father, he had passed me and was reaching for the latch of the door in the wall. I jogged a few steps after him and then stopped. He might not know I had been meeting with Alana. If she was preparing for another festival, I didn't want to get her in trouble.

I found Hahl in his tower bent over his enormous tome, apparently unimpressed with the fact that he had just met with the King. I didn't even wait for his permission to enter.

"Why hasn't Alana come to worship at the Hitching Post of the Sun?" I demanded.

Hahl's anger flared, and his yellow eyes churned. Something more than anger emanated from him. Was it triumph?

"I told you once not to bother with such trivialities," he said. "She performs her duties, as she must. She is no concern of yours." Hahl returned to his book.

I wasn't about to give up that easily.

"Last time she didn't come, she was preparing for a ceremony," I said. "Is there another ceremony coming soon?"

An emotion of deep satisfaction came from Hahl. "Yes," he said. "She is preparing for the equinox celebration that will occur in a few days."

"What occurs at this celebration?" I asked. I knew there was no equinox this early in the year. It was still mid-summer.

Hahl glanced up at me again. "Why? Do you wish to purify it

before you have even seen it?" His voice was hard and mocking.

I wanted to twist his ugly skeleton head from his shoulders. "I'm trying to learn what you are supposed to be teaching me," I said.

Hahl strode toward me. I stood my ground. The power sparked on my fingertips. After what Ufel told me, I wasn't frightened of Hahl anymore.

"Yes, I am your teacher," Hahl said. "And I will decide what you learn and when you learn it. You will be told what you must know the day of the celebration, as before."

Ross's anger filled my mind. I could do it. I could do it now. I could start with Hahl, but I was no killer. I would find another way. I spun on my heels and retreated to my room.

As I crossed the courtyard under the shadow of the great sundial, the ground of the temple rolled under my feet, and an agonizing groan echoed off the walls. I stumbled and staggered until the rolling stopped. Somehow, I knew earthquakes were not normal around here. I broke into a run. Maybe if I went to the altar in the room called the Navel of the Earth below the sundial, I could do something to help the temple.

As I raced down the corridor, I found a little Roinan girl standing by my door holding a large tray.

"Hello," I said, "let me take that." She handed it to me but didn't rush off like I thought she would. She was a beautiful child with large, black eyes and a round, pleasing face. She couldn't have been more than seven or eight years old.

She stared at me.

I shouldered through the door and set the tray on the table. The child crept into the doorway, watching me.

"Are you hungry?" I asked. I pointed at the food.

She shook her head. Then she stepped through the door and stole up to me, reaching out one small hand to tug at the sleeve of my robe. She pointed with the other hand toward the door.

"What?" I asked. "You want me to follow you?"

I hesitated. The temple was in pain. It wanted me to do something right now, but the Roinan worked for Alana. Could Alana have sent the little girl? Maybe Alana knew what to do to help the temple.

The girl nodded vigorously and grabbed my hand.

"All right," I said. "Where are we going?"

The little girl never said a word. She dragged me off into the underground corridors. She led me deep into the tunnels under the temple. I called up a ball of light into my hand as we descended. Cold, damp air hung silent and unmoving in the corridor. Water dripped somewhere in the distance. Now and again, the sound of clawed feet scuffled over the stone floor. The little Roinan girl never stopped to rest. She tugged relentlessly on my hand.

I almost tripped over her when she stopped before a large wooden door and gestured at it.

"You want me to open it?"

She nodded.

I tried to lift the latch, but it was locked. "Do you have the key?"

She shook her head.

"Okay," I said. I had used the power to blast a hole in the ceiling of a chamber. Why not use it to open a locked door?

I placed my hand on the door and called up the power. It entered the door, and the latch clicked. I pushed the door open with a smug feeling of satisfaction. This power was pretty useful. I hadn't tried anything dramatic since the last test, remembering that the power could do strange things to my body. The door groaned on its rusted hinges as the girl shoved it open.

A waft of foul, stale air slapped me in the face. I covered my nose and mouth with my robe, raising the ball of fire and sending it into the room ahead of me. It pushed back the blackness and spilled across Alana's body dangling from rusted chains clamped around her wrist. Three other bodies sagged against the far wall, and a pile of human bones had been tossed into one corner.

My heart leaped into my throat. I bounded the few paces to Alana's side. A trickle of dried blood smeared her arms. Her white robe was torn, dirty, and stained red. Her head sagged to one side. She appeared to be dead.

The breath caught in my throat. I lifted her head and brushed the hair away from her face. "Alana," I said. "Alana."

She stirred at the sound of my voice.

"Wait," I said. "I'll get you down." At least she was still alive.

I called up the power. The locks clicked, and the chains fell away. I caught her as she fell away from the wall and lowered her to the dirty straw that littered the floor.

She opened her eyes, and my breath caught in my throat. Where once her beautiful black eyes had sparkled and danced, now the deep pits of her eye sockets had been partially filled with a horrible gray fluid.

"Alana," I whispered as I stroked her face. "What happened to you?" I fought to keep the tears in.

Her lips trembled. She spoke in a deep, scratchy voice devoid of the song that had always been there before. It was horrible to hear coming from her lips.

"I can't see," she croaked. Her hand crept to her throat. "They found out and came for me."

"The priests did this to you?" I asked, already knowing the answer. Alana gave a feeble nod.

Tears trickled down my cheeks. The horror at what they had done to her burned in my chest. They had blinded her, ripped out her eyes and destroyed her beautiful voice.

"I'm sorry," I said. "This is all my fault."

If I had left her alone, none of this would have happened. I brushed a dirty smudge from her face as tenderly as I could. I loved her. Not until that moment, when I had nearly lost her, did I realize it.

"Hang on," I said, struggling to speak past the horrible knot in my throat. "I'll help you."

I grasped her hand in mine and sang. As the power reached out to her, a rush of pain and anguish filled me like I had never known. My voice faltered, but I struggled to keep singing. The pain sank deep roots into her soul. Only someone with long practice could cause that much pain without killing. The anguish burned in my chest, and I pinched my eyes shut, forcing myself to continue.

The power gushed out of me, taking my own Light with it. As I sang, the power filtered through her body, mind, and soul, searching out all of the damage and replacing the pain with a portion of my own Light. As my Light healed her damaged soul, her breathing deepened, and the tension ebbed from her body.

When the power finished, I let the song die, and I sat back on my haunches. Sweat trickled down my face. A great emptiness had expanded inside me, a vast unfillable pit. I trembled as the sores spread on my hands and burned on my face. I glanced toward the door and found the little Roinan girl quivering with wide, wondering eyes, and fear etched on her face, but she didn't leave.

Alana was now breathing deeply with her eyes closed. The anguish had left her face, and the color had returned.

Weak from my exertions, I whispered, "Alana, are you all right?"

She opened her eyes, and I jerked in shock. The hollows had been filled by a pearly-white fire that swam and churned within them. I stared and fought back the tears again. Why had the power not fixed her eyes? Even as I thought it, I knew the answer. Her eyes were gone. The priests had torn them out in some cruel form of butchery the Light could not heal. A fire started in the pit of my stomach and spread to every inch of my body. Ross joined me in his fury.

"Kell," she said. Her voice was still harsh and unpleasant. "I hoped you would come." She looked at me like a lost child. "How did you find me?"

A slender hand crept up to her throat again at the sound of her own voice. A tear trickled down her cheek.

I had failed to heal her voice, as well. I hesitated for a moment in awkward silence before I pointed to the little Roinan girl. Then I realized she might still be blind, but Alana gave the girl a weak smile and held out her hand to the child. The child came and took it.

"Thank you," she said, squeezing the child's hand.

The girl smiled shyly.

A look of surprise crept over Alana's face. "Kell, what happened to you?" she asked.

I touched the blisters and scabs forming on my face. "It happens when I use the power too much," I said. "It'll go away."

"I'm sorry," she whispered.

I took her hand. "Don't say that. I would give anything for you."

She swallowed as a single tear slid down her cheek.

"The others?" Alana said.

At first, I didn't understand her, but as she craned her head toward the wall where the other bodies hung, I scrambled to my feet and let each of them down from their chains.

I recognized the large man as the one that tried to kill Durr. The other two were women, one old, one young. Where their eyes should have been, I found empty sockets oozing a black substance like what

I had seen on my mother and on the plant in Einediau's garden. I touched each person in turn and searched for their Light, but it was gone. I wondered if these were the women who dared defy the priests during the procession. Suffering and death seemed to be the fate of anyone who crossed them.

I glanced back at Alana and shook my head.

"They tortured them in front of me," Alana said. "They wanted to punish me."

My stomach rolled, and I thought I might be sick. Glancing around the room again, I found the doll that struck me in the chest during the procession laying crumpled against the wall. I picked it up. The face was still shredded, but the needle had been removed. I handed the doll to the little girl. She held it close and bent over to whisper to it.

Alana struggled to sit up. I stooped to help her rest against the wall.

"Tell me what happened," I said as I crouched beside her.

"Lowthelian came to tell me that the priests wished to see me," she said in the harsh, croaking voice. "I came and found Llaith and Einediau. They threw me in the cell, and then they came and…" Her voice broke. Tears ran down her face. "They took my eyes and my voice and said I was to be the sacrifice at the fall equinox. Then they tortured me."

Horror and rage strangled in my throat so that I couldn't speak. Llaith, I could have guessed. Even Durr wouldn't have surprised me. But Einediau? He seemed like a deranged old man who cared for nothing but his garden.

"Why did they take my eyes?" Alana choked on a sob, and I enfolded her in my arms. She clung to me as the little girl patted her hair.

I struggled to understand why they had done this. Why had they murdered the two women and tortured Alana? The fall equinox was months away. They had just renewed their power. Deep down, I knew why, and so did Ross. Revenge. Revenge for me daring to question them. They wanted to show me who held the real power. This is what they would have done to me and my mother had Ross not found a way to send us to safety.

"For the Light of the body is the eye," I quoted. I had seen the phrase written on the wall in the Navel of the Earth. "The eye reveals the inner Light of a person, so they attacked your eyes to blind you and to torture you."

I pulled away and grasped Alana's face in my hands so I could peer directly into her eyes. "This is why your eyes are now white and pure. They reflect the beauty and purity of your soul."

Alana licked her trembling lips.

"I won't let this happen again," I said. The rage inside me roared to be set free. Ross was with me. Father and son agreed the time had come. At that moment, something snapped inside me, and I clutched at my head.

The temple surged into my mind in a desperate rush of urgency. Thin, golden writing appeared on the stone of the wall. It wasn't strong and bold like it had been in the Navel.

"Now." The words said. "Or. All. Is. Lost."

The temple convulsed. A long black crack ripped through the stone. The wall wavered, and a curved black claw stabbed through, trying to widen the tear. It was part shadow, part substance with a jagged, serrated edge, sharp as a blade.

Alana screamed. The child clutched Alana's arm with a little whimper as the eyeless face of a beast thrust into the room, swiveling from side to side, searching for something or someone. Horror gripped my chest in a tight fist. The beast sniffed, following a scent. It shot its claw toward me, and I stumbled back with a cry of surprise. The very fabric of the temple was being ripped apart. Monsters from some other time or place had come hunting for me.

I raised my hand toward the crack and sent the power to attack the monster clawing its way through. A shriek sounded. The monster writhed. A second beast rushed in behind it, tearing at the rent, widening the hole. Behind them surged a mass of beasts, dark as night, jostling one another in a frenzy to reach the gash in the temple wall.

The temple convulsed again. Bits of the ceiling fell. The beasts snarled as the gap widened. I focused the power and blasted them from the rent. The beasts vanished, and the rent closed.

A desperate urgency washed over me to mingle with the anger and the horror. I had to act today. I had taken too long to find my mission. The temple had been trying to tell me all along. Now that

I knew my task, I struggled to control the rising panic that filled my chest. I still had to make sure Alana and the Roinan girl were safe. But I was *so* tired.

Alana clutched at my arm with an expression of pure horror. The child was crying.

"What was that?" she asked.

"The temple is being attacked," I said. "We have to go."

Alana glanced to where the crack had been. "By what?" she asked.

"The priests and their evil," I said. "How do you feel? Do you think you can walk?"

She nodded. The child and I pulled her to her feet, and she took a few experimental steps.

"I feel fine," she said. "I'm just a little tired. But you look terrible."

"I'll heal," I said.

Her slender hand crept to her throat again. New tears trickled down her cheeks.

"They stole my voice, too," she whispered. "I'll never sing again."

I held her close. "I'm sorry," I said. "It's my fault."

She pushed me away.

"No," she said. "It's *their* fault. They can't tolerate anyone defying them. We did, and since they can't harm you, they took me."

I bowed my head. By harming her, they hurt me in the worst way possible, but I wasn't going to argue with her. What happened *was* my fault, and I knew it.

Alana grabbed my hand and squeezed it. Then the Roinan girl seized Alana's hand and pulled. I glanced over at the three bodies by the far wall.

"What can we do for them?" I asked.

Alana paused and turned her swirling, white gaze on them. "They dared to defy the Keepers," she said. "Once we are safe, I will send Roinan to collect them. At least we can give them a decent burial."

The temple rumbled, and a long crack split the stones. Bits of the ceiling cascaded around our heads.

The little girl tugged again.

"We better go before this place collapses on top of us," I said.

Terrible, rending music burst into my mind. It sounded like the temple was shrieking in pain. The terror and urgency sweeping into me from the stones of the temple made me stumble. I was too late. The temple was dying. I had chosen Alana over the temple, and now the temple would die. But I couldn't have made any other choice.

We rushed headlong down the tunnels, desperate to escape before it was too late.

"Where is she taking us?" I asked. "I need a place to hide you, while I…" I couldn't tell her what I planned to do.

"I think she's taking us to such a place," Alana said. "Let's see where she goes first."

Moments later, I realized we were nearing the great chamber of the Navel of the Earth. Another tremor rippled through the temple. The dreadful music faltered, and the urgency faded to a resigned horror. The temple knew it was dying and had given up.

"Hurry," I said to the girl. I had to find the priests before it was too late.

We rounded a corner, and the Roinan girl stopped dead in her tracks.

Chapter Twenty-Two
The Cleansing

I SENSED HIS presence before I saw him. Pushing past Alana and the girl, I planted myself in front of them. Alana snatched up the girl into her arms and backed away. Llaith filled the corridor, his great red eyes boiling in fury, his long black hair flowing around him as if a wind were blowing. He clutched a round glass ball the size of a baseball that burned blood-red in one hand. A vapor of black mist swirled around him.

At that moment, I realized I was staring death in the face. Llaith had become the thing he so admired, and he had come to kill. He pointed a long bony finger at me. The stench of him choked the corridor.

"You defy the Keepers?" he growled. "You would weaken the Light and give your power to She-Who-Would-Not-Sing. You shall pay."

Before I could react, he held up the crystal ball of crimson fire and a fountain of red-hot light shot from the ball to slam into my chest. It dove deep, searching for my Light. I stumbled backward, and, for an instant, I sensed the clutching fingers of death raking my soul, grasping at my Light the way they had when I first touched the skull in Llaith's chamber. This glass ball must be some new toy he had created to focus his power.

My own power flared in response. Llaith shrieked and flew

backward in a shower of red sparks. I advanced. The familiar tickle at the back of my brain intensified as Ross urged me on.

If this is what Llaith wanted, then so be it. I might as well start with him. He was the worst of the lot. He had earned the right to be the first to be purged.

Llaith clawed his way to his feet. He tried to muster another jet of light, but I threw it back into his face. I sent the power toward him, willing it to seize his Light. I waited for the familiar tingle and warmth of the Light of a living thing sweeping into me. But something wasn't right. I couldn't draw his Light to me.

Panic clutched at my throat, and I felt my Light falter. I struggled to breathe. My chest tightened, and my stomach rolled over. I had miscalculated—just as my father had done. I wasn't powerful enough to do what Ufel thought I should. I was going to fail, and Alana and this little child who had tried to save her were going to die with me. The priests would never let them live after this.

Llaith sent a stream of red light, and my power caught it. I tried to draw it again, but I couldn't. What was I thinking? I was still ignorant of this invisible power, while Llaith had had centuries to probe the depths of his. He was more powerful than I believed. I underestimated him and all the priests because I had defeated the objects they created so easily.

Llaith started to laugh—a deep, mocking laugh, broken by the sickening clatter of his teeth as they smacked together in mirth.

"Fool," he bellowed.

As I struggled, Ross burst into my mind with an image of the two round stones I carried in my pocket. I glanced back to find Alana and the little girl cowering against the wall. Rage overwhelmed my despair. He would not hurt Alana again. I was sick of him laughing at me and treating me like I was stupid. I sent a great wave of power surging toward him. It lifted him off his feet and slammed him into the wall.

Ross forced the image of the two stones into my mind again. The image burned so powerfully I couldn't concentrate or see clearly.

I shoved my hands into my pockets, desperate for any possible help before Llaith came at me again. I yanked the stones out. They glowed at my touch—one bright yellow like the burning sun and the other a soft silver like the light of the full moon—and I understood.

The Cleansing

The rush of comprehension made me reel and stumble. I had been so blind.

Images of circles and squares swam in my memory. The serpent of time devouring its own tail. The union of day and night. Male and female. Past and present. Light and darkness. Wholeness and fragmentation. They were pairs, not opposites. Complementary pairs. The eye was really a stone set in the palm of a hand. The layout of the temple symbolized order amid chaos, union, and perfection—the cosmic creation.

Everything the priests had been teaching me had been about this. I could never control the power of Illurien until I accepted who I was. Until my soul, mind, and heart were one. Until I united the powers of day and night, until my power united the spectrum of Light. This was my role. The writing on Dairen's stone came back to me. "Sun and moon are one in thine hands." Seren taught me that the sun and moon were the eyes of the day and night and represented the union of light and dark.

I gripped a stone in each hand as Llaith crawled to his feet. The goosebumps erupted all over my body as if charged with electricity. A flood of power overwhelmed all other senses, and all I could see was Llaith filled with his putrid Light. I had been sent to purify it. To cleanse it of the evil that festered inside him. To sweep away the darkness.

With this realization came the sudden knowledge that I would die. I had been sent by Illurien to be the sacrificial lamb, the cost of so great a task could only be my life. I glanced back at Alana before facing Llaith. I would die to save her and all the children the Keepers would no longer be able to murder. I would die to avenge my father and mother. I would die to release my friend Ufel from his agonized existence. I would die to save all creation from the darkness.

The power flowed out of me in a great enveloping wave. I staggered as the Light swallowed Llaith in an invisible wall of energy. The glass ball in his hand shattered. He screamed and writhed in agony as the Invisible Light drained his power.

Llaith's Light filled me with loathing. Death and emptiness poured into me. Despair, pain, suffering, hate, jealousy, greed, selfishness—all the emotions that made Llaith who he was had been drained into my soul. It was a fetid, rancorous presence, and I struggled to end it as quickly as possible. Llaith thrashed and jerked.

He screamed a high-pitched and tormented "nooooo" that echoed down the corridor. He twitched and then lay still. The black swirling vapor roiling around him lifted into the air and dissipated. His robe sagged over the empty skeleton as his bones clattered to the floor. His hair splayed out around him, seeming even more grotesque against the white cobblestones.

I stared down at the glowing stones in my hands. They were hot. The writing on them burned and throbbed in unison like a heart was pumping power through them. Somehow, they had channeled my power in a way I couldn't do on my own. I sensed their incredible age. They must have been created in the beginning, eons ago when the Light was pure and the worship uncorrupted.

With that idea came the sudden knowledge that they had been touched by Illurien herself and prepared for the Promised One. I was meant to find them. Somehow, the temple had known. The usual weakness and pain that followed using the power didn't come. It was like the stones had increased my ability to withstand the effects of the power.

I tore my gaze from the stones to stare at Llaith's crumpled remains. Red liquid spilled from his eyes to pool underneath him. I could only contemplate him with pity. What a fool he had been. He had grown so confident in his own power and so hungry for life that he was willing to do anything to keep it. Anything.

The clicking sound of running skeletal feet forced me to spin from the hideous remains as Durr burst out of a side tunnel and skidded to a stop. He stared at Llaith and the red fluid dripping from Llaith's eye sockets. Fear and anger surged out of Durr. His blue eyes boiled.

"What have you done?" he cried.

I glanced at the stones in my hands. "The cleansing has begun," I said.

The rage and terror I experienced before had been replaced by a new understanding of what I must do. The Light that had been Llaith was so dirty and so evil that only his death could purify it. Ufel had been right. Llaith would have clung to that life no matter the cost. Most of the others would, too. They would never change willingly. Maybe they couldn't. Maybe they had become so accustomed to their own darkness that all the true Light had been smothered in them.

Durr stared at me in open horror for a moment before he fled.

I started after him and then stopped. "Take Alana to my quarters," I said to the Roinan girl. "And lock the door. I will come as soon as it is finished." I spun to chase after Durr.

"Kell," Alana's harsh voice cut through the corridor, and I paused to glance over my shoulder at her. "Please come back to me," she said.

The anguished concern on her face sent a knot into my throat. I wanted to tell her how much I cared for her. How sorry I was that I would never see her again, but if I did, she might do something rash—something dangerous—and get herself hurt. I couldn't have that. I was doing this so she would never be hurt by these priests again. I pinched my lips tight and nodded before I sped after Durr.

If it had not been for Ross, I would have become lost in the tunnels. He led me out near the sundial. This is where the priests would choose to make their stand at the center of their power.

I sprinted around the corner of a building and slid to a stop. Hahl, Durr, and Einediau gathered in front of the sundial. I glanced around for the others, but they weren't there. I had no plan. I didn't even know if I could defeat them all. I simply knew that I had to face them.

Hahl spoke first. "You have betrayed the Light," he said. "You must be punished."

I advanced until I stood a few yards from him.

"I finally understand my mission," I said. "I don't want to do it, but I must. You've given me no choice. It doesn't need to get ugly."

Durr growled. "All along, you have been ready to serve her. I saw it in the Mirror. You would destroy us and place She-Who-Would-Not-Sing upon the throne of Illurien."

I shook my head. "No," I said as I held up the stones. My robe rubbed against the sores forming on my skin, but I had to ignore the discomfort.

Hahl gave a visible start at the sight of the stones. Confusion and fear coursed through him as he exchanged glances with the other priests.

"I possess the Cosmic Stones," I continued, "prepared by Illurien herself to protect the temple. She has given me a portion of her Light, which governs all things. I have been sent to use these stones and the power of her Light to purify the pollutions you have introduced. I've united the light of day and night as they were always meant to be, just as I have united the colors of light. Light and darkness cannot exist alone, just as pure Light contains all the colors of the Keepers."

The temple convulsed again, and a horrible, high-pitched screeching burst into my mind. The sundial burst apart with an ear-splitting crack. The air in between me and the priests shimmered. A kaleidoscope of color flickered along the edge of the rent that widened until a black head with no eyes or nose burst through the rent. Einediau and Hahl gasped and stumbled backward. Durr didn't appear surprised.

I sent a bolt of power into the rent. The monster opened its jagged maw and roared as the Invisible Light slammed into it, thrusting it back into the rent.

"You see what you have done," I shouted. "You have so fragmented and polluted the Light that you have disturbed the balance. *You* have laid the foundation for the undoing of the Light—for the chaos of oblivion. Your temple is under assault from the darkness, and, rather than unite to protect it, you torture innocent people within it." I paused to let them consider this. "I did not choose this mission, but it is mine to perform, and I will do it. I must."

Durr and Hahl roared together, launching themselves at me. I stumbled backward and fell as their power lashed into me. Hahl landed on top of me with his bony hands clutching at my throat. Yellow flame leaped from between his fingers, searing my flesh.

The power exploded from me in a sudden, furious blast. Hahl flew high into the air twisting grotesquely amid his flapping black robe. Before I could catch my breath, Durr was on me, sending great jets of icy-blue water he conjured from somewhere into my eyes. The tiny molecules solidified and stabbed into my face, scouring my eyes and flesh. I cried out as the wall of tearing, biting particles flung me backward to skid and bounce across the cobblestones. Again, my power flared, and Durr screamed in rage and pain as he stumbled and slipped to bounce with a horrible crack against the cobblestones. His water evaporated into a thick mist.

Hahl crawled to his feet as the ground cracked all around my body, and great roots climbed from the soil beneath to encircle my limbs and chest. One crossed over my throat and started to squeeze. Einediau loomed over me, his green eyes swirling, an emerald light dancing on his fingers.

"Green is *my* Light," he said. "And I am bound to it."

Hahl pointed one finger at me, and a narrow beam of yellow fire cut through my robe and bored into my chest. My scream of pain and terror gurgled in my throat as I choked and gasped for air. I couldn't move or run. I could barely breathe. The roots held me tight as Hahl's beam of fire cut its way to my heart.

Somehow the stones remained in my grasp, and I summoned the power. It caught Hahl's beam and wrapped itself around Einediau's roots. The roots withered as I drew in their Light and caught hold of Einediau's power. Hahl realized what I was doing too late as my power grasped his narrow beam and drew it in, siphoning his Light from him.

He struggled to break free, but I held him as I crawled to my knees, breaking Einediau's roots. Hahl's Light was not as filthy as Llaith's had been, but it was still tainted by many evil deeds. Einediau's Light was not so polluted, but it, too, held the stain of consent and participation in centuries of murder and torture.

I thought of Alana and what Einediau helped Llaith do to her, and I renewed my efforts to withdraw his Light. The pain of it sent me groveling on the cobblestones. The polluted Light filled me like a great geyser that had been forced down my throat. It burned and tore at the fabric of my soul. My power struggled to contain it. I could not survive using the power like this.

Hahl and Einediau screamed and writhed. The Light of Illurien sought to reclaim their Light and drew it in relentlessly, irresistibly, despite their reluctance. I couldn't have stopped it once it began if I had wanted to.

The Cosmic Stones seared my hands. The smell of burning flesh saturated the air, and the terrible pain made me cry out. I struggled to drop the stones, willing the power to stop, to let me release the stones before they charred my hands to useless cinders. I needed to regain my sense of balance, but the power continued. I could feel Hahl and Einediau failing. Their Light was almost gone. It couldn't be much longer. I set my teeth and tried to control the awful agony.

A few more seconds.

A searing pain stabbed into my back. I gasped. Something hard scraped against my ribs. I sagged forward with a groan and rolled over to find Durr towering above me with a long, thin knife in his hands.

"I may not be able to resist your power," he cried, "but I can still kill you with cruder weapons." He leaped toward me.

A boiling cloud of bright orange flame caught Durr in the air, flinging him backward like a rag doll. The roar of it filled my ears, and its heat singed my skin.

Ufel slid to a stop beside me. "Heal yourself, quickly," he said.

How could I do that? I had only ever healed others. I gritted my teeth against the pain. Warm blood spilled down my back. My breath came in short, stinging gasps. Durr had pierced one of my lungs. I closed my eyes and tried to focus on the pain. It felt like someone had shoved a red-hot iron between my ribs.

I fought to keep the panic down. I couldn't die. Not yet. I let the stones fall to the cobblestones. My hands still smoked, and I stared at the melted skin in my palms. The images of the stones with their intricate writing and been seared into my flesh. I gasped at the fire in my lungs and called for the power. The Light flared, but nothing happened. I struggled against the sinking despair. Ufel had been wrong. I couldn't heal myself. Illurien hadn't given me the power so I could serve myself. I was a servant of the Light. I struggled to my knees, gasping at the pain and the need for more air. I had to finish this before it was too late.

Durr regained his feet. His smoking robe hung in tatters around his skeletal frame. "What are you thinking?" he demanded of Ufel. "Do you realize what he has done?"

"Yes," Ufel said, "I know what he is doing, and I know it is what has been prophesied. So do you—only I accept it, and you do not."

"Traitor!" Durr roared. "He would deliver his power to *her*."

"Yes," Ufel said. "You and I are the traitors. *We* polluted the Light. You know as well as I do that only then did the Light begin to fail, and it has been failing ever since. We should never have listened to Llaith. He led us astray, and we followed—though we all knew better. We followed because we were tantalized by the idea of living forever to serve the Light. It was a fool's dream, and it has brought nothing but sorrow." Ufel's voice quieted. "Now, let it go, Durr," he said. "We have lived far too long already."

Durr responded with a great sheet of blue light that caught Ufel in the face, snapping his head back with a loud crack. Ufel flew several yards, falling limply to the stone pavement with a clatter of bones. I stared down at him in horror. Durr leaped toward me again, but this time I caught the hand with the blade, and the power surged into Durr. He screamed, trying to wrench his hand free of my grasp, but I held him. The power had changed. I glanced at my free hand and saw the golden light of the Sun Stone pulsing through the writing seared into my palm to the rhythm of my own heartbeat. We had become one. I no longer needed to hold the stones to harness their power.

Draining away Durr's light was like drinking toxic water. It flowed smoothly and almost pleasantly, but it was so contaminated that it overwhelmed me. I stumbled backward, trying to keep Durr's blade from my throat as he still struggled to drive it home. Durr's Light left with a quiet snap, and he clattered to the ground.

I fell to my knees, gasping in the air and tasting blood in my mouth. Sweat fell in sheets all over my body, dripping to mix with my blood on the white cobblestones. I struggled to my feet and staggered to Ufel's side. When I touched him, he shuddered.

"Do it quickly, Promised One," he said. "Release me from this pain."

"Ufel, I'm sorry." I choked on the last word as tears sprang to my eyes. I had grown fond of him—especially in the last few days.

Ufel raised a trembling skeletal hand to grasp mine.

"It is as it should be," he said. "I thank Illurien you've come. Now, please, Promised One. You swore an oath to me. Please."

I placed a hand on Ufel's brow. Not much Light remained to be withdrawn, but I drew it in as quickly as I could. Ufel sighed as the last of the Light left him.

I sank back on my haunches. A wave of dizziness made my head spin. I didn't have much time now. My life's blood was pumping out through the hole in my back. My lung was filling with blood. I sagged with exhaustion. So filled with anguish. So filled with foul, toxic Light that I thought I would burst and spill it all over the courtyard.

The temple convulsed so violently that I fell to my hands and knees. It was dying. I had to save it. The ground exploded underneath me, carrying me away in a fountain of earth and stone. I struggled to get my bearings as the fountain of earth crashed to the ground and piled on top of me, crushing the life out of me. Footsteps clicked against the stone and stopped in front of me.

"Eons we have served the Light," Dairen said, "and you come to undo all that we have worked so long to build. You have destroyed the knowledge of ages and ages. Knowledge that may never be regained."

I lifted my head, struggling against the crushing weight on my chest to peer up at Dairen. Blood dribbled from a dozen wounds on my head and face.

"You misunderstand your mission, Promised One," Dairen continued. "We'll have to wait for another." He raised his skeletal claw, and indigo flame arced from it. I caught the flame on my hand and held it.

"No, Dairen," I choked. "I do not misunderstand. You have polluted the Light far too long. This is the only way to purify it. I'm sorry. But it must be done."

Dairen raised another fountain of stone and drove it toward my head to crush me, but I called up the power with all the energy I could muster. It exploded into the stone with the roar of a thousand jet engines, spraying it in every direction. I crawled to my feet, choking on the dust.

"It has to be done," I gasped. Dairen sent a sheet of violet light into my face, but I caught it with the Light. I staggered against the sundial for support. Dairen's Light flowed into me. He struggled to resist as the fear of death gripped him.

"You play with me like you did the diamond," he said. "Such power. Please, Promised One. Such power." I snatched the rest of his Light, and he collapsed.

I fell to my hands and knees, gasping for breath. Blood and sweat dripped from my head, leaving red stains on the white stones. I had no energy left. Darkness swam before my eyes. Pain laced every fiber of my being. I was coming undone. The use of the Light was tearing me apart. Even breathing caused me searing agony.

"Promised One?" I started and looked up. The mingled sweat and blood dripped from my nose and chin and stung my eyes.

The Cleansing

Seren gazed down at me.

I crawled to my feet, leaving bloody handprints on the sundial as I struggled to keep my balance. The emotions coming from Seren were wild and confusing.

"Has it come to this, Promised One?" he asked.

I nodded.

"Is there no other way?"

I clutched at the sundial for support.

Seren gazed at me for a long moment and then chanted in a low beautiful voice.

> The pulse of life, the coldness of death.
> A touch, a song, a simple breath.
> The eternal flame will burn no more.
> Water cannot flow o'er the shore.
> The strength of the earth he will sift like sand.
> The light of the star will fly to his hand.
> The seven colors will cease to be.
> Only the Promised One will be able to see.

> Life and death are one in his hand.
> Fire and water obey his command.
> Earth and star, he can mold with a touch.
> Rainbows fade within his clutch.
> The lost and forgotten shall return.
> Upon his palms, the Light will burn.
> Light unseen descends from the skies.
> Only the Promised One will hear their cries.

Then he repeated the last two lines. "Light unseen descends from the skies. Only the Promised one will hear their cries." Seren gave a resigned sigh. "Now, I understand the song," he said. "It was not only to tell us how to recognize the Promised One. It was to tell us that we each would die at his hands."

Seren bowed his head, and that sense of peaceful, quiet resignation I sensed in him that first night emanated from him more powerfully than ever.

"I once told you," he said, "that with understanding comes

acceptance. With acceptance comes peace. I now understand, and I accept it. I go in peace."

He knelt before me and bowed his head. I hesitated.

"I'm sorry," I said. "I didn't want it to be this way."

"I know, Promised One. Do what you must."

I placed my hands on his warm skull and withdrew his Light. Seren's Light was the purest of them all. With the Light came a peace that was as powerful as had been the evil of the others. Seren exhaled and slumped forward. I caught him and lay him gently on the stones. The task was done.

Chapter Twenty-Three
To Hear Their Cries

MY WHOLE BODY trembled. I sank to my knees again. It was finished, and I was still alive. As I blinked at the gathering darkness, my breath came in short, ragged gasps. The temple trembled, and a great rent tore through the courtyard. The buildings around me crumbled, tumbling to the ground in a dull roar. I stared in confusion as the sense of terror and suffering coming from the temple mingled with my own. I swayed where I knelt. What had gone wrong? Why was the temple still in pain? Why was it still being torn apart?

A strange sensation crept over me—a feeling of incompleteness. I glanced around and found Hahl and Einediau sprawled on the stone. They were still alive. I crawled over to them, fighting against the nausea and confusion. I had to finish it while I still could. I couldn't fail, not now. Not after everything I had done. Alana was counting on me. My mother was counting on me.

Ross stirred and sent me an image of a young man with a shaved head, holding my mother in his arms. The warmth of his love brought tears to my eyes. My father was counting on me, too. I had to do this for them.

I placed my hand on Einediau's wrist and withdrew his remaining Light. Then I crawled to Hahl. I placed a hand on his skull. Hahl still struggled. Bitterness and anger kept him alive—but just barely. He clutched at my throat. I caught his hand and withdrew the last of his

Light. His was the oldest Light. It had had many centuries to mature and grow in power. Its quality was different from the others.

Sores had erupted all over my body. My breathing came in ragged gasps as the fire burned in my lung. Despite the pain, I experienced a moment of triumph as the last of Hahl's Light failed, but my satisfaction was cut off in a burst of agony exploding in my mind.

A violent tremor shook the temple to its very foundations. My whole being filled with the cries and screams of the dying priests and of all of their victims. The chorus of pain and anguish overwhelmed me. I collapsed to writhe against the cobblestones. A great fountain of white light burst from my chest. My head flew back against the stones, and I arched my back, screaming and screaming and screaming. How could a body endure such pain?

All the power I drained from the priests had built up inside me like a pent-up fountain, waiting to burst. It surged forth, tearing at the fabric of my soul. Ross also screamed in pain and anguish. The barrier between us collapsed, and I understood.

Ross had rent his soul to remain in the tomb so he could end the priests' reign of terror. Now, the last remaining pieces of his soul were being ripped away. He was dying a second time. Ross had known he would die when the task was done, but that knowledge did not make his passing any less painful.

That pain was only increased by the knowledge that he was leaving behind the son he had thought he would never meet again in life—a son he had also led to his death. Ross reached out in desperation as the last shreds of his being were torn from me, leaving behind a memory of a baby cradled in his mother's arms and a young man tenderly stroking the infant's cheek.

A powerful emotion of love and regret swept past the pain for an instant. Then he was gone. My father was dead. I knew I would soon join him and my mother.

The searing agony surged anew, entering every fiber of my being—agony such as I never thought a person could experience and live. My soul cried out to be released.

The great arcing beam of white light that exploded from my chest connected to the point of the sundial, which drew the Light into itself. The sundial shivered, and the great crack healed without a trace. The memories, lives, and thoughts of the priests gushed past my consciousness in a blinding and confusing rush, at once beautiful and foul. All the pain they had ever inflicted ripped through me in great, raking waves of anguish. The temple trembled and shook.

Then the Light tugged at my own being, at my own Light. I resisted. I tried to control the power. I struggled to cling to the little Light that made me who I was. Not yet. I didn't want to die. Not yet. I needed to know Alana was safe—to tell her that I loved her.

But I couldn't stop it. Bit by bit, piece by piece, my soul tore free. My Light flowed toward the sundial. I pinched my eyes closed against the unimaginable pain. I tried to focus my last thoughts on Alana and then on my father and mother and the new image I now had of us as a family. It was like being given a photograph, only better. Because I could feel and remember my father's love. *I'm coming,* I thought.

As quickly as it began, the pain ceased. A brilliance surrounded me as I sagged back against the cold stone like a rag that had just been wrung out. A woman of unsurpassing beauty descended and stood before me, wreathed in the most pleasing Light. This woman's beauty and power so far exceeded the one I had seen in the Mirror as to make that one seem common.

This was Illurien, the Goddess of All Creation. She smiled at me and touched a finger to the top of my head. In a rush, my fragmented soul returned and settled comfortably back into place, repaired and whole. Ross was no longer there. I was alone again.

"Well done, my child," Illurien said with a voice that rang like the purest crystal. It sang with all the melodies of nature—rushed like the crashing of waves against the shores—so profoundly beautiful that it was painful to hear.

In the air behind her, my mother stood smiling down on me. She was so happy that a knot formed in my throat, and tears slipped from my eyes.

"I'm sorry I left you, Mom," I whispered.

Then my father came striding toward her through the air. Mom opened her arms wide, and they gathered each other into a long embrace. I ached to be with them. To join them.

Illurien shook her head. "Your time is not yet, Promised One. You still have much to do and much to learn." She touched my cheek, and she was gone.

I lay staring up at the pale sky. Thin vapors of cloud floated lazily in the sea of blue. I tried to move, but I couldn't. The experience had drained me. I didn't feel any more pain, but my body had no strength. I struggled to understand all that had happened, but I couldn't focus my thoughts.

A shadow fell across me. I blinked up into Lowthelian's swimming silver eyes. Her black robe was wrinkled and dirty. Why was she wearing a black robe again? Tears dripped from her eyes as she loomed over me. I tried to stop the violent shaking that spread through my body. My vision blurred in and out of focus, but I could see the tears streaking her cheeks.

"I'm all right," I muttered.

She sobbed. "I don't want to do it, Promised One, but I must."

I blinked at her, trying to bring her face into better focus. Something in her voice filled me with dread. Then I realized she was pointing a black, shiny staff at me. Where had I seen that stick before?

She spoke in a tremulous voice. "She commands, and I must obey. I have served her ever since they did this to me." She gestured to her eyes. "They maimed me in both body and soul because I would not obey, but she has been a good mistress. She only punishes me when I fail. And I seldom fail, Promised One."

"What?" I said.

"I've hunted the Chosen who escaped the Great Cleansing, and I have killed the new Chosen who were sent. I destroyed their Light while the priests have grown weaker. But you came to the chamber, and Llaith found you before I could."

Horror filled my soul. "You?" I said. "*You* killed my mother?"

Lowthelian paused. "Your mother?" Then her face assumed a knowing expression. "You were the baby, Ross and Delwyn's baby," she said. "Were you at the rock somewhere? Is that where the chamber was? Is that why she was digging?"

She shook her head and swallowed. "I should have guessed," she said. "But it doesn't matter now. I destroyed your book to keep you from learning too much, but now you've killed all of the priests for me."

Her voice grew louder and more agitated.

"Now, when I kill you, She-Who-Would-Not-Sing will ascend

to the throne of Illurien and throw Her down. Darkness will reign forever. I will be rewarded beyond all the Beings of Light. I alone have remained faithful."

Lowthelian gazed at me with a frown while I wrestled with the implications of what she was saying. Then she convulsed with a maniacal cackle of laughter that rang through the courtyard. The echo rebounded around us as she bowed her head and grew quiet— very quiet.

"I have never loved a Chosen One," she said. "It was easy to kill them. But you? I don't want to do it, Promised One, but I must. It is required."

She said the last words with grim finality and pointed the stick at my head.

I reached for her. "No," I whispered, completely defenseless. I tried to rise, but my arms and legs were as heavy as lead. "No," I said again.

I had just been snatched from the jaws of death only to be dropped back in. When I reached for the power, it stirred feebly. I was too weak to control it. The horror choked me. Lowthelian, my friend, the one I had saved, was going to kill me. I struggled with the horror until I thought of Seren. I stopped resisting and lay back. There was nothing I could do. A quiet resignation filled me. I might as well face death as serenely as Seren had done.

Lowthelian stopped trembling, and her face was grim and pale. Her silver eyes churned wildly. "Goodbye, Promised One," she said. "I will miss you."

Someone wearing a flowing white robe slammed into Lowthelian, who cried out and fell sideways. A jet of black light shot from the end of the stick with a crack and exploded into the cobblestones beside me. They disintegrated with a roar and a shower of stone and dust. The two women struggled until Alana leaped up, brandishing the black stick in her hand, a triumphant smirk on her face. Lowthelian rose and yanked a thin dagger from under her robe. They circled.

"You spoiled little princess," Lowthelian spat. "Thought you could save him from me? Save him for yourself?" She noticed the Cosmic Stones I had dropped and bent to pick one up. The silver light of the stone flared, and she staggered back, trying to drop it.

But the stone clung to her. Lowthelian screamed in pain and terror. She shook her hand, desperate to free herself. Then she snarled in frantic horror. Her face twisted in rage, and she leaped toward me. I raised a feeble hand to ward off the blow of the dagger.

"Kell!" Alana screamed in terror.

My hand touched Lowthelian's as the knife descended, cutting into my forearm. My palms burned, and the power surged from me in a great arc of brilliant, white light that lifted my body from the ground.

Lowthelian flew high into the air, her arms and legs flailing. She shrieked and slammed against the sundial with a loud crack before sliding to the white cobblestones, leaving a streak of silver liquid behind her. She lay still. The silver Moon Stone rolled away from her charred hand.

I glanced up at Alana. Her face had drained of color. Tears wet her cheeks. Footsteps and shouting echoed through the temple before I tumbled into darkness.

Chapter Twenty-Four
Only the Promised One

I AWOKE WRAPPED in a soft, warm blanket to the sound of quiet singing. I knew the song, but the voice was strange. It had a harsh, scratchy quality to it, and it couldn't stay on pitch. I tried to focus on the odd feelings in my chest and mind. Something was missing that should have been there. That sense of being split in two was gone. My soul was whole and alone.

The memories of Ross came rushing back. The father I had never known had shared my mind for weeks with neither of us knowing who the other was. I recalled the image of my young mother holding me in her arms, and my father caressing my cheek. I blinked at the sudden rush of tears. I missed his presence.

Through all the confusion and terror I had experienced in the temple, my father had been there to help me. He struggled to teach and prepare me, and, in the end, he is the one who revealed the secret to unlocking the power. With this sorrow came an overwhelming sense of pride. My father hadn't been a deadbeat dad. He had sacrificed his life, not once, but twice to stop the evil the priests introduced into the world. My mother sacrificed everything to keep me safe and then sent me back home to find the power and complete my father's task.

I wiped at the tear that slid down my cheek and into my ear before turning my head toward the song. Alana stopped singing and gazed down at me with pure, white eyes and smiled. The little Roinan girl sat in her lap, holding the doll I had given her. She stared at me with a sober expression. A rush of affection filled my chest as I remembered what Alana had done. She risked her life to save mine.

My head swam when I tried to sit up.

Alana placed a slender hand on my shoulder to restrain me. "Don't be in such a hurry, Kell. You should rest while you can."

"Alana," I said, "what happened? Lowthelian?"

"Hush," she said. "I'll tell you. Everything is all right."

I lay back, searching her face, still unaccustomed to the harsh voice and white, swirling eyes.

"Lowthelian is dead," she said, "and so are the priests."

"The stones," I interrupted. "Where are the stones?"

Alana pointed to a little stand where the stones sat on a white cloth. "I picked them up for you."

"Thanks," I said.

"The ceremony of burial," Alana said, "will take place tomorrow if you wish to attend. My father waited for two weeks for you to wake, but he says he can wait no longer. The people need to know what has happened."

"Two weeks?" Why was I not dead? Using the power to destroy the priests should have killed me. The power had torn me apart. The only reason I was still alive was because Illurien had restored my Light, and then Alana had saved me from Lowthelian. But how had I not died of dehydration?

"Yes, Kell. It has been two weeks off and on. You came around enough to drink a bit. Anyway, my father arrived just as Lowthelian attacked you. He and his guards came running, but she was already dead."

"She's the one who killed the Chosen," I said. "She murdered them all. She killed my mother."

Alana nodded. "I heard her as I was trying to get close enough to stop her without being seen. She betrayed the Light. The priests must have known and punished her."

Alana shivered, and I remembered how I had found her dangling from the chains in a filthy cell.

"Are you okay?" I asked.

She grinned. "You healed me well."

Not well enough, I thought, or her voice and eyes would have been healed.

She must have read the expression on my face. Her smile faded, and she wiped at a stray tear that escaped down her cheek. I reproached myself for endangering her by insisting that she help me. I wanted to explain this to her, but she didn't give me a chance.

"My father has had the priests' bodies removed," she continued in a subdued whisper, "and the temple gates are locked. The temple has been cleaned, and the damages repaired. The King waits to know what the Promised One wishes him to do."

I stared at her, but she wouldn't look at me now.

"He wants to know what *I* want to do?" I asked. "I have no idea."

I placed a hand on my forehead and felt the rough scar on my palm. I looked at it and found the perfect image of the stone imprinted in my melted flesh. The other hand was the same. Why hadn't Illurien healed my hands? I traced the ridges of the scars with my fingers. Did she think I would need to wield the power like that again? The thought disturbed me. I knew I wouldn't survive it.

I glanced back at Alana. "I really don't have any idea."

Alana gave me a shy glance. "I have ideas—if the Promised One would hear them."

"Of course," I said. "The priests are destroyed, and the Light has been purified, but what are the servants of the Light supposed to do?"

Alana placed a hand on my arm. "I will explain," she said.

After Alana returned to the palace, I slipped out of my room before the sun was up. Silence filled the temple. An eerie sense of destiny and loneliness swept over me as I descended the corridor toward the Navel of the Earth. My mother and father had once strolled these corridors. I had been born within these walls. Tens of thousands of Chosen Ones had lived and loved, suffered and died in this place. Here I was, the only person alive inside its walls. Not even Ross shared my mind anymore. I had never felt so alone. The temple had never felt so old and so at peace. I couldn't tell if it was the peace of the grave or the peace of healing.

Still, I needed to know—to make sure I had succeeded—that I had healed the temple. Alana's white churning eyes and rough voice never let me forget that I had failed her. What if the temple was the same? What if I had only managed to save part of it?

I hesitated at the door to the Navel of the Earth, inspecting the wide altar, feeling the beauty of the Light that filled the room. Would it speak to me again? Did I want it to? I stepped up to the altar and placed my hands on its warm surface. I waited for the music to fill my head or the writing to appear. Nothing happened.

"Hello," I said. "Are you there?"

Golden letters formed on the stone surface between my hands. "Hello, Promised One."

I shivered. "Are you healed?" I asked. "Are you safe?" It felt strange talking to a building, but I had to know.

Peaceful angelic music filled my head. "I am whole," it wrote. I was about to lift my hands away with an incredible sense of relief when more writing appeared. "She comes," it wrote. "Shadows come. Time is broken."

"What does that mean?" I asked.

"You go. Shadows come. Time broken."

"Go where?" I asked.

"Protect Chosen."

A jolt hit me. "Are more Chosen coming? When? Where are they?"

"She comes."

"Okay," I said. "You're not answering my questions."

"Thank you, Promised One," it wrote.

I pulled my hands from the altar. "Yeah, well, you're welcome, but I haven't got a clue what you're trying to say."

I turned to the wall to find my father's and mother's names. Mom's name came first. It was the third Delwyn on the list. Then Dad's followed. This was proof they had been here. That I had a family. I recalled the image my father sent me of them holding me, and their love and warmth filled me. I had found my father, just like Mom wanted. Yet, I was still alone.

The temple said it was whole, but I wanted to see for myself. I strode to the sundial in the great courtyard. The great crack that had broken its smooth white surface was gone. The stone was smooth and polished like nothing had happened to it. When I stepped into Einediau's garden, the energy and life pulsed in greeting. I pinched a leaf of the plant that had been sick, searching for any residue of the illness, but the plant hummed with life and vitality.

I paused at Durr's Mirror of Light and wondered if I should look but decided against it. I already had enough puzzles to work out. The water of the lake was its usual deep blue with its mirrored surface. The fountain at the far end splashed into it. I bent to dip my fingers into the water, expecting the surge of malice and evil I had found lurking there, but nothing happened. The lake appeared to be just a lake of pure water—no longer a repository for darkness.

Everywhere I went in the temple, I searched for any signs of the illness and evil, but I could find no trace. Maybe the temple was truly whole. What could the temple's message mean then? Shadows were coming, and time was broken? If it wasn't broken here, then where could it be broken? How would I fix it?

Several days later, I stood with Alana, gazing out the window of Hahl's tower. The city stretched out beneath us, a checkerboard of red-tiled roofs and whitewashed walls. The palace soared above the city on the neighboring hill. Far off mountains, loomed purple and blue on the horizon.

The priests' burial had been quiet. I couldn't tell from their grim faces whether the people accepted me or not. One man with long brown hair stared at me with a sour expression, and I wondered if he might not stir up trouble.

I addressed the people and assured them the time of renewal was come, and they now had the opportunity to spread the true worship of the Light. I didn't think it had been much of a speech, but Alana assured me it had been inspiring.

We buried the priests together in one of the mounds beyond the walls of the city and set a great black stone to guard the entrance. I carved the epitaph myself with the invisible power. "Light and Truth. May They Endure Forever."

I ordered the cleaning and rebuilding of the library, though I had few books to place in it. Roinan cleared the bodies of the Chosen, which had been unceremoniously stuffed into the rooms beneath the temple, and buried them in the green mounds beyond the city.

It was a terrible sight to see the shriveled bodies of the Chosen being carried from the temple that should have been their home and refuge. They had died for so little—been slaughtered so seven men could defile the Light in a bid to live forever and keep the power of the Light for themselves. They had become parasites feeding off the Chosen. Mere leeches. The memory of their foul Light still sent shivers through me. Every now and then, a peculiar ache burned in my chest as if the great rent where the geyser of Light had spilled their evil into the sundial would never be healed.

Alana and I were now the last servants of the Light. The temple had said more Chosen were out there, and I was supposed to protect them. But how? If they did come to the temple, how would I find them? What should I do with them?

Illurien had said, "Your time is not yet, Promised One. You still have much to do and much to learn." But she hadn't told me what that was or how to learn what I needed to know. I hadn't forgotten the evil I discovered prowling in Durr's pool, the black ooze that seeped into Einediau's garden, the monsters with claws and no faces, and the little dots of evil light that had threatened me.

These things still lingered somewhere, even if they had been driven from the temple. I had no idea where to find them or how to deal with them if I did. I also remembered what the Mirror of Light had shown me—the creeping shadows in human form, the image of the young man standing on the beach, and the girl bent over the drawing. Of all the things the Mirror had shown me, these were the ones I still didn't understand. Should I go searching for them? Were they the next Chosen? Would the shadows threaten them?

There was also the song of the Promised One that Seren had taught me. I hadn't fulfilled all the purposes mentioned in the song. I may have purified the Light here in the temple, but I hadn't completed the circle of time, united the scattered fragments of Light, or done anything to bind the Light to the world. All of this must be what Illurien referred to when she said I still had work to do. I had no idea where to even begin.

"Alana," I said as I drew the small book I had found in the altar from my pocket. "Do you think your teacher would translate this? I think it holds a lot of secrets about the worship of the Light that we may need."

"It will take time, Promised One."

"Yeah, well, we seem to have a bit of that now. I'll take it to him myself. I want to see this archive of his and pick his brain to see what he knows. Maybe you can convince him to have copies made for our new library."

"He'll do anything I ask," Alana said and smiled.

"Now, the real adventure begins," I said.

Alana studied me with her creamy, white eyes. She had a strange expression on her face. "Tell me this," she said, "will you stay?"

I stepped back from her to see her better. She was serious. "Where would I go?" I asked.

"I can lead you to the chamber in which you arrived. As the Promised One, you could send yourself back to where you grew up."

I stared at her. The thought hadn't occurred to me since the cleansing. If I could do that, couldn't my father have done it when the priests locked him up in the chamber? Then I remembered that he was already dying when they put him in. He wouldn't have had the strength to use it.

And I wasn't sure that I wanted to go back to Ohio. I could go and see what happened to my mother's body. I could go back to high school and see Dean again and maybe even go to college. I could, but what good would it do?

I lifted Alana's hands in mine. "This is my world," I said. "I was born here. I belong here."

Alana gave me a sad smile. "Will you be happy?"

"As long as I have you," I said.

A tear trickled down her cheek. Her lips quivered. She averted her gaze. "You can't want someone whose face, voice, and soul have been mutilated."

I pulled her close and hugged her tight. "Your eyes reflect the purity of your soul. Your life is a song, as you once said. Let's make it a song worth singing."

I held her at arm's length, looking into her white eyes. Then I leaned in and kissed her. It was a gentle, lingering kiss. Her lips were warm and soft.

We parted and smiled awkwardly at each other. The cool breeze came in through the window and stirred Alana's black hair. I smelled the fragrance of flowers.

Alana's lip trembled. "Only the Promised One will be able to see how to set things right," she said.

I studied her lovely face and prayed that she was right.

Continue the adventure in Book Two *The Rending.*

Thank you for reading *Worlds of Light: The Cleansing.* **Please take a few minutes to leave a review on Amazon.**

As an independent publisher, I have to compete with the big five publishing houses and their big bank accounts. Your review will help me reach a broader audience.

Please accept a free story by signing up for my email list at www.jwelliot.com

ABOUT J.W. ELLIOT

J.W. Elliot is a professional historian, martial artist, canoer, bow builder, knife maker, woodturner, and rock climber. He has a Ph.D. in Latin American and World History. He has lived in Idaho, Oklahoma, Brazil, Arizona, Portugal, and Massachusetts. He writes non-fiction works of history about the Inquisition, Columbus, and pirates. J.W. Elliot loves to travel and challenge himself in the outdoors.

Connect with J.W. Elliot online at:
www.jwelliot.com/contact-us

Books by J.W. Elliot
Available on Amazon and Audible

Archer of the Heathland
Prequel: *Intrigue*
Book I: *Deliverance*
Book II: *Betrayal*
Book III: *Vengeance*
Book IV: *Chronicles*
Book V: *Windemere*
Book VI: *Renegade*
Book VII: *Rook*

Worlds of Light
Book I: *The Cleansing*
Book II: *The Rending*
Book III: *The Unmaking*

The Miserable Life of Bernie LeBaron
Somewhere in the Mist
Walls of Glass

If you have enjoyed this book, please consider leaving an honest review on Amazon and sharing on your social media sites.

Please sign up for my newsletter where you can get a free short story and more free content at: www.jwelliot.com

Thanks for your support!

J.W. Elliot

Printed in Great Britain
by Amazon